GOLIATH

-A RYAN MITCHELL THRILLER-

BY

RICHARD TURNER

1

Dublin, Ireland
July 2nd, 1922

T he sound of sporadic gunfire echoing through the narrow streets of Dublin sounded to ten-year-old Patrick Murphy like the rolling thunder from a summer storm brewing somewhere in the distance. Cautiously peering around the corner, he saw that the street was deserted. With a smile on his dirt-smeared face, he realized that his luck was holding.

For days, Irishmen fought one another as soldiers from both the Irish Republican Army and the Provisional Government battled for control of Dublin. Patrick looked back over his shoulder and waved to his brother sitting behind the wheel of a borrowed white paneled truck, O'Doul's Butcher Shop emblazoned on the sides in large blue lettering. A moment later, Liam, Patrick's older brother, waved back and drove to the corner before stopping to let him climb back on board the truck.

Sitting beside his brother was a man they had only met this morning. He wore a long gray trench coat and a cap pulled down low on his head. The man had short red hair and a stern-looking face. His name was Mister Lewis, or so he said, and that was all they needed to know. On the floor of the truck sat a large battered wooden box with one of Mister Lewis' leg resting on top. His constant fidgeting with a pistol in his hands made Patrick uneasy. He had seen weapons before as his older brother was a volunteer with the government militia, but their passenger seemed overly nervous, as if expecting something to happen.

Slowly, they drove out of the city, making their way past a couple of heavily armed police checkpoints that were busy looking for gunrunners and IRA sympathizers. After driving for an hour, they began to approach the outskirts of Old Conna Village when Mister Lewis brusquely told them to turn off the paved road and into an empty farmer's field. Parking the truck, Lewis ordered Liam and Patrick to remain in the cab while he stepped outside to conduct his business. Grabbing the heavy wooden box in his arms, Lewis climbed out of the truck, walked out into the middle of the open field, lit a cigarette, and stood there as if he were waiting for a train to come by and pick him up from the middle of nowhere.

Patrick looked over at his older brother, who seemed relieved to be free of their mysterious passenger even if only for a short while.

"What's the fella doing?" asked Patrick.

Liam shrugged. "I haven't the foggiest clue," he replied. "I was told to drive Mister Lewis wherever he wanted and to not bloody well get caught doing it. That's all I know Patrick me boy, aside from the fact that I'm getting fifty pounds for a few hours' work."

Patrick may have been a young boy, but he knew his family did not exactly work within the law. His father and oldest brother were in prison and yet, for all his youth, he somehow knew that someday he would be, too.

After a half hour of sitting and staring at Mister Lewis sitting on his box, Patrick heard the sound of an engine in the distance, gradually growing louder as it drew closer. Rolling down the window, Patrick stuck his head out and looked into the sky. Gray clouds hung low, blocking out the sun. Turning his head, he was surprised to see an aircraft emerge out of the clouds like a hawk diving down out of the sky after its prey. It was unlike any other he had ever seen in his life. It was a monoplane, with a single engine mounted in the nose of the craft, painted all white, except for a long red streak that extended all the way down the fuselage of the plane.

Seeing the plane, Lewis stood and waved his arms in the air.

A moment later, the plane seemed to leisurely bank over in the air and began to line itself up with the farmer's field.

2

Patrick could barely contain himself; he had never seen a plane so close before. He made to leave the cab when his brother firmly grabbed him by the arm and pulled him back inside. His eyes narrowed, telling him that he had best stay put.

With a huff, Patrick sat back on the bench as the plane swooped down and effortlessly landed in the pasture. *The pilot looked like he had done this before*, thought Patrick, his eyes glued to the plane.

Lewis stood up, grabbed the wooden box, and waited for the plane to come to a complete stop. The plane's engines remained on, ready to take off at a moment's notice.

Patrick chaffed at being cooped up inside the cab of the truck when all the excitement was going on outside. Thrusting his head out the open window, he saw Lewis throw his cigarette onto the ground and walk over to the idling plane. A door on the side of the plane opened and out stepped a beautiful woman with long golden-blonde hair. She was wearing a green leather jumpsuit with a gray fur collar. Seeing Lewis, she stepped down and waited while he opened the box. Peering quickly inside, she looked back over her shoulder and called out. A thick-necked man with broad shoulders climbed out of the airplane, took the box from Lewis, and handed him an identical one in return. Without saying a word, Lewis moved back from the plane, a new box clenched firmly in his hands. The woman and the large man turned and climbed back inside the plane, closing the door behind them. The plane's engine grew loud as it began to taxi down the field. Bouncing once or twice on the uneven ground, the plane slowly lifted off and flew off into the clouds out of sight, as if it had never been there at all.

"Now remember this, Patrick: if ever asked, you never saw a thing today, ok?" said Liam, his voice full of warning as Mister Lewis made his way back to the truck.

Patrick simply nodded, wishing he could have gotten a closer look at the plane.

Lewis walked over to Liam's side of the truck and without uttering a word, he handed him the wooden box. Reaching over, Liam grabbed hold of the box. Placing it down on the floor of the truck, he sat up and looked over at Lewis. His eyes instantly grew wide as a pistol was thrust inside the cab. Before he could move, it fired. Blood and gore flew onto the glass windshield; the sound of the gun discharging inside the cab was deafening.

Patrick jumped right out of his seat. His heart pounded like a jackhammer inside his chest. Spinning about in his seat, he fumbled to open his door, when another shot rang out. The glass window beside Patrick's head exploded, showering him with sharp shards of glass. With his heart racing away in his chest, Patrick pushed as hard as he could before the door suddenly flew open. Patrick spilled out of the truck and hit the ground running. He needed to get away and hide. Seeing an apple orchard barely a hundred yards away, he sprinted as fast as he could towards it.

Tears streamed down his face as he ran. Another shot split the air. Patrick felt the bullet pass by his head. The trees loomed large. With one last burst of speed, he ran into the orchard. Without looking back to see where Lewis was, he ran deep into the woods, seeking safety inside from his attacker. Suddenly, he felt his foot catch onto something. Falling head over heels, he tumbled down onto the wet ground.

A voice called out, "Give yourself up, you little bastard, and I'll make it quick."

Patrick did not intend to give himself up. Quickly looking around, he saw a thick bush nearby. Scrambling on all fours, he dove under the scrub and lay there silently. He fought to control his ragged breathing, fearing that the man would hear him and come over to kill him. A moment later, he could see a pair of feet.

It was Lewis. He stopped where he was and looked around, searching for his quarry.

Patrick fought back the tears and the terror in his heart. He knew if he made a sound, he would be as dead as his brother. How was he going to tell his mother that Liam had been murdered? With her husband and eldest son in jail, they relied on Liam for income. With him gone, they would be penniless.

"I know you're around here somewhere," called out Lewis menacingly. "I don't have all day, you little bastard. Show yourself."

The feet grew closer.

Did the man know where he was? Patrick jammed his hands over his mouth; he was afraid to make a sound.

"You're lucky I have to be somewhere, or you'd be as dead as your brother," yelled Lewis. "You had better not say a thing, because if I ever hear that you did, so help me God, I will track you down and put a bullet between your and your mother's eyes," snarled Lewis angrily.

No pleaded Patrick silently.

The feet turned and walked away.

Patrick lay under the bushes, silent, and afraid. A moment later, the sound of the truck starting startled Patrick. Lying there with his heart still racing, he heard the truck driving away back down the road they had come up earlier.

Patrick waited until he could not hear the truck anymore before warily crawling out from his hiding place, his face covered in dirt and tears. Looking down, he saw that he had soiled himself. As he walked back to where he had last seen his brother, Patrick's feet felt like they were made of lead. Each footstep was labored and hard. He did not want to see what had happened to his brother. Trancelike, he walked to where they had parked in the open field.

A bloodied shape lay face down in the field. Knowing, but not wanting to believe that it was his brother, Patrick could no longer hide his fear and let out a mournful wail as he dashed over to his brother. Dropping down onto his knees, hesitating, he slowly reached over, grabbed his brother by his shoulders, and pulled the lifeless body into his. Sobbing uncontrollably, Patrick held on tight to his brother. He wondered what had been in the box and why someone would kill to keep it a secret. It was a question that would haunt him for the rest of his life.

2

North-West Africa
June 10th, 1931

Like some kind of ancient, monstrous creature breaching the waves, the Royal Airship *Goliath* effortlessly floated up through the thin gray evening clouds. Her skin shone silvery white from the brilliant full moon hanging high in the night sky. Shadowy and almost spectral, the massive craft left the wispy tendrils of the clouds behind and steadily climbed into the dark embrace of the night sky.

The *Goliath* was the latest and most-expensive showpiece vessel of Lord Angus Seaford, a blunt Scottish self-made multimillionaire who had a singular vision that trade throughout the British Empire would one day be by air, not by sea. He envisioned a world where fleets of airships, owned by him, would fly their goods and passengers all across the British Empire, from London to New Delhi, to Cape Town and back again. Trade and control over the seas was what gave Britain an unrivalled empire over which the sun never set. Seaford saw a new realm of the air and he wanted to be the man to control it all. His growing passion (or obsession, some would say) had driven him to take the costly risk of financing the building of the airship out of his own pocket to the unheard-of tune of almost three and a half million pounds sterling.

The craft was the largest ever made in England. It measured over 250 yards long and had a forty-five man crew, all of whom were veterans of the burgeoning airship business. The *Goliath*

6

was propelled at a steady 100 kilometers an hour by five powerful eight-cylinder diesel engines, each mounting sixteen feet solid oak twin blade propellers. Nestled comfortably within the craft were sixty luxurious passenger cabins and an elegant five-star dining room that served meals easily rivalling any found in Paris or London. Two promenade decks with windows running down both sides of the airship allowed the passengers a view, unlike anything anyone had ever seen before. There was even a spacious lounge and an asbestos-lined smoking room where Lord Seaford would entertain guests after the five-course evening meal. As it was in English society of the day, most of the passenger space was on the upper deck with the kitchen, washrooms, and crew accommodation. Much of the inner workings of the craft were located out of sight on the lower deck. The massive airship was steered from the control car located well forward under the lower deck and was only accessible by a ladder that led down from the chart room. *Goliath* spared nothing for the comfort of its privileged passengers.

Seaford had ensured that all of the major media outlets throughout the country were on hand to cover the maiden launch of Great Britain's pride, the *Goliath* as it took off from Southern England to the cheering adulation of thousands of well-wishers. Revving its powerful engines to full power, the *Goliath* turned away from her home and effortlessly floated off into the bright summer sky.

Crossing over the channel, accompanied by several intrepid flyers hired by the papers to record the event, the *Goliath* headed for its first stop in Paris, where Lord Seaford and his amazing airship were the toast of the town. After only one short night's stay, several new passengers joined the flight. They then flew on to Rome where a crowd of thousands of onlookers raucously cheered as the *Goliath* moored itself on the outskirts of the city. With an eye on showing the world what could be accomplished from the air, Seaford harried the ship's captain to continue with their voyage. After only a brief stop to refuel, the *Goliath* soon continued on her journey and traveled south out over the warm blue waters of the Mediterranean Sea. It headed towards its next destination, Nouakchott, the capital of Mauritania, in French West Africa. Their final destination was Cape Town, South

Africa. Once there, Seaford had told the press that he intended to hold a news conference and announce to the world his plans for a fleet of airships that would become the new vessels of commerce for the twentieth century and beyond.

Inside the airship's control cabin, Captain William Wright stood silently; his steely blue eyes watched intently as the duty officer gave an order. Instantly, the ship's helmsman acknowledged the order, then spun the wheel over to starboard, steering the *Goliath* southwest towards the small French military airstrip, still many miles distant. Captain Wright was considered by his employer to be a steady and dependable captain, a man who never failed to bring his ship, cargo, and crew home safely. His blue naval-style uniform looked as crisp and clean as when he had dressed earlier that morning. A stickler for dress and discipline, Captain Wright believed in setting an example for his much younger crew to follow. He was always first on shift in the morning and the last senior officer to leave at night. Reaching over, Wright rested his hand on the side of the wooden cabin; he could feel the powerful rhythmic vibration of the engines. Somewhat superstitious, Captain Wright always felt that it was good luck to touch his craft and feel the almost living power of his vessel before turning over the duties and responsibilities to the night duty officer. A smile crept across his weathered face. It may have been the maiden voyage of the *Goliath*, but it was Wright's final duty call as he was planning to retire after an illustrious forty-five year career.

"Mister Young," said Wright as he looked down at his gold pocket watch and then over at the slender junior officer standing patiently beside him. "It is now midnight, you have the ship. I expect you to wake me should the need arise."

Lieutenant Young respectfully raised his hand to his cap. "Aye sir, I have the ship," said the young officer confidently.

Captain Wright patted the young officer on the shoulder and climbed up the ladder into the darkened chart room. Looking about, Wright saw that the room was empty; not that he expected anyone to be there at this hour. Straightening out his tunic before stepping out onto the main passageway that ran like a long metal spine through the body of the airship, Wright looked aft towards the crew quarters. He thought about having a quick walk through to see how the men were doing before turning in for the night. Instead, he decided to make his way up to the passenger deck and the lounge, where he had no doubt that Lord Seaford and several of his equally rich friends would still be up playing cards and drinking the night away. It was none of Wright's business what his employer did, but he could tell that Seaford was gambling and drinking far more on this flight than any other time that they had travelled together before. Turning, Wright clasped his hands behind his back and started walking down the dimly lit corridor, when the hair went up on the back of his neck...something was wrong. Suddenly, he heard the unmistakable sound of a pistol firing. His blood instantly turned cold in his veins. *Who the hell was firing off a gun on board a vessel filled with massive highly flammable hydrogen cells? It was sheer madness.*

Another shot fired.

Wright, his heart pounding away in his chest, looked down the corridor and saw a dark shape stumble out of a room and tumble onto the carpeted floor. Fighting the fear gripping his stomach, Captain Wright ran over to the body lying face down on the floor. A dark stain of blood was already seeping out from underneath the man. Slowly, Wright turned over the body and saw that it was his junior radio-operator, a bloody hole now blasted into the poor man's chest. Laying the body back down, Wright stood and cautiously walked towards the open radio room. Stopping at the door, Wright could hear the sound of someone inside smashing the radio sets to pieces. It was as if the man did not care if anyone heard him.

Summoning up his courage, Wright took a deep breath, stepped inside the door, and froze. He could not believe his eyes. Standing there with an axe grasped tightly in his hands was Lord Seaford. His red hair was a mess and his deep-green eyes were ablaze with a maniacal look.

"My God, sir what are you doing?" said Wright as he looked around at the destroyed radio equipment.

"I'm sorry, Captain," mumbled Seaford. "I had to do it. I had to do what needed to be done."

Not a word of it made any sense to Wright as he carefully edged forward, his hands at his sides. "What needed to be done, sir?" Wright calmly asked Seaford.

9

Seaford suddenly raised the axe above his head. "Stay where you are, Captain!" screamed Seaford, spittle flying from his mouth. "I've already killed tonight. Don't make me kill you too!"

The ghastly image of the dead radio operator filled Wright's mind. His fear faded as anger swelled inside his chest. Had the man gone mad?

"Easy now, sir," said Wright, trying to get the lunatic to lower his axe. "Why don't you tell me what the problem is, and I'll see what I can do about it."

"It's too late for that now," sobbed Seaford, as tears welled up in his bloodshot eyes. "No one can know what has happened here."

Wright inched forward. A flicker of sadness registered in Seaford's eyes. The axe lowered slightly. In a flash, Wright launched himself at Seaford, grabbing the axe in his hands. In an instant, the two men tumbled from side to side inside the tiny room, trying to wrestle control of the deadly weapon. Wright was the larger of the two, but Seaford fought back like a man possessed by a demon. Back and forth the men staggered, smashing into overturned chairs while destroyed radio components crunched under their feet.

"What the hell is going on in here?" yelled a voice from outside.

A second later, a crewman stepped inside and threw himself into the fight. Seaford struggled in vain as the two men soon overpowered him; the axe was forcibly taken from his hands. Captain Wright, his heart still beating wildly, ordered the crewman to first tie Seaford up. A minute later, with Seaford firmly tied to a chair, the crewman headed off to wake the sleeping master-at-arms so he could break out a pistol and a set of handcuffs from the airship's tiny armory.

Captain Wright put the axe down on a far table, removed his tunic, and placed it over the body of the unfortunate radio-operator. Saying a quick prayer for the man, Wright turned and looked towards Seaford and was surprised to see tears streaming down the man's face.

"Sir, pull yourself together. What the Devil is going on here?" asked Wright, shaking his head at his employer, a broken man.

Seaford said nothing, meekly lowering his head in shame.

Wright bit his lip in anger and frustration. What could have possibly made Seaford want to kill a defenseless man and try to stop any communication of the event? A sudden chill ran down Wright's spine. Stepping out from the room, Wright looked down the long passageway towards the back of the airship.

A low rumble echoed throughout the *Goliath* followed a second later by a violent explosion that rocked the massive airship from side to side, throwing Wright off his feet and onto the floor of the radio room. Struggling to rise, the captain did not need to be told what had happened. Somewhere in the bowels of the ship, a catastrophic explosion had just occurred, and Wright knew who had caused it. Looking over at Seaford, he knew the man was mad and had doomed them all.

From the tail section of the airship a ghastly wall of fire and destruction raced, picking up speed as it shot forward, instantly breaching and tearing apart the gas cells that held hundreds of thousands of feet of highly-flammable hydrogen. Like a creature bursting from the pits of hell, the bright orange wall of flame consumed all before it.

Captain Wright clenched his fists in frustration and anger. He knew that it would be mere seconds before the *Goliath* would lose its structural integrity and begin its death spiral towards the ground thousands of meters below.

Already, the once-proud airship started to list forward, tilting its nose downwards.

"What the hell have you done?" yelled Wright angrily at Seaford as the horrible noise of the craft tearing itself apart filled his ears.

Seaford raised his head, looked into Wright's rage-filled eyes, and mouthed one word: "Sorry." An instant later, scorching flames ripped through the cabin, incinerating Wright and Seaford.

Far below, a massive sandstorm whipped across the desolate and rocky terrain while burning debris rained down from the night sky like a bright, unexpected meteor shower. The *Goliath* plummeted down to the ground, her crew and passengers lost in the vast expanse of Africa for decades to come.

3

**The Philippines
Present Day**

The sun slowly crept below the green hills surrounding a small camp nestled against the banks of the swollen Cagayan River. Long shadows crept along the ground, soon covering the encampment as the once bright world turned to dusk. With the darkness approaching, the jungle slowly came to life. The local wildlife called to one another, filling the air with a cacophony of noise.

Jennifer March stepped out of the large green military-style tent that she and several other people had been using as a makeshift office. Standing there, her hands on her hips, she took in the symphony of the night. Running a hand through her short caramel-colored hair reminded Jen that she had not had a decent shower in over a week and was not likely to get another one for a few more. Her lithe physique was hidden under a pair of baggy khaki-colored shorts and a loose-fitting shirt tied up around her taut midsection. Brushing some dirt off her warm brown arms, Jen began to wonder if she would ever feel clean again.

Just shy of thirty, Jennifer March had recently thrown herself into her work with a renewed passion and vigor to avoid having to deal with the messy implosion of her two-year relationship with an older colleague. It had been comfortable at first but ultimately it was doomed. Jen wanted to know that it was going somewhere; however, her boyfriend would always avoid the issue whenever she raised it. One day, six months ago, she'd had enough. Packing her bags, she moved back in with her mother in Charlotte, North Carolina, and steadfastly refused to talk with anyone about her decision to leave. At the expense of everything else, her work had now become the only focus in her life.

Three months ago, a local farmer who was clearing the land along the riverbank to plant crops for his family stumbled upon the mangled wreckage from what could only be an old military transport plane. After calling the authorities, the plane was identified by a professor from the University of Luzon. Unmistakably, the wreckage was the remains of an old U.S. Dakota transport plane that had crashed sometime during the Second World War. Having lost numerous planes to probable mechanical breakdowns or enemy action during the war over the Philippines, the U.S. State Department financed a dig. They were eager to identify the plane and to repatriate the remains of any US servicemen killed in the crash.

Forensic archaeology was far from Jen's field of expertise, but when the original team leader went down with appendicitis a day before the team of grad students was due to leave, Jen volunteered to step up, but only if she was allowed time off from teaching to write a book about their findings. Arriving in the capital, Luzon, Jen and her gang of a dozen graduate students were met at the airport by her counterpart on the dig, Professor Carlos Laurel. Laurel was a large and jovial man who wore pop-bottle glasses and a constant smile across his broad face. Jen and Laurel instantly hit it off, and a strong bond soon developed between the two disparate groups of students living and working shoulder to shoulder in the heat and humidity of the Philippine jungle.

Her stomach rumbled loudly, reminding Jen that once again she had worked straight through lunch. Turning in the direction of the communal mess tent, Jen walked over and joined a short lineup of local workers mixed in with Filipino and American grad students, all loudly chatting away like a gang of old friends. Jen slowly made her way forward to the cooks. Seeing the meal, she cringed. It was to be another meal of chicken, rice and steamed vegetables. With a weak smile on her face, Jen grabbed her food and looked around for a seat to eat her all-too-routine supper meal. Finding a quiet spot, Jen sat down in a far corner of the mess tent, dug out a small black notebook from a pocket in her shorts, and reviewed her day's work while she disinterestedly picked away at her meal.

"May I join you?" said a voice with a strong Filipino accent.

Looking up, Jen saw Professor Laurel standing there with a heaping tray of food. With a quick smile, she motioned for him to join her at the empty table.

Jen felt the table dip as Laurel sat down.

"A good day, wouldn't you say?" said Laurel as he helped himself to a heaping forkful of rice.

"Oh yes, very much so," Jen replied, thumbing through her notebook. "The serial numbers found on the engine block were the clue we needed to positively identify which missing plane it could possibly be. I emailed the Department of Defense the photos taken this afternoon of the engine, along with its serial number. I suspect that by tomorrow morning we should have a flight manifest of those U.S. and Filipino service personnel who are still listed as missing on the flight. From there, we can go about expanding the search for the remains if any have survived this long."

"The jungle is not too kind on the dead. If the local animals did not cart off the remains after the crash, then they would have decomposed very quickly in this humid climate. For the families' sake, I hope we do find something that can be returned home and buried with some dignity," said Laurel solemnly.

Jen thought about Laurel's words for a moment and added, "Amen to that." She was about to go over her thoughts about the tomorrow's dig with Laurel when a small, lean, bespectacled Asian-American girl wearing a tight-fitting Lady Gaga world tour T-shirt walked over to their table holding a plate with nothing but vegetables on it.

"Can I join you two, or is this not business talk?" asked Alanis Kim, looking enviously down at the empty spot at the table.

Jen shrugged her shoulders and pointed towards an empty spot on the bench; Laurel did not even bother to look up from his food.

Kim slipped down onto the chair and cleaned her cutlery

with a napkin before cutting up some broccoli. "Oh, I hope I wasn't intruding?" said Kim mischievously.

Jen shook her head. She had noticed that Kim had an overly active imagination and had become the de-facto team gossip. Nothing escaped her vigilance. An innocent smile or friendly wave at an associate was instantly turned into the latest romance or secret affair between seemingly unconnected colleagues, all of which was meticulously recorded and posted on Facebook and Twitter for the world to read.

"You should really slow down when you eat," lectured Kim as she watched Laurel finish off his plate of food until not a scrap remained.

A loud belch escaped Laurel's mouth. He patted his belly and smiled over at the horrified student.

"You should eat more," said Laurel, "you might be able to attract a man if you put some weight on. I like my women with a bit of meat on them."

Kim scrunched up her nose at the thought. "I guess that takes Professor March out of the equation then."

"Kim, really," said Jen, shaking her head at the graduate student's foolish remarks.

"I have a beautifully round girlfriend waiting for me in Manila," said Laurel with a warm smile on his face. "I'm going to get a coffee and perhaps some cake. Can I get you two beautiful ladies anything?" asked Laurel, rising from the creaking table.

Both women asked for a cup of green tea, but no cake. Laurel smiled politely and went off to fetch the order. A minute later, Laurel returned and handed a piece of cake heaped with icing to Kim with a smile on his face that said *you had better enjoy it*.

They spent the rest of the evening talking about what they hoped to accomplish the next day. Feeling fatigued, Jen turned in early and was out seconds after her head hit the pillow.

The next morning began like any other. There was a quick, chaotic breakfast of coffee and scrambled eggs, immediately followed by the daily brief from Professor Laurel on the activities ahead, which to Jen always seemed more like a sermon. After that, the students broke down into their respective teams and went about the painstaking work of carefully excavating the crash site.

As Jen had predicted, an email file was waiting on her computer in the morning from the DOD. It was the flight manifest of the doomed flight known by its call sign, Whiskey-35. Skimming the document, Jen saw that seven American and five Filipino servicemen had been on the plane when it disappeared over the jungle on March 3, 1945. The plane had been bound for Manila, but when it failed to arrive on time, a search was initiated. After two weeks of fruitless effort, the search was called off and the flight was officially listed as missing.

That was, until today.

Jen smiled to herself; things were going as planned. She quickly printed off a couple of copies of the flight manifest (one for herself, the other for Professor Laurel) and stepped out from the dingy tent into the bright morning sunlight. Slipping on a pair of sunglasses, Jen headed off into the already humid morning to look for Laurel to tell him that they had the information they had been waiting for.

The crash site was marked off with yellow barrier tape in the rough shape of an airplane. All around the dig, students, and local workers toiled side by side; most had grown used to the stifling heat and humidity that seemed to envelop the site throughout the long day.

Jen soon found Laurel, his head down, looking over some mangled remains that vaguely looked like a plane's steering wheel. Walking over, she looked at the bent wheel and wondered how the men felt in the last seconds before the crash, knowing they were going to die. A cold shiver ran down her spine. Shaking such thoughts from her mind, Jen handed Laurel a copy of the flight manifest. Together, they began to discuss the next step in trying to find the crew's remains, when an excited voice called out. Jen and Laurel trotted over to the site of the commotion. A group of students and locals were huddled around a freshly dug hole. Gently prying the people apart, Jen and Laurel stepped down into the hole. The smell of fresh earth wafted in the air.

"What do you have there, Joseph?" Laurel said to one of his

16

students.

"Professor, I found this," said the student proudly as he held up a pair of rusty-looking military identification discs.

Laurel took them in his large hand and reverently examined the discs, his mind taking in every minute detail. "Where exactly did you find these, Joseph?" asked Laurel, his voice serious.

"Right here, sir," said Joseph, pointing to a patch recently dug in the dark earth.

Laurel bent over, his large frame blocking the dig from view. Brushing more dirt aside, Laurel found a pair of broken glasses embedded in the earth. Picking them up, Laurel rubbed the dirt off them and stared down at the distorted shape.

"My God, do you think we have found one of our missing soldiers?" asked Jen, peering down at the objects in Laurel's meaty hand.

Laurel stood and looked around at the anxious crowd of students peering down into the dig. "These items belonged to one Sergeant Thomas Henry. He is one of the crewmen listed as missing on the flight manifest, so we have the first evidence of remains from the crash," said Laurel, looking into the inquisitive faces of the grad students. "Now the real work begins," announced Laurel.

A murmur raced through the crowd of onlookers.

"What are you all doing standing around and gawking?" said Laurel with a huff as he helped himself out of the hole. "Come on, everyone, there's still plenty of work to be done before the sun goes down tonight."

With that, the crowd broke up and went back to work, excitedly chatting away about the find.

Laurel reverently handed Jen the dirt-covered items and headed off to supervise another part of the dig.

Jen stood there staring down at the mangled pieces of metal in her hand and wondered who Sergeant Henry was, and if he still had any living relatives back in the States. She was about to return to her tent to catalogue the find, when the sound of automatic gunfire tore through the air. Jen instinctively flinched at the noise and turned to look in the direction of the shots.

Already, there were people screaming and struggling to get away from the gunfire. A young man, his hand held to a bloody wound on his head staggered past Jen. Fear filled his eyes.

More gunfire suddenly erupted from another direction.

Jen froze in her tracks. She did not know which way to turn. People were panicking all around her, running, screaming and crying as they were forced towards the center of the camp.

A man wearing an ill-fitting camouflage uniform emerged from behind a tent fired a burst into the air, and with a crooked smile, walked towards Jen, a rusted AK47 clenched tightly in his hands.

"You, that way," yelled the man at Jen as he pointed towards the camp's mess tent.

Jen stood there wide-eyed staring down the barrel of the still-smoking AK.

"Now," said the man forcefully, raising the assault rifle until it was aimed at Jen's head.

Jen instantly snapped out of her stupor and darted towards the mess tent, almost stumbling over the body of one of their local workers, a ragged bloody hole in his back. Her mind screamed in horror at the sight, but Jen fought to stifle a scream as she joined the mass of sobbing and terrified students corralled in the mess tent.

A minute after it had begun it was all over. An uneasy silence filled the camp.

Jen sat at a crowded table like everyone else; her hands were locked together on top of her head. It was truly an uncomfortable position, but Jen dared not move. The last student who did got a rifle butt to the head for his troubles. Jen saw that the men guarding them were mainly dressed in rags and old uniforms and wondered if they were anti-government rebels. She was confused; she had been told the area was safe. Looking around, Jen could not see Professor Laurel anywhere. She closed her eyes and silently prayed that somehow he had managed to get away to warn the authorities. A moment later, her hopes were instantly crushed as a dead body was dragged across the red dirt path between the rows of tents, a hole blasted in its skull. Jen's heart skipped a beat when she saw that it was Laurel. A couple of girls screamed and broke out crying at the sight of the professor's bloodstained body.

Jen bit her lip. She had to do something, but what? She was

at a loss; she had never been so scared in her entire life, but she knew that somehow she had to fight the fear and stay calm. With this many American and Filipino students in one place together, someone inevitably would be coming to help them—she hoped.

The tent doors opened. A man in immaculately pressed camouflaged fatigues entered the tent. He stood a solid six feet tall, with wide, powerful shoulders, short blond hair, and unforgiving dark blue eyes. *A cold-blooded killer's eyes* thought Jen. This was a man to be feared. He was unlike the others; they were Filipino, while he was white and looked decidedly European to Jen. Nonchalantly, the man stopped in front of the frightened group, dug out his cell phone from his pocket, and made a quick call. Once done, he put the phone away and fished out a piece of paper.

"Good day, my name is David Teplov, and you are all now under my protection. There has been some trouble in the local area, and I have been dispatched to bring you all to a safe location," said the man in Russian-accented English.

"But you murdered Professor Laurel," defiantly protested one of the local workers.

"If you speak another word, I will make sure that you join him," Teplov replied with a cold lizard-like smile, as he looked out over the crowd of terrified faces.

The once-defiant worker turned his head away and tried hiding behind a student.

"Now, let's all be civil about this. I want to see Miss Jennifer March," said Teplov.

Fear gripped Jen's stomach. Why did they want her and not someone else?

For a moment, no one moved.

Teplov looked over the crowd and shook his head. With lightning-like reflexes, he drew a Russian-made MP-446 9-mm semi-automatic pistol, walked towards Alanis Kim, and jammed the gun into the petrified girl's face. "Stand up now, or I will blow this girl's brains all over the ground," snarled Teplov.

Kim whimpered in fear and tried to pull her face away from the cold pistol jammed against her glistening forehead.

Teplov tightened his grip. Kim screamed.

Jen stood, hatefully staring towards the killer. "I'm Jennifer

March. Please don't hurt her. I'm begging you. You have me. Now please, put your pistol away."

Teplov smiled as he slowly pulled his pistol away from Kim's terrified face, placed it back in its holster, and looked over towards Jen. "There now, that's better."

"What could you possibly want with me?" said Jen, looking around at the worried faces of the students and locals alike.

"That is not important right now. I have a jeep waiting at the edge of the camp for you," said Teplov with a wave of his hand. "As for the others, they will be joining you shortly once a couple more of my trucks arrive."

Jen stood there not believing a word. The look in the killer's cold eyes told her that he could not be trusted. She could not just leave the students there; they were all looking to her for leadership now that Professor Laurel was dead. She tried playing for time, hoping that by some miracle, someone would come and help them. "I have your word that my people will be unharmed if we come with you?" Jen asked as she locked eyes with Teplov.

"Miss March, I have not given you my word, not once, but if it will make you come with me, then you have it," Teplov said with an artificial smile on his face.

Jen knew she had no choice. Feeling as if she were deserting everyone to a certain death, she nodded. Walking out of the tent without saying another word, she made her way towards an idling beat up, old-looking military-style Hummer jeep. Waiting at the far end of the camp were a couple more Hummers. A young thug wearing a red beret, green shorts and nothing else opened the rear passenger door of the lead Hummer. Jen felt the man leering at her, but defiantly, she held her head high as she silently climbed into the back of the vehicle.

Teplov barked some orders in Tagalog, the local language, to the men guarding the students and climbed in the passenger side of the vehicle. He looked back at his hostage. "Hang on, the road out of here is a little bumpy," Teplov said with a grin.

Jen stared back at him; she may have been scared out of her mind, but there was no way that she was going to let him see it in her eyes. Crossing her arms over her chest, she sat back with a defiant look on her face.

Teplov laughed aloud, turned around and with a wave of his

hand, the driver slowly pulled away from the camp.

Jen looked out of the vehicle window at the people she was leaving behind. She prayed that Teplov would keep his word and not harm anyone else, but deep down, Jen knew that he was probably going to kill them all.

4

High above the dig site, like an eagle soaring on the winds, a small, almost invisible unmanned aerial vehicle (UAV) turned and began to follow a convoy of vehicles as it snaked its way along the bumpy red dirt road. Painted ghost gray to blend in with the sky, the UAV was nearly impossible to see, its high-tech cameras sending a feed directly to a laptop computer over twenty kilometers away.

Jen March sat dejectedly in the back of the Hummer as it bounced up and down the rough track that passed as the local highway. She bit her lip and wanted to cry. Jen could not fathom why anyone would want to kidnap her for ransom. Neither she nor anyone in her family had any real money. It made absolutely no sense whatsoever. Who would be so monstrous as to plan to kill seventy students and locals just to cover her abduction? Despondent, she was about to hunker down deeper into her hard seat, when suddenly out of the corner of her eye she saw a vehicle, like a charging rhinoceros, burst out of the thick jungle. An instant later, with a loud crunch of compacting metal, it smashed headlong into the side of the closest Hummer behind them, sending it spinning off the road and into the tropical forest.

Nate Jackson, a heavyset African-American, held the jeep's steering wheel tight in his large hands. The impact of hitting the Hummer at over fifty kilometers an hour had instantly crumpled the Land Rover's engine bumper guards and shaken up Jackson and his passenger. Quickly spinning the wheel around in his hands, Jackson expertly turned the vehicle onto the road, only a few meters behind Jen's Hummer.

"Aren't you glad we were wearing seatbelts?" said Jackson's passenger, Ryan Mitchell.

"I hope they weren't," said Jackson with a wide grin on his face.

"Time to lose our company," said Mitchell as he unbuckled his belt, turned about and crawled over his seat until he was standing in the open back of their Rover, his hands resting on a machine gun mounted on the vehicle's roll bar. Quickly, he pulled back on the charging lever and loaded a round from the belt already inside the GPMG. With his shoulder jammed tight into the butt of the weapon, Mitchell aimed it squarely at the cab of the Hummer behind them.

The driver of the Hummer saw Mitchell and tried swerving from side to side, but with thick jungle on either side of the narrow dirt road, he had nowhere to go.

Taking aim, Mitchell slightly lowered the weapon's sight and let loose a long burst of 7.62 mm rounds into the engine block of the Hummer. Within seconds, steam and black oily smoke rose from the stricken engine. The Hummer lurched forward, started to slow, and stopped moving altogether, a cloud of steam blocking it from view.

Seeing that the vehicle was no longer a threat, Mitchell turned about and jumped back into his seat. He could see the lead Hummer with Jen inside it trying to get away, but the awful road conditions combined with Jackson's driving skills meant that they were not going to escape that easily.

"Now what?" said Jackson over his shoulder to Mitchell.

With a bang, Mitchell slammed home a fresh thirty-round magazine into his M4 rifle. "I don't know, I honestly hadn't thought that far ahead," said Mitchell as he charged the weapon.

"Wonderful," said Jackson under his breath as he changed gears and floored the gas pedal, instantly narrowing the distance between the vehicles.

"What the hell is going on? Who are those people?" screamed Teplov at his equally perplexed driver.

"I don't know, sir," the young man replied.

Jen squirmed around in her seat. Looking out the rear window, she could see a jeep racing towards them, like a lion

23

chasing down its prey. She had no idea who they were, but for the first time since this awful day had begun, Jen dared to hope that she might be saved.

"Pull up beside them, I'll try to shoot out their tires," said Mitchell as he raised the M4 into his shoulder.

Jackson shook his head; this was something that was easier said than done, and only in the movies. Edging up slowly, Jackson brought Mitchell in line with the rear driver's side tire and held his breath.

Mitchell took quick aim and fired off a three-round burst into the tire. The sturdy tire did not shred but started to leak air from the holes shot into it by Mitchell.

Waving his hand forward, Mitchell signaled to Jackson to speed up so he could shoot the driver's tires, when the loud pinging sound of automatic gunfire hitting the back of their jeep caught their attention. Pivoting around in his seat, Mitchell was surprised to see the battered Hummer they had smashed off the road speeding up behind them. He hoped they had dealt with them in one blow, but it was not to be.

"God damn it," said Jackson as he bobbed and weaved his head while bullets flew past him. Jamming his foot down on the gas, he sped up and shot past the lead Hummer, intending to use it as a shield. "Think of something, will you, Ryan? We need to ditch that other vehicle, and fast."

Mitchell looked over his shoulder and smiled to himself. Pressing his throat-mic, Mitchell gave a quick set of orders to the UAV operator, watching the struggle on his computer from their base camp, and settled back down in his seat.

"Mind telling me what you're thinking, Captain?" said Jackson, struggling to keep their battered jeep on the bumpy road.

"I hope UAVs aren't too expensive," said Mitchell as the shadow of their UAV suddenly raced over them like a massive bird of prey diving down.

A second later, the driver of the battered Hummer following Jackson's jeep was horrified to see the image of a large flying object hurtling towards him. He did not even have time to scream. With a loud crash, the UAV smashed straight through the front windshield, instantly killing the driver and the lead passenger before its near-full fuel tank exploded. A bright orange fireball shot up into the sky as the Hummer was incinerated.

"The general is gonna be pissed when he hears what you did," said Jackson, slowing down as he tried to force the last Hummer off the road.

"He can bill whoever these people are working for," replied Mitchell, as he once more unbuckled his belt and crawled back to the machine gun. Mitchell's patience was growing thin; the shot tire was not deflating fast enough for him. Taking the weapon off safety, Mitchell fired a short burst into the Hummer's hood; right away, the vehicle started to slow down.

Keeping pace with the Hummer, Jackson slowed down his jeep and pulled over beside it, leaving plenty of room between Mitchell and his target.

With the GPMG aimed at the driver's compartment, the driver's door to the Hummer slowly opened and an AK was dropped unceremoniously onto the dirt road.

"Show us your hands," said Mitchell, keeping the machine gun trained on the Hummer.

A pair of shaking hands emerged from behind the door.

"Good, now get out, slowly," ordered Mitchell.

The driver, shaking in fear, stepped out of the vehicle, his eyes wide as he stared over at the weapon trained on his chest.

"Lie down," said Mitchell firmly, leaving no doubt in his voice that he meant business.

Nodding, the driver got down on the road and lay there vibrating in fear.

Jackson grabbed his M4, chambered a round and hauled his frame out of the jeep and stood there, warily eyeing the vehicle.

"You inside, play it smart, let the girl go and slowly step outside," said Mitchell. "Don't do anything foolish. I'd fill you with a ton of lead before you could grab a weapon."

Teplov sat there silently, staring out of the open driver's-side door at the people who had ruined his plans. He knew he had no recourse; he was trapped. Gritting his teeth, Teplov swore under his breath at his bad luck. This was supposed to be an easy assignment: grab the American from the dig site, eliminate everyone else there, and make it look like the work of rebels. It was not supposed to be this way. He was not a fanatic; he was just a man doing a job, and dying was not part of the bargain.

"Get out," said Teplov to Jen, his voice bitter with defeat.

Jen slowly opened her door, showed her hands like the driver had and stepped out of the back of the Hummer. A feeling of relief washed over her the instant she stepped out of the vehicle.

"Ok, miss, now keep it calm, and slowly walk over beside me," said Jackson to Jen, all the while never taking his eyes off the Hummer.

Jen nodded and walked over beside Jackson. She saw that he was built like a defensive lineman in the NFL and easily dwarfed Jen's more diminutive figure.

"Now you," ordered Mitchell to Teplov. "Throw out any weapons you have and crawl out through the open driver's-side door. Make any sudden moves and I promise that I'll turn you into Swiss cheese."

A moment later, a pistol dropped out of the Hummer. Mitchell could hear a man swearing away in Russian as the last occupant of the vehicle emerged; standing there with his hands by his sides, he stared defiantly at Mitchell and Jackson.

Mitchell lowered the machine gun, grabbed his M4, jumped down from the Rover, and walked cautiously towards the Hummer. Looking at the imposing solid frame and cold, uncaring eyes of the man standing in front of him, Mitchell knew he was dealing with a professional and not one of the local thugs they had already dealt with today.

"Ok, mister, hands on your head and slowly get down on your knees," said Mitchell as he waved towards the dirt with his rifle barrel.

With a look of disgust, Teplov reluctantly did as he was told.

Mitchell carefully walked forward, picked up the discarded pistol and then, before Teplov knew what was happening, he was pushed onto the ground and a set of handcuffs was quickly slapped on him.

Rolling over to look up at the man who had dared to touch him, Teplov looked into the blue-gray eyes of his opponent and swore an oath: no matter the cost, he would find a way to get revenge on this impertinent man.

Mitchell left Teplov in the dirt and strolled over to Jackson and Jen. "Are you all right?" he asked Jen, with a reassuring smile on his face.

"Yes, I guess so," replied Jen, looking at the men dressed in US military MultiCam fatigues who had just saved her life. "Who are you guys? Are you with the army?"

Jackson let out a little chuckle.

"No, miss, we're not with the army; at least, not anymore," said Mitchell, as he offered his hand. "Where are my manners? My name is Ryan, Ryan Mitchell, and this mountain of a man standing beside me is Nathaniel Jackson."

"Nate," said Jackson, in a deep booming voice while offering his large hand in greeting.

Jen shook both men's hands. She looked over at Mitchell, taking in his intense blue-gray eyes. She saw that he stood just over six feet and had a trim athletic build. Mitchell had thick brown hair cut short. His skin was tanned. She could tell that he was a man who spent a lot of his life outdoors. Jen thought that Mitchell had a rugged, confident air about him, which she suspected women liked. She suddenly realized that she was staring. Blushing, she looked away.

His friend was a tall African-American with a smooth-shaven head, large broad shoulders, and strong muscular arms. Jen thought he looked like a man who could hold his own easily in a boxing ring.

Jen realized she was standing there, not saying a word. She spoke, "Oh, sorry; my name is Jennifer March, but please call me Jen."

"Jen it is then," said Mitchell, smiling at her before stepping to one side. "Yuri, send a sitrep," said Mitchell into his throat-mic.

Yuri, their UAV operator, quickly filled him in and then jokingly asked Mitchell how much per month he wanted deducted from his pay to cover the loss of the drone.

In the distance, a police car with its siren blaring sped towards the stopped Hummer, leaving a red dust cloud behind it.

"Cavalry's coming," said Jackson dryly.

"Better late than never," said Mitchell, looking over at the worried look on Jen's face. "Don't worry about your friends,

27

they are safe," said Mitchell, as he fixed his gaze on Jen's alluring deep brown eyes.

Tears welled up in Jen's eyes at the news. "How do you know that?"

"It's a case of dumb luck really, but Nate and I and several others were over here helping to train the Philippine national police's latest counter-terrorism unit and by pure accident, we spotted several vehicles heading in your direction. Yuri, my UAV operator, wanted to show off his new toy to the class, so he followed the convoy until they stopped short of your camp. When we saw armed men jumping out of the back of several Hummers, we knew it wasn't going to be a friendly house call. Nate and I decided to come after you while the remainder of my training team under command of the Philippine counter-terrorism team leader swung in via chopper. It turned from a training exercise into a live-fire confirmation in real short order."

Jen wiped the tears off her cheeks, smudging red dirt across her face.

Mitchell smiled and handed Jen his camouflage neck scarf so that she could clean herself up.

A police cruiser came to a sliding halt beside the Hummer. Two officers got out. Mitchell filled them in on what had happened. Grabbing Teplov by the arms, the police dragged him away and placed him in the back of their car before speeding off back the way they came.

"So, shall we take you back to your camp?" said Mitchell to Jen.

"Yes, thank you," said Jen, more composed now that her tormentor was gone.

Ten minutes later, Jackson turned off the mud-filled road and headed towards a group of Philippine special police who were standing around with several overjoyed students happily congratulating them for saving them.

Alanis Kim saw Jen sitting in the front seat of Mitchell's jeep. In an instant, fear changed to elation. She broke into tears as she ran forward and threw herself into Jen's arms. Both women sat there for a moment, not daring to let the other go for fear of losing one another once again.

Mitchell and Jackson left Jen alone with Kim, and together

they walked over to a small, young Asian-looking woman dressed in fatigues like them. She was busy helping dress the wound on an injured local. Samantha Chen was the team medic, but her short stature meant nothing; she was just as deadly with a rifle as any man on the team. Sam, as she preferred to be called, stood just over five feet tall with a petite but firm build. Her dark-brown eyes burned with a passion to be the best at everything she did. A former airborne medic, she was a professed adrenaline junky and loved to free climb and parachute whenever she could. Standing beside Sam was a tall, slender man with a thick black goatee. Gordon Cardinal, a Canadian from the Rockies, was the team's sniper and surveillance expert. Whereas Sam was excitable, Cardinal was as cool as a mountain glacier; nothing ever seemed to faze him. Relationships in their business were frowned upon, but Mitchell turned a blind eye to Sam and Cardinal's blossoming romance. He reasoned that if he did not see it, he did not know about it.

"How did it go?" Mitchell asked Cardinal.

"Smooth, really smooth," he replied. "We were on them before they had a chance to kill them all."

"They're actually quite good," Sam said proudly of the police special unit. "Not a single terrorist got away. Unfortunately, five people were killed before we got here."

Mitchell reached out and squeezed her arm. "We did the best we could. There are a lot of people alive here today because of what we and especially our police counterparts did. We should be proud of ourselves."

Sam smiled and went back to her work.

The adrenaline built up in his system slowly left Mitchell's body, making him start to feel fatigued. Slinging his rifle, Mitchell decided to check on Jen one last time before rounding up his team and heading back to their camp. As he wandered through the camp, students and locals alike came up and shook his hand. This was not normal; Mitchell's people usually did their work in the shadows, without notice, and without thanks. In his mind, he reasoned that he and his team were simply doing their job.

Mitchell and Jackson had known each other for years, serving on numerous deployments to Afghanistan together. Both former U.S. Army Rangers, they had recently been enticed to leave the service and come to work in the world of private security. Reticent at first, both men decided to take a leap of faith and retire from the army to a more stable life that paid far better than the military ever could when Jackson's eldest son got into trouble with a local street gang during his last deployment.

"Mister Mitchell…Mister Mitchell," called Jen from behind a growing gaggle of police and students.

Mitchell walked towards her. A bright, warm smile on her face greeted him.

"I'm glad you that found me, I wanted to see how you were doing," said Mitchell. "It's not every day that a person gets kidnapped."

"Mister Mitchell, I'm doing quite well, thanks to you and Mister Jackson," said Jen.

"Please, call me Ryan," said Mitchell, smiling.

"Ok then, Ryan," said Jen, stressing his name in jest.

"We will be leaving soon, but I was wondering when you might be heading back to the States and what your plans might be when you get back home?" asked Mitchell.

Jen looked into Mitchell's eyes and saw that this was a man that she could trust. She suddenly felt herself staring again. *Keep it casual* flashed in her mind like an alarm bell going off. "We've been told by the police that they are going to leave some men with us tonight, but we have to wrap up our dig by tomorrow morning and head back to Manila for a flight out of the country," said Jen.

"Prudent move, it's not too safe around here, not after what happened today."

"No, I guess not."

Mitchell canted his head, trying to catch Jen's attention. "You still haven't said what you plan to do when you get back to the States."

Jen smiled at Mitchell's attention. "Why, Mister Mitchell, are you trying to ask me out?"

"The thought just came to me. It may seem a bit forward, but in my line of work hesitation never pays off," Mitchell said with a smile. "I know several good restaurants in New York City, if you were interested in some fine dining."

Jen smiled. "I would love that, but I happen to be living with my mother in Charlotte, North Carolina right now."

"Good thing I know several good restaurants there as well," said Mitchell, not backing down.

Jen felt out of sorts; first a kidnapping and now a man she just met asking for a date in the middle of the jungle. There was no way she could explain this one to her mother. "Ok, you win, Mister Mitchell; dinner when I get home. Now, how will I get in touch with you?"

Mitchell dug out his wallet and with a smile, he handed her a business card before turning about to rejoin his team, leaving her standing where she was.

Jen watched him fade into a crowd of milling soldiers. A smile broke across her face. She suddenly felt alive, hoping that her heart was not going to take her down the wrong path again. She could tell that Mitchell was unlike any man she had ever met before in her life. Holding onto the card, she stood there, knowing that she could not wait until they met again.

5

The Yacht – *Imperator*
The Black Sea

The small red MD-500 helicopter flew through the hot afternoon sky, cruising along 1,000 meters above the dark blue-green sea, easily doing two hundred kilometers an hour. The pilot had yet to push the small but versatile craft to its limits. Sitting stone-faced beside the pilot was an attractive woman in her late twenties. Her pale, almost porcelain-white skin and long black hair gave her the look of a model. The pilot, a mid-forties, blonde-haired ex-Russian police chopper pilot, had picked up the woman from a private airstrip just outside of Istanbul. He was under strict orders not to talk to his passenger, and that suited him fine. Most people talked too much for his liking; however, this one looked almost statue-like, sitting there saying nothing, doing nothing, just staring straight ahead, ignoring the world flying past beneath her. The silence may have been welcome, but for some indefinable reason, she made the pilot quite uncomfortable. The sooner he landed and was rid of his passenger, the better it would be. He knew from his flight briefing that this was going to be a quick visit followed immediately by a return flight straight back to the private airstrip, where a Lear jet was waiting on standby. All he had to do was fly the helicopter, keep his mouth shut, forget his passenger was ever in his helicopter, and an easy fifty thousand dollars was his.

A minute later, the luxury yacht *Imperator* emerged like a welcoming island on the blue horizon. Relief flooded through the pilot; he wanted this task over with as soon as possible. He quickly radioed the ship that he had their guest and began banking to the right, so he could align his helicopter with the massive boat's rear helipad.

At 120 meters in length, the *Imperator* was the fifth largest luxury yacht in the world. Crewed by forty, it could comfortably accommodate twenty guests at a time in the most-lavish rooms imaginable. For its rich occupants and visitors, it had all the usual features such as an indoor theatre, two heated pools, and a huge dining room along with many additional unseen defensive measures such as black-market Russian made ship-to-air missiles, a mini-sub, and the latest in surveillance and mine detection systems. This vessel did not want to be bothered.

Dmitry Romanov watched silently on the ship's closed surveillance system as the helicopter came in and effortlessly landed on the deck. At fifty-five years of age, he was a man at the height of his game. The heir presumptive to the long-vacant Russian throne, Romanov claimed he could trace his family lineage as far back as the beginning of the House of Romanov in 1613. His family had lived in Paris ever since the Russian Revolution in 1917; however, recently, Romanov had decided to move back to the land of his ancestors and had bought land outside of Moscow and built a palatial mansion for his family to live in. He had always known affluence and prestige; his father was a wealthy executive who died when Romanov was in his teens. Although young, Romanov quickly took the reins of his father's business. Driven by an insatiable desire for wealth and power, he was a multimillionaire by age eighteen and a billionaire before he turned thirty, with offices and holdings all over the world. Oil and natural gas were the two commodities that Romanov continually sought. If they were out there hidden deep underground, he seemed to know where to look and never let anyone or anything get in his way. His shares of companies involved in oil exploration in Russia and West Africa were unmatched; his profits soared by the day. He rarely traveled anywhere except aboard his yacht, safe and secure from his rivals and the prying eyes and ears of many a hostile power.

He had short black hair along with a neatly trimmed circle goatee, both always immaculately kept. Romanov was by choice a vegetarian; this, combined with his avid love of swimming, kept him trim and in outstanding shape. Today, Romanov was casually dressed in a pair of white slacks with a blue and white striped nautical-looking short-sleeved shirt. His bright cognac-brown eyes burned with an intensity that showed his razor-sharp intellect and unparalleled drive to dominate and control the world around him.

A young woman in her late twenties dressed in a snug teal jumpsuit quietly entered the high-tech office and walked over beside Romanov. She easily stood six feet tall and anyone admiring her physique would see that she, like her father, was fanatical about her physical condition. Her face was angular with hauntingly deep-set hazel-colored eyes. The young woman's long black hair was tied in a ponytail that went halfway down her muscular back. She was unmistakably her father's daughter.

"Is she really back so soon?" asked the girl, as she peered up at the screen as the helicopter doors were opened by two of Romanov's well-armed security personnel. She pursed her lips and took in a deep breath as she intently watched her twin sister, equally attired in a jumpsuit, this one tan as she stepped onto the ship's deck.

"Yes my dear Alexandra, your sister Nika is home," replied Romanov, lovingly patting his daughter's well-manicured hand.

Alexandra and Nika Romanov were identical twins. They not only looked alike, but they also always dressed alike. Thousands of kilometers could separate them, yet they would always arrive on time dressed in exactly the same outfit, just in different colors. This was the only way that her parents could tell them apart as children.

"She looks tired," said Alexandra sympathetically, as she watched her sister slowly climb down a set of metal stairs leading down from the helipad.

"Don't worry too much, I am sure that your sister has done her part and has obtained what we are looking for," said Romanov.

Alexandra watched impassively as her sister walked, under escort, from the helipad through the main deck of the yacht towards her father's office, located in the luxurious aft lower level. "Father are you sure we are not pushing things too fast?"

asked Alexandra, as she smoothly moved behind her father's tall antique eighteenth century wooden chair.

"Alexandra, my dear, this is not like you. You are starting to make me nervous," said Romanov, reaching up and lightly squeezing his daughter's soft pale-skinned hand. "Your sister is the most-resourceful person I know at obtaining, how would you say, the unobtainable. If she is back, then she has the missing pieces of the puzzle with her."

Alexandra looked down at her father and smiled at him. "Perhaps I am being overly melodramatic, but please remember father, we are risking everything we own on this venture, and I for one won't relax until we have what is rightfully ours."

"Your mother would be proud of the women you have both become, but Alexandra, you worry too much my dear; it's truly not good for you." Tamara Romanov, the girls' mother, died almost ten years ago from cancer. Alexandra, the more pragmatic of the twins, had taken over the role of matriarch and looked after her father and his business affairs with cold efficiency.

Seconds later, there was a knock. The door to Romanov's office slowly opened and one of his impeccably dressed security guards entered the room. "Sorry to intrude sir, I have your daughter waiting outside the door," said the guard respectfully.

"Very good, show her in," said Romanov.

With a nod, the guard opened the door and politely waited for Nika to enter the room.

With a slight nod to the guard, Nika strode into the room, locking eyes with her father. Her twin sister was standing guardedly behind him like an eagle waiting to pounce on some poor field mouse. She quickly scanned the room and with an unconcealed smirk, she noticed that her father had extensively re-decorated the room since she was last aboard. There were several new paintings by Van Gogh and Rembrandt adorning the walls, along with four ancient Chinese vases from what Nika suspected was the Third or Fourth Century. The magnificence of the room was designed deliberately to awe Romanov's guests, but all it elicited from Nika was a bored, indifferent shrug. Money and material gains no longer interested her. She now only lived for the rush that came with her high-risk lifestyle. Nika always knew that she would die young and yet somehow, deep down inside her cold heart, she welcomed it.

Romanov saw the uncaring look in his daughter's unemotional brown eyes and realized with a heavy heart that he was losing her. Ever since her unfaithful husband's death from an overdose last year, his beloved Nika had embarked on a self-destructive path. Until now, he had been able to manage it, but seeing the lost look in her eyes, Romanov knew things were getting worse. Standing, he smiled warmly, walked towards Nika, and wrapped his arms around her. He gave her a long hug followed by a quick kiss on each cheek.

"Please my beloved, please come in and take a seat," said Romanov cheerfully, as the guard pulled out an ornately carved chair that had once belonged to Louis XIV of France for her.

Nika sat and looked up towards her father. "I am sorry to say father, but I cannot stay long," said Nika with an accent that, like her sister's, was a mix of French and Russian.

"Nika, please reconsider," replied Romanov, perplexed at his daughter's behavior. "My dear, we haven't seen you for months, and now you are already planning to leave. Please, say you will stay at least for one night."

"No, father, I cannot. In fact, I need to be on my way shortly, if I am going to make my next appointment in the States," said Nika brusquely, as she reached into a pocket pulled out her silver cigarette case, removed one and lit it. She knew her father had never smoked a day in his life and thoroughly detested the smell of it, but she did not care; she needed a smoke, and that was all there was to it.

Alexandra could see the game her sister was playing, and she shot her sister a look that said *back off now...or else.*

Nika saw the expression on her sister's face, shrugged and ignored her.

Romanov saw what was happening. He struggled to smile. "Nika my dearest, please reconsider and stay," he said, his voice almost pleading.

Nika removed the smoldering cigarette from her lips and crushed it in an ornate and expensive-looking China cup on the table.

Both Alexandra and her father winced at the latest display of rebellion from Nika.

36

Alexandra's blood was boiling. How dare her sister act so disrespectfully in front of their father! "If you are not going to bless us with a visit," said Alexandra, her words dripping with venom, "then please tell us, what is so important that you had to fly here to tell us only to have to leave right away?"

"Later," said Nika curtly.

Romanov watched his daughters as they verbally sparred with one another. He never said it aloud, but he had always encouraged his daughters to be competitive, even with each other. It was the only way to survive in the real world. People will use you up and spit you out if you do not learn to use them first.

Nika slowly undid a zipper on her breast pocket, and pulled out a small green memory stick, which she carefully laid on the table in front of her.

Alexandra reached over and snatched it, examining it. She was not surprised to see that it was marked top-secret, and had come from the South African Ministry of Defense.

"So, what did you have to do to obtain this little gem?" asked Alexandra, as she eyed her sister.

"Not too much," said Nika, as she poured herself a tall glass of ice-cold water. "It was remarkably easy. I appealed to the loneliness of a very young and forlorn corporal far from home, who also happened to work in the computer section located deep inside the South African Ministry of Defense. He was instantly smitten by me and, after a few days of toying with him, I simply had him download the information that I was looking for."

"What about the corporal?" asked Romanov.

"Oh, he had an unfortunate accident. They fished his bloated body from the Jukskei River yesterday," said Nika, without a hint of remorse in her voice.

"Most unfortunate for the young man," said Alexandra dismissively, as if they were talking about the weather.

"Love can be fatal," said Nika with a cold smile as she poured herself another glass of water.

A sudden thought occurred to Romanov. Perhaps Nika's husband was helped along with his suicide; he was not putting anything past his daughter these days. With a forced smile, he asked, "What are the chances his theft of key defense

37

information will be discovered?"

"Nil, absolutely none," Nika said confidently. "The late corporal uploaded a virus that I provided to him after he had downloaded the information that I needed. It will take their IT experts weeks to de-bug their system and by then the files will be horribly corrupted. The theft will go unnoticed for weeks; by then it will, of course, all be too late for anyone to do anything about it."

Romanov smiled at his daughter's ingenuity.

"Have you looked at the files?" asked Alexandra, her voice suddenly trembling with anticipation as she spoke.

"Oh, most definitely; everything, and I do mean everything, is on that memory stick. Father, all you have to do is give the go ahead to Colonel Chang and what you seek will be yours," said Nika.

Romanov said nothing. He stared proudly at Nika and turned towards Alexandra. "Take the stick and download all the information into our secure computers. Make sure you encrypt it before sending it on to Colonel Chang. Let him know that he can back-brief me via video-teleconference on his plan to secure the packages tomorrow morning at 1000 hours," said Romanov.

Alexandra nodded, picked up the stick, and placed it in her pocket for safekeeping.

"Nika, you have done wonderfully," said Romanov. "Since you have taken the time to personally deliver this truly wonderful news to us, why do you have to leave?"

"Father, I have an entirely reliable source in the U.S. that has provided me with information that the American woman your people failed to grab in the Philippines will be back home tomorrow night," said Nika as she inattentively swirled the ice around in her crystal glass.

Romanov smiled. "Do you think you can you get your hands on her?"

Nika locked eyes with her father. "Have I ever failed you?" said Nika boastfully.

"No, not once, my dear," Romanov said as he patted his daughter's hand.

Nika stood. "Now, I have wasted too much time already. I must be going." Nika wrapped her arms around her father, looked over at her sister, and shot her a smug, almost taunting, self-righteous smile.

Romanov and Alexandra stood there watching as Nika exited the room and was escorted to the waiting helicopter. When she arrived on the helipad, Nika turned towards the nearest camera and playfully waved goodbye, just before climbing into the passenger door of the helicopter.

Romanov shook his head at his daughter's increasingly unpredictable behavior, before sitting down in his favorite leather chair. Reaching into his leather briefcase, he pulled out an iPad and opened it to today's *New York Times*. The headline read *Another deadly week of unrest sweeps Moscow —Can President Ivankov survive?*

He smiled to himself and looked towards Alexandra and thought about the revolution he was secretly financing. "These zealots are creating more havoc than I had truly hoped for when we initially agreed to support them and their foolish uprising," said Romanov, genuinely impressed with the chaos and carnage sown by the latest bombing at an army barracks on the outskirts of Moscow.

Alexandra looked over her father's shoulder at the news headline; a crooked smile crept across her face. "The Russian current government is nothing more than a glorified dictatorship. It will naturally overreact and crack down even harder on the rebels, causing more disenfranchised people to turn to them, thereby creating the opportunity for someone willing to take the chance to lead Russia and her people out of this mess."

Like a cat, Alexandra slinked over and sat down beside her father. "As I planned, Father, we only need to keep the West's intelligence agencies focused away from what is really going to occur. The plan is pure genius in its simplicity. I have it from very well-placed and highly reliable sources that your name is already being whispered on the lips of some very nervous Chinese, Japanese, and European officials as the possible savior of Russia and *their* precious supply of oil and natural gas. Your well-cultivated, pro-western stance, and proven track record as a formidable global business leader, makes you their knight in white shining armor," said Alexandra smugly.

"They are all fools who have become addicted to the cheap

oil and gas I have been selling them," said Romanov contemptuously.

"Most assuredly, father, I expect that by the end of next week, the West will be begging you to step in and become the de-facto ruler of Russia. As it should be, the House of Romanov will resume its rightful place as the leader of the nation."

"This is all truly excellent news. Now, all we need is the right catalyst, and we will be richer and more powerful than any family in the history of the world. Alexandra, do you think Chang and his band of overly well-paid mercenaries can pull this off?" asked Romanov.

"If Nika is right, and the information contained on the memory stick is 100% accurate, then Colonel Chang is the man to do it. After all, he does not come cheap. People like him care more about their reputations than anything else. He will deliver what we are after," replied Alexandra confidently.

Romanov smiled and lovingly patted his daughter's hand. "You and your sister truly do make me proud."

Alexandra smiled at her father as she stood, removed the memory stick from her pocket, and rolled it in her hand for a moment, wondering to herself what their world would look like in a matter of weeks. Snapping herself back into the here and now, she strode out of her father's office, leaving him alone with his thoughts.

6

Polaris Operations Complex
Albany, New York

About thirty kilometers south of Albany, New York, comfortably nestled against the Hudson River, is a small run-of-the-mill gas station that also sells local antiques left over from estate auctions. Its owners, a retired Hispanic couple originally from California, make a respectable profit selling gas and the odd antique to passing tourists. Although no signs exist, the gas station is the only distinct landmark indicating the turnoff that leads to the Polaris Complex. A dirt road full of potholes that get worse by the season gently meanders behind the store and then disappears off into the thick pine-filled woods which surround the three hundred acres that are part of the Polaris Complex, with its administrative buildings and extensive training grounds.

The brainchild of Major-General Jack O'Reilly, U.S. Army (retired), Polaris Operations (Global) is a discreet, private organization that specializes in unique problem solving, military, police and civilian training, along with consulting services that will go anywhere in the world at a moment's notice. Although in competition with the larger companies in the US and Great Britain, General O'Reilly made sure early on that he and his people only ever dealt with legitimately elected governments and internationally recognized organizations such as the UN and other international Non-Governmental Organizations. To date, most of his clients only required low-level training, conducted either in their home nation or on Polaris' wide-ranging grounds themselves. Weapons handling, advanced driving, small unit tactics and police training could all be handled by his expert crew of retired military and police personnel working seven and twenty-four. No one could apply for a position there; all of O'Reilly's people were handpicked. Many of them were enticed away from their parent organization to come and work for him for considerably more money. He had four field teams, of which only one, Mitchell's, worked on the more challenging and dangerous missions approved and overseen exclusively by O'Reilly himself.

It had snowed through the night, but as the gray light of dawn crept into the world, the snow slowed and then stopped, leaving the picturesque countryside looking like a Christmas card. The bright yellow sun shone down on a refreshingly beautiful winter's day.

Mitchell turned his beat-up blue Jeep Wrangler onto the dirt road by the gas station, heading into the snow-covered woods. Music blared inside the cab, and Mitchell drummed his hands on the steering wheel to the latest tunes from U2. A heavy blanket of snow covered the fir trees lining the road, weighing down their boughs, giving the entire area a decidedly Christmas look to it.

Having turned thirty-one the month prior, Ryan Mitchell felt that life was going his way. A graduate of West Point, Mitchell had chosen to serve in the army. He sought out a series of ever-challenging positions within the army and soon joined the U.S. Army Rangers, a principal part of the U.S. Special Operations Command. After several tours in Iraq and Afghanistan, his superiors identified Mitchell as an officer who would do well in his career. However, he would never hold a key position in the higher echelons of the military because he would never adapt to being stuck behind a desk more than being in the field. Mitchell did not regret his choice to leave the army; he was never comfortable with the idea of playing the political games that came with the more senior appointments he would have assumed in the service. Although he would not admit it, Mitchell had grown increasingly frustrated with the seeming civilian indifference to the years he and his comrades spent overseas.

When he was unexpectedly called by General O'Reilly to join his organization, Mitchell jumped at the chance to take his life in a new direction. It was a decision he would never regret.

Lost in his thoughts, Mitchell almost forgot to slow down when a closed gate barring his way suddenly appeared in front of him, as he approached a sharp curve in the trail. Slamming on the brakes, Mitchell cursed as the jeep slid to a less than graceful halt, mere inches from a locked metal fence.

"You'll need to pay more attention next time, Mister Mitchell," yelled a man in his sixties wearing a rumpled blue uniform, as he stepped out from a well-camouflaged guard shack and ambled over beside Mitchell's idling jeep. Although he knew almost everybody who worked at Polaris by sight, Pat McGregor still diligently checked everyone's IDs—he did not want anyone getting in on his watch.

"Sorry about that, Pat. That's what, the second-or third time I've done that?" said Mitchell as he flashed his ID and reached down for his travel mug filled with home-brewed coffee.

"Try again, mister," said McGregor. "You forget every single time, and we go through this damned routine time and again," scolded McGregor as he looked over Mitchell's less than pristine-looking jeep.

"Well, at least I'm consistent," joked Mitchell as he took a long swig of coffee and put his ID away. "Many people in today?"

"A few folks came in last night to do who knows what, but overall it's a fairly quiet day. The usual staff is in though; you know, the general, his secretary, and some of the other under-appreciated security folks like me," said McGregor as he stepped back into his shack and flipped a switch to open the creaking metal gate. Although the gate looked antiquated, there were cameras and motion sensors covering every centimeter of the perimeter. The security staff boasted that a squirrel could not get onto the grounds without their knowledge. However, they could not explain a family of deer that seemed to come and go as they pleased.

"Thanks, Pat," said Mitchell with a wave as he changed gears and drove off down the snow-covered path. A couple of minutes later, Mitchell pulled up his jeep in front of a large gray building that looked more like a storage warehouse than an office complex. It may not have been architecturally pleasing to the eye, but the main Polaris Complex building was very utilitarian. Located inside were the head offices for the various branches that ran the organization and where General O'Reilly personally held all of Mitchell's pre-mission briefs.

Mitchell jumped out of his jeep and headed to the closed front doors. His tall, athletic frame was dressed for the weather in a warm blue ski jacket, dark blue jeans, and a pair of worn brown leather hiking boots.

Inside the building were several rows of metal detectors manned by ex-service personnel who had retired from the military or police forces due to injuries suffered while serving. Mitchell knew the drill. Before passing through the metal detectors, he handed over his sidearm, a Swiss-made 9mm SIG Sauer P220, to Harry Chappell, a lanky ex-marine who cleared the weapon before placing it in a safe box under his desk.

Mitchell waved to Chappell and, whistling to himself, he sauntered through the detectors, signed in and walked down the long highly polished corridor until he came to a set of stairs that led directly up to General O'Reilly's office. Taking two steps at a time, Mitchell charged up the stairs. With a loud bang, he flung the door open to O'Reilly's personal assistant's office.

Tammy Spencer, a beautiful African-American woman in her early thirties, who had lost a leg in Iraq, did not even bother to look up. "I don't know why you insist on doing that, Ryan Mitchell. I have you on the surveillance cameras the instant you enter the building," said Spencer as she tapped a small screen on her desk with her pencil. Today, she was wearing a New York Jets football jersey instead of one of her usual eye-catching dresses.

"Casual day at work today, Tammy?" asked Mitchell.

"Captain Mitchell, if you must know, I am in here on my own time during the holidays, so the general lets me dress as I please," shot back Spencer as she finally looked up at Mitchell with her appealing deep-brown eyes.

"Don't get upset Tammy," said Mitchell defensively. "I didn't mean any offence. I just look forward to seeing you dressed to the nines, since I work with the people I do. Your outfits tend to brighten my days. Besides, I'm still betting the Vikings will do better this year," said Mitchell.

"They may be from Minnesota like you, but I doubt they'll do very well this year. Their quarterback was injured last week, and with him gone, your team is doomed," said Spencer, as she shot Mitchell an enticing smile. "Now, Captain, enough chit-chat. General O'Reilly is in his office, and he's waiting for you, so please go in."

Mitchell winked at Spencer and turned away from her desk. For as long as Mitchell had worked for O'Reilly, he had innocently flirted with Tammy. It was just for fun; she was getting married in the New Year to a New York City police officer whom she had met while they were both on active duty in Basra, Iraq. Straightening out his ruffled appearance, Mitchell headed the last few feet down the carpeted hall to O'Reilly's office.

The door was open; Mitchell respectfully stopped at the entrance and knocked.

Major-General Jack O'Reilly looked away from his laptop and saw Mitchell standing there. Although retired, O'Reilly kept himself in superb shape and still looked as if he could throw on his college uniform and play football with men more than half his age. His head was smooth-shaven and the only concession to growing older that he allowed himself were the silver-rimmed glasses that he wore to read.

On seeing Mitchell, a smile broke on his broad face. "Come on in, Ryan, come on in," boomed O'Reilly's deep voice.

A thirty-five-year veteran with the U.S. Army, O'Reilly had spent most of that time in the U.S. Special Operations Command and had been the first African-American to command the first Special Forces Operational Detachment-Delta, an elite and highly secretive Tier One Special Forces organization that spearheaded America's global counter-terrorism fight. A few years back, he had been offered a more senior operations position in the Pentagon, but when his wife was diagnosed with cancer, he decided it was time to stay home more often and established Polaris.

Mitchell stepped inside the office and was met by a smiling O'Reilly, who eagerly shook his hand.

"It's damn good to see you, Ryan. Come in and have a seat," said O'Reilly with a wave of his hand. "Take off your jacket and stay awhile."

Mitchell took off his winter jacket, revealing a well-worn army issue green fleece sweater underneath.

"Take the boy out of the army, but you can't take the army out of the boy," kidded O'Reilly, as he looked over Mitchell's mix of military and civilian attire.

Both men sat down. O'Reilly reached over and poured them both a steaming hot cup of coffee from the carafe on his desk.

"How is Diane doing, sir?" asked Mitchell, inquiring after O'Reilly's wife.

"She has good days and bad days, but thankfully, there are far more good ones than bad."

Both men sat silently for a moment.

O'Reilly smiled and handed Mitchell a coffee. "Ryan, you and your people did really great work in the Philippines."

"Thanks, General. Honestly, it was purely by happenstance that we stumbled upon those thugs. It was also a plus that the Philippine Counter-Terrorist unit that we had been training was as ready to go as it was. A lot of the credit really belongs to them," said Mitchell humbly.

"You're being too modest again, my boy."

"Just calling it as I see it, sir."

"Well, some people don't see it that way, and that's why I asked you to come by today," said O'Reilly as he leaned forward and yelled down the hallway. "Tammy, could you please get Mister Samuel Kim on the line? Thanks."

Curiosity got the better of him. Mitchell raised an eyebrow.

"Do you remember a young Asian-American girl named Alanis Kim among the students at the dig site?" asked O'Reilly.

Mitchell scrunched up his face and shook his head. It had all happened so fast. The only name and face he truly remembered was Jen's.

"Well, don't feel bad if you can't remember her, but she remembers you and her really rich father wants to thank you personally," said O'Reilly as he waited for the call to be put through.

Mitchell felt embarrassed. He cleared his throat and said,

"General, there's really no need for this. I just did what I was trained and what you pay me quite well to do."

"I knew you would say that, but a billionaire client with many wealthy friends is always a good thing to have on our side. Consider this a little PR work for the firm."

O'Reilly's phone rang. He picked it up and spoke for a few seconds before placing the speakerphone on. "Please go ahead, Mister Kim. I have Captain Ryan Mitchell in my office with me."

"Thanks, General," said a voice with a slight Hawaiian accent over the speaker. "General, my wife and I would like to personally thank your organization and especially Captain Mitchell for the outstanding work that he did in rescuing our Alanis from those savages."

Mitchell leaned towards the speaker. "Sir, thanks for that. It means a whole lot to the team; I'll make sure that everyone involved knows of your gratitude."

"You're far too modest, Captain. My wife and I were horrified when we heard what had happened," said Kim.

"Sir, I was just doing my job," said Mitchell as he winked at O'Reilly.

"You had best watch out, General, or I just might steal him away from you," said Kim teasingly through the speaker.

"Don't you dare," said O'Reilly with a chuckle. "I haven't gotten my substantial investment in him back yet."

"Once again, gentlemen, please accept our heartfelt gratitude for all you have done. I know that I've kept you all far too long at this time of the year," said Kim.

"Thanks, sir," said Mitchell and O'Reilly in unison.

"Oh, one last thing before I go, and I don't want to hear either of you say that isn't necessary. I have had my accountant wire a half-million dollars into your company account. I would like to see it distributed as a bonus to the men and women on the ground who risked their lives for my Alanis," said Kim, choking up over the line.

"Thank you for that, sir. I'll personally see that it gets distributed equitably before I go home today," said O'Reilly.

"Goodbye, and all the best to you and your folks," said Kim before hanging up.

O'Reilly terminated the call and with a bear-like grin, he looked over at Mitchell. "So, Ryan, what are you going to do with your 100K?"

Mitchell was speechless for a minute. "General, I doubt I deserve that much."

O'Reilly raised his hand to cut off the conversation. "Don't be foolish. You and all your people will get 100K each. It's only fair," said O'Reilly.

"Thanks, sir, I really don't know what else to say."

"Ryan, for the next month you and your team will be moved into reserve status," said O'Reilly. "Take some time to relax and spend time with your family."

"Well, with that much time off and a spare 100K in my pocket, I think I'll see about having a date tonight with a beautiful woman whom I met in the Philippines."

O'Reilly turned curious. "Is she here in New York?"

"No; actually, she lives in Charlotte, North Carolina, so I had best book a flight and get my ass in gear if I am to attend a charity fundraiser event with her tonight."

O'Reilly chuckled. "A charity event in North Carolina? You do realize that this will undoubtedly be a black-tie event, so you'll need to dress up for once in your life."

"Black-tie," repeated Mitchell. His mind raced, wondering if he would be able to rent a tuxedo before heading to the airport.

Seeing the look on his face, O'Reilly asked Tammy to book Mitchell's flight and to find him a tuxedo rental shop on the way to the airport.

"I almost forgot, one thing before you leave," said O'Reilly as he rifled through a file on his desk. "It would appear that the man you detained and then handed over to the police in the Philippines has escaped."

Mitchell raised an eyebrow. "What happened, sir?"

"An investigation is still ongoing, but it would appear that he somehow managed to bribe some guards and made his getaway sometime during the night last week."

"He didn't seem too happy with me and Nate. We'll have to add him to our database of people we've managed to piss off recently."

Mitchell shook O'Reilly's hand and with a promise to call

tomorrow to let him know how the date went, Mitchell left the office. He was almost past Tammy Spencer's desk when a troubled look on her face caught his eye.

"Ryan, it's truly awful," said Spencer, her voice choking with sorrow.

"What's wrong, Tammy?" asked Mitchell

"It's Russia again. Someone set off a series of car bombs at several apartment buildings. CNN is reporting that there could be hundreds, if not thousands of dead and injured."

Mitchell looked at the images of devastation on the TV and felt a sudden chill crawl down his spine. His instincts told him it was about to get a lot worse, although he could not predict that it would soon involve him as well.

7

Northern Province
South Africa

The sky turned dark as a storm rolled in off the Indian Ocean.

Out to sea, looking like a flock of malevolent prehistoric birds, six large dark shapes dropped from the leaden clouds, diving straight towards the churning gray seas below. Straightening out barely fifty meters above the waves, the helicopters switched off their running lights one by one; darkness quickly enveloped them.

Sohn Gun-Woo briefly looked down and studied his instrument panel for the thousandth time since taking off. Having spent countless hours over the past ten years flying at night wearing night vision goggles, for Sohn Gun-Woo it now seemed as natural to him as breathing.

A former North Korean Army Major, Sohn was a natural at flying the ungainly-looking MI-18 Hip helicopter. Outside it had started to rain, dropping visibility to a few hundred meters, but that was not Sohn's biggest concern. Looking left and right over his shoulders, he was relieved to see that his wingmen, two additional MI-8s, were flying close by in a tight V-formation with his own craft in the lead. Sohn knew flying this fast and close was dangerous to try during the day. However, at night wearing NVGs, it could be a sure-fire recipe for disaster. One small error by any one of the pilots and they would all crash into one another and end up as a flaming ball of wreckage plummeting towards the Indian Ocean. Flying in such a tight formation required nerves of steel and had taken weeks of practice to perfect. His co-pilot, a former Ethiopian Air Force pilot, interrupted his thoughts and spoke over the intercom to say that they were now ten minutes out from their objective. Sohn acknowledged the information and casually dipped the nose of his helicopter. As one, the formation dove closer to the waves to avoid detection as they crossed over into South African territory.

Flying barely one hundred meters behind the three troop-carrying helicopters were two additional empty MI-8s and one massive Hind-D attack helicopter, a monstrous Soviet-era helicopter that looked more like a medieval dragon than the sleeker attack helicopters used throughout the West. The Hind-D was armed with a 12.7mm machine gun under the nose cone; mounted on its small wings were four 57mm rocket pods, two on either side. Finally, on each wingtip were several AT-6 Spiral anti-tank missiles just in case the assault force ran into anything larger than a truck on their objective. It truly was a machine made for killing.

Sohn reached down and flipped a switch on his instrument panel. In the back of the helicopter's spacious cabin, a red light came on, warning his passengers to prepare for landing. So far, it had gone as planned, but now Sohn felt his stomach tighten as he grew nervous. Looking towards the horizon, Sohn searched the deteriorating night sky for their planned landing zone.

Nestled between two hills was an insignificant farming community of barely one hundred souls. Many of the local farmers had lived there for generations, making a good living by raising and selling cattle. A few kilometers south of the village was a small isolated ranch that had been abandoned by its original owner. About five years ago, a quiet stranger from Johannesburg bought the farm and had it completely refurbished.

The front door to the home opened. Jan Dornberg, a balding man with a large belly that hung over his belt, stepped onto the front porch of the old-fashioned looking wooden farmhouse. He felt the cool night air on his face. The smell of rain was in the air; he knew that it would not be long before it stormed. Calmly looking down at his watch, he saw that he barely had five minutes before the planned arrival of the helicopters. A former member of the South African Special Forces, Dornberg was not what he appeared to be. To the local farmers of the tiny village of Georgetown, he was a simple, but reclusive farmer who never bothered his neighbors and in turn they never paid much attention to him.

Inside, he felt nothing, nothing at all at the horrific act he was about to do. His beloved wife of twenty years had been murdered during a home invasion in Durban nearly eight years ago. Ever since then, Dornberg had been shuffled around from one unimportant desk job to another. That was until five years ago, when he ended up on the farm as a glorified night watchman. Approaching mandatory retirement, Dornberg had become an alcoholic and had slowly grown more and more disenchanted with his lot in the world. Unexpectedly, a mysterious and beautiful brown-eyed stranger approached him one day. The stranger asked him about making five million dollars to betray the country that no longer gave a damn about him. He never once hesitated.

Trying to act casually, he walked over to where two men were idly standing in front of his farmhouse smoking cigars and laughing about something. Dornberg suspected they were talking about him; his blood started to boil. *Damned ingrates*. He knew from experience that both men, who were security personnel, carried semi-automatic pistols hidden carefully under their scruffy blue work clothes. Dornberg silently cursed his luck. Once a month, like clockwork, an inspection team disguised as farmhands came up from Johannesburg to check on the security of the farm and its hidden cache. He thought he had it all worked out to the minute, but these troublesome men had come one week after the last team had visited, thoroughly screwing up his plan. As he walked towards the unsuspecting men, using the shadows, Dornberg calmly drew his silenced South African made Vektor 9mm pistol from inside his bulky dark-green jacket. Keeping the gun discreetly hidden behind his back, Dornberg, with a pleasant smile on his face, waved at the two unwary guards. They simply nodded in recognition and turned their backs on him to continue their conversation as the first flash of jagged silver lightning ripped across the darkened sky, sending eerily-shaped shadows dancing across the vast open plain.

His mouth dry with fear, he could feel his heart jackhammering away inside his chest. Dornberg closed the distance, quickly looking around to make sure no one else was watching. He brought his pistol up and in rapid succession, fired off two bullets into the skulls of the guards, killing them both instantly. Dornberg had never killed a man before. Looking down at the dead bodies, a cold sweat wrapped itself around his body. He struggled to keep himself from throwing up. Taking a deep breath to calm his fraying nerves, Dornberg strode over, kicked the bodies to make sure they were dead and then dragged the lifeless bodies behind some nearby bushes. Satisfied that no one would see the corpses until it was all over, Dornberg strolled back calmly towards the farmhouse. When he did not hear any alarms coming from the small command post hidden deep below the building, Dornberg knew that he had pulled it off. Now all he had to do was wait for his accomplices to arrive.

Another bright flash of jagged silver lightning lit up the dark night sky followed instantaneously by a deep boom of thunder in the distance, startling Dornberg. *This could not end soon enough*, he thought. Reaching deep inside his jacket, he retrieved three small handheld infrared strobe lights. Looking down, Dornberg saw that his hands were shaking and his stomach felt like he was going to lose the battle and be sick any second. Fighting the guilt and growing doubt nagging at his conscience, he took one last long look around to make sure it was safe, before activating the markers. With an underhand pitch, learned from playing cricket in his youth, Dornberg threw the markers out onto the open grassy field directly in front of the farm. The markers were invisible to the naked eye; only someone wearing night-vision gear could even hope to detect them blinking on and off. The approaching storm clouds thundered ominously. Dornberg carefully removed the silencer from his pistol and put them both away in his jacket. Taking out a cigarette, Dornberg lit it. He had done his part; now, it was up to the others. Taking a seat on the deck, he waited for the approaching helicopters to arrive.

Inside the lead helicopter, Colonel Chang Ji-Hun saw the warning light come on, bathing the cabin in a deep red hue. Calmly, he removed his headset and stood inside the spacious interior of the MI-8 Hip. With his thick mop of salt and pepper hair and a black eye patch over his left eye, Chang looked more like a seventeenth-century pirate than a highly skilled mercenary. Raising his hand, Chang indicated to his men that they were two minutes out from their objective. Silently, his team all gave him quick thumbs' up in unison and started to unbuckle themselves from their mesh canvas seats along the walls of the chopper. Chang, a former North Korean Special Operative, who saw the folly of working for despots when he could be deciding his own fate, looked into the faces of his men. Most were in their early to late thirties. All were veterans of many years with the North Korean, East European, or African Special Forces. Many of his men had taken part in clandestine raids to conduct sabotage or gather intelligence throughout the world. Their cool and confident demeanor showed on their expressionless faces.

Chang was wearing full battledress with a chest rig that held ten AK magazines along with numerous fragmentation grenades. He made his way to the back of the helicopter so he would be the first man off once they hit the ground. Chang had never failed in a mission, and he knew that this was the most-lucrative mission he had ever planned in his entire life. He had studied the objective for weeks and was confident that he knew everything there was to know about it. He did not expect much in the way of resistance, but he never knew until he arrived at the position. Chang knew that no plan, no matter how carefully thought out, ever survived contact with the enemy. He, like his men, had to be able to adapt and overcome their opponent quickly if they were to pull off this lightning-fast raid.

Major Sohn's hands were starting to get sweaty inside his skin-tight leather gloves. Looking into the night, he was becoming concerned. Although equipped with a state-of-the-art GPS system, the only way he knew that their contact was waiting and that it was safe to land was via the IR strobes. He was positive that he should have seen the IR markers by now. Sohn, fearing that something had gone wrong on the objective, was about to break radio silence, when suddenly he caught a glimpse of something flashing out of the corner of his eye.

With a relieved smile on his face, he saw that the IR indicators were flashing on and off as bright as a bonfire in the night, indicating that it was safe to approach the farm. Letting out a deep sigh, Sohn banked the helicopter over towards the beacons. Now that they were mere seconds away from landing, he broke radio silence for the first time since leaving base. Sohn sent the code word *Eagle* three times over the radio to ensure that his message was heard. Knowing that no reply was coming back, Sohn once more switched the radio off and started to slow the helicopter down so he could land smoothly in the field directly in front of the farmhouse. As they had practiced numerous times on an isolated farm in Mozambique, Sohn's Hip helicopter would land first, rapidly disembark his men, keep rolling forward and quickly take off to be followed by the next chopper waiting in line. If things went well, all of Chang's team would be on the ground and in action in less than sixty seconds.

A sound caught Dornberg's ear: a rhythmic beating, somewhere out in the dark, growing closer by the second. His pulse raced as he saw the helicopters start to emerge out of the rain like monstrous bats sent from hell itself. Though the glass windshield was blackened out, Dornberg could see the lead pilot bathed in a red light as he brought his helicopter into land. The rotor-wash from the powerful blades stirred up dirt and pebbles on the field, showering Dornberg with small, annoying pieces of debris. He barely heard the yelling coming from behind him over the noise of the helicopter. Turning around, he saw two guards armed with assault rifles emerge from the front door of the house, waving towards the approaching swarm of helicopters. Without even bothering to aim, Dornberg brought his pistol out of his jacket and emptied an entire magazine into the two men, sending their lifeless bodies tumbling down the front steps onto the dirt. All pretense of duplicity was gone now. Dornberg tossed the empty gun onto the ground and picked up an assault rifle belonging to one of the dead guards. Checking that it was loaded, Dornberg stood staring into the rain as the lead helicopter was now barely thirty meters from him, closing in fast.

Inside the Hip's cabin, a green light flashed on. Instantly, Colonel Chang pulled up on the latch holding closed the large bulbous rear doors of the Hip. No sooner had the helicopter touched down, when Chang kicked open the doors, jumped out and led his men out of the back of the chopper and into the cool rain coming down on the open field. Quickly fanning out, Chang's men took up positions and waited just the briefest of times until their helicopter lifted off into the night, its rotors momentarily blinding them with a storm kicked up by the powerful downdraft from the departing Hip. Knowing that another Hip was mere seconds behind them, Chang stood and, with a wave of his hand, he and his men rose like wraiths coming out of the ground and rushed towards the brightly lit farmhouse. A large man moved towards Chang. He tensed. Seeing the two dead bodies lying on the dirt behind the man, Chang suspected that he was their contact and not an enemy target. He was about to call to the man when a shot rang out from a window in the farmhouse. The large man seemed to stagger forward. A moment later, blood burst forth from his mouth; he fell to his knees and tumbled sideways onto the wet ground. Chang ran past the body; the man did not matter to him, but his mission tonight meant everything. He had no time for the dead and dying; that would come later. He'd barely made it ten meters when all hell broke out. Fire erupted from the front windows of the farmhouse. Men screamed and fell. Chang's well-trained mercenaries reacted and promptly returned fire. Breaking down into two-man fire-teams, they continued to push forward; one man fired while the other dashed forward a few meters and started to fire at their enemy. The noise was overwhelming. The sound of Chang's men returning fire combined with the rotor blades from the incoming Hips made it impossible for Chang to communicate with his men. Unlike American Special Forces, not all of Chang's men had night-vision gear, and only the squad leaders had personal radios. None of this bothered him. It was his decision to keep things simple. All the men on the mission tonight were highly trained and handpicked by Chang. He was confident that they could deal with any opposition that they might find here tonight.

Suddenly, the night sky lit up as rockets from their supporting Hind helicopter tore into the front windows of the farmhouse. Blinding explosions ripped open the front of the building as if it were made of paper. Chang instinctively ducked as glass and wood flew everywhere. A large chunk of the front door sailed over Chang's head and smashed into splinters on the ground behind him. Looking back, Chang was relieved to see the last Hip leaving the landing zone. A smile broke on his blackened face. He now had all fifty-five men of his mercenary team on the ground. The gunfire began to slacken from the burning farmhouse. Chang stood and without any care for his own well-being, called for his men to stand and follow him. A loud cheer rang out as Chang and his men dashed forward, firing small bursts from their assault rifles into the wrecked house at any target of opportunity.

Chang was the first man to reach the steps leading into the building. He pulled his AK-74 tight into his shoulder as he advanced over the destroyed remains of the front of the burning farmhouse. Pausing for a moment to see if anyone could have survived the initial rocket attack, Chang decided not to take any chances and hurled a Russian-made anti-personnel grenade through a blown-out window. He heard it bounce along the floor; three seconds later, it went off. The noise and concussion of the blast rocked the shattered wooden walls of the wrecked house.

Two mercenaries rushed over and joined Chang. Just as they had rehearsed at their mock-up in Mozambique, he waved at his men to kick in what was left of the shattered door and then as a group, they dashed inside the smoldering house. The interior of the old farmhouse was a complete wreck. Several mangled bodies and destroyed pieces of furniture were scattered across the hardwood floor. Chang took a step forward, but had to brace himself from slipping in a puddle of blood as he stepped past a severed limb. Looking for any further sign of opposition, Chang saw none.

A moan rang out from the far side of the room.

Chang turned towards the sound and walked over to see who had survived the volley of missiles from the Hind attack helicopter. He saw a young black woman in South African military fatigues, her round face covered in blood, struggling to get up on her hands and knees. She was in shock and did not realize that Chang was standing over her. Seeing that she was the only survivor, Chang lowered his weapon until the barrel rested on the back of her head. Without flinching, he fired two rounds into the woman's skull, splattering her blood and brains all over the floor. He did not care about the cold-blooded murder of the girl; it was no more troubling to him than stepping on a bug with his boot. Cradling his AK in his arms, Chang headed towards the kitchen. All around him, his men broke down into their pre-determined search teams and started their deadly and methodical clearance of the house. A shot rang out somewhere in the building but was quickly and abruptly silenced by the overwhelming firepower from Chang's highly trained killers.

With a smile on his hard face, Chang let himself relax for a moment. So far, so good, it was all going to plan. Chang, accompanied by his radio operator, strode into the kitchen and stopped by the fuse box on the wall. Reaching over, he found that it was locked.

Chang's radio-operator stepped forward, reached into a pocket, pulled out a skeleton key, and quickly popped opened the locked box. Chang grabbed a Maglite from his chest-rig and shone it inside the fuse box. He counted the fuses until he found the sixth one. Pressing it in with his thumb, Chang was rewarded by the sound of a hidden door sliding open beside the stove.

"Ingenious," said Chang in perfect English as he stared at the open elevator. "Call in the exterminators," said Chang to his radioman.

A minute later, two men dressed from head to toe in chemical warfare suits and wearing military gas masks walked into the kitchen. Chang nodded to them and pointed towards the open elevator. Both men returned the nod and stepped into the elevator. In their hands were canisters of deadly Sarin nerve gas. Chang closed the door behind them and looked down at his watch. So far, they had been on the ground for no more than five minutes. They had twenty-five more before any police, alerted by local farmers, would arrive. While he and some of his men cleared the house, Chang knew that his deputy was busy establishing a defensive perimeter around the building to keep the authorities at bay for as long as it took.

A huge broad man with short black hair and a long scar across his left cheek entered the kitchen. Chang nodded at Ivan Kolikov, an ex-Russian Spetsnaz sergeant, and his deputy for the raid. "Are the bug specialists in the hole?" asked Kolikov as he looked at the closed elevator door.

"Yes, and I suspect that we shall hear from them shortly,"

said Chang, watching the time burn away on his watch.

"Good. I'll get the bomb experts up here and then call in the two empty choppers," said Kolikov with a mock salute before heading back out into the pouring rain.

Seconds later, the door to the elevator slid open; a dark-skinned man stepped out without his gas mask on. "It's clear down there," said the man in a thick Somali accent.

"How many?" asked Chang.

The Somali mercenary held up two fingers, indicating how many South African security personnel were now dead.

Chang thanked the man. He had expected more, but most must have died under the rocket barrage from the Hind. Stepping into the elevator, Chang pressed the only button on the wall. A moment later, he felt the elevator start to descend. From studying the secret files provided to him by Alexandra Romanov, Chang knew the basement level built thirty meters below the surface held South Africa's last line of defense. Something that had been hidden away for years and was not supposed to exist: two nuclear bombs.

Built during the Cold War, South Africa once had had an arsenal of six known and two undisclosed nuclear bombs. With the approaching end of Apartheid, South Africa openly and willingly dismantled its six bombs and declared itself a nuclear-free state. However, even the new leadership of the country saw the wisdom of keeping a secret nuclear deterrence and continued with the clandestine maintenance of two nuclear bombs. It was a decision they would now live to regret.

Chang moved out of the elevator and was met by the other member of the exterminator team. With a quick handshake, he stepped over the dead bodies of two South African bomb technicians, their vacant, accusing eyes staring up at him. With a grin from ear to ear, he walked straight over to the two nuclear bombs. Chang saw that the white-painted bombs were three meters long and strapped down onto sturdy metal tables. Chang knew that these bombs were designed to be delivered from the air.

The sound of men chatting away excitedly as they exited the elevator caught Chang's attention. They nodded their heads in greeting and moved past him, carefully starting to unlock the bombs from their cradles so they could be quickly placed onto the waiting heavy-duty carts for transfer to the surface.

Chang watched his men work as fast as they could. They knew just as well as he did that time was not on their side, but they could not afford to be sloppy around such lethal devices. Ten minutes passed; the first of the bombs was on its way to the surface. Chang looked at his watch and cursed. They had, at most, five minutes before a police car arrived. Leaving his technicians to their work, Chang jumped into the elevator and headed up to the surface to prepare a reception.

Outside, the rain had stopped. The air smelled fresh and appealing to Chang after being cooped up for the past ten minutes in the stale air of the smoldering farmhouse's basement.

Out of the night came one of Chang's helicopters. It smoothly pivoted around in the air and landed with its rear doors already open. Two men waited inside the Hip ready to receive its deadly cargo. A minute later, the first bomb was dragged out of the house by a dozen of Chang's men who quickly loaded it onto the waiting MI-8. Chang watched with satisfaction as the helicopter lifted off into the darkness and headed towards their rendezvous, a ship docked in an isolated cove on the coast of Southern Mozambique. Turning his head, Chang saw a man run over to him and excitedly point into the distance. He saw red flashing lights of two police cars racing down a dirt road towards the destroyed farmhouse.

"Damn, I was hoping we would have avoided the authorities," muttered Chang, as he reached for the radio. Swiftly passing on orders, he turned to see his second empty Hip helicopter start to descend into the open field.

Soon, the police cars were within two hundred meters of the farm when a pair of wire-guided anti-tank rockets raced out of the pitch-black night sky and slammed into both cars, tearing them apart. Brilliant red fireballs shot into the sky, marking where they had been demolished. Chang's support Hind helicopter flew out of the night, straight over the top of the wreckage, and opened up with its cannons to ensure that no one survived.

Kolikov walked over beside Chang. "Sir, the last bomb is on its way up."

"Good news," Chang replied, patting his subordinate's arm. "Hurry, let's get it loaded and get out of this godforsaken country."

Five minutes later, with the second bomb secure, Chang stepped onto the last helicopter. He took one final look around at the death and devastation that he and his men had wrought tonight and smiled to himself. After all, it was not every day that you made fifty million dollars for thirty minutes' work.

8

Charlotte
North Carolina

M itchell got out of the polished jet-black stretch limo, checked himself over one more time in the car's passenger-side mirror and, with a bouquet of flowers in hand, he headed up the short flight of stairs to the front door of a two-story brick building that dated back to the turn of the last century. Mitchell rang the doorbell and waited. *It's cool and damp outside, but not too uncomfortable for a late December evening*, thought Mitchell, as he waited patiently for someone to answer the door.

Tammy Spencer had outdone herself. From arranging his flights, to finding him a tux, to hiring him a limo, Mitchell had only to meet the timings laid down by Spencer and the date would go perfectly. She finished by reminding him that this was how it should be done and if a woman wanted it done right, then she had to do it herself. He made himself a mental note to buy her a dozen roses when he got back to New York.

On the other side of the glass door, a light switched on. A small dog started yelping and digging furiously at the door. Mitchell heard a female voice shoo away the dog. A moment later, the door slowly opened.

A thin black woman in her late fifties, dressed in a stylish blue pantsuit, stood there looking Mitchell over.

With survival instincts honed on the battlefield, Mitchell instantly smiled and handed over the flowers to the surprised woman.

"These are for you Mrs. March," said Mitchell, hoping that she would fall for the ruse.

Mrs. March smiled at the flowers and looked past Mitchell at the waiting limo. "Please, do come in, Mister Mitchell. My name is Corrine. Jennifer will be down shortly," she said as she took the gift and inhaled the fragrance of the freshly cut flowers. "Thank you very much, Mister Mitchell. It's been an awfully long time since anyone has bought me such lovely flowers."

"I'm glad you like them, ma'am," said Mitchell, as he stepped inside the warm hallway. The corridor was adorned with several generations of family photos and the usual memorabilia from the many family trips taken across the States over the years.

"Mister Mitchell, I understand that you work for a private security company and that you had a hand in saving my daughter last month in the Philippines."

"I did my part, ma'am."

"Oh please, do stop with all of this ma'am nonsense. You're making me feel old. Please call me Corrine," said Mrs. March as she delicately extended her hand to Mitchell.

"Sorry, a strict upbringing from my mother followed by ten years in the army will make anyone overly polite," replied Mitchell as he gently shook Corrine's warm hand.

"Jen, your date is here," yelled Mrs. March down the hallway.

"Coming Mom, I'll be down in a minute," said a distant voice.

"I wouldn't call it a date," said Mitchell, skirting around the issue. "It's more like I'm accompanying your daughter to a charity auction."

"Mister Mitchell, you brought me flowers, you look extremely handsome in that stylish, form-fitting tuxedo of yours, and you have rented a limousine. In my day that would be some special date," said Mrs. March with a mischievous wink.

Mitchell's face flushed. For the first time in a long time, he was tongue-tied and genuinely embarrassed.

"Coming," an approaching voice said lyrically.

"Mister Mitchell, I believe you already know my daughter, Jennifer," said Mrs. March with pride.

Mitchell turned, instantly captivated at the sight of a

beautiful woman standing there. Jennifer March hardly looked like the disheveled and grime-covered woman he had last seen a month ago in the Philippines. She stood there wearing a pair of open toe high-heeled shoes with a long black sleeveless dress that hugged her lithe physique. Mitchell noticed that her face was well proportioned, with deep-brown eyes that seemed to glow in the light. She wore a pearl necklace with matching earrings that accented her warm brown skin. Her hair was a radiant caramel color cut stylishly short around the ears.

"Good evening, Ryan, long time no see," said Jennifer playfully as she extended her hand in greeting.

Mitchell stood there for a moment before he realized that he was still staring. "Oh yes, of course, good evening Jen," stammered Mitchell as he took her hand.

Jennifer lightly took his hand, feeling a reassuring warmth radiate from his touch.

"Is it cold out?" asked Jen as she dug inside her purse for her lipstick that she lightly applied to her full lips.

"You should be ok tonight, dear. Mister Mitchell has a limo waiting to take you on your date," said Mrs. March teasingly, clearly enjoying the moment.

"It's not a real date, Mother," said Jen, before Mitchell had the chance to. "We have to get going, so don't stay up too late. The auction should end around one, so I should be home by two, or three at the latest," said Jen as she gave her mother a quick kiss on the cheek.

Mitchell opened the front door for Jen. The driver, seeing them coming, got out and opened the side door of the waiting limo. Once Jen and Mitchell were comfortable, the limo driver edged out into traffic then and headed for the Charter House in Downtown Charlotte.

"This is quite nice. Not what I had been expecting at all," said Jen as she looked around the limo. "After seeing you in the Philippines, I half-expected you to pull up in a rusty old jeep wearing blue jeans and a down-filled jacket."

"Funny you should say that, but I received a bit of a surprise holiday bonus this year, so I could afford to rent this limo," said Mitchell.

"A jeep would have been fine with me as well."

"Well, when you come up to New York, I'll have to take you for a ride with the top off. Now Jen, would you like a drink?" asked Mitchell as he eyed the well-stocked mini-bar.

"Yes, a gin and tonic would be fine."

Mitchell poured them both a drink and sat back to enjoy the ride. The traffic was not bad, considering the hour. They made good time as they drove east on West Boulevard.

"The flowers for my mother were a nice touch. A little over the top, but nice nonetheless," said Jen as she sipped her drink.

Mitchell chuckled. "I actually bought them for you, but once I saw your mother giving me the eye as if I were a raw recruit, I instantly panicked and changed my tack. I thought she might be easier on me if I gave them to her instead; sorry."

Jen broke out laughing, almost spilling her drink in the process.

"Glad you thought it was funny."

"My mom, bless her heart, is a little over-protective of me these days. You must have made quite the impression. She's never that nice to any of my gentlemen callers; not that there have been that many recently."

Mitchell looked deep into Jen's beautiful eyes and said, "I find it hard to believe that someone as stunning as you doesn't get many dates."

Jen turned away. "Please, Ryan, you're making me blush."

"Sorry, that wasn't my intention," said Mitchell. "I honestly find it hard to believe that you cannot get a date."

"I was seeing someone," said Jen, looking uncomfortable, "but that all fell apart in the spring. Being a historian isn't the most glamorous of professions and besides, most of the men I work with are already married."

"Well tonight, I for one am glad for that," said Mitchell as he toasted Jen with his glass.

"But enough about me, Ryan Mitchell. Why isn't a handsome man like yourself married?" asked Jen good-naturedly as she took another sip of her drink.

"Who says I'm not?"

Jen playfully slapped Mitchell on the arm. "Don't even joke like that! It's not the slightest bit funny."

"Sorry again," said Mitchell. "Like yourself, in my line of

work it's hard to find someone to spend time with, let alone settle down. I was engaged once, but that was a while ago."

"Oh dear, what happened?" asked Jen.

"When I was on my first tour of duty in Afghanistan, the supposed love of my life ran off and eloped with my older brother."

Jen sat there speechless for a moment, and then hit Mitchell's arm again. "You're awful. Quit toying with me."

Mitchell downed his drink in one gulp. "I'm not. It's all true," said Mitchell with a slightly sour look on his face.

"Oh, I'm sorry. I didn't mean to pry," said Jen as she took his hand.

"Family dynamics will never be the same. Christmas is always awkward at my parents' house, but it turns out that I dodged the proverbial bullet on that one as she has become, shall we say, high maintenance for my poor brother."

"Damn," said Jen as she finished her drink.

"All true; scout's honor," said Mitchell with a flash of the two-fingered scout salute.

Jen giggled and changed the topic. "So, please, tell me about your work and the people you work with. The ones I met in the Philippines seemed like quite an eclectic group."

Mitchell grinned at Jen's use of eclectic. He'd never heard his friends referred to like that before. Scoundrels, yes, but never eclectic. "Well, we all work for an organization known as Polaris Operations."

"Polaris, that seems like an odd name," said Jen.

"Not really if you knew our boss, Major-General Jack O'Reilly. Polaris is the North Star. The general chose it because it has both a modern and historical context. If you know where the North Star is, you can find your way home. The Underground Railway taught it to escaping slaves, to help guide them to freedom in the north. We may not be as noble, but I find it an apt name in today's environment."

"And your friends?"

Mitchell collected his thoughts. "Well, as you know, Nate and I met in the army. We were both Army Rangers working together in a combined NATO Special Operations Task Force assigned to track down and eliminate HVTs."

Jen scrunched up her face. "HVT. What is that?"

"Sorry, army-speak. It means a high-value target. It could be anything from a key Al Qaeda or Taliban leader, to a command and control node, or perhaps even an IED factory, all of which needed dealing with to ensure that they were no longer able to influence the fight."

Jen did not need to be told that Mitchell was talking about killing terrorists. After another sip, she said, "Sounds really dangerous."

"Yes, it can be if you don't take the time to plan and resource it properly."

"You did ok rescuing me on short notice," said Jen with a warm smile on her lips.

"That was a case of blind luck more than anything else. Not the best way to conduct business, if you want to stay alive long enough to retire and enjoy your grandchildren."

"And your other teammates?" asked Jen.

"Sam was a medic in the 82nd Airborne attached to the organization and Cardinal was from a Canadian sniper team that supported many of our operations. The only one not from our time in Afghanistan is Yuri. He's a Russian black marketer, who sort of fell into our laps a while back. His contacts throughout the world are invaluable to a team like ours."

"Fascinating," said Jen. "Truly fascinating, it all sounds far more exciting than being a simple old professor of history."

"It sounds glamorous, but I live out a duffle bag and can't remember the last home-cooked meal I ate," said Mitchell.

"Well, I'll have to have you over for dinner. My mom would love the company, and she cooks a mean meatloaf."

Mitchell smiled. He found himself truly relaxing in Jen's warmth and easy-going manner. "Sounds like a date."

Looking at his watch and then over at Jen, Mitchell said, "The traffic is starting to slow down. We're not going to be late, are we?"

"No, these things always start with a few cocktails, followed by some overly pretentious and boring people talking art and other such foolishness, as if they were all experts on such things. The charade usually runs a good hour before the auction actually begins. As long as we get there by nine, we should be ok."

Mitchell thought about it for a moment. Even with a small delay, they would still arrive with plenty of time to spare. He shimmied over to the bar. "Since we have time to kill, can I offer you another drink? And from here on out, I promise that the conversation will be neither pretentious nor boring," said Mitchell as he waved his empty glass.

Jen beamed a smile back at him. "Sure, why not?"

9

Charter House
Charlotte

Mitchell and Jen got out of the limo at the entrance to the Charter House. Stepping up to the driver's-side window, Mitchell quickly spoke to the driver and, offering Jen his arm, they headed inside.

The three-story Charter House was until recently an exclusive high-end art studio for the haute rich. Coming under new management, the old building had received a much-needed facelift and had diversified its activities to include an art gallery, offices, and a floor solely dedicated to auctions.

As soon as they stepped inside the warm building, Mitchell realized that he was no longer in his comfort zone. He could see several politicians, several professional athletes, and at least three media personalities with their camera crews in tow, hovering around for an interview. Everyone in the room was well-dressed in suits and outfits that would have quickly bankrupted Mitchell.

Jen could see the uncomfortable look on Mitchell's face, so she slipped her arm into his and gently pulled him towards a sculpture on the far wall. Along the way, they both helped themselves to a free flute of expensive champagne.

"So, Jen, what exactly is your interest here tonight? Not that I'm objecting to spending time with you," said Mitchell as he sipped his champagne.

"It's for a pet research project that I've been working on for a number of years. I'm hoping to get my hands on several books that are being auctioned off here tonight. They once belonged to the estate of Charles Reid, a member of the board of inquiry into the loss of the British Airship *Goliath* over Africa in 1931," said Jen with a twinkle in her eyes.

Mitchell shrugged his shoulders, having never heard of the loss of the *Goliath*. "What on earth is your interest in a long-lost airship?"

Jen turned and smiled. "Well, for one, they never found more than a few pieces of debris. It was widely rumored at the time that the *Goliath* had been sabotaged."

"Curious, I guess," said Mitchell, toying with her.

"Ryan, I'm a history professor, but ever since I was a student, the *Goliath* has always held a certain indefinable fascination for me. A lost ship, rumors of sabotage and murder. You know all that cloak-and-dagger stuff. It really fascinates me."

"Yeah, it's great fun until someone starts shooting at you," replied Mitchell.

"Ryan, quit it," said Jen, as she playfully hit him on the arm. "I'm serious about this. I want to write a book about it."

Mitchell took Jen's hand and looked deep into her striking brown eyes. "If you write about it, I'll be the first to buy it, even if it means this ex-soldier will need a really expensive dictionary with lots of pictures to help me with the big words that I am sure you'll use."

Jen just giggled and led Mitchell over to the far side of the gallery to a table where a couple of young people, also dressed in tuxedos, were busy registering people for the auction. She dug in her purse, showed their invites to a girl working at the desk, and was handed a numbered paddle. Turning it over, Jen saw that the number was seventy-five.

Seeing the number, Mitchell let out a quiet chuckle.

"What's so funny?" asked Jen.

"That's my old army regiment," exclaimed Mitchell. "The 75th U.S. Army Rangers, I was with them for most of my time in the service. Rangers lead the way," said Mitchell proudly, as he told Jen his regiment's motto.

Mitchell and Jen joined the growing line of impeccably dressed people heading up the stairs to the second floor. Once there, they moved off to one side and took a seat at the back, deciding to leave the front rows for the more serious buyers in the crowd. Mitchell picked up a program. Thumbing through the booklet, he saw a diverse collection of items going on the auction block, from modern art to antique firearms to several unopened trunks from estate sales.

Mitchell leaned over to Jen and whispered in her ear. "You know, I almost forgot to ask you. What's the charity we are supporting here tonight?"

"It benefits a local chapter of the Wounded Warrior Project," solemnly replied Jen.

"Damn! I wish I'd known. I would have brought more money," said Mitchell loudly, bringing unwanted stares of disgust from several nearby couples.

Jen tapped his hand consolingly, "It's all right, Ryan, they take all major credit cards here. Besides, if it means that much to you, you can help me win my bid."

"Deal," said Mitchell enthusiastically.

A dour looking African-American gentleman in a tuxedo entered the room, walked over to the podium at the front of the room and with a loud bang of his gavel, began the auction. The first item up for bid was a sculpture that did not garner a lot of attention, but with a few well-placed quips from the auctioneer, the crowd came to life and the serious bidding began in earnest. Soon the auctioneer had his rhythm. He played the crowd for all they were worth. The man was a consummate master at getting the people to bid outrageous amounts for items they did not really need, nor want.

"I've never been to an auction before, but if I had to, I'd say this guy's good," said Mitchell admiringly to Jen.

"It doesn't hurt that several of the local news outlets are here tonight covering the event," said Jen, as she motioned her head over towards a reporter eagerly waiting with her camera crew to talk with the people once the auction was over.

"What item are we after?" asked Mitchell, like a kid waiting for his turn at bat.

"We're up next," said Jen, sitting up in her chair to get a better look at the stage.

Mitchell leafed through his brochure until he found the next item. It was a set of three books from an estate sale.

"Ok, here goes," said Mitchell, getting into the spirit of the evening.

The bidding started at two hundred dollars. Jen instantly raised her paddle.

The auctioneer raised an eyebrow at the paltry bid, shook his head, and asked if anyone wished to raise the price. An elderly woman sitting up front who had not bid on anything so far tonight raised the bid to three hundred.

Not to be outdone, Jen instantly raised it to five.

Most people in the room did not seem to care about the seemingly insignificant items up for bid and began to chat amongst themselves.

The auctioneer looked down at the woman in the front row and tried cajoling her to bid higher. Unfortunately, it worked all too well and soon the bid stood at one thousand dollars.

The room grew silent as some of the disinterested buyers watched with fascination as the old woman and Jen sparred over some moldy-looking books. The bidding soon topped five thousand dollars.

"Damn, this is exactly what I was hoping to avoid," said Jen, biting her lip. "That woman has no need for those books; she is just pushing the bid higher to look good in front of her wealthy friends."

"Well, I for one don't like being outdone by anyone, even if it is for charity," said Mitchell as he gently took the paddle out of Jen's hand. Instantly, Mitchell stood and yelled, "Ten thousand dollars."

The auctioneer's face lit up. He looked down at the woman, hoping that she might take the bait. She hesitated for a second, chatted with a friend sitting beside her, and slowly looked over her shoulder towards the imposing-looking man who had just upped the bid. Seeing Mitchell standing there with his hands draped across his chest, looking like a man spoiling for a fight, the woman shook her head in defeat.

The auctioneer's gavel smashed down and with that, Mitchell and Jen became the owners of three books.

Mitchell handed the paddle back to Jen with a look on his face as if he had just won the state lottery.

"Ryan, you didn't have to do that," said Jen, more than a little surprised at Mitchell's bold move.

"You said I could help," said Mitchell with a shrug, "so I helped."

"I didn't expect you to spend that kind of money. It's just a set of books. I could have looked elsewhere for my material."

Mitchell shook his head. "No way, tonight I am your escort. You wanted those books, and I wanted to donate to the Wounded Warrior's Charity. I know several ex-service men and women who rely on that charity and honestly Jen, I don't give a damn about the money; I can always make more of it in my line of business. All in all, I think things turned out quite well tonight."

Jen affectionately slipped her arm into Mitchell's, leaned over and gave him a quick kiss on the cheek. "Thank you, you're a unique man Ryan Mitchell. I truly do appreciate your help here tonight."

Mitchell did not say a word. He just sat there and enjoyed the moment. For the first time in a long time, Mitchell found himself not thinking about his job. He was truly enjoying his time with Jen.

A short while later, the auction concluded with the sale of a set of paintings by local African-American artists that were the highlight of the auction, and with a player from the Hornets sitting in the front row bidding for the first time tonight, they fetched over one hundred thousand dollars. With a loud bang of the gavel, the auction finished. The crowd congratulated themselves and slowly headed downstairs for more post-auction drinks. Everyone wanted a chance to mingle with the local celebrities and, more importantly, to be seen by the media.

Mitchell and Jen grabbed a couple of flutes of champagne and found a quiet corner to be by themselves.

"Now what?" asked Mitchell, looking around the room.

"In about half an hour, they will ask people to pay for their items," said Jen.

Mitchell looked at his watch. It was getting late, but he felt as if he were getting his second wind. The smell of Jen's perfume was intoxicating and inviting. He was about to say something, when he eyed the woman who had been bidding against them.

She locked eyes on them and started walking over.

"I hope we haven't ticked off the wrong person," said Mitchell, only half-joking, into Jen's ear.

"Good evening," said the woman, delicately extending her hand.

"Good evening," said Jen as she took the woman's white-gloved hand and lightly shook it.

"I just wanted to congratulate you on your purchase tonight, dear," said the dignified looking African-American woman, who appeared to be in her early seventies. She was dressed in a long dark-blue dress and wore a pair of diamonds in her ears that were larger than most women's engagement rings.

"Thank you," said Jen, with a flash of her pearly white teeth.

"I didn't really want those old books, but I just wanted to help out. However, after seeing your boyfriend glaring at me, I was too afraid to keep going," said the woman.

Mitchell and Jen exchanged a smirk between them.

"I am sorry about that, ma'am," said Mitchell as he delicately shook the woman's gloved hand. "I sometimes get a little too competitive for my own good."

"Well, it's nice to know the money will be going to those veterans who truly need it," said the woman as she turned to leave.

Mitchell stepped forward. "Ma'am, if you truly do care, they accept donations all year round. If you look over by the entrance, there's a table set up to take donations," said Mitchell, pointing to the table.

"Oh, right you are," said the woman as she fumbled with her purse. "Your bid was ten thousand, wasn't it?"

"Yes, ma'am," replied Jen.

"I didn't catch your name. Mister...?"

Mitchell felt awful for forgetting his manners "Mitchell, my name is Ryan Mitchell, and my friend's name is Miss Jennifer March."

"Very well, Mister Mitchell, Miss March. I too can be competitive when the mood strikes me," said the woman, as she fished out her checkbook. "Would you mind coming with me, dear?" said the woman to Jen, as she took her by the arm and walked with her over to the waiting table.

Jen returned a few minutes later with an astonished look on her face.

"What is it?" asked Mitchell inquisitively.

"She...she donated twenty thousand dollars," stammered Jen.

Mitchell was suitably impressed. "Who was she?"

Jen shook her head. "I haven't a clue, but you seem to be able to bring out the competitive side in people, Ryan, I'll give you that."

They were about to look around for one last drink when the auctioneer announced that people could pay for their items or make arrangements to do so in the next forty-eight hours. Mitchell and Jen decided to pay now with Mitchell's credit card and collect the items later the next day. When they arrived to pay, Jen eyed the smallest of the three books, picked it up and with a giddy smile, she excitedly exclaimed that the book was no less than the personal diary of Charles Reid. She held on to the book like a teenage girl getting the latest vampire romance novel. She left instructions for the delivery of the other two books, while Mitchell paid for their items.

Mitchell could see the obvious excitement written across Jen's face. "I can see it was money well spent," said Mitchell, as he took Jen's arm and led her towards the entrance of the building. Jen was far too engrossed in the diary to acknowledge Mitchell. He left her inside the building and stepped outside into the cool night air to look for their limo. Looking up and down the street, Mitchell was a little peeved when he could not see their limo anywhere. Checking his watch, he realized that he had arranged for it to arrive in ten minutes' time. Quickly, he stepped back inside the warm interior of the building.

He found Jen still with her nose deep in the book. Smiling to himself, he realized that she was enthralled with their purchase; it was going to take some sweet talk to get her back out into the real world. "The limo isn't there yet. It should be here in another ten minutes," said Mitchell, trying to get Jen's attention.

"Uh-huh," replied Jen distractedly, without looking up.

Mitchell stood there watching people leave in expensive-looking cars that he had only read about in car collector magazines. There was a steady stream of people leaving, when three men dressed in jeans and long black leather jackets appeared from out of nowhere, brusquely pushed their way inside, and started looking around. Mitchell saw the serious and determined look on their faces; instantly, he knew something was wrong. Clearly, none of them were patrons of the arts. Mitchell watched as they walked over to the auctioneer and swore under his breath as the man pointed the three men in their direction. From the way the men moved purposefully towards them, Mitchell judged them as being either ex-police, or former military. He did not like the way the men's jackets bulged, the telltale sign of concealed weapons. Quickly looking around for another way out, Mitchell was frustrated to see other patrons idly waiting around for their rides, blocking their only exit.

The men stopped in front of Mitchell; the closest man was easily over two meters tall with broad shoulders. He menacingly stood there looking down at Mitchell, when another man came inside and joined them. Mitchell could not believe when he saw it was the thug from the Philippines.

"Good evening again, Mister Mitchell and Miss March. How nice that you decided to get together after all the unpleasantness of our last encounter," said David Teplov with a smile.

Jen's heart skipped a beat. Without even looking up from her book, she instantly recognized the voice of the man who had tried to kidnap her.

Mitchell ground his teeth. He was hoping to BS his way out of the auction house, but as soon as he saw Teplov, he knew they were trapped.

Jen finally looked up and recoiled in shock when she saw Teplov standing so close to her and Mitchell. "Ryan, what's going on? Why are these men here?" asked Jen, suddenly feeling very scared.

"Now, Miss March, just stay calm and come with us," said Teplov.

Mitchell stepped between Teplov and Jen. "I think we'd rather stay here and have another drink," said Mitchell, as he quickly checked out the competition. He was not carrying a gun, but all of the thugs were most likely armed and by the cold looks on their faces, they were no doubt proficient in the application of violence.

Jen's heart started to race as one of Teplov's thugs brought out a pistol and aimed it right at Mitchell's heart.

"Don't try any foolish heroics, Mister Mitchell," said Teplov with a nod. "Just quietly move outside with us."

Mitchell realized that any commotion would instantly result in his and Jen's deaths. Reaching back, Mitchell took Jen by the hand and followed one of the men out the door, closely trailed by the man with the pistol. His mind raced. What could he do? Mitchell knew that he probably could take out the man behind him, if he were fast enough, but that left the other men, and Jen would most likely be killed before he could take down anyone else. Mitchell cursed under his breath at their dilemma. Squeezing her hand, he pulled Jen closer to him.

Jen nervously grabbed Mitchell's arm. "What's going on, Ryan?" she said, fear creeping into her voice. "They're after me again, aren't they?"

"I don't know; just stay calm, and we'll be ok," said Mitchell, trying to keep things composed. He watched as one of the thugs spoke into a small Motorola. A moment later, a white Chevrolet van seemed to appear out of nowhere and came to a screeching halt in front of the auction house. No sooner had the van stopped when the passenger-side door was flung open. Mitchell and Jen were motioned towards the idling vehicle. One of the thugs painfully thrust his pistol hard into Mitchell's back as a warning not to try anything, or they would both die. Before Mitchell could say a word, Teplov reached over and roughly grabbed Jen by the arm, pulling her away from Mitchell. With an evil glint in his eye, he threw her into the back of the darkened van.

Mitchell's heart skipped a beat as Jen disappeared from sight. Anger ripped through him; he had to do something. In the instant before Mitchell could even move to help, his world exploded in searing white light and pain. The man behind him had jammed a police issue Taser into Mitchell's back, causing electricity to instantly race throughout his body. His muscles involuntarily contracted, causing him agonizing pain as his legs buckled out from underneath him. He tumbled down onto the pavement, jerking from side to side from the searing current still coursing through him. Mitchell tried to focus, but all he could see were brilliant flashes of white light in his mind as he suffered through the painful electrical assault on his body. Mercifully, five seconds after it began, the attack was over.

Mitchell moaned in agony. Painfully, he rolled over only to see his attacker jump into the waiting van. Blinking his eyes to clear the white dots still clouding his vision, Mitchell could have sworn that Teplov smiled and waved at Mitchell before slamming the door shut. With an ear-splitting squeal of its tires, the vehicle raced off into traffic, leaving Mitchell agonizingly gasping for breath on the cold sidewalk.

From inside the building came a tall black man wearing a tuxedo, who quickly helped Mitchell to his feet. "Are you all right? Do you need help?" asked the man as he reached into his pocket for his cell phone.

Mitchell looked into the traffic and saw that the white van was fading away as it blended in with all the other traffic heading east on Central Avenue. Clumsily, Mitchell pushed away from the man helping him and staggered like a drunk towards the busy road. Taking a deep breath, Mitchell sought to calm his nerves and clear his aching head and body. The cold night air filled his lungs. He knew he had to act fast if he was going to help Jen. Looking around, Mitchell saw an older blond-haired rocker trying to look and act much younger than he was. He was waiting with two young models hanging off him while a sleek black BMW Z4 was driven over by a valet.

The car came smoothly to a halt in front of the auction house, its twin turbo-charged engine purring away as only a finely tuned high-performance automobile could.

Mitchell instantly decided on his course of action. Groggily launching himself forward before the star could even leave the sidewalk, Mitchell whipped out his company ID and lied, "Police, I need your car."

The rocker hesitated and with that small window of opportunity, Mitchell jumped into the idling car. Slamming the door behind him, Mitchell pressed the gas pedal to the floor. The car leapt forward. Mitchell changed gears as fast as he could as the car sped away; he never heard the man cursing him from the sidewalk as he raced into traffic. The three hundred-horse power engine roared to life. Mitchell drove the car like a man possessed, quickly weaving in and out of traffic as he tried to spot the escaping white van lost to him in the busy nighttime traffic. The 1980s hit *Rebel Yell* blared from the car's sound system as Mitchell floored the accelerator.

Pain racked his body. He had never been tasered before. It even hurt to breathe, but Mitchell shook his head to clear the cobwebs and dug deep inside and tried to shut out the pain as he changed gears and sped after the van. The traffic was heavy, but Mitchell just ignored it and drove down the middle of the road, disregarding the cars swerving to get out of his way. Red lights did not even slow Mitchell; he simply jammed his hand on the horn and charged headlong through the steady stream of cars, hoping not to hit, or get hit by, anyone.

Jen lay scared and miserable on the floor of the van as it made its way east. Her heart was racing wildly. She fought to stifle a scream of fear; she could feel the cold metal from a pistol jammed against the side of her head. It was happening all over again. Why would anyone want to kidnap her? None of this made any sense to her. Closing her eyes, she said a silent prayer and wondered how Mitchell was doing and if he were even still alive.

With a sharp blast of the horn, Mitchell changed gears and whipped around a car that was foolishly doing the posted speed. The more he drove, the more enraged he became. He cursed himself for being caught off guard without a sidearm; it was a mistake he vowed never to repeat. Even though he was streaking through the traffic, Mitchell still had not seen the white van and was beginning to feel in his gut that somehow he had screwed up, that somewhere they had turned off and that he had lost Jen to the thugs. A car suddenly stopped in front of him; Mitchell's heart leapt into his throat. He barely had time to swerve around the car into the blaring horns of the oncoming traffic. Mitchell continued to speed his way down the middle of the road. An oncoming black SUV honked its horn. A second later, the driver's-side mirror on Mitchell's car exploded into thousands of tiny fragments as the two cars narrowly missed hitting one another.

Suddenly, a few hundred meters in front of him, Mitchell saw the van. With a loud roar of the engine, Mitchell jammed the car into fifth gear and sped after the van, hoping to close the distance before the vehicle had the opportunity to turn off onto a side street.

The white van's driver was an ex-member of the Charlotte police force who had worked the streets for years before being expelled for corruption. Now, he did not care where the money came from, only that he was paid well for his services. Carefully threading his way through the traffic, trying not to draw the unwanted attention of any police cruisers, the driver couldn't wait to get his share of tonight's profit. Taking a quick look in the driver's-side mirror, he caught a glimpse of an expensive-looking black car weaving its way through the nighttime traffic towards them. The hair on the back of his neck instantly went up; someone was after them. Gritting his teeth, he swore. He told his boss that they should have killed the man. Instead, they had followed orders and only used a Taser on him. Now, the driver had no doubt that he was the man in the car following them. Shaking his head in frustration, the driver gripped the steering wheel, changed lanes, and sped up.

Mitchell saw the move, changed gears, and rocketed between two cars, missing them by mere inches until he was only a few car lengths behind the van. As he got closer, it dawned on him that he had not yet thought through what he was going to do next. He didn't have a gun and although his car was fast, it would not last very long if the driver of the van decided to play bumper cars with him. Mitchell needed help. Reaching into his pocket, he pulled out his iPhone and quickly dialed 911. As soon as the operator came on, Mitchell blurted out where he was and the make of the car he was following, and got off the line. He needed to concentrate on his driving, not on answering the many questions surely to be asked by the operator.

The white van turned suddenly onto a side street; its tires screeched loudly in protest at the sharp turn. Looking in his mirror, the driver cursed when he saw that their tail had also made the turn. The man was good; he had to give him that. The pursuing car's driver was relentlessly closing in on the back of the van.

"Boss, I hate to spoil the party, but we've got company," yelled the driver over his shoulder. "Behind us, there's someone driving a black BMW, and he's been following us for the last couple of blocks."

Teplov moved to the back of the van and looked out the rear windows; his mood instantly soured as he watched Mitchell change lanes and race around a red mini-van until he was right behind them. He shook his head; he knew he should have pushed his employer to allow him to kill Mitchell, but she had been adamant that they avoid the police. That was not going to happen now as he could hear sirens closing in on them.

Suddenly, from out of nowhere, three police cruisers turned onto the street, their sirens blaring, lights flashing red and white. They rapidly closed in behind Mitchell's car and joined in the pursuit.

"No one said this was going to be easy," said Teplov, shaking his head. Mumbling to himself, he reached down and grabbed an AK-74M fitted with a grenade launcher underneath the fore stock. Making sure the weapon was loaded with a high-explosive round, he steeled himself and then threw the rear doors of the van open, quickly raising the AK tight into his shoulder.

Mitchell's eyes focused instantly on the business end of an AK. He did not even think; acting on pure adrenaline and the instinct of self-preservation, Mitchell turned the wheel hard over to the left and floored the gas pedal just as the weapon opened up. Bullets streaked through the air. Mitchell was fast, but not fast enough as rounds chewed through the passenger-side headlight while the remainder of the burst struck the asphalt instead of the BMW. Speeding up, Mitchell flew past the van, placing himself squarely in front of the vehicle.

Teplov could not believe that he had failed to stop the BMW. Looking back, he saw the police cars close in behind the van. Teplov knew that it was only a matter of minutes before a police chopper joined in the pursuit, making it near to impossible for them to get away. With a smile on his face, he decided to give the authorities something else to worry about tonight besides them. Dropping to one knee, he brought up the AK and emptied a full magazine into the nearest police car. They never had a chance as the glass windshield imploded, spraying glass and bullets into the doomed passengers. The driver died instantly in a hail of bullets, his hands still holding the wheel as his lifeless body slumped over. A second later, the car drifted over into oncoming traffic. With a loud crunch of compacting metal and glass, the front of the police car hit a bus, crumpled in, and was sent flying through the air straight into the next police car, exploding into a bright-red fireball that shot up into the night sky.

"That'll do," said Teplov as he slammed the rear doors shut. The Russian mercenary handed off his AK and made his way to the front of the van. Seeing Mitchell's BMW right in front of them, his blood began to boil. Swearing at the top of his lungs, he told the driver to smash Mitchell off the road.

With a smile on his face, the driver jammed his foot down on the gas pedal. A second later, the van leapt forward like an enraged bear chasing down its prey.

Looking through the rear-view mirror, Mitchell saw the van speed up. It closed the distance in the blink of an eye, hitting the rear end of Mitchell's borrowed BMW, easily destroying the bumper, and crushing in the trunk several feet. Mitchell felt the impact shake the car. This would not do. Speeding up, Mitchell moved his BMW a car length away. Looking ahead for a moment, Mitchell saw more red and white flashing lights racing towards them. Whatever happened now, Mitchell knew the men in the van were rapidly running out of time.

With another loud crunch, Mitchell felt his car being rammed from behind. With his hands grasped tight on the steering wheel, he fought to keep his battered vehicle from spinning about on the slick road. He'd had enough of this crap. The police were not getting there fast enough for him. Slowing down slightly, he pulled into the lane beside the van and waited until he was even with the vehicle. Deciding that it was now or never, Mitchell swerved over, striking the van with his much lighter sports car. Sparks flew, like a swarm of fireflies in the night, as the metal crunched in on both vehicles, but mainly on Mitchell's stolen BMW. Keeping the wheel turned over, Mitchell hoped to force the van into a parked car, causing it to stop.

"Jesus Christ, Johnson!" screamed Teplov at the driver. "Get us off this street before we all get killed and get rid of that fucking car if you can. It's really beginning to piss me off!"

With a grin on his face, the driver applied the brakes and turned his wheel slightly, striking Mitchell's car on the rear passenger side and causing it to spin around like a child's toy on the road. Without waiting to see what happened to Mitchell, the driver expertly sped up, aiming to turn down an upcoming street.

Mitchell ground his teeth in anger, as he fought to regain control over his spinning car. Reaching down, he pulled up on the emergency brake, turned the steering wheel hard over, released the brake, and then floored the accelerator as the car's tires noisily gripped the road, taking off once more in pursuit of the escaping van. Mitchell saw the van just as it turned onto a side street. He sped up and soon found himself weaving in and out of the infuriatingly slow traffic on a one-way street.

"Damn, that bastard is persistent," yelled the driver over his shoulder. "He's back and closing on us, for God's sake. Teplov, do something, will you?"

"I've had my fill of this crap for tonight. Time to finish this off," snarled Teplov as he got out of his seat, made his way to the back of the van and then angrily grabbed his AKM-74 from the man holding it for him. Putting in a fresh thirty-round magazine, he kicked open the rear doors of their van; cold air instantly rushed inside. He could see Mitchell two cars back. Taking careful aim, the thug fired a 40mm high explosive round into a cab driving right behind them. With a bright yellow flash, the car exploded, sending the hood of the engine cartwheeling skyward along with hundreds of deadly fragments of shrapnel flying into cars on both sides of the street. Behind the destroyed cab, cars smashed into one another as they slammed on their brakes, trying to avoid the flaming wreckage.

"Yeah, that'll do nicely," said Teplov dryly as he admired the devastation behind them. His work done, he slammed the van's rear doors closed.

Seeing the cab disintegrate right in front of him, Mitchell never hesitated. With his foot jammed down on the gas pedal, he shot through the burning wreckage, barely missing a mangled piece of engine lying in the middle of the road.

The van's driver was looking in his rear-view mirror when suddenly, from out of a darkened alley, a speeding police cruiser ran straight into the side of the van. Neither driver had been expecting the collision. Inside the van, people were thrown around like rag dolls as the vehicle tumbled over from the force of the impact. Sliding on its side, the van came to a sudden jarring stop when it plowed into the back of a parked tow truck.

Mitchell saw the collision; his heart missed a beat at the thought of Jen being injured or killed. He quickly geared down, bringing the car to a screeching halt a few meters short of the smoldering wreck. Mitchell leapt out of the BMW even before it had come to a complete halt and darted for the rear doors, praying that Jen was all right.

Just before he got there, the back doors spilled open, and a man with an AK in his hands fell out onto the road. He looked bruised and disoriented.

Mitchell needed a weapon.

Without hesitation, he dove onto the man, knocking the wind out of him. Both men tumbled to the ground. Sitting up, Mitchell slammed his right fist into the stunned thug's face, breaking his nose. Hauling off again, Mitchell brought his fist straight down on the man's jaw, breaking it and knocking him out cold. A loud painful grunt escaped the man's lips as his body went limp. Rolling over, Mitchell grabbed the man's dropped AK, quickly checked that there was a round in the chamber, and then stood with his weapon at the ready. Edging towards the back of the van, Mitchell flipped the change lever to fully automatic with his thumb, raised the rifle into his shoulder, spun on his heels, and faced towards the open doors just as another thug tried getting out. Mitchell recognized him as the man who had tasered him. White-hot anger instantly ran through him. The goon saw Mitchell standing there and foolishly tried to bring a pistol up, only to be cut down by a quick burst from Mitchell's weapon. The thug staggered back onto the side of the overturned van and then slid to the ground, dead. Quickly scanning around, Mitchell saw no more movement. Carefully moving over to the open doors, Mitchell cautiously peered inside the darkened van. He saw another one of their attackers lying in an unnatural heap. Mitchell realized that he must have broken his neck upon impact. His eyes searched for Jen. His heart raced when he could not see her. He was about to dive inside the van, when he heard a moan somewhere in the dark.

"Jen is that you?" called out Mitchell. "Are you all right?"

"Yes, I landed on someone," replied Jen. "What happened?"

"A police car slammed into your van. It's lying on its side."

Relieved that she was alive, Mitchell was about to crawl in and help Jen out when the sound of sirens filled the air as four police cruisers came to a screeching halt behind Mitchell.

"Drop your weapon and lie down on the ground," said a commanding voice from one of the police car's speakers.

Mitchell was still as mad as hell, but he knew better than to turn around with an AK in his hands. Slowly, he lowered the weapon and got down as ordered. Seconds later, he felt his arms pulled behind him as handcuffs were quickly locked in place. Mitchell let out a deep breath and tried to focus his mind as he tried to figure out what was going on. *Why had someone gone through so much trouble to try to kidnap Jennifer March twice?*

In the dark of an unlit alleyway, David Teplov stood with a handkerchief to his bloodied head, injured during the crash. He had decided that discretion was the better part of valor and had crawled away the instant he heard gunfire. He knew that he had failed once more to get his hands on Jennifer March. With a burning hatred building inside him, Teplov silently watched the police as they hauled Mitchell off the ground and placed him in the back of one of their waiting vehicles.

A former member of the Russian Armed Forces, Teplov had a reputation for obtaining the unobtainable for his clients.

Glaring at Mitchell sitting in the back of a police car, he ground his teeth and vowed never again to allow his employers to stop him from killing Mitchell on sight. The man had cost him millions in trained fighters, but more than that, he had severely damaged his reputation. Stepping back, Teplov walked down the darkened alley, dug out his phone, and made a quick call. A few minutes later, a silver-gray Mercedes SUV pulled up. Getting inside, Teplov gave directions to the driver and then sat there silently contemplating his next move. Twice foiled by the same man, Teplov could not afford failure in his line of work. Teplov dug out his phone and reluctantly made another call.

Nika Romanov answered. "Do you have what we are after?"

"No," replied Teplov bluntly.

"What do you mean, no?" asked Nika.

"You didn't tell me that she was going to be with the same American who screwed things up for me in the Philippines," said Teplov angrily.

The line went silent for a moment.

"So she got away again?" asked Nika, her voice as cold as winter.

"Yes."

The air went uncomfortably silent again.

Nika broke the silence. "I don't believe in coincidences. That man has meddled in my affairs twice. I do not care what it takes, but I want him dead. Do not fail me again, Teplov. Kill him and anyone else who gets in your way from now on."

"Gladly," said Teplov, relishing the thought of eliminating Mitchell. He vowed to himself that no matter what it took, Mitchell was going to suffer horribly before he died.

10

**Polaris Complex
Albany, New York**

General O'Reilly walked into the briefing room, holding a thermos of coffee. He was dressed casually in a pair of blue jeans and a warm gray turtleneck sweater. O'Reilly saw Mitchell and Jen sitting there in jeans and a pair of old army sweat tops, looking like they hadn't slept in days. Taking a seat, O'Reilly poured them both a piping hot cup of coffee and then sat back in his seat while they waited for the others to arrive.

Mitchell's first call had been to O'Reilly to explain what had happened.

Telling Mitchell to stay where he was while he made a few calls, O'Reilly's first one was to Polaris' deputy leader, Luis Ortiz, a former Miami police commissioner, who in turn contacted some old friends with the Charlotte police. Almost right away, Mrs. March was taken into police protection and moved to a safe house in Concord. Once Corrine was safe, a Lear jet was hired to safely bring Mitchell back to New York for a debriefing. At her insistence, Jen tagged along to add anything she could to help put whoever it was behind all of this behind bars.

Ortiz sauntered in with a box of fresh donuts and laid them on the table. When no one moved, he opened the box, grabbed the closest one, and popped it into his mouth. Ortiz had short black hair that was graying at the temples. He was short and stocky, with a permanent smile on his face. Having met O'Reilly when he was serving on a counter-narcotics operation in Latin

America, the two had become close friends. When O'Reilly established Polaris, Ortiz was offered the position as his deputy to oversee all of the police training that occurred in the complex and elsewhere.

Everyone sat in silence as O'Reilly's two best intelligence experts came in and sat down on the opposite side of the table from Jen and Mitchell.

The first was Mike Donaldson, a tall, lanky Texan, who had been an intelligence officer with the US Air Force. He had a full head of white hair and a few extra pounds on his midsection. Donaldson was the senior analyst at the complex. His junior partner was Fahimah Nazaria, a stunningly beautiful Iraqi-American, dressed from head to toe in a conservative dark-blue outfit. Fahimah had graduated from Harvard with honors and followed that up with a graduate degree in Middle Eastern Studies. Recruited straight out of university, Fahimah was the fastest-rising member of the "Office of Dirty Tricks," General O'Reilly's planning and intelligence department.

O'Reilly quickly made the round of introductions.

"Ryan, I heard what you told me and what the police passed on to Luis," said O'Reilly as he sipped his coffee, "but why don't you tell me in your own words what really happened the other night?"

Mitchell went over the events of the evening from the time he arrived at Jen's until he was dragged away by some of Charlotte's finest. Jen added what she could, but she found that Mitchell seemed quite adept at giving these kinds of briefs. She saw that Mitchell had an eye for detail and seemed to be able to recall the events in far greater clarity than she could. O'Reilly sat there quietly while Fahimah and Donaldson respectfully grilled them over the details of the story, trying to find some meaning to the kidnapping attempt.

"As far as I can tell, the only common denominator in both kidnapping attempts in Charlotte and in the Philippines, seems to be you, Miss March," said Donaldson.

"I have to agree," added O'Reilly.

"But they also may be looking for something that she had or was working on," added Fahimah. "The books you bid on, what were they about?" asked Fahimah, while she typed away on her laptop.

Jen cleared her throat. "They were from an estate sale and once belonged to a Mister Charles Reid. He was a former British subject who was a member of the Board of Inquiry into the loss of the British Airship, the *Goliath*. The ship was lost on June 10, 1931, somewhere over Mauritania, West Africa."

Ortiz's phone rang. He walked out into the hall to take his call.

"These books were they valuable?" asked Donaldson, looking through his notes.

"No, I don't believe so," answered Jen.

"This keeps getting worse by the hour," said Ortiz as he re-entered the room and took his seat. "That was the Charlotte chief of police on the line. He said that the man Mitchell knocked out at the crash site has been found dead in his hospital room. His throat had been slit from ear to ear, and those books you were just talking about have disappeared right out of the police evidence locker."

"Good Lord!" exclaimed Jen at the news.

"For the right price, Miss March, you can get anything, and I do mean anything done. Even in a police station," said Ortiz regretfully, shaking his head.

"It would appear that we are dealing with someone with very deep pockets," said Mitchell.

Donaldson looked over at O'Reilly. "Sir, those books may be more valuable to someone than Miss March believes."

"General, I think I may have found something that may be useful," added Fahimah without looking up from her computer. "I believe I have found a living relative of Charles Reid, a Mister Francis Reid."

"Where does he live?" asked Mitchell, his tired eyes suddenly coming to life.

"Alaska. Palmer, Alaska to be exact, it is just north of Anchorage. He is a retired schoolteacher. He wrote a small book on the *Goliath's* disappearance a number of years ago and if the web is to be believed, he is considered an expert on the subject. I think I can get my hands on his book electronically," said Fahimah.

"Great, email it to me when you can," said Mitchell. "Have

you ever heard of this man before?" he asked Jen.

"I read his book a few years ago. It's more of a family history than a definitive work on the loss of the *Goliath*, but he may have additional information on the disappearance that he's just never found the time to publish," said Jen.

"Palmer, Alaska. I've never been in that neck of the woods before," Mitchell said, his mind switching into overdrive. "But I bet I could be up there in a matter of hours."

O'Reilly looked over at Mitchell. "What are you thinking, Ryan?"

"I want to meet this man. I would like to know all I can about the *Goliath*. It may help me understand what is so important about it and perhaps shed some light on why some people seem hell-bent on getting their hands on Jen."

"Ryan, don't forget this has become a police matter, not a company one," said O'Reilly, gauging Mitchell.

"Sir, I got it one hundred percent. I agree. It is a police matter in Charlotte, North Carolina, not Alaska, and you know that I would never do anything to jeopardize or tarnish the good name of the company, but I need to find out what's going on. Jen's in real danger, and I want to find out why. You've put me on leave for a month, so technically this wouldn't be on the company's time. All I would need is access to the staff should I have a question or two that needs answering," said Mitchell.

O'Reilly smiled and shook his head at Mitchell. He knew the man would go even if he told him not to. He could see the concern in Mitchell's eyes for Jennifer March. "All right then, Ryan. Since you are officially on leave, you can do as you wish, but let me pay for the flights," he said as he handed Mitchell a gold-colored company credit card. "But at the first sign of trouble up there, you hand the problem over to the local police and get your ass back here pronto."

Mitchell thanked O'Reilly and happily took the credit card.

"Now that that's settled, I can have you flown back to your mother later today," said O'Reilly to Jen.

"Sorry sir, but it's my neck on the line here, and I also want to know why this is happening," said Jen firmly. "If you and the police think that they may try for my mother, to get to me, I'm not just going to sit back and wait for it to happen. I'm well and truly pissed now and want to help. No offense to Ryan, but he knows almost nothing about the *Goliath*, whereas I've spent years studying the airship. He doesn't realize it, but I am more valuable to him then he knows right now."

Mitchell was about to open his mouth when Jen raised her hand, cutting him off.

"I'm coming and that's all there is to it, mister," said Jen, leaving no doubt in her voice.

O'Reilly smiled. "Well, I'll get Tammy to book the flights and arrange for a rental at the other end. Consider this an early Christmas present."

Sitting back in his seat, Mitchell shook his head at Jen, who smiled back at him. He only hoped that their trip could shed some light on the growing puzzle. Before it was over, they would face an even greater and more dangerous mystery.

11

Oil Exploration Vessel – *Romanov Star*
South Atlantic

A bitterly cold wind whipped across the open helipad, buffeting the gold-painted helicopter as it maneuvered to land. The helicopter, a Eurocopter Dauphin, seemed to hover for only the briefest of times above the heaving deck. The pilot's eyes were fixed on a man in a yellow survival suit standing on the pad with bright orange paddles in his hands, indicating the pitch of the ship. Judging that the time was right, the pilot brought the copter down as if he were landing on a pillow instead of the deck of a vessel rolling around in rough seas.

Seeing the rotor blades slowing, another sailor dressed in a survival suit darted forward, opened the passenger-side door, and helped Alexandra Romanov from the helicopter. No sooner had they cleared the rotors than the pilot revved up the craft's powerful engines. Gracefully the helicopter rose from the deck and then headed back out of the storm and towards the safety of the mainland.

Wearing a dark-blue outfit with matching down-filled parka and rain pants, Alexandra was dressed for the downpour soaking the deck of the ship. She followed her guide along the cluttered deck of the oil exploration ship, the *Romanov Star*. The spray caused by the cold slate-gray waves breaking against the sides of the vessel felt like a thousand needles poking into any exposed skin. This, combined with the rocking motion of the ship, made movement for those unaccustomed to rough seas extremely treacherous. Alexandra found herself having to grab hold of anything she could to prevent herself from being tossed around like a rag doll on the slippery deck as she fought her way towards the ship's bridge.

The *Romanov Star* was one of three ultra-modern exploration vessels owned by the Romanov business empire. It had a unique design with a twin hull, better known as a SWATH (Small Waterplane-Area Twin Hull). To most people, it looked like a super-sized high-tech catamaran, but the ship was designed to have its floats below the surface, thereby giving it greater stability on rough seas. That notion was lost on Alexandra as she swore that she still felt every wave in her stomach as they struck the ship.

Opening the door to the bridge, Alexandra happily stepped inside away from the freezing storm and quickly removed her rain-soaked parka and rain pants, revealing the form-fitting green jumpsuit that she was wearing underneath. Taking a breath, she almost fell over as her nostrils were assaulted by the noxious smell of stale cigarette smoke and body odor from the unwashed men jammed inside the cramped bridge. Before she could say a word, a piping hot cup of sweet tea was handed to her; she gladly cupped it between her frozen hands, trying to get some feeling back into them.

A skeleton crew of men fiercely loyal to the Romanovs currently manned the ship. Alexandra knew these men were in it for either the cause or the money; either way, she knew that no one onboard was going to say a word about what was happening.

"So where are they?" Alexandra asked as she took a seat beside a pimply-faced technician who looked young enough to still be in high school.

The young technician had been so engrossed in his work that he had not heard her enter the room and was startled when she spoke. "Oh my," said the youth, looking up at Alexandra's sleek figure, causing him to drop the pen he had been absentmindedly chewing on. "One second," said the engineer as he called the ship's captain over.

A man with a thick mane of gray hair walked over and stopped in front of Alexandra. His huge belly hung over his belt and his stained clothes looked like they had not been washed in days, perhaps weeks. "So, to what do we owe the pleasure of a visit from one of the boss' daughters? How can we humble employees help?" mockingly asked the captain, with a strong Greek accent.

Alexandra's nostrils rebelled at the overpowering reek of body odor coming from the man. "For starters, Captain, have you ever thought of taking a shower?" said Alexandra.

A loud, raucous laugh burst out from the other men in the bridge; the captain even joined in.

"Our hot-water lines have been acting up recently, so none of us has had a shower nor washed any clothes in over a week," replied the captain proudly, as he patted his giant stomach.

Alexandra shook her head; she knew the Romanovs were not paying them to be clean, just to do their job. "I won't belabor the point, Captain. I came aboard to see the packages."

The captain leaned over his shoulder, barking a set of orders at several of the younger men on the bridge who moaned aloud and then reluctantly started putting back on their wet-weather clothing.

Alexandra also cringed at the thought, but she knew that she would have to go outside into the squall once more if she wanted to personally verify that Chang had lived up to his end of the bargain.

Five minutes later, Alexandra Romanov found herself struggling along the deck of the ship as it rose and fell with the tall dark waves. Each time the ship dipped, her stomach felt like it was going to come out of her mouth. She vowed to herself to never do anything this foolish ever again. The aft deck of the ship was like an obstacle course, only ten times worse. Equipment had come loose in the storm and littered the deck, making walking along the slick surface a dangerous proposition.

The lead man stopped beside an ordinary-looking sea container fastened to the deck of the ship. Alexandra nodded at the man and with that, he bent down and unlocked the metal doors. With a loud screech, one of the doors opened. Alexandra felt herself shivering, not from the cold, but from anticipation as she moved inside the poorly lit container. It was barely warmer than a fridge inside, but Alexandra was thankful to be out of the rain. Pulling the hood of her jacket back, Alexandra ran her fingers through her rain-drenched hair and walked towards a pair of large wooden crates secured to the floor of the container to prevent them from moving around in the rolling waves.

"Open them up," ordered Alexandra.

The men quickly did as they were told and soon both crates' lids were removed, exposing the bombs.

Alexandra felt butterflies in her stomach as she stepped forward and looked inside each crate. The nuclear bombs looked sleek and somehow almost sexual to her. A smile crept across her pale features. She stood for close to a minute gazing down at the bombs, her heart racing in her narrow chest, before ordering the men to seal them up once more.

With the bombs secure, Alexandra left the sea container and reluctantly stepped back into the raging storm. She quickly pulled her hood up around her face and leaned forward as she struggled to make her way back to the bridge. Once there, she demanded to be patched through to her father on a secure line and then with the line established, Alexandra smiled as she passed on a single word: *RETRIBUTION*.

12

City of Palmer
Alaska

The trip so far turned out to be uneventful. Catching an early-morning flight out of JFK Airport, Jen and Mitchell transferred onto another flight in Seattle and then flew on to Anchorage, Alaska, where they rented a dark-blue Jeep Cherokee. After quickly setting up the GPS, Mitchell drove out of the city and soon found himself driving on the Glenn Highway heading north towards Palmer. Mitchell found the drive through the snow-covered countryside to be relaxing as it reminded him of his home growing up on a farm. Additionally, it gave him time to think.

As they drove alongside the Matanuska River's tree-lined shore, Jen saw that it was covered in a thick layer of glistening snow and ice that reflected brilliantly like diamonds in the bright sun. She had never been to Alaska before. The quiet beauty, combined with the fact that they were thousands of kilometers away from Charlotte, made her feel somewhat more relaxed that she had been in days. Through his window, Mitchell could see groups of kids chasing each other over the river's icy surface or playing games of hockey close to shore, taking him to another time when he was a kid in northern Minnesota. The world was a simpler place then, and Mitchell thought back on it nostalgically before turning his thoughts back to the here and now.

Mitchell slowed the car down when he saw the sign for Palmer, where Reid had his cottage. Checking his GPS to make sure he was in the right spot, Mitchell turned off the road and headed onto a curved snow-covered trail that led towards an expansive frozen lake. With a reassuring smile at Jen, Mitchell drove for about a kilometer through a thick pine forest until they saw a tall wooden A-framed house that faced out onto the lake. It looked almost too quiet except that the snow had been recently ploughed away from around the house, indicating that someone was home.

Stopping in front of the house, Mitchell called the number he had been provided by Fahimah and waited for someone to answer. After a few rings, Charles Reid answered his phone and told Mitchell to come around the side of the cottage to the garage, where he was busy working.

Bundling up, Jen and Mitchell got out of the car into a sharp cold wind blowing up off the lake. Taking Jen by the hand, Mitchell led them around the side of the cottage where they found the garage, its side door open. Mitchell knocked once and then together they stepped inside, both happy to be out of the wind.

Mitchell stood there for a moment, almost disbelieving what was in front of him: it was an old fashioned looking Ice Speeder. It was at least eight meters long and was painted all red with silver lightning bolts shooting down the sides. Sitting atop three large skis, the enclosed box-like speeder had a powerful fan attached to a powerful-looking engine mounted on the back, which would propel it across the ice at breakneck speeds. As a kid in Minnesota, Mitchell had seen a more modern version of the old speeder racing along the frozen lakes in the dead of winter, but he had never been in, let alone driven, one before.

"Hello, Mister Reid," called out Mitchell.

"Oh, yes...sorry, I didn't hear you come in," said a voice from inside the speeder.

A second later, the side door opened and a small man in his eighties, wearing a grease-stained set of outdoor coveralls, climbed out. Mitchell made the introductions.

"She's a beauty, isn't she?" said Reid as he looked admiringly at his speeder.

"It sure is," said Mitchell. "How old is it?"

"She's from the 1950s. I found her languishing away in a neighbor's barn. I've been restoring her for the past few winters now," Reid said proudly.

"Does it run?" asked Jen.

"Like the wind," said Reid with a twinkle in his eye. "Now, why don't you come inside and let me make you both a hot cup of coffee, and you can tell me why you young folks decided to fly all the way to Alaska in the dead of winter just to talk to me."

Reid led Mitchell and Jen inside his rustic cabin. He threw the kettle on while he got out of his dirty coveralls, and washed up.

An old German shepherd, seeing new visitors in the house, trotted over from the living room and guardedly sniffed Mitchell's outstretched hand. Once satisfied that he posed no threat, the dog nudged Mitchell's hand, and he obligingly scratched behind her ears.

"Sandy, he's a guest," said Reid to his dog. Hearing her name, the German shepherd dropped her head and slinked off into the kitchen to lie down on a worn red woolen blanket, her head resting between her paws.

The cabin interior's first floor was one large room with dozens of photographs from multiple generations adorning the walls. Jen marveled at the thousands of books piled high in bookcases all over the floor and spread out along the walls. Reid probably had as many books as a small library. A set of highly polished wooden stairs led up to the second floor where the bedrooms were located.

Reid poured them both a hot cup of coffee and then asked them to join him at an old wooden table in the middle of his small kitchen.

Jen thanked him for his hospitality and then got right down to the purpose of their visit. Together they told Reid what had happened in the Philippines and at the auction house, hoping that the old man could shed some light on why people may have wanted to kidnap her, and if he thought that the *Goliath* had any bearing on what was going on.

Reid sat there drinking his coffee and when they were finished talking, he shuffled over to a nearby bookcase by the stairs and rummaged around for a while before returning with several binders of notes that he had amassed over the years while researching the disappearance of the *Goliath*.

Jen's eyes lit up wide at the sight of the binder. Being an historian, she saw the binders as mini-gold mines of information. Perhaps the answer lay hidden somewhere in the man's voluminous notes.

Reid sat back in his chair and ran a hand through his thinning white hair. "Here is all the original source material that I have on my uncle's fascination with the loss of the Royal Airship *Goliath* over Africa in 1931," explained Reid as he spread the notes about on the table. "It kind of turned into a bit of a family obsession, you might say," Reid explained as he looked down at the hundreds of pages and photos covering the table.

"Wow, you could say that," said Jen as she looked over the worn and yellowed pieces of paper, her mind soaking in everything she could about the *Goliath*.

"Sir, do you know why they didn't ever find the *Goliath*? And what is so damned important about her?" asked Mitchell.

"Well, Mister Mitchell, those are both good questions," said Reid as he took a sip of his coffee and then continued. "First things first, my uncle was certain that the man behind the *Goliath*, Lord Seaford, had actually grossly mismanaged his company's funds and was heavily in debt to his creditors. He even wrote that he believed that Seaford was going bankrupt when the *Goliath* disappeared. Rather conveniently, his widow received millions from the insurance Seaford took out on his airship before it left England. However, with creditors demanding to be paid, his company folded shortly afterwards," explained Reid.

"And the search?" asked Mitchell.

Reid smiled and then said, "For weeks, the French authorities scoured the desert, but found nothing. Over the years, several privately-funded expeditions have only managed to find some small pieces of wreckage in the desert outside of a tiny village called Ouadane, in Mauritania, but no one to date has ever found the *Goliath* herself. I've always felt that if she is still out there, she'll be found near the area known as the Eye of the Sahara, a truly massive naturally-formed rock feature that can be seen from space," explained Reid. "I never went to Mauritania myself, couldn't afford to, not on my salary, but my uncle did once, decades ago. The locals told him that a massive sandstorm lasting for days tore through that region about the same time that the *Goliath* disappeared."

"So it could still be out there then, buried under tons of sand?" said Mitchell.

"Yes, Mister Mitchell, exactly. I, like my uncle, truly do believe that she's waiting to be discovered someday."

Mitchell absentmindedly rubbed the couple of days' growth on his chin. "Well, that's something, then. But why would someone still care after all these years?"

"That part's easy," said Reid, looking straight into Mitchell's blue-gray eyes. "Greed, Mister Mitchell, simple greed. The *Goliath* was carrying a fortune in her cargo hold when she disappeared."

"How so?" asked Jen, looking up from a photograph of the lost airship. "Aside from the jewels and personal belongings carried by the passengers on the flight, I've never come across any reference to anything that would lead me to believe that there was a fortune to be found in her remains."

Reid rummaged around on his table, grabbed a piece of paper, and then laid it out in front of Mitchell. "The flight manifest listed at least a dozen British and French millionaires as passengers. Their jewels alone would be worth tens of millions on today's market, but that pales in comparison to what was loaded onto the *Goliath* during its brief stopover in Paris," said Reid with a smile as he reached over and topped up their cups.

"I take it you have an idea what that fortune might be?" said Jen.

"Oh, I know exactly what it is," Reid replied, smiling over at Jen.

Both Jen and Mitchell sat there staring at Reid, waiting for him to speak.

"Have you ever heard the strange but true tale of how the Romanov crown jewels were loaned to Ireland by the Bolsheviks after the Russian Revolution?" asked Reid.

"No," said Jen and Mitchell in unison.

"Well then, let me tell you," said Reid. "For a sum of twenty-five thousand US dollars, the crown jewels were loaned to the Irish government, but they were never placed on display. Instead, they were hidden away in the home of the mother of the

Irish envoy to the United States. However, trouble soon brewed in Ireland and civil war broke out. During the Battle of Dublin, the jewels were repeatedly moved around to ensure that they didn't fall into the wrong hands. It was during one of these moves that the jewels were smuggled out of the country and replaced with flawless replicas."

"So, you're telling me that the ones on display in Moscow are fakes?" said Jen disbelievingly.

"Yes, that's precisely what I'm telling you," replied Reid bluntly. "In fact, the Russians themselves know it and have spent decades and billions of rubles looking for them all over the world."

"Being the only non-historian here, what exactly constitutes the Russian crown jewels?" asked Mitchell.

"There are the sovereign's crown, which would have been worn by the Czar, along with the consort's crown, and a scepter and orb," explained Reid. "You can easily find information on all of them on the web."

Jen leaned forward in her chair. "Sir, that's quite the claim. Can you prove any of this?"

"My uncle obtained the sworn testimony of a fellow called Father Patrick Murphy, before he died of throat cancer in 1974. He claims to have helped transport the jewels to a rendezvous outside of Dublin during the fighting, where the jewels were switched and his brother was murdered. He was lucky to survive, himself. When he finally arrived home and told his mother what had happened, he learned the truth behind his family's participation in hiding the jewels."

"But you said that they were placed onboard the *Goliath* in Paris," said Mitchell.

"That I did," he replied. "The jewels were smuggled out of Ireland by a pro-monarchist group who had decided to safeguard them until a Romanov heir could be returned to the throne of Russia. However, no secret ever stays a secret forever. Soon, Red agents began to close in on the hiding place of the jewels, so it was decided to move them far from Paris and to the home of Lord Roberts, a British sympathizer, who lived in Durbin, South Africa. Unfortunately, the jewels never arrived, as they were lost along with the *Goliath*."

"Well, I can now see why someone would be very interested in finding the *Goliath*," said Mitchell. "But why the fixation on Jen?"

"That, Mister Mitchell, I cannot answer."

13

Outside, a heavy blowing snow had blanketed Mitchell's rented car with a thick layer of fresh snow.

Silently, a shape moved out from the snow-covered pine trees lining the road to Reid's cottage. Slowly, the form coalesced into that of a man dressed in military-style winter white coveralls. Clenched firmly in his hands was an AK-74 with a long suppressor on it. Stopping a meter away from the driver's side of the rental car, the man raised his AK to his shoulder, took aim, and noiselessly fired off three rounds into the vehicle's engine block, instantly disabling it.

Cautiously, the man looked about and then, with a slight wave of his hand, four more men, all dressed in white, emerged like ghosts out of the blowing snow and walked over to the assassin.

"All right, I want this done quickly and quietly. Listen up: I do not want the woman to be harmed in the slightest. As for the old man, keep him alive long enough for him to give us what information he has. After that, kill him. The other man inside is a former US soldier and is highly dangerous, so don't hesitate, kill him on sight," said Teplov to his men, his voice as cold as the blowing snow falling to the ground, covering their tracks.

The thugs nodded their acknowledgement. With precision learned from years of brutal fighting deep inside Chechnya, the men silently fanned out and took up fire-positions around the building.

Teplov was pleased with the operation thus far. It had taken a lot of money to get his weapons of choice delivered to Alaska on such short notice, but Teplov always knew how to find men who only needed money to look the other way. Like his men, all

Teplov cared about was money, lots of money, and as long as it flowed he was willing to take the risks. A series of quick clicks sounded in his earpiece. A crooked smile crept across his scarred face. His men were all in position and ready to begin the assault.

Inside the cottage, Sandy raised her ears. Something troubled her. Sitting up, she began to growl at the front door.

"Be quiet, Sandy," ordered Reid.

Mitchell looked over at the dog and instantly felt his pulse race. He had been with teams who had used dogs in Afghanistan, and knew that the dog was bothered by something unseen. Something dangerous.

The dog growled deeper. Sandy slowly crept towards the front door, baring her teeth to ward off the approaching threat.

"Sandy, come here," said Reid, firmly snapping his fingers to get the dog's attention.

Mitchell's instincts kicked into high gear. "Mister Reid, do you have any guns here?" asked Mitchell as he looked around for an exit. He gritted his teeth. He had underestimated the persistence of his opponents. He would not do that again.

Reid nodded, walked over to a closed wooden closet in the kitchen, and then opened the doors, revealing an old double-barreled shotgun.

Mitchell practically sprinted over and snatched the shotgun out of the closet.

Sandy growled again and moved over beside her master, defiantly protecting him from the invisible danger.

"What's going on, Ryan?" asked Jen nervously.

"Not sure, but I don't think we're alone," answered Mitchell.

Pleased to see that Reid kept his shotgun in pristine condition, Mitchell grabbed a couple of slugs, swiftly loaded them in, and then slammed the shotgun closed. Hurriedly, he stuffed more shells into his pockets. Taking a deep breath to calm himself, Mitchell pointed the shotgun at the front door.

"Sir, is there another way in or out of here?" Mitchell asked Reid over his shoulder, his eyes fixed on the door, expecting to see an unwanted guest at any second.

"The only other door is the one we came in leading to the garage," replied Reid, reaching for his thick red hunting jacket.

"Is your car in there?" said Mitchell, edging back from the front of the house.

"My car's in town, getting repaired. It was giving me trouble, so my friend Julie gave me a lift in and out of town yesterday," Reid replied apologetically.

Mitchell was about to say something, when suddenly, the world around them exploded in a hail of bullets, broken glass and wooden splinters as gunfire tore through the house. Reid never had a chance. Hit dozens of times in his chest, he staggered backwards, and then fell straight back onto the floor, dead.

Mitchell barely had time to pull Jen to the floor, instantly covering her with his body.

The deadly torrent of bullets tore through the cottage, sending bits of wood and furniture spinning through the air. Mitchell tried lifting his head to see where the gunfire was coming from, but with the volume of fire tearing through the house, he couldn't see a thing. Their opponents were too well hidden. Unlike before, Mitchell knew he was facing professionals.

Jen screamed; the noise was deafening as bullets continued to tear the old wooden cottage apart. It was as if a giant was outside taking a buzz saw to the whole place. Wooden debris and pieces of chewed-up books rained down on Mitchell and Jen.

The shooting suddenly stopped. Silence filled the air.

Mitchell knew what was coming next. Moving away from Jen, he quickly brought the shotgun up to his shoulder and took aim at the front door.

Simultaneously, the front and back doors of the house exploded inwards. The doors shattered into thousands of pieces by the force of the shaped charges placed against them.

Mitchell felt the explosions deep inside his body. His ears rang from the blasts.

"Stay down," yelled Mitchell at Jen just as a white shape suddenly appeared in the blown-out entrance to the house. It smoothly dropped to one knee and raised its AK, intent on spraying the inside of the house with a deadly fusillade of bullets before entering.

Mitchell did not hesitate, pulling back on the first trigger, the shotgun roared in his hands. Flames leapt from the barrel of the old weapon as the 12-gauge pellets hit the attacker square in the chest. The force of the impact threw the man backwards and out into the yard. His dead body lay there as falling snow slowly covered his bloody chest.

Spinning around on the floor, Mitchell aimed the shotgun over the top of Jen and towards the destroyed back door. Without waiting for a target to appear, he counted to two in his head and fired.

The Russian thug coming in the back door had not anticipated anyone surviving the initial assault on the house. His complacency cost him as he stepped into the opening and was hit by the blast from Mitchell's shotgun. Screaming in pain, the man tumbled forward as the pellets tore into his groin and upper legs. The man let go of his rifle as he fell onto the floor, reaching down in agonizing pain for his bloodied legs. In anguish, the man rolled around on the floor, swearing at the top of his lungs in Russian.

"Grab the notes and let's go," said Mitchell to Jen as he stood and quickly loaded a couple more shells into the shotgun. "Stay behind me," said Mitchell firmly. Jen nodded. Behind them, Sandy lay silently on the floor beside her master.

Mitchell looked around quickly at the dead man at the front of the house and the wounded one at the back and instantly decided that their best chance of survival lay in getting as much distance as they could from their attackers. He knew that he had only delayed, not stopped, their assailants. With the shotgun firmly tucked in his hands, Mitchell edged towards the destroyed back door.

Cold air rushed in, cooling Mitchell's sweating body as he edged forward, carefully peering out into the blowing snow. He was relieved to see that there were no more thugs waiting for them outside, but something told him to be wary. It would be dark soon, but not soon enough.

The wounded thug cursed Mitchell and made a move for a pistol jammed into his chest harness.

Mitchell saw the motion out of the corner of his eye. Instinctively, he lowered the shotgun butt straight onto the man's head. With a loud thud, the man was knocked unconscious, his body a bleeding heap on the hardwood floor.

Seeing the wounded thug's AK lying on the floor, Mitchell bent down and picked it up, checked the magazine to see that it was full, and then handed the shotgun to Jen, who took it but gave Mitchell a look that said she had no clue how to use it.

"Point it at the bad guys and pull the trigger if you have to," whispered Mitchell, his voice barely loud enough to hear. "We need to get to the garage," Mitchell said, motioning for Jen to keep close behind him.

Jen nodded; she was scared beyond belief, but trusted Mitchell with her life, so she did as she was told.

"Ok, let's go!" said Mitchell as they quickly darted into Reid's musky-smelling and dimly lit garage. There was no heat inside. Mitchell could see his breath and feel the growing cold starting to envelope his sweating body.

Mitchell knew there was only one way out. Running to the closed front door of the garage, he unlocked the door and opened it barely an inch before doubling back and opening the side door on the ice speeder. Quickly ushering Jen inside the aged speeder, Mitchell jumped in and closed the door behind them. The interior was bare except for two old canvas chairs bolted to the floor for the driver and a passenger. Mitchell took a seat behind the controls and looked down at the paint-chipped console, trying to find the ignition.

Jen pointed at a large red button on the driver's side. "I think that might be it," she said, crossing her fingers for luck as Mitchell reached down and pushed the button. A split second later, with a loud bang, the engine loudly coughed and sputtered to life.

Quickly looking down, Mitchell was happy to see that there was a gas pedal and a hand brake to control the speed of the craft. Deciding that there was no time to waste, Mitchell smashed his foot hard on the gas and felt the speeder lurch forward. A second later, they hit the garage doors, throwing them open. Blowing snow instantly rushed inside, blinding Mitchell for a moment, but he was not going to hesitate nor slow down. With a sharp turn on the half-moon shaped driver's wheel, Mitchell turned the speeder away from the house and headed towards the frozen lake, leaving a swirling white cloud of powdered snow in his wake.

Teplov stepped into the doorway of the wrecked cottage; wood and glass crunched under foot. His blood boiled as he stared down at the lifeless body of one of his men. Having not heard from the other attacker, Teplov knew that he was either dead or incapacitated. He shook his head in disgust. How could one man be such a pain in the ass?

Teplov keyed his throat-mic. "Anatoly, Isaak, this is Teplov, I think both Pasha and Petya are down," said Teplov, his voice unemotional as he reported the news. "Stay alert, I think they got out through the back door," Teplov added, as he walked through the house to confirm his nagging suspicion about his men. Heading into the kitchen, Teplov saw Petya lying by the back door. He was still breathing, but his legs were a bloody mess. Teplov doubted that he would live much longer from the loss of blood and the onset of shock. Time was against them; he could not spend the time to care for the wounded man, nor could he risk him being taken by the police alive. Lowering his rifle, Teplov fired a bullet into the dying man's skull, sending him on his way. Finding he could no longer control the anger racing through him, Teplov lashed out with his foot, sending a small coffee table flying against the far wall, shattering it to pieces.

Suddenly, the sound of an engine coming to life in the garage outside caught Teplov's attention. Edging to the back door, his weapon at the ready, Teplov was stunned to see an old red ice speeder burst out of the garage, picking up speed as it raced off towards the frozen lake. Quickly firing off two shots, he ran forward to get a better view, only to be blinded by a blowing wall of snow thrown up by the escaping speeder's fan.

Teplov snarled into his mic at his accomplices, "Get back to the car right now, or I'll leave you for the police!" Seeing the speeder reach the lake, Teplov swore, turned on his heels and then dashed back through the trashed house and out towards their waiting H2 SUV.

"I hope there's a working heater in this ice box," said Jen as she rubbed her cold hands together, trying to get some feeling and warmth back in them. Neither Jen nor Mitchell had had the time to grab their warm winter clothing during the attack, so both now sat in the speeder, shivering in the cold. Looking over the control panel, Jen saw a small toggle switch. Reaching over, she flipped up the switch and hoped for the best.

Seconds later, warm air started to blow into the cabin of the speeder. Jen leaned forward and put her hands over the precious vent, letting the heat warm her near-frozen hands.

Mitchell was happy to feel the heat start to warm the cabin. The snow was coming down in thick clumps, making it more difficult by the second to see through the plastic windshield of the speeder. The last thing he wanted to do was smash into a sunken log sticking through the ice or run head-on into an outcropping of rocks. To do so would mean serious injury or death inside the old vehicle.

"Any idea where we're going?" asked Jen as she looked over at Mitchell.

"I think we're heading south. So, we're going in the right direction back towards town," replied Mitchell optimistically.

Reaching over, Mitchell rubbed the steadily fogging up window with his hand, trying to see outside as he drove the speeder down the lake through the deteriorating winter storm.

"Hopefully, we should be in Palmer in the next five to ten minutes," said Mitchell as he peered out of the frosty windshield, trying to discern any landmarks that they may have passed earlier, hoping that they might help tell him where they were.

Jen was about to say something, when suddenly through the swirling snow, a dark object appeared directly in front of them. Mitchell thought for a second that it was an abandoned ice fishing hut and was about to steer around it, when the mass started to race towards them. At the last second, Mitchell realized that it was a vehicle.

The sound of bullets tearing into the side of the speeder made both Mitchell and Jen reflexively duck their heads down as the car raced past barely a meter away from them, a man wildly firing his AK from his open window.

"Who the hell was that?" a terrified Jen yelled as Mitchell looked over her shoulder at the Hummer as it disappeared into the thick blowing snow.

"It would appear that our friends are back. They must have a really good GPS, and some top-of-the-line snow tires on their damned Hummer," said Mitchell as he floored the speeder's gas pedal. The engine surged as the speeder skimmed over the icy surface of the frozen lake. Mitchell knew the speeder was old and probably wouldn't take much more punishment, but he didn't care. At that moment, he needed all the power the aged vehicle could give him.

In the SUV, the driver, Anatoly, a blonde-haired man, cursed as he turned the wheel hard over in his calloused hands. He felt the tires of his Hummer struggling to grip the snow and ice beneath him. Letting go of the accelerator, Anatoly turned into the slide and felt his vehicle's tires grab the ice. With a practiced move, he swiftly turned the vehicle around, floored the accelerator, and then, like a charging Siberian tiger, the Hummer sped back into the blowing whiteout and after the fleeing speeder.

"Don't let them get away this time," Teplov said from the passenger seat as he loaded a fresh magazine into his AK.

His blood was up. He smiled to himself; the hunt was on again.

Mitchell strained to see if the car was still after them; his frustration when he realized the storm was getting worse by the minute. All he could see now was the snow as it accumulated on the speeder's windshield. Looking over, Mitchell saw that their side mirrors were caked in snow, rendering them useless.

"Do you think we lost them?" asked Jen, trying to see their pursuers in the whiteout.

"They won't quit, not now. Unlike us, they don't need to see where they're going. All they need to know is how to read their GPS' electronic map," answered Mitchell.

"At least we're both in this awful weather," Jen said, hoping that their adversary was as blind as they were, but somehow, knowing her luck, she doubted it.

Mitchell gripped the speeder's steering wheel hard the instant he heard the sound of their adversary's vehicle engine rapidly approaching from somewhere behind them in the blinding snow. Turning his head just in time, Mitchell saw the Hummer emerge out of the blowing snow like a charging tiger intent on getting its meal. With a loud thump, the Hummer smashed into the driver's side of the speeder, easily crumpling the thin aluminum box towards Mitchell's legs.

Mitchell cursed under his breath. He was growing desperate. Taking a deep breath, he turned the speeder into the Hummer, hoping to cause their attacker some damage as well.

Instantly, both vehicles swayed from side to side like drunken prizefighters. The Hummer may have been heavier, but the speeder had the advantage of mobility and traction on the ice. With a quick flick of the wrist, Mitchell turned the speeder away from their attacker and sped off, hoping to use the cover of the blowing snow to escape.

"We can't keep this up forever," said Mitchell as he reached down and picked up the AK that he had taken from the wounded thug. "Jen, I need you to take over," he said as he edged out of his seat, making room for her.

"I was hoping you would ask," said Jen with a smile as she jumped from his seat and quickly took over the speeder's controls from Mitchell. "Guns are your forte, but I can drive and now that I'm scared out of my mind I'm sure I can drive like the wind."

Mitchell patted Jen on the shoulder and then moved over to the side door of the speeder. Looking out the tiny side-door porthole, Mitchell couldn't see more than ten meters into the blinding snow. He tensely gripped the rifle and turned his head towards Jen. "Ok. I know this going to sound crazy, but I want you to trust me on this one. Jen, I want you to slow down."

"Are you nuts?" said Jen over her shoulder. "I thought we wanted to get away, not give in."

"We'll never outrun them, so let's have them come to us," said Mitchell, grinning.

"Ryan, I hope you know what you're doing," Jen said as she reluctantly took her foot off the gas pedal. Instantly, the vehicle began to slow down to a mere crawl along the ice.

Anatoly cursed the weather as he peered into the near-impenetrable wall of snow. He had been in many whiteouts in Russia but never one when he was in pursuit of someone over a frozen lake. His stomach was in knots. If he failed to find the Americans, Teplov would surely gut him and his partner without hesitation. Peering down at the GPS, he saw that they were nearing the shoreline of the lake. Suddenly, a dark shape in front of them emerged through the snow.

It could only be one thing, thought Anatoly. Speeding up, he raced to close the distance before they tried to escape once more.

Mitchell saw the Hummer coming towards them. Taking a deep breath, he opened the door. Instantly, a bitter cold wind whipped inside, freezing Mitchell to his core.

Suddenly, the front ski on their speeder hit the top of an ice-covered boulder sticking through the ice, sending it bouncing up into the air. Mitchell barely had time to shoot out his free hand and grabbed onto of the open door, stopping himself from being thrown out of the vehicle and onto the frozen lake.

"Sorry," called out Jen, "I must have hit a rock or something. I think we're getting close to the shoreline. I'll try to take us back out onto the lake."

"No! Keep going straight. If it sucks for us, it will for them too!" yelled Mitchell, as he struggled to pull himself back inside the speeder. Turning his head, Mitchell saw their opponent's car racing towards them. Grabbing the AK, he brought it up to his shoulder and took aim.

Jen yelled something, but Mitchell never heard her; his mind was too fixed on the vehicle speeding towards them.

The Hummer was now only seconds away; it was so close that Mitchell did not even need to aim. Flipping the AK's selector to full auto, Mitchell pulled the trigger and held it down as he emptied the entire thirty-round magazine into the vehicle. Bullets shot into the windshield of the approaching Hummer, shattering the glass and tearing into the hapless driver, his body jerking violently as the bullets struck his body.

The dead driver's hands still clenched the steering wheel. His lifeless body slowly slumped over, turning the wheel hard left. Blinded by the blowing snow and wind whipping inside their vehicle, Teplov struggled to reach over and pull the dead driver away from the wheel. Jamming his foot down hard on the brake pedal, Teplov fought to bring the SUV to a stop before they hit something and ended up flipping over on the ice.

Slamming the speeder's side door closed, Mitchell dropped the empty AK onto the floor, shook the snow from his body, and then made his way over to Jen. Sliding down into the passenger seat, Mitchell looked over at Jen and smiled. If she was scared by everything that was happening around her, she surely didn't show it.

Peering out of the frosted windshield, Mitchell saw what he took to be a cottage set back from the edge of the lake. "Jen, head over to the right," said Mitchell, pointing towards the dark shape in the distance.

Jen nodded and then turned the speeder towards land.

They were less than ten meters from the shore when disaster struck. Unseen in the blowing snow was the top of a log lodged deep in the ice. The speeder hit the log head-on. Instantly, their speeder came to a bone-jarring halt. Jen screamed as she was thrown forward by the impact, her head hitting the dash, knocking her out cold. Blood poured from a deep gash on her forehead. Mitchell raised his arms to cover his face as he flew straight through the plastic windshield, his body tumbling end over end until he came to a stop beside a small ice-fishing cabin.

With his hand raised to block the blowing snow, Teplov brought the battered SUV to a halt beside the destroyed speeder. Grabbing his AK, he jumped from the vehicle, ran over to the side of the speeder, and pulled open the side door. Thrusting his weapon inside, he expected Mitchell to be there waiting for him. Instead, all he saw was Jen lying face down on the dash, slowly being covered by the snow blowing in through the damaged front end of the vehicle.

"Get her and put her in the car," said Teplov to the last surviving thug with him. Gripping his AK tight in his hands, Teplov moved to the front of the speeder and looked around for Mitchell. The wind had picked up, making it hard for him to see more than a few meters in front of his face. Looking down, he could not find any tracks leading away from the destroyed speeder. *If Mitchell had survived the impact, he was long gone* reasoned Teplov. Turning around, he ran back and helped Jen into the back of their SUV. Covering her with a blanket, he jumped into the driver's seat and then turned the vehicle towards the shoreline. Minutes later, they were on the road heading back towards Palmer, where he intended to steal another vehicle and then make their way to Anchorage where a private jet awaited his return. It had been a costly venture, but Teplov had obtained the woman for his employer. With this one act, his tarnished reputation was restored. Now, an even more challenging mission lay ahead for him in the deserts of West Africa.

A numbing cold filled Mitchell's body. Lying there, he saw the impact repeatedly in his mind. He tried to move, but found that he was pinned underneath something. Forcing his near-frozen eyelids open, he saw that his feet had come to rest under a bench that had sunk into the snow, pinning him to the ice. Out of the corner of his eye, a dark shape appeared. It seemed to hover over him for a moment, before reaching down for him. With a painful tug, Mitchell felt his legs being pulled free. He tried to speak, but found that his vision was narrowing. A second or two later, he blacked out.

14

Jen was bleeding. Reaching over, Mitchell found himself unable to reach her. Slowly, she began to drift further and further away from him. No matter how hard he tried, he could not reach her. He began to panic. Suddenly, Mitchell sat straight up. Opening his eyes, he saw that he was lying on a bed inside a small log cabin. The small room was lit by a couple of old oil hurricane lamps that reminded Mitchell of his uncle's old cottage on Lake Michigan. He could feel the welcoming heat coming from an aged lead-belly stove on the far side of the room. The smell of percolating coffee filled the air.

"Good evening there, young fella," said an unfamiliar voice.

Slowly turning his head, Mitchell saw a man with bright blue eyes and a caring face with a long white beard, wearing a faded red sweater, sitting on a chair beside the bed smiling at him.

"Let me guess, I'm at the North Pole and you're Santa Claus," said Mitchell weakly.

The man let out a deep laugh. "No, Mister Mitchell, you're not in the North Pole, and if you ever heard my wife talk about me, you would know that I'm far from Santa Claus," said the man as he ran his hand through his thick beard.

Taking a deep breath to clear his aching head, Mitchell looked down and saw that his arms were covered in fresh bandages. His mind went back to the crash. Instantly, his heart began to race.

"There was a woman with me, did you find her as well?" asked Mitchell.

"Sorry, I only found you lying out there in the snow," replied the man. "There were tire tracks leading away from your demolished speeder. Perhaps she took a ride to the hospital with those people?"

"Yeah, perhaps," said Mitchell, knowing that Jen had been taken hostage by whoever had attacked them and was probably out of the country by now.

"You're damned lucky that I was up here doing some ice fishing, or you would have frozen to death out there, Mister Mitchell. I heard a loud crash and decided to see what happened that's when I stumbled across you."

"Thanks," replied Mitchell earnestly. "How come you know my name?"

"When I stripped you down to warm you up, I checked your wallet and found your ID. I've already called your work to let them know that you're all right. They told me to pass on that a Mister Jackson would be up here in the next day or so to take you back home to New York," said the man.

"So, sir, what do I call you?" asked Mitchell.

"Oh, you can use my first name. Please call me Chris," replied the man with a broad smile as he offered Mitchell, his hand.

Mitchell shook Chris' hand and then tried sitting up, only to find his vision blur.

"Whoa there, you need to lie down, son," said Chris, helping Mitchell to lie back on the bed. "You've probably got a concussion, so you need your rest," he said as he pulled up the sheets.

Mitchell was too tired to resist. A minute later, he was fast asleep, his mind searching for answers: where was Jen and why did they want her? These were questions, for the moment, that had no answers, but before long, they would be answered in blood.

15

The Yacht – *Imperator*
Coast of Mauritania

Jen paced back and forth inside her locked cabin, as if she were a tigress kept in a cage far too small for her. She was dressed in a loose-fitting teal blue jumpsuit and wore a pair of leather sandals on her feet. When she had awoken from her drug-induced sleep, Jen had yelled and screamed to be set free, but found that her pleas went unanswered. Her cabin was her prison cell. Meals were brought to her by a pair of armed men who were constantly on guard outside of her room. The same questions kept running through Jen's mind: why would someone go to such great lengths to kidnap her, and why was she onboard a ship?

Just as Jen was about to lose her cool and lash out at the nearest piece of furniture, the door suddenly opened; a stone-faced guard motioned for her to follow him.

Jen's stomach clenched in a knot; she had wanted to be set free, but now that the door was open, Jen was not so sure that she wanted to leave her room. Nervously nodding her head, she stepped out into the corridor and fell in behind the hulking guard. They walked in silence down a long carpeted corridor until they came to a set of metal stairs leading up to the next deck. Jen could smell the warm salt air as they climbed up until they arrived on the main deck, where they walked out into the open. The bright sunlight was hard on Jen's eyes. She raised a hand to block the sun as she looked around. Jen was amazed to see that she was being held on a multi-leveled luxury yacht, not some rundown rust bucket as she had half-imagined in her mind. The guard led her to the stern of the yacht where a tall man dressed in khaki pants and a light-blue shirt stood looking over the railing at another ship anchored a few hundred meters away.

None of what was happening made any sense whatsoever to her.

The guard stopped short of the man, then told Jen to take a seat on a white leather chair looking out over the warm, deep-blue Atlantic Ocean.

Sitting there, with her arms crossed, she looked at the other ship anchored nearby. It looked to her like a high-tech catamaran on steroids. On the aft deck, it looked as though men were preparing a dirty orange painted sea container to be moved. Jen began to wonder what was going on, when the loud rhythmic sound of a powerful helicopter's blades beating through the air filled her ears. Looking up, Jen saw a large camouflaged military helicopter fly right over their ship and maneuver itself into position, hovering just above the catamaran. A man with a pair of paddles guided the noisy helicopter down until it seemed to hang effortlessly in the air just over the sea container. Ever so slowly, the helicopter descended until it was no more than a couple of meters above the container. Right away two men jumped up, grabbed the chains secured to the sea container, and then latched them onto a hook on the bottom of the helicopter, before jumping down from the container. Barely a second later, the helicopter took up the slack and then, with its engines revving for all they were worth, the helicopter and the container steadily rose up into the cloudless sky. Jen watched with rapt fascination as the helicopter and its cargo seemed to leisurely bank over, then pick up speed as it headed away from the catamaran, flying towards the sandy shore in the distance.

The tall man turned about and looked over at Jen; his cognac-brown eyes seemed to be studying her. Suddenly very uncomfortable at the man's unwanted attention, Jen tried to look away.

A waiter dressed in an all-white uniform walked over and handed Jen and the man each a cool bottle of Perrier. With a nod, the server departed, leaving Jen and the man alone on the deck.

"Good afternoon, Miss March," said the man with a smile.

"I hope that you are finding your accommodations satisfactory."

Jen looked at the man and saw that he had short black hair along with his neatly trimmed circle goatee. He looked to be in superb physical shape. Jen figured that he was in his fifties and judging by what she had seen of his yacht, he was unbelievably rich. Lifting the bottle, Jen took a swig of her Perrier, felt the cool liquid soothe her parched throat, and then spoke, "Yes, my room is quite satisfactory." *If you like being held hostage* thought Jen.

"That's good to hear," said the man as he took a seat across from Jen. "Miss March, you must be very puzzled by what is going on. First off, let me introduce myself. My name is Dmitry Romanov, and as you have no doubt already figured out, you are no longer in Alaska."

"By the smell of sand mixed with spices coming from the mainland, I would say we are somewhere off West Africa. I did some charity work here a few years back. The aroma is quite distinctive," said Jen.

"Well done, Miss March. To be precise, we are currently anchored off the coast of Mauritania," said Romanov as he leaned forward in his seat. "Now, you must be full of questions as to why I have brought you here. You can ask me anything you like."

"Ok then, Mister Romanov, why am I here?" said Jen, getting straight to the point.

"Miss March, I am here looking for my past as well as my future. You see, there are some items belonging to my family that were lost in the desert decades ago, and I have been told by someone very special that you, and you alone, are the key to finding them for me," said Romanov with a bright gleam in his eyes as he spoke.

Jen shook her head. Placing together the Romanov name and the story of the missing jewels she'd heard in Alaska, Jen instantly knew what the man was looking for.

"Mister Romanov, I'm a history professor, not an archaeologist," explained Jen. "If you're looking for the Romanov crown jewels reputed to have been on the *Goliath* when it disappeared, I'm sorry, but I may not be the best person for the job. I hope this isn't all a big misunderstanding, and that you have the wrong Jennifer March."

"Oh no, Miss March, I am quite certain that you are precisely the person I am looking for, and shortly you will help me retrieve what rightly belongs to my family. What I want is still buried somewhere out there, waiting for me to come and find it," said Romanov, waving his arm towards the distant shore.

Jen looked towards the windswept shoreline, wondering if Romanov could possibly be right. She was genuinely intrigued, but still failed to see where she fit into his scheme to find the *Goliath*.

"The information found with you in Alaska has proven to be most useful," said Romanov. "But it does not provide the missing piece of information that I need."

"Sir, those weren't my notes," said Jen, slowly becoming exasperated with the man. "Your people murdered the man who wrote them. As I already said, I'm not an archaeologist."

Romanov stood and looked down at Jen. "Miss March, I know this, and if there had been another path to follow I would have taken it, but you have been chosen."

Jen looked into Romanov's cold eyes and asked, "Chosen by whom?"

A smile emerged on Romanov's face. "Miss March, like my forefathers, I am a true believer in mysticism. Ever since I was a young man, I believe in my ability to shape and control my own destiny. With the guiding hand of Madame Yusuf, an old Romanov family confidant, I have never once failed to achieve whatever I set my mind to. It was Madame Yusuf who told me about my future and the part you would play in it. Her mother was the spiritual advisor to Czar Nicholas II's wife Alexandra. She is a psychic and true believer, like myself."

Jen couldn't believe what she was hearing. She shook her head, unable to decide if the man was mad.

"I see the doubt in your eyes, Miss March," said Romanov. "Please, let me explain. It was Madame Yusuf who told me that in order to secure my future, I must first sow chaos in my homeland, which I have done by financing revolution throughout Russia. Secondly, she told me to find my past here in Africa, and that by finding my family's jewels, I would gain credibility with my future subjects in my homeland. Lastly, she told me that you, and you alone, Miss March, would lead me to the jewels. Surely, it's clear even to you that you have a part to play in this grand endeavor."

Jen sat back and looked over at Romanov. "Sir, honestly, I don't believe in mysticism or psychic abilities. It's nothing more than carefully posed questions designed to draw the right responses out of the people seeking guidance," said Jen.

"Well, Miss March, we will have to agree to disagree on this matter, and I hope for your sake that you allow yourself to embrace your hidden abilities, or things might not go so well for you and your mother," said Romanov coldly.

"You have me, you don't have my mother," Jen said defiantly. "She's in protective custody with the police."

Romanov smiled wickedly at Jen. "I am sorry, but that is not quite accurate. She *was* in police protective custody, but now she is on her way here. My people found her safe house and took her from it earlier this morning."

"You bastard," snarled Jen as she jumped up from her seat.

A guard instantly appeared with a pistol in his hands aimed straight at Jen's head.

"I think we have finished our little discussion for today, Miss March. I need to place a call to a friend in Moscow," said Romanov as he stood. "I will see that your mother is brought to you the instant she arrives." With that, Romanov walked away, leaving Jen sitting there trying to control the growing hatred in her heart for the man.

16

Moscow
Russia

An anonymous tip called into a local radio station had diverted the authorities. The usual daily traffic passing by the Kremlin was quickly rerouted to a side street, where it was searched by the police and armed forces for weapons and explosives being smuggled into the capital for the rebel forces. Before long, a column of traffic snaked back more than two kilometers from the police checkpoint.

The checkpoints, once confined to the roads around government buildings, had spread throughout the city, making life difficult, if not unbearable, for many Muscovites. Knowing there was nothing he could do about it, Anatoly Grekov sat back in his tanker truck, turned on his radio, and patiently waited his turn to drive through the checkpoint. He was looking forward to delivering his supply of gasoline to a nearby gas station and then getting home to his wife and newborn child before it got too late in the day. Like many young Russians, all he wanted was the opportunity to look after his family and make a decent and honest wage doing so. Growing restless, Grekov took out a picture of his child from his wallet and smiled. Their son would be three months old tomorrow and he could not wait to take him in his arms as soon as he got home. Unlike his father, he hoped for a large family with many sons.

The truck in front of him pulled forward through the checkpoint. A police officer cradling a submachine gun in his arms nonchalantly waved for Grekov to move towards him.

Placing his son's picture back in his wallet, Grekov changed gears and then slowly drove forward until waved to a halt by the police officer.

Several vehicles back, a thin, blonde-haired driver watched Grekov pull up to the roadblock. Reaching down into a small backpack, the man removed a disposable cellphone and then dialed a number. Instantly, there was a bright flash of light, immediately followed by the noise of the blast as Grekov's truck evaporated in a massive explosion. A blinding orange and red fireball shot straight up into the sky. Along with it, the police checkpoint vanished in the blink of an eye. Instantly, fifteen other vehicles around Grekov's truck were consumed in fire as the blast wave and shrapnel ripped through everything they hit. Flame, smoke, and confusion spread out like ripples from a rock thrown into the water.

The thin man who had detonated the bomb via his cellphone watched his handiwork with some satisfaction, and then calmly jumped out of the cab of his vehicle. In the ensuing chaos, he quietly walked into the nearest alleyway. Soon the man disappeared among the throng of people jostling with one another trying to get away from the rapidly spreading fire. Whistling to himself, the man knew that the best suicide bombers were the ones who did not even know they were.

17

The White House
Oval Office

President Donald Kempt switched off the television and wearily sat down on the dark-green leather couch. A youthful man with a thick mop of premature gray hair, he was the first president elected from the state of North Dakota. With a daily stream of bad news about the deteriorating situation in Russia flowing into the White House, he felt the full weight of his job pushing down upon his shoulders. He wondered why anyone one would ever put themselves through such torment to be president. He was not even sure that he had the stamina to go through this for another four years. Shaking off such thoughts for another day, he turned his attention towards the members of his staff.

Several members of the president's National Security sat quietly in the room, but with the holiday season upon them, several of the usual key staff members were still noticeably absent.

"I know what CNN is telling me, but what is the true situation in Russia, and how much longer can President Ivankov keep a lid on the growing unrest?" asked the president, throwing the question out to the room.

Dan Leonard, the president's National Security Advisor, a white-haired former Chairman of the Joint Chiefs of Staff, took out his reading glasses, placed them on his wide nose, and started to read the latest information that he had received from his various field offices. Leonard cleared his throat and then spoke.

"Mister President, things are getting worse by the minute over there. Martial law was established throughout the country earlier tonight, but that did not prevent a suicide bombing at the Domodedovo International Airport in Moscow. This attack resulted in the deaths of at least forty-five Americans, nearly all university students, along with a hundred and sixty-five other foreign nationals who were all waiting in line to board a plane out of the country. It's still a confused situation at the airport, but our field personnel over there are working closely with the local authorities to try and get an accurate count of our casualties." Leonard did not make eye contact with the president as he continued to thumb through his file. He found what he was looking for and continued. "My opposite number in the Russian government says that he believes that at least another one hundred and eighty-five Russians were killed earlier in the day when a tanker truck full of fuel was detonated outside of a police checkpoint in the heart of Moscow, and hundreds more have horrific wounds from the fire. It may take them a couple of days to confirm their exact totals, as these figures also include those potentially incinerated in the blast."

"My God, this is worse than Iraq at the height of the insurrection," said David Grant, the Vice President. Grant was a Texan, ten years older than the President; he was a popular man with hawkish views on national security. He squirmed forward in his chair and said, "Damn it all. We need to do more to help the Russian government before they fall to this cabal of nationalist terrorist groups. Russia's the number two exporter of oil in the entire world, and I don't need to remind anyone that any interruption in the flow of that oil would have a crippling effect upon the economies of Europe, China and Japan. Our own economy isn't as strong as we had predicted earlier in the year. We cannot sit by idly and allow the world to spiral into a depression that would make the 1930s look like child's play. It wouldn't sit well with the voters."

The president shot Grant a 'not now' look for his last comment.

"Sir, I have to agree with the VP. It's in our best interests to push Congress for another multi-billion dollar aid package to their military and law agencies before all is lost. To do nothing would be suicide with the electorate," said bookish-looking John Morillo, the current Director of the FBI.

"What about ties to known terror organizations? Has anyone taken the time to see if these attacks are their handiwork?" threw out the vice-president as he took a sip of coffee. "We hurt them badly in Iraq, Somalia, and Afghanistan. I have no doubt that they're looking for ways to strike back at us. I know right-wing groups don't normally mix with Islamists, but stranger things have happened, especially when it is in both of their interests. We know that they're always looking for new and more imaginative ways to strike here in the States."

Voices rose in the room at the mention of another possible attack on the United States.

"Ladies and gentlemen, please, we're getting ahead of ourselves," said the president, trying to keep his team focused on the problem at hand. "The issue now is what do we do to prevent the fall of a friendly government?" President Kempt paused for a moment to ensure he had everyone's attention. "I hate to say it, but we should acknowledge the fact that it may already be too late for President Ivankov; pro-Western or not, he has failed to contain this worsening crisis."

"What about Dmitry Romanov?" threw out the vice-president. "He is definitely pro-Western and is reputed to have ties to the Romanov royal family, something that would sit well with hardliners in both camps. Hell, he could easily be seen by many as a compromise candidate for the Presidency."

President Kempt sat silently, lost in thought for a few moments. "You may be right, Dave. He may be the only option left to us in a couple of days if Russia continues to fall apart," said the president firmly, wishing things were not so dire.

No one said a word, but the implications were clear: the US needed to be ready to step in and help oversee the peaceful transition between Romanov and Ivankov. No one wanted a reactionary nationalist government with access to Russia's vast nuclear arsenal. Events were spiraling out of control, and they had to be prepared to act and act decisively to ensure that Russia did not collapse into total anarchy.

"Mister President, I have met Romanov on several occasions over the years. With your blessing I will start exploratory talks immediately," said Grant to the president.

"I don't want this to get out into the media that we are looking at replacing President Ivankov," said the President firmly. "Dave, treat this as a social call and nothing else right now. Ivankov still represents the horse I'd like to back in this race, but we need to be prepared to act should he continue to falter."

There was a knock at the door. An aide entered the room and without saying a word, he walked over to Dan Leonard and handed him a note. As the Chairman of the NSA read the note, the color drained from his face. "Oh God, no," blurted out Leonard.

"What the hell is it?" asked the vice-president.

Everyone in the room leaned forward in their seats as they waited on Leonard's next words.

Leonard hesitated; he seemed to be searching for the right words to say. "Mister President, the South African Ambassador is asking to see you immediately. It would appear that they were not 100% honest with the world about their nuclear disarmament program. It would appear that they retained two nuclear bombs as a means of deterrence, but they have been reported as stolen," said Leonard as he sat back and blankly stared out of the window.

"Do you mean to tell me that there are two nuclear bombs loose out there?" shouted the Vice-president.

"It would appear so," replied Leonard.

No one in the room noticed as President Kempt sank deeper into his couch and seemed to age several years in an instant.

18

Polaris Complex
Albany, New York

It took Mitchell and Jackson the better part of four days to make it back home to New York. Between getting checked out at the hospital to make sure he could fly, the interviews with the local police about Reid's murder and a snowstorm closing the airport, Mitchell was a tense bundle of nerves ready to explode by the time he arrived at the complex.

Mitchell headed straight for the conference room. General O'Reilly and Fahimah were already there waiting to debrief him on what he had learned in Alaska, then in turn fill him in on what they had been able to uncover on the *Goliath*.

Before boarding his plane, Mitchell had taken the opportunity to email Fahimah a series of questions and ideas he had come up with after thinking about what Reid had told him about the disappearance of the airship. The news that Jen's mother had been taken from a safe house and that three police officers had been killed further infuriated Mitchell. Someone was seriously pissing him off, and he intended to make that person pay.

As Mitchell entered the room, O'Reilly looked genuinely happy to see his protégé back and relatively unhurt. Fahimah gave Mitchell a quick smile and then handed him a briefing package that she had prepared about the *Goliath* for him to read over later.

It took over an hour for Mitchell to go over his run-in with the Russian thugs in Alaska. Both Fahimah and O'Reilly took copious notes, digging into the story to make sure Mitchell did not leave out any detail, no matter how insignificant it may have appeared.

Once Mitchell finished his debriefing, Fahimah picked up a remote and turned on a screen on the far wall. The first picture was a grainy black and white image of the airship *Goliath* flying over the shores of Dover on her way to Paris.

"The Royal airship *Goliath*, at over 250 meters in length, was the greatest airship of her time and the largest ever built in England," said Fahimah as she changed the image on the screen.

A picture of the planned route of the Goliath came up.

"From England, the *Goliath* headed first to Paris and then on to Rome. From there it was scheduled to arrive at a French military airstrip on the outskirts of Nouakchott, the capitol of Mauritania, to refuel, but as history records, it never made it."

Fahimah made eye contact with Mitchell and then continued. "Ryan, I looked into Mister Reid's hypothesis that the *Goliath* went down in the region known as the Eye of the Sahara and compared that with its original flight plan, and the difference is quite substantial," explained Fahimah as she brought up a picture comparing the scheduled flight plan over Africa and the suspected location of the wreck. Mitchell took a deep breath as he studied the screen and saw that the navigational error, if it occurred, would have been well over 100 kilometers.

"Winds could account for some of that," pondered O'Reilly, "but I find it hard to believe that a seasoned captain would have allowed his airship to run that far off course."

"Unless he wasn't aware that someone was tampering with the navigational instruments," said Jackson as he walked into the room, holding a box of his favorite donuts.

Mitchell stood and shook his friend's hand before helping himself to a less than nutritious breakfast.

Jackson took a seat and looked over at Ryan. "Before I took a trip up north to visit Santa and bring your sorry ass back home, Fahimah, on a hunch, asked me to do some research on the navigational means available to the *Goliath*," said Jackson. "I can assure you that there was no GPS in 1931. The poor long-suffering navigator had to use a sextant to measure the angle between the sun, stars, or planets, and the horizon, and then plot that location on his map. While you were on vacation in the great white north, I paid a visit to the Intrepid Sea, Air, and Space Museum and had one of the old hands there show me how a sextant works. I have to tell you it takes an experienced hand to work these finicky pieces of kit," said Jackson before swallowing a donut whole.

"So you don't think a navigational error could have sent them that far off course?" asked Mitchell.

"I doubt they hired any person off the street to navigate a multimillion dollar piece of hardware around the world. So no, I don't think so," replied Jackson.

"There's another possibility," said O'Reilly. "Ryan, your email said that Reid believed that the airship's builder, Lord Seaford, was up to his eyeballs in debt."

"Yes sir, that is what Reid believed," said Mitchell.

"What if Lord Seaford tinkered with the sextant to ensure that they ever so slowly, over a couple of days flying, went inexorably off course?"

Mitchell looked over at Jackson.

"Don't look at me, I needed my daughter to set up my new iPhone. I suppose anything is possible," said Jackson, not committing himself either way. "Look, if there's a will, there's always a way."

"Ok, so, if we go with the theory that the *Goliath* went incrementally off course and crashed in the desert, where could she be?" asked O'Reilly, looking intently up at the map on the screen.

Fahimah brought up a satellite image of the Eye of the Sahara.

Mitchell studied the image as he took a sip of his coffee. The Eye of the Sahara looked like a series of massive concentric circles extending out from a large central dome. It appeared to Mitchell to be the result of an ancient meteorite strike.

Fahimah looked up at the image. "The Eye of the Sahara, located near the town of Ouadane, has a circumference of over forty kilometers and is made up mainly of rock and sandstone. It may appear to look like an impact crater, but it is, in fact, the remnant of a collapsed geologic dome that has eroded away over millions of years to give the uniform shape that you see on the screen," explained Fahimah.

"I'll have to take your word for that," said Jackson with a wink at Fahimah as he reached for another donut.

Fahimah ignored Jackson and continued. "Captain Mitchell, I looked into the sandstorms that were described in Mister Reid's notes and found several references to them in the diary of a Foreign Legion Officer, and in the notes made by a French merchant living in Ouadane at the time of the *Goliath*'s disappearance. I found credible evidence that there was indeed a massive sandstorm during that time that lasted for about a week. Roads, several villages, and many ravines that had been there before were all swallowed up by the storm."

"So she could be out there still," said O'Reilly, growing more intrigued by the minute.

Mitchell looked at his mentor. "General, I truly do believe that the *Goliath* is out there, and I have no doubt whatsoever that Jen's kidnappers believe so too," said Mitchell. "I'd wager everything I have that there is where they'll go next."

A grin appeared on O'Reilly's face; he knew that Mitchell was already planning his next move. "So, what do you want to do?" asked O'Reilly.

"Sir, I know this isn't company business, but I'm on leave, so I'm going to Mauritania to try to pick up Jen's trail and get her and her mother back," said Mitchell firmly.

"You can count me in too," said Jackson, grinning. "You young officers always need supervision."

"Well, Ryan, while you were away, it became company business," said O'Reilly, smiling at both Mitchell and Jackson. "A certain Miss Alanis Kim, you remember her wealthy father, don't you?"

Mitchell nodded. Although they had spoken only a week ago, it now seemed a lifetime.

"Well, somehow Miss Kim's family learned about Jennifer March's kidnapping and she convinced her father to put up the money to get her back. Mister Kim told me that money was no object, so it looks like your team just jumped from reserve to active status."

"Captain, knowing that you would be heading out shortly, I took the liberty of putting together a country file for you and your team," said Fahimah with a mischievous sparkle in her eyes. "I've also included translated copies of the two diaries describing the storm; it may help guide you to where Jen's kidnappers could be going."

Mitchell always felt himself to be a good judge of character. Looking over at Fahimah, Mitchell knew a good thing when he saw it. "General, this is going to be the most-complicated thing we've ever done on such short notice, and as I don't speak Arabic as well as certain members of the organization, and since Mauritania is an Islamic Republic, I'd like to drag Fahimah along with the team as our intel expert. I promise not to put her in harm's way."

"The hell you don't speak Arabic, you just don't speak it good enough," said O'Reilly, correcting Mitchell. "Besides, French is widely spoken there as well, but I get your point."

O'Reilly looked over at Fahimah. The excitement etched on her face was barely held in check at the prospect of her first field assignment.

"Ok, you can borrow Fahimah, but you'd better promise to look after her," said O'Reilly, shaking his head in defeat.

"Scouts' honor general," said Mitchell. "Besides, what could possibly go wrong?"

19

Romanov oil refinery
Atar, Mauritania

Like an eagle circling on the warm air currents of the noonday sky, the gold-colored helicopter, bearing the Romanov logo of a white two-headed eagle with a sword clutched between its claws, slowly began its descent onto the shimmering helipad. As soon as the wheels touched down, several armed guards dashed over, opened the rear doors, and held them open while the helicopter's passengers climbed out.

Jen stepped out into the blistering heat and instantly started to sweat. The overpowering smell of oil combined with dusty sand assaulted her senses as she fell into line behind Dmitry Romanov and several of his well-armed bodyguards. The refinery stretched as far as Jen could see. *There are thousands of people who must work here day and night*, Jen thought.

Corrine March held onto Jen's hand for dear life; she had no idea what was going on, but knew that it was nothing good. Mrs. March tried to keep up, but Jen could tell that she was scared. With a tight squeeze of her mother's hand, Jen tried to tell her that it was all right and that help would come.

Since arriving onboard the *Imperator*, Jen and her mother had been inseparable. Mrs. March had been placed in Jen's cabin, where they spent hours for the first time in years talking to one another. Jen was relieved when they stepped inside an air-conditioned building and were handed a couple bottles of cool water. Jen gave one to her mother and then opened her own. The cold liquid felt refreshing after the scorching dry heat outside.

The building was an enormous storage hangar, which looked to Jen like it could easily house a couple of 747 Jumbo Jets inside and still have plenty of room left over. The rhythmic sound of their feet hitting the concrete floor echoed through the expansive area.

Jen looked around and spotted the sea container that she had seen airlifted off the catamaran yesterday. Its hinged doors stood wide open. Inside, Jen could see what she took to be a couple of long white metal pods. A cordon of tough-looking and well-armed thugs stood around it, their weapons at the ready. They did not look like locals to Jen. She suspected that Romanov had a private army of ex-military personnel from all over the world in his employ.

At the sound of the approaching footsteps, a pair of twin women walked out from behind the container. Jen was astonished to see them dressed identically in loose-fitting cargo pants and long-sleeved shirts. The only difference was that one was dressed in tan and the other in charcoal black. Jen studied their faces and saw a cold and calculating look in their eyes—a look she had seen before. She knew that they were Romanov's daughters.

"Ah, my dears, I am so happy to see you again," said Romanov as he embraced his daughters.

Jen could tell that the one in tan was not as pleased to see her father as the one in black.

Stepping back, Romanov waved Jen and her mother over. "Ladies, I would like you to meet my daughters, Alexandra and Nika," said Romanov proudly.

Jen felt like a piece of meat about to be sold at the auction, the way the twins disdainfully eyed her up and down.

"So this is the woman who will provide you with the Romanov crown jewels," said Nika dismissively.

Jen took an instant dislike to the one dressed in tan, the one called Nika.

"I have no doubt of that, and neither should you," said Romanov curtly, signaling that the conversation was over.

With a snap of his fingers, Jen and her mother were led away and given seats at the far end of the hanger, well out of earshot of Romanov and his daughters.

"Father, I have something to show you," said Alexandra excitedly to her father.

With a nod, Romanov stepped inside the sea container, his heart racing with anticipation. Right away, he saw, strapped securely onto a couple of industrial-grade steel tables, the instruments of Armageddon. Edging slowly forward, Romanov could barely breathe. He now held in his possession the means by which he was going to right history and forever change his family's destiny. His plan was going flawlessly. Once he obtained the crown jewels, he would be able to seize control of a nation begging for a strong man—for a Romanov.

"Father, the Russian bomb expert will be here tomorrow to check the bombs over and ensure that they can be armed and remotely detonated," explained Alexandra.

"Yes, very good," said Romanov as he tenderly ran his hand over the casing of one of the nuclear bombs, like a lover's thigh.

"Once they are ready, I will have them immediately flown back to the *Romanov Star* for onward movement to Iceland. I don't want anything to get in the way, so I will personally see to the final preparations," said Alexandra.

"Of course, my dear," said Romanov.

"What about the black woman?" said Nika scornfully. "When will she provide you with the location of the *Goliath*?"

"I have that already. Madame Yusuf and I spoke for hours last night, and I know precisely where to look. Miss March is here to provide us with the jewels," said Romanov, looking over at Jen and her mother at the far end of the hanger. "You have my word that we will soon have what is rightfully ours."

"Father, all I need are the coordinates, and I can be there with a crew to commence digging in a matter of hours," boasted Nika.

"Patience, Nika," said Romanov. "I will give you what you need tomorrow morning. Now, I must call Madame Yusuf and talk about my plans for Iceland," said Romanov as he turned his back on the container and strode away, leaving his daughters alone to contemplate the next day's events.

20

Saharan Desert,
Mauritania

T he twin-engine Antonov AN-32 flew over the vast Saharan Desert, cruising along at 450 kilometers an hour. Since leaving Algiers, the plane had flown steadily at just over 8,000 meters above sea level. The sturdy Russian transport plane used by many countries throughout Africa had come at a steep price, but using one to fly into Mauritania only made sense to Mitchell if they wanted to avoid any unwanted attention. Yuri Uvarov removed his headset, turned the controls of the plane over to his co-pilot, a trusted accomplice from his earlier days as a black market smuggler, and then climbed out of his seat. He pulled his long black hair back into a bushy ponytail and then headed to the passenger compartment to join the remainder of Mitchell's team.

Seeing Yuri approaching, Mitchell gave Jackson a little nudge to wake his sleeping friend. No matter where they were or what they were doing, Jackson could always find a way to grab forty winks. It was something Mitchell could never do.

Since leaving the States, Mitchell, Jackson, Fahimah, Sam, and Cardinal had first flown to Charles de Gaulle Airport in Paris; from there, they hopped a flight to Algiers. It was there that they linked up with Yuri and boarded the AN-32 for the last leg of their long journey into Mauritania.

Jackson rubbed his eyes and sat up. His stomach rumbled loudly. "Is it time to eat yet?" asked Jackson, looking around the cabin for some food.

"After the brief, you can eat to your heart's content," said Mitchell as Fahimah handed out briefing packages to everyone in the cabin.

"Ok folks, first things first. Mauritania is a less than stable country. It is an Islamic republic, and the current government is made up of the former heads of the armed forces. They were voted in during an election last year that was roundly criticized by the West," said Fahimah as she perused her notes. "There is wide-spread discrimination by the Arabic-dominated regime against the nation's black population. Unbelievably, it is one of the few places left in the world where slavery is still openly practiced."

"Wonderful place to vacation," murmured Cardinal before getting a sharp shot in the ribs by Sam.

"Any hint of rebellion by the population is brutally suppressed by the military. The Arab Spring was an abject failure here, with hundreds killed and many more missing, presumed dead as well," explained Fahimah.

"All of this means that we need to tread lightly and do nothing that will bring the heat and light of the Mauritanian Police upon us, as I for one don't want to rot in some African jail for the rest of my natural life," said Mitchell.

"So what's our cover?" asked Jackson, pretending to flip through the notes provided by Fahimah.

"Ok, this was really short notice, so I did the best I could," said Yuri with his thick Russian accent as he reached into his grungy-looking canvas pack and pulled out a handful of fake passports. "I haven't changed our names or pictures; our cover story is that we are a documentary film crew scouting locations for a show on the desert," said Yuri as he handed out the passports. "All of the visas and stamps have been entered into the passports. It cost me a lot of money, but they will fool the customs officials at the airport."

"Equipment?" said Sam, eyeing the less-than-flattering picture in her passport. She quickly decided that she needed to get a better one taken when she got back to the States.

"All in the back," said Yuri. "I bought cameras, computers, satellite phones, and plenty of other top of the line Japanese stuff. Trust me, we will look like real movie people," said Yuri proudly.

"Transport?" asked Cardinal.

"I have a trusted friend who still has connections at the airport. We have two old army Land Rovers waiting there for us to pick up once we arrive," said Yuri.

"Ok, then, everything is set. The plan for us is quite simple," said Mitchell, looking into the eyes of his teammates. "We'll split into two teams. Fahimah, Nate, and I will work together while Sam and Cardinal will work as the other. We'll start in the south and you two can start in the northern end of the Eye of the Sahara. We'll do hourly calls to pass on any news," said Mitchell. "Yuri, as per, I want you to be our leg on the ground. See about renting a helicopter in case we need to leave in a hurry."

"If I can't find one to rent?" said Yuri.

"Then get ready to steal one. If things go pear-shaped, there's no one sitting around waiting to come to our aid. Besides, we can always beg for forgiveness after the fact," said a grinning Jackson.

"Questions?" asked Mitchell. As he had expected, there were no questions, only a dogged sense of determination to get the job done in the eyes of his friends. He was proud of them all and trusted them with his life.

"Ok then, we're set," said Mitchell. "I'm counting on whoever kidnapped Jen to be in the country by now. All we need to do is find them, and then follow them back to where they're holding her and her mother."

"Then what?" asked Cardinal.

"Then we go in, get them out, and if need be, kill whoever gets in our way," said Mitchell, his voice steeled with resolve. "If you find yourself in a spot of trouble, don't hesitate. These people won't hesitate to kill you, so give them the same courtesy."

21

The Eye of the Sahara
Ouadane region, Mauritania

Like a pair of giant birds of prey, two large military transport helicopters dove out of the cloudless sky, their shadows racing along the desert floor. In unison, they banked over and, one after another, they touched down on the rim of a rocky plateau overlooking the expansive Eye of the Sahara. No sooner had they landed than the back doors of the MI-8s opened, disgorging men in desert fatigues carrying a variety of assault rifles and machine guns. Quickly, they fanned out and set up a secure perimeter. Some were Mauritanian army regulars while others were a team of Chang's men. The helicopters, their holds empty, revved their powerful engines and then leapt back up into the sky.

A minute later, a golden helicopter dropped from the sky and landed in the center of the perimeter, sending up a billowing cloud of dust and sand. The instant the engine switched off, the doors to the helicopters opened. David Teplov and Colonel Chang climbed out and together they looked around at the desolate terrain that stretched as far as the eye could see.

Colonel Chang pulled a tan desert cap out of his trouser pocket and then placed it onto his head. He had always hated the heat and the endless sand of the desert. The overwhelmingly dry heat always made him think of what it would be like to be trapped inside an oven. Chang preferred the more temperate climate of his native North Korea, but he went where the money was, and at this moment in time, the money was in the Saharan

Desert.

David Teplov, his hands grasped firmly around his AK-74 stepped over beside Chang. A new scar ran down his left cheek from the shattered windshield glass that had flown everywhere when his SUV had been hit. He had yet another reminder of his many brushes with death. He'd decided to come along with Chang to ensure that Dmitry Romanov's orders were followed to the letter.

A slender man with dark east African features walked over and stopped in front of Chang. "Colonel, the perimeter is now secure. The Mauritanian lackeys have the outer perimeter, and we patrol the inner cordon," reported the man.

Chang nodded and thanked the man.

Teplov stood silently looking out over the rocky and hilly desert, reminding him very much of his time as an eighteen-year-old conscript in Afghanistan. He had learned his trade there, and once he had realized he was good at killing, he'd never looked back.

Chang smiled as his deputy, Ivan Kolikov, sauntered over and handed him a cool water bottle. "Good work, Ivan. Tell the men that they should be prepared for a stay in this location for up to a couple of days," said Chang as he retrieved a satellite phone from his chest rig. He quickly called Romanov to tell him it was now safe for them to fly out to the dig site.

Stepping over to the edge of the rocky cliff, Chang looked down and saw nothing that even remotely looked like a crash site. As far as the eye could see there were rocks, sand, jagged red dusty colored hills and still more rocks. He checked his GPS one more time, just to make sure that they had not landed in the wrong spot. The coordinates checked out; he was precisely where he had been told to go.

Chang shrugged his shoulders. If this is what Dmitry Romanov wanted him and his men to do, stand guard over some worthless rocks, who was he to complain? He knew he would be well-paid. Opening his water bottle, Chang took a deep swig of cool water, looked out over the desolate and unforgiving landscape, and wondered how long they would have to wait until their employer and all the excavation equipment showed up.

22

Ouadane,
Mauritania

The desolate silence of the desert was broken as a dust-covered Land Rover trailing a cloud of dust behind it came to a grinding halt at the side of what had once been a paved road. Even though the engine had been switched off, the battered and rust-covered vehicle's engine continued to shake and rattle as if it were alive.

Long snake-like sand dunes had built up alongside the road from the strong winds whipping across the Sahara from the north. Anyone foolish enough to drive into one while speeding would have found it to be like hitting a brick wall head on, with the same result to their car.

Jackson applied the parking brake, reached down, grabbed a bottle of water, and then chugged the lukewarm liquid down, quickly emptying the bottle. Looking over, he saw Mitchell checking their location on an old worn map with his handheld GPS. "I should be navigating," said Jackson. "We all know officers, even retired ones, can't read maps."

"Well then, we only have the NCOs like you to blame for not teaching us properly," shot back Mitchell without looking up from his map.

"Ouch, that hurts Ryan," said Jackson, feigning pain in his chest.

"Where are we?" inquired Fahimah from the back seat.

"If our GPS is working, and if I'm reading this right," joked Mitchell, "then we're only a couple of kilometers outside of our first stop, the village of Ouadane."

Their sat phone rang. Fahimah picked it up and chatted with Sam and Cardinal for a couple of minutes before hanging up.

"Sam says they are currently heading cross country towards the northern end of the Eye of the Sahara and have seen nothing but camels and millions of rocks for the past hour," reported Fahimah.

"Well, at least they've seen camels," said Jackson. "This has been one long and boring drive from the capital."

"That's ok," said Mitchell. "I'm happy to keep it quiet for now."

Jackson shrugged his shoulders as he started the Rover, released the parking brake, and then steered their vehicle back onto the atrocious potholed path that masqueraded as a road.

Five minutes later, the village of Ouadane came into view. Built as part of the trans-Saharan gold trade route, the Portuguese had established an outpost in 1487, but eventually had to abandon it when the gold dried up. A once thriving outpost now mainly lay in ruin. Sand-colored dwellings with thick high walls hugged the narrow road that zigzagged like a maze through the center of the town.

Jackson pulled over near a small dilapidated-looking government building on the far side of the settlement. An old and tired police officer, who looked like he had not washed or pressed his faded blue uniform in weeks, sat out front. A rusting AK lay across his lap.

Mitchell jumped out, accompanied by Fahimah, who pulled up her headscarf to cover more of her head. Pointing at the map, Mitchell assisted Fahimah by asking the police officer the best spots to look for a documentary movie shoot at the southern end of The Eye of Sahara.

The policeman looked disinterested and shrugged his shoulders at each question until Mitchell dug into his wallet and offered him a one-hundred-dollar bill for his help. Instantly, the old man burst to life and enthusiastically pointed with his nicotine-stained fingers at several prominent features on the map that he thought would offer an excellent backdrop for a film.

Mitchell thanked the man and paid him for his help.

Fahimah was about to crawl back into the jeep, when she

spotted a group of young women dressed from head to toe in traditional long dark robes, standing around chatting and pointing at the Land Rover and the new strangers in town. Strolling over, Fahimah flashed a winning smile and quickly engaged the women in conversation. A few minutes later, she thanked the women and then walked back to the Land Rover and climbed in.

"Any luck?" said Mitchell, looking back at Fahimah.

"Yes, quite a bit, actually," said Fahimah as she dug out her water bottle. "The women said that there haven't been any strangers other than us stopping in town for at least a week."

"Damn, I was hoping that someone with a lot of digging equipment would have come through here. I would have thought that this is the logical route to take with heavy equipment to a crash site."

"Well, they did say something else that caught my attention," Fahimah said before taking a swing of water.

Mitchell and Jackson locked eyes on Fahimah and waited.

"For the past couple of nights, helicopters, lots of them, have been heard flying over the village heading to and from the Eye of the Sahara."

A grin broke across Mitchell's face; it could only to be the people looking for the *Goliath*. If they were there, Jen would also be there.

"One more thing, the women said that men with guns are out on the main roads keeping people from going anywhere near the Eye of the Sahara," said Fahimah.

"Sam and Cardinal need to know this," said Jackson as he dug out the satellite phone.

"Good call," said Mitchell. "Tell them to hole up where they are until nightfall and wait for the helicopters to appear, and make sure that you warn them to use caution and avoid the armed patrols."

After a minute, Jackson finished the call. "They've gone to ground in a wadi. I think we should do the same."

"I agree," said Mitchell.

An hour later, Jackson pulled off the bumpy road and drove their Rover across the rocky terrain until they came to a slight depression in the ground. Deciding that it was the best spot around to hide in, Jackson parked the jeep. Right away, Mitchell and Jackson jumped out, grabbed a dirty sand-colored tarp from the back of the jeep, and then built a roof over the side of the vehicle, giving themselves some shade from the scorching sun.

While Jackson looked for a good observation post, Mitchell dug into their gear in the back of the jeep. He was pleased to see that Yuri had ensured that their equipment was custom-made to order. Hidden inside the camera cases were a couple of brand new NVGs. A false bottom built into the back of the Rover hid two brand new Russian made AKS-74U carbines along with several already loaded banana-shaped magazines. After a less than scrumptious meal from their ration packs, the group settled down for the evening.

Mitchell took the first watch. Rummaging through his knapsack, he pulled out a gray fleece sweater and then took a seat alongside a rocky outcropping, resting his back against it. Mitchell could see that they had an unobstructed view for kilometers all around them. Looking up into the clear night sky, Mitchell was always amazed when he was deep in the desert at the unbelievable view of the stars without all the light pollution from a city blocking them out, and how damn cold it got once the sun went down. Towards the end of Mitchell's four-hour shift, Jackson ambled over, plunked his massive frame down beside Mitchell, and handed him a cup of hot coffee. Mitchell thanked him. Together they sat in silence, listening to the noisy banter of a couple of jackals calling to one another across the lonely breadth of the desert.

"Sounds like someone is looking for a date," joked Jackson.

"Yeah, but I bet she's coyote ugly," said Mitchell in reply, which garnered a disapproving moan from his friend.

"Worst joke of the mission," said Jackson.

Mitchell took a sip of his coffee and then looked over at his friend. "I really appreciate you coming along, but you know you didn't have to," said Mitchell. "You've earned a break; no one would have said a word if you'd taken the time to be around your son."

Jackson nodded. "Daniel's doing fine these days. We've hired a private tutor who works with him three nights a week after school to get his grades back up to where they should be, and ever since he joined the high school football team, I've seen a profound change in him; he's finally found something to focus on," said Jackson. "Besides, my mother-in-law is coming to visit over the holidays so a little time away for me isn't a bad thing."

Mitchell chuckled and then suddenly stopped. Turning his head, he looked up towards the night sky. A faint rhythmic sound like a train riding the rails somewhere out in the dark caught his attention. Instantly, both men jumped to their feet and began scanning the horizon for the location of the noise.

Turning his NVGs on, Mitchell's vision was instantly bathed in bright green. Slowly turning in place, Mitchell tried to locate what could only be the helicopters the locals had reported hearing.

A couple of dark shapes flying nap of the earth emerged out from a nearby valley and then started to climb towards a craggy ridgeline in the distance.

Mitchell quickly adjusted his NVGs to get a better picture and instantly recognized the helicopters as MI-8 Hips flying without any running lights on. They seemed to rise up for a moment, banked over to the left, and then swiftly disappeared from view. Mitchell grinned; they had them. Grabbing their gear, Mitchell and Jackson sprinted down to the Land Rover. Quickly grabbing his map, Mitchell marked the position where the helicopters had vanished.

It looked to be no more than ten kilometers cross-country.

Jackson placed a quick call to Sam to let them know what they had seen, and that they were going to check it out right away.

Hearing all the commotion, Fahimah shot up, wide-awake. Pulling her blanket over her shoulders, she walked over to the side of the Rover to see what was going on. Mitchell quickly filled her in and then told her to pack.

"It's time to do some night driving, cross-country no less," said Mitchell to Jackson with a grin on his face.

"I hate driving by NVG," grumbled Jackson.

"Ok then, I'll drive."

"No way, Captain, you're bad enough with a map. I sure as hell ain't gonna let you drive cross-country by NVG."

"Your call," said Mitchell as he dug out the two AKs from the back of the jeep. Slamming home a thirty-round magazine in his AK, Mitchell pulled back on the charging lever, loading a round into the chamber. His mind fixed on one goal: finding and rescuing Jen and her mother before the sun came up.

23

The Eye of the Sahara,
Mauritania

Jen felt her stomach flip over as her helicopter dove out of the night sky. Although a good flyer, she rarely flew in a helicopter and had never been in one flown by an ex-military pilot who acted as if he were still flying in Afghanistan trying to avoid surface-to-air missiles. Grabbing onto the nearest handhold, Jen closed her eyes. Just as she thought she might lose her last meal, the moment quickly passed. Jen sat uncomfortably rocking back and forth in her seat, berating herself about having eaten before boarding the chopper for the scariest ride of her life.

The inside of the helicopter was blackened out with only the green lights from the pilot's controls lighting up the cabin, making it seem far smaller than it really was.

Turning her head to look outside, Jen could not see a thing in the pitch-black night. She doubted her mother was enjoying it any more than she was, as she was squeezing Jen's hand so tightly that it almost hurt.

Jen took a deep breath to calm her nerves as the helicopter banked over sharply and then abruptly slowed down as it positioned itself to land. A moment later, its wheels touched down on the rock-strewn surface on top of the ridge.

Their guard, a youthful-looking woman with a strong Scottish accent, quickly unbuckled herself and then helped Jen to unbuckle Mrs. March from her harness.

The side door on the helicopter opened and cool, refreshing air rushed inside. Jen stepped through the open door and took a deep breath. Taking her mother by the hand, they followed close behind their guard as she led them towards a well-lit white canvas tent guarded by several well-armed thugs. Jen was not surprised to see Romanov waiting for them, his hands resting on his hips with a faint smile on his lips.

"My dearest ladies, I am so glad that you could come here tonight," said Romanov as if welcoming old friends.

"I didn't think we had a choice," said Mrs. March, glaring at Romanov.

"You didn't," he replied, still smiling. "Now, ladies, I have some good news that I wish to share with you both."

"You're letting us go?" said Jen sardonically.

"No, but just as Madame Yusuf foretold, we have found the remains of the *Goliath,* resting in a deep crevice not very far from here," said Romanov.

"Then you don't need us," Jen said.

"Au contraire, I need you to find the crown jewels for me," replied Romanov. "Madame Yusuf was quite specific about that. She insisted that you had to be here to tell me where to look in the wreckage."

Jen bit her lip to stifle a scream. So much seemed to be riding on her, but she had absolutely no clue how she was going to pull off the miracle Romanov's mystic claimed she was capable of doing.

Romanov snapped his fingers and then turned his back on the women as he stepped inside the tent. Two well-armed men moved over beside Jen and her mother and waved for them to follow Romanov. Stepping inside, Jen saw that there were several tables covered with debris collected from the crash site. A couple of white-lab-coated technicians were busy photographing and recording everything. On the table nearest to her were some personal effects from the crash: glasses, watches, and the occasional pitiful item of singed clothing were all that remained of the passengers and crew of the doomed airship.

A feeling of melancholy overcame Jen. This was not a dig to find answers about the past to help explain why the *Goliath* had disappeared. This was nothing more than a naked grab for wealth and power.

A flame flickered in Romanov's eyes while he stared at Jen,

knowing that shortly she would bring him one step closer to his goal. Once he had the jewels, he would be able to offer the hardline nationalists a symbol from the past, a symbol with which he would ultimately cement his hold on Russia. However, Romanov had no intention whatsoever in sharing his newfound power and wealth with the nationalist fanatics that he had so carefully financed and nurtured. Once installed as ruler of Russia, he would unleash the army against the rebels and exterminate them all, like so many unwanted vermin.

"Now, ladies, we are wasting precious time. Please come with me, I want to show you the crash site," said Romanov.

Led by a couple of Romanov's thugs, Jen and Mrs. March walked to the edge of the ridge. Stopping, they looked down into a brightly-lit excavation site. Jen edged forward as her curiosity grew. Peering down into the ever-growing hole dug out of the hard rock and sand, she could see tall industrial searchlights illuminating the dig site, making it seem as bright as day inside the pit. At least two hundred Mauritanian soldiers slogged away with pick and shovel to remove the tons of debris covering the mangled remains of the *Goliath*. Jen had not known what to expect at the crash site, but the partial remains of the outer structure of the airship thrust out of the sand like the rib cage of some long-dead giant prehistoric beast. Looking around, Jen saw more well-armed men walking the perimeter of the site, keeping a watchful eye out into the pitch-black desert. They were a mix of nationalities and sexes. They did not look like the men in the pit; these people all looked like hardened killers to Jen. Just looking at them made a cold shiver ran up her spine.

Romanov walked over and stood beside Jen and her mother. In his hands was an iPad tablet with a computer-enhanced schematic of the *Goliath's* superstructure superimposed upon the dig site.

"Now, Miss March, take a look at this and tell me where I should have my men dig," said Romanov.

Taking the tablet in her hands, fear gripped Jen's soul. She had no idea where the jewels could be. Looking at the image on the screen, Jen saw that the Goliath must have hit the ground nose first, as it appeared to have collapsed in on itself upon impact. She'd spent countless hours reading about the *Goliath*, but now, looking down at the image on the screen, Jen found it hard to discern one part of the airship from another.

Romanov turned his cold gaze on Jen. "Well, Miss March, where are the jewels?"

Jen fought to control the panic growing inside her mind. She looked down at the screen and froze. There was no way in hell she could possibly know where the jewels were.

The sound of a pistol being loaded snapped Jen out of her paralysis. Looking over, she felt her heart sink. Romanov stood there with a gun pointed at her mother's head.

"Jen, please!" pleaded her mother.

Her heart was racing in her chest. Jen bit her lip and then looked down at the image; nothing was coming to her. She felt like screaming at the top of her lungs that she was not what Romanov believed she was when she heard the hammer on Romanov's pistol being pulled back. Fearing for her mother's life, Jen closed her eyes and then jabbed her finger on the screen and held it there.

Romanov calmly released the hammer on his pistol and walked over to see where Jen was pointing on the schematic. Her finger rested on a spot no more than twenty or so meters from where the soldiers were currently digging.

"See, Jen, I knew you could do it," said Romanov as he gently took the tablet out of her shaking hands.

Jen was about to say something, when her mother moved over beside her and wrapped her arms around her. Both women looked at one another, wishing that they could wake from the horrid nightmare in which they found themselves trapped.

Romanov saved the image on the screen and at the top of his lungs, called over the dig supervisor to give him new orders.

Looking over at Romanov, Jen could not decide if she had given him what he wanted or only bought them a few more hours of life. There was no doubt in her mind that the instant Romanov got what he wanted, he would have them both killed. Holding her mother tight in her arms, Jen took a deep breath and then peered up into the night sky. With a prayer on her lips, she wondered where Mitchell was and if he was even alive. Something deep down told her that he had survived the crash and would never rest until he found her. With a small smile on her lips, Jen knew that as long as she was alive the chance existed. He would come for her. Suddenly, the night seemed less dark; there was hope.

24

Sweat ran like a stream down Jackson's forehead. The rough ground, strewn with rocks as big as their Rover and deep holes spread throughout the uneven desert terrain, made driving hard at the best of times. Driving in the dark with NVGs was proving to be quite the challenge for Jackson.

It took them close to an hour to cover the ten kilometers from their hiding spot to the sheer cliff rising a hundred meters into the night sky like an impenetrable rock wall barring their way ahead. They were relieved to find that this portion of the desert seemed devoid of anyone else. If the army was busy looking for intruders, thankfully they weren't doing it in this area.

Jackson parked the vehicle in a dry river gully and climbed out of his seat with his shirt glued to his body from perspiration.

Grabbing his AK, Mitchell moved over beside Jackson, who was busy shaking out the tense muscles in his forearms. Removing his NVGs, Mitchell let his eyes begin their adjustment to the clear star-filled night.

"Now, what are we going to do? And please don't tell me that we're going to climb that cliff in the dark," said Jackson, rubbing out the ache in his neck.

"Ok then, I won't tell you, but limber up, old man," said Mitchell as he slung his rifle over his back.

Turning about, Mitchell walked over beside Fahimah and said, "Sorry to do this to you, but you're going have to stay here while Nate and I see what's going on up there."

Fahimah nodded her head in understanding.

Mitchell moved over to the jeep, dug under his seat, and then pulled out a Russian-made 9mm Makarov pistol. "Can you work this?" Mitchell asked as he handed the pistol to Fahimah.

With a wink, Fahimah pulled the slide lever back, chambering a round. "Mister Mitchell, I may be an intelligence analyst, but I try to attend all the range practices I can back at the complex."

Mitchell smiled at Fahimah and grabbed one of the hardened briefcases they had stowed in the back of the jeep. Opening it, he removed something that looked like a child's toy. In Mitchell's hand was a mini UAV that looked to Fahimah like a giant insect. It had four rotor blades on arms that extended out from the body of the craft and a powerful mini-camera that could send back images in clear or in thermal. Switching it on, Mitchell quickly checked that all of its systems were working before placing it on the hood of the Rover.

"Ok then, let's see what we can see," said Mitchell as he moved his finger over the mouse pad of a small control tablet. Instantly, the UAV rose into the air. Moving his finger from side to side to get a feel for the UAV's capabilities, Mitchell looked up at the cliff face and then sent the UAV climbing up into the night sky.

Fahimah and Jackson stood quietly, watching the feed on another small-handled screen.

It took the UAV mere seconds to reach the top of the cliff. Hovering in the dark, the UAV swung around so its camera could observe and record what it could see. Switching the camera over to thermal, Mitchell scanned the rocky terrain, looking for heat signatures that could indicate if soldiers were moving around up there. Seeing none, Mitchell sent the UAV up higher into the night sky. A few seconds later, the brightly-lit dig site came into view. The UAV's distance was limited to one kilometer; it might make it over to the site, but then again, it might not. Mitchell decided not to press his luck. Banking the craft over, he looked for anyone hiding among the rocks but found that the ground was cold and empty. He had seen enough and quickly brought the UAV back down to the Rover.

"Ok, if we're not back by first light, get the hell out of here. Don't linger a moment longer than you have to," said Mitchell firmly to Fahimah. "Contact Sam and Cardinal and tell them what we're doing. If you ever feel that your life is in danger, don't hesitate. Make your way to their location as fast as you can."

Fahimah nodded and then wished Mitchell and Jackson luck as she put the UAV away in its case.

Grabbing a couple of extra water bottles, Mitchell closed the door to the Land Rover and then walked over to Jackson, who was busy jamming as many magazines as he could into his chest-rig.

"Ready for a little night-time stroll?" said Mitchell, looking up at the cliff face in front of them.

"As long as I don't have to climb a sheer rock face in the dark, I guess so," said Jackson, knowing that was exactly what they were about to do.

Fifteen minutes later, Mitchell rolled over onto the rocky ledge and lay on his sweat-soaked back, staring up into the brilliant night sky as he inhaled deeply, filling his aching lungs with much-needed oxygen. Millions of stars shone in the darkness of space. Across the heavens, a shooting star raced past and quickly disappeared from sight. Mitchell superstitiously made a wish, and then turned back to the edge of the cliff as a hand thrust itself up onto the ledge. Mitchell reached down, grabbed Jackson's hand, and then helped pull his huffing and puffing friend up onto the top of the cliff.

"Just for the record, Ryan Mitchell, former U.S. Army Ranger Captain...I hate you," said Jackson. Rivers of sweat poured down his face as he opened his canteen and took a long deep gulp of refreshing water.

"I know, Nate, but don't forget that we still have to get down the same way we came back up," said Mitchell cheerfully as he took his AK off his shoulder and cradled it in his arms, ready in an instant should danger arise.

Jackson felt every spare pound on his frame. He took another long swig and made himself a promise to lose some weight once this was all over.

A breeze made its way across the plateau like an unseen river, bringing with it the smell of diesel. The rhythmic hum of generators and the glow from powerful lights danced on the horizon just over a kilometer away.

Mitchell dug a small pair of binoculars from his vest pocket and looked towards the light. He couldn't see a thing, but his gut instincts told him that Jen was out there somewhere.

"Come on," said Mitchell, helping his exhausted friend onto his feet.

For the next half-hour, Mitchell and Jackson cautiously approached the position. They moved stealthily, using whatever cover they could, constantly on the lookout for any sentries who might have moved away from the dig site. So far, their luck had held. They had yet to see a living soul on the ridgeline when suddenly, Jackson let out a surprised yelp as he tripped over something and came crashing to the rocky ground. Mitchell was about to tell Jackson to be more careful, when a shape rose unexpectedly from the ground. Like a ghostly specter rising from the grave, an astonished soldier took one look at Mitchell, flung down his AK, and then ran off into the night.

"Damn it, they're always in pairs, find the other one," snapped Mitchell at Jackson as he sprinted after the fleeing soldier. Mitchell knew that they must have stumbled upon a couple of soldiers who had decided to take a quick nap rather than do their job.

The uneven ground was strewn with rocks, but that didn't slow Mitchell down at all. Adrenaline raced through his veins. He had to catch the soldier before he warned anyone else. The escaping soldier was fast, but not fast enough. Mitchell closed the distance to mere meters. Hearing Mitchell behind him, the man turned to look over his shoulder, only to strike a rock and lose his balance. Staggering like a drunk, the soldier started to tumble head over heels. Mitchell instantly dove at the man, using his weight to pin him to the ground.

Struggling to rise, the soldier found himself outmatched by Mitchell's size and strength.

Mitchell couldn't risk the man alerting his comrades. Balling up his right fist, he smashed it hard into the soldier's face, knocking him out cold. Holding still for a moment to make sure they had not inadvertently alerted any other sentries, Mitchell bent down, tore several strips from the soldier's shirt, and then quickly bound and gagged the unconscious man.

A few minutes later, with the incapacitated soldier slung

over his shoulder, Mitchell returned to where he had left Jackson. Another unimpressed Mauritanian soldier lay hog-tied on the ground. Mitchell tossed his still-sleeping companion down beside him.

"I found these lying on the ground next to Sleeping Beauty," said Jackson, holding up a pair of old looking AK-47s.

"We'll take them with us," said Mitchell as he looked down at the tied-up sentries. "I bet these poor sods are out here all night with no relief, and that's why they were sleeping."

Jackson smiled. "That means they weren't expecting anyone to come around to check on them, either. The door is wide open. I do love sloppy soldiering."

Mitchell turned and looked towards the dig site. "Shall we see what the hell is going on?"

"Yeah, let's," Jackson said, hauling the extra AKs onto his back.

Romanov's cold, uncaring eyes stared at Jen and Mrs. March as they sat down on a bench outside the tent with a warm blanket draped around them. He had no doubt that Jen would soon deliver what she was expected to, so there was no real need to keep her mother alive anymore. He had thought about killing Jen too, but decided to keep her around a little while longer, just in case he needed her. The question was not when, but where he would have Mrs. March killed. Picking up his Motorola, Romanov called for Teplov and his daughter Nika to join him.

Mitchell slowly crawled up beside a large boulder that vaguely looked like a coyote howling at the moon, and brought his binoculars up to his eyes. Below him, he could see the brilliantly-lit dig site. He let out a low whistle as he surveyed the area. Hundreds of soldiers frantically worked away at removing the sand and rocks as fast as they could. It reminded Mitchell of an old black-and-white Hollywood film in which a Pharaoh used an army of slaves to build the pyramids. Mitchell zoomed in on several jagged pieces of the metal superstructure projecting out of the sand. It looked to him like the carcass of some large animal after the buzzards had gotten to it. Turning away, Mitchell noticed a couple of large tents near the dig; he could see well-armed mercenaries walking back and forth on guard in front of the tents. A chill descended on Mitchell; they were not Mauritanian conscripts, but well-paid mercenaries. They would be much harder to deal with than the poorly-trained soldiers guarding the outer perimeter of the site.

Jackson maneuvered his large frame in beside Mitchell. "See anything?" he asked, barely above a whisper.

Mitchell handed him the binoculars. "We're in the right spot, all right, but things just got a whole lot more difficult," Mitchell said as he pointed out to Jackson the well-armed mercs patrolling the inner perimeter.

"I see fifteen of 'em," Jackson said, lowering the binoculars. "Those odds aren't great."

Mitchell grinned. He knew Jackson was worth a dozen men in a fight, but tonight they needed to be quiet. Rushing in with guns blazing would not help their cause. "No, those odds aren't spectacular. Fifteen or more well-armed mercs against two poorly armed former Rangers? I pity them."

Jackson turned to his friend and spoke. "Seriously, Ryan, what do you want to do?"

Mitchell thought about it for a minute and then grinned at Jackson. "Well, we didn't come this far not to look around. I want you to stay here and cover me. If I'm not back in an hour, make your way back to Fahimah and then link up with Sam and Cardinal."

"No way, I'm coming with you," protested Jackson.

Mitchell looked into his friend's eyes. He knew Jackson would move heaven and earth for him; his loyalty and friendship were never in doubt. "Nate, two of us snooping around out there are more likely to be discovered a hell of a lot quicker than one. I need you to cover my back and come up with something to get us out of here, should things turn ugly."

Jackson knew Mitchell was right, but did not want to admit it. "Ok, you win this one, but you had best get your butt back here in an hour, or you'll have to answer to Master-Sergeant Jackson. You got it," said Jackson as he shook Mitchell's hand.

Crawling backwards like a thief in the night, Mitchell vanished into the shadows.

Mrs. March lay in Jen's arms, fast asleep. The toll of the past few days had caught up with her. Jen sat, rocking back and forth while her mother slept. Looking up, Jen felt a horrible chill crawl down her spine the instant she saw Nika and a tall man walking towards Dmitry Romanov. Staring at the man, Jen fought to stifle a scream. Fear instantly knotted her stomach. He was the same butcher who had killed Professor Laurel in cold blood and tried to kidnap her in Charlotte. She looked around for a place to run, to hide, but she couldn't move. Jen knew she could never leave her mother alone with these monsters.

Nika Romanov was dressed in a form-fitting tan one-piece outfit. She chatted in hushed tones with her father for a moment. Seeing Jen, she left her father's side and, with a menacing smile on her face, strolled over to where Jen was cradling her mother in her arms. Nika looked down at Mrs. March; her face was devoid of any emotion.

Jen's skin crawled just looking at the woman; she thought the woman had the cruelest eyes that she had ever seen.

"She looks exhausted," said Nika. "Let's put her down on a cot in my father's tent."

"It's ok; if you don't mind, I'll hold onto her for now," replied Jen.

"I wasn't asking," Nika said threateningly.

Jen reluctantly nodded and allowed one of Chang's men to pick her mother up in his arms. Mrs. March was carried over to an adjoining tent and then delicately put down on a green army cot. Jen carefully covered her with a warm woolen blanket.

Nika waited until Jen was finished and then stepped forward until she was mere inches away from Jen's face. "I think my father puts too much faith in you," said Nika, her loathsome eyes boring into Jen's.

Jen wanted nothing more than to smash her fist into the revolting woman's face. Keeping her head proudly held high, Jen stood her ground and pushed back. "I suspect your father has more faith in me than he does in you or your sister."

A flicker of anger rippled across Nika's face. "Your time will come soon enough, and I'll see to you personally," snarled Nika, before turning on her heels and storming out of the tent.

Stepping over to the entrance of the tent, Jen looked into the cool night and then ran her hand through her hair, letting out a deep breath. She wondered if the night could get any worse.

Mitchell moved carefully until he was about one hundred meters away from the dig site. Throwing his AK over his shoulder, Mitchell stood up and sauntered forward, deciding that it would be best if he tried to hide in plain sight. If he kept out of the light, Mitchell thought he might be mistaken for one of the guards. Making his way towards a couple of jeeps parked just outside of the searchlight's glare, Mitchell quickly checked the vehicles and was relieved to see that they both had keys in their ignitions. A sigh of relief escaped his lips; so far, fortune was still smiling on him. Looking about, Mitchell was about to go and check out a couple of tents in a nearby depression when he suddenly froze in his tracks. Standing there, barely fifty meters away illuminated in the entrance to a tent, was Jen. His heart raced as a smile crept across his face at seeing Jen alive and unhurt. Mitchell knew he had to get closer. Rummaging through the back of the jeeps, Mitchell found a discarded keffiyah. Grabbing it, Mitchell wrapped it freely around his head to mask his face as best he could. With his AK held loosely by his side, Mitchell walked towards Jen.

The night air was starting to get cold. Jen felt a shiver crawl down her back. She wrapped her arms around her chest to keep herself warm. She took one more look into the near pitch-black night, seeing nothing but the dark empty expanse of the desert. She was about to step back inside the tent to warm up when she saw one of Romanov's hired goons suddenly appear out of the dark. Jen thought it was odd, but it looked like the man was walking straight towards her. The hair on the back of her neck went up; something was not right. Jen was about to take a step back, when the man suddenly lunged at her. In a flash, a hand was thrown over her mouth and another around her waist. Jen, her heart pounding in fear, fought desperately to break free. She struggled for all she was worth, but found herself dragged into the dark. Jen felt herself pulled down onto the hard, rocky ground. A thought flashed through her mind. Was this what Nika had meant when she left? Was she going to be raped and killed now that she was not of any use to the Romanovs anymore? If she was going to die, she was not going to allow her attacker to get away unscathed. Turning her head, Jen lashed out and dug her teeth deep into the man's hand; a second later, she tasted the warm coppery taste of blood in her mouth.

"Goddamn it Jen, that hurts," said her attacker in English.

Pulling down his scarf, Mitchell looked into Jen's deep brown eyes. He had never been so happy or relieved in his life to see someone alive. Mitchell raised a finger to his lips, telling Jen to be quiet.

Jen's eyes lit up; she couldn't believe it. Letting go of her pent-up emotions, Jen threw her arms around Mitchell's neck and pulled him in tight.

"Easy does it, Jen," said Mitchell quietly, trying to pull Jen away from his neck. "You'll choke me if you keep it up."

Jen let go and looked into Mitchell's blue-gray eyes. "How on earth did you find me?" she asked, barely above a whisper.

"It's a long story, but we have to get moving before we lose the cover of night," Mitchell said as he went to stand.

Jen hesitated.

"What is it?" asked Mitchell, helping Jen stand up.

"I can't go without my mother," said Jen, worriedly looking back towards her tent.

Mitchell swore. "She's here with you?"

"Yes, she's fast asleep in that tent," Jen replied, looking back towards the tent.

"Can she run?" asked Mitchell.

Jen shook her head. "She's exhausted and wouldn't make it ten feet before we were both shot by the guards."

Mitchell bit his lip in anger. He could not believe that he had come all this way only to have to turn back without Jen.

"Ryan, I'm sorry, but you'll have to leave without me," said Jen.

"I can't leave you here, not after finding you," said Mitchell, tightly holding onto Jen's hands.

"Ryan, I trust you with my life. You'll just have to find me again," said Jen, with tears welling up in her eyes. "A man called Dmitry Romanov is financing this dig. He has an oil refinery just to the west of here. I have no doubt that Mother and I will be there by tomorrow evening once he finds what he's looking for out here."

Mitchell started to say something when Jen leaned forward and gently placed her lips on his.

Jen stood up with a weak smile on her face. "Get going, Ryan, and find a way to get us home. Do you hear me, mister?" she said, fighting back the tears.

Mitchell reluctantly let go of Jen's delicate hands and took a step back away from her. He fought to keep his emotions in check. He couldn't believe his bad luck. To make it this far, only to have to turn back tore at him. Mitchell knew that Jen was right; he had to leave her and try again.

Reaching over, Mitchell gently wiped a tear from Jen's face. She grabbed his hand for a second time, and then let it go. Without saying another word, she turned her back and quietly walked back out of the shadows towards her tent.

Mitchell wanted to run after her, but knew that it would be pointless. He had to get going. A rustling noise from behind made Mitchell instantly spin around. He found himself looking straight into the face of a startled guard. The man had thought Mitchell was one of his men chatting with a girl and had walked over to see what was going on. Without hesitation, Mitchell swung the butt of his AK up and struck the thug in the stomach, knocking the wind out of him. The man doubled over in pain. Bringing up his rifle, Mitchell swiftly brought it down hard onto the man's head, knocking him onto the rocky ground. Mitchell did not care if he had killed him or not. Unlike the Mauritanian conscripts, this man chose to be here. He was someone who killed for money, and that made him a target. Mitchell dropped onto one knee, brought up his rifle, and quickly scanned about to make sure that he was alone. Deciding it was time to head back and join Nate, Mitchell's stomach dropped when he heard the distinct whoosh sound made by a flare arcing up into the night sky. Without hesitating, he flung himself to the ground. A second later, the flare popped open, bathing the desert in an eerie mix of bright green light and long dark shadows as it rocked from side to side in the wind, slowly descending from the sky. Raising his head slightly, Mitchell could see armed men running towards where he had left Jackson.

After a few seconds, the flare burned itself out, plunging the world back into darkness. Jumping up, Mitchell sprinted towards the empty jeeps.

Shots rang out into the night: Jackson was being hunted.

Teplov heard the flare rocketing up into the air. Instantly, he snatched up his Motorola and screamed into it, demanding to know what was going on.

Only confused and garbled messages came back over the Motorola.

Cursing, Teplov threw the Motorola in the corner of the tent. Grabbing his AK, Teplov ran to the open entrance to see another flare floating through the air.

Automatic gunfire filled the air. Tracers shot back and forth in the dark.

"Stay with Mister Romanov and the women," snarled Teplov at the two closest mercenaries, as he sprinted off in the direction of the gunfire.

Mitchell ran as fast as his legs would carry him. Turning a sharp bend in the trail, Mitchell saw the jeeps. An armed man had already jumped in the nearest jeep and was trying to start it. Mitchell did not bother to slow down. Leaping over the back of the jeep, Mitchell landed beside the startled driver. A solid right hook sent the man tumbling out of the jeep. Jumping over into the driver's seat, Mitchell released the park brake, changed gears, and then slammed his foot on the accelerator. Like a hunting dog straining at a leash that is suddenly released, the vehicle leapt forward, churning up sand and rocks behind it as Mitchell sped off into the dark.

Mitchell did not bother with the headlights; he knew they would only draw unwanted attention and gunfire. Turning the wheel hard over, Mitchell headed in the direction of the gun battle, his AK resting close by on the seat next to him. As he drove cross-country, the jeep bounced up and down like a bucking bronco, as Mitchell seemed to hit every rock in his path. Driving like a madman, Mitchell knew that he had to close the distance to his friend, before it was too late.

Another flare flew through the night, again illuminating the desert for all to see. Mitchell could see muzzle flashes coming from all around Jackson's position. A soldier who had foolishly tried rushing forward was cut down. Another soldier popped his head up to take a shot only to have it shot off instead. Jackson was a crack shot and was proving it tonight.

Teplov stopped in his tracks. His anger instantly boiled over. He could not believe his eyes. There was Mitchell, barely a hundred meters away from him, driving a stolen jeep out of their supposedly secure camp. He didn't even bother to aim. Firing from the hip, Teplov emptied his entire magazine in the direction of the vehicle before throwing the empty weapon away in a fit of rage.

From somewhere out of the night came two soldiers running, frantically trying to get Mitchell's vehicle to stop. Paying them no heed, Mitchell kept his foot jammed all the way down on the gas pedal. One of the men rushed out in front of Mitchell, waving his hands, trying to get Mitchell's attention. Without even bothering to slow down, Mitchell rammed the vehicle straight into the man, sending him spinning over the top of the jeep like a rag doll, his body landing behind the jeep in a bloody and shattered heap. The other soldier, seeing what had happened, stopped in his tracks and went to raise his rifle only to be dropped by a well-aimed burst of automatic fire from Jackson.

The sound of rounds flying overhead sounded like a whip cracking right next to his ears, but Mitchell ignored them as he quickly rounded a tall boulder behind Jackson's hiding spot and then slammed on the brakes.

"Move your ass, Nate!" yelled Mitchell.

A long burst of automatic fire ripped from Jackson's AK, pinning several men in a gully below him before he jumped up and sprinted down the slight embankment. He did not so much jump in as tumble into Mitchell's waiting jeep.

"Drive," muttered Jackson as he tried to catch his breath.

Mitchell changed gears and thrust down as hard as he could on the aged jeep's gas pedal.

Another flare streaked across the night sky, opening up right above Jackson's old fire position. Gunfire erupted as a group of soldiers stormed the abandoned position.

Jackson pulled his seat belt over and locked it in place. Looking over his shoulder, Jackson saw long shadows creep along the desert floor as the flare burned itself out. They were safe for now in the darkness as they hurriedly drove away from the dig site.

"That was a bit too close for comfort," said Jackson, slapping home a fresh magazine into his AK.

"What happened?" asked Mitchell as he finally slowed down and tried not to hit every boulder and rock on the ridge.

"One of our sleepy-headed soldiers must have gotten loose. Before I knew it, there were people crawling all over my position. I had to do something or I was going to get caught," explained Jackson. "What about you?"

Mitchell looked over at Jackson. "I found her."

"So where is she?" said Jackson, looking in the back of the empty jeep.

"She wouldn't come," said Mitchell.

Jackson sat there speechless for a moment. "What do you mean, she wouldn't come?"

"Her mother's with her. She wouldn't leave without her. We just have to figure a way to get them both tomorrow from Romanov's refinery," said Mitchell, his mind racing as he tried to determine his next course of action. He needed a plan to get Jen and her mother back. "Get a hold of Fahimah on your sat-phone and tell her to pull back immediately and RV with us in Ouadane."

Jackson nodded, dug out his phone from his chest rig, and passed on Mitchell's directions to Fahimah.

In the distance, Teplov ground his teeth, knowing that his quarry was escaping him yet again. "Not this time!" swore Teplov. Turning on his heels, he saw the answer to his problem. A smile broke on his face. In the distance sat an MI-8 helicopter, its crew already warming up its engine in anticipation of taking off. Grabbing a radio from a passing soldier, he gave a set of orders to Chang. His eyes burned with hatred. *This time, there will be no escape*, thought Teplov.

25

A small horned lizard darted out from under its hiding place and looked into the once quiet night. It sat there with its head raised, wondering what was going on, when it suddenly heard a strange noise approaching quickly out of the dark. A second later Mitchell's jeep turned a bend, barely missing the lizard, which had wisely scrambled back under its rock for safety.

Mitchell had no idea where he was going. He tried to keep the camp behind him and the cliff they climbed earlier off to his right. The narrow trail they were on bent slightly to the right and then began to meander down off the ridge towards the desert floor.

Both Mitchell and Jackson let out a deep breath when the jeep finally touched down onto a sandy desert track leading away from the dig site. Looking up at the stars, Mitchell soon found the North Star and guessed that they were now more or less going in the right direction, heading west towards Ouadane.

The sat-phone suddenly rang, startling both Mitchell and Jackson.

Fahimah reported that she was on the move and that Sam and Cardinal were moving to join her as well. Mitchell was relieved that she at least was safe. Fahimah was his responsibility. Thankfully, she was proving to be more than capable of looking after herself in stressful situations. Mitchell made a mental note to talk to General O'Reilly about making her a permanent member of the team once they got back home.

"Now what, boss?" said Jackson as he looked over his shoulder for any sign of pursuit.

"We're going to RV with the rest of the team and find out all we can about Dmitry Romanov and where exactly his oil-refinery is so I can come up with a plan to rescue Jen," said Mitchell.

"Well, when you say it..." Jackson's voice trailed off. "Hard right, now!" yelled Jackson as he pivoted around in his seat and brought his AK up to his shoulder.

Mitchell did not hesitate. Cranking the driver's wheel hard over to the right, he slammed his foot down on the gas pedal. Instantly, the vehicle leapt forward, just as a bright-red streak of tracers from a 12.7mm machine gun lanced out of the night sky, chewing up the dirt where the jeep had been a mere second before.

Jackson fired furiously up into the darkened belly of the MI-8 as it flew overhead, hunting them.

The sound of bullets striking the undercarriage of the helicopter sounded like hail bouncing off corrugated iron. With an armor-reinforced belly, there was no way that Jackson's AK fire had any hope of bringing the flying beast down.

Chang's deputy, Kolikov, adjusted his NVGs on his head and then looked out the side window of the MI-8, hoping to catch a glimpse of his prey. He cursed the door gunner for opening up too early. Looking down, he could not see Mitchell's jeep in the green image of his glasses. Turning in his seat, he ordered the pilot to turn about and come back over Mitchell's last position, hoping to finish him off with the next pass.

"These people are starting to piss me off," said Mitchell as he spun the wheel and aimed the jeep for a dry riverbed. The old vehicle bounced up wildly as Mitchell pushed the jeep's suspension to the point of breaking as he tried to find some cover before the helicopter made another pass.

The sound of rotor blades grew louder as a dark object sped towards the jeep, its menacing dark shape silhouetted against the star-filled sky.

Mitchell struck the steering wheel with his hands, willing the jeep to go faster.

Jackson took aim and fired off the remainder of his magazine, hoping to hit the large front windshield and, if he was lucky, kill the pilot of the MI-8.

Kolikov saw the muzzle flash below and instantly heard the sound of the bullets striking the front of the helicopter. A lucky round struck the windshield right in front of the pilot, shattering the glass inwards. Instinctively, the pilot raised a hand to protect his face and pulled hard on the joystick, banking the helicopter up and away from the bullets striking the craft. A second later, Kolikov heard a long burst of machine-gun fire from the right-side door gunner's heavy machine gun letting loose.

Mitchell felt and heard the sound of bullets hitting the back of the jeep, ripping anything unlucky to be back there to ribbons. The ground soon angled down and Mitchell steered the jeep into a dry riverbed. Looking desperately in the dark, Mitchell saw a large rocky outcropping about fifty meters away that presented the best place for cover. Sliding to a halt, Mitchell and Jackson jumped out of the jeep and ran for the cover of the outcropping, just as the sound of the helicopter's rotors filled their ears. A second later, the MI-8 flew right over their hiding spot, firing off a long burst towards the empty jeep, tearing it to pieces.

"We can't stay here forever," said Jackson, removing his empty magazine and replacing it with a fresh one.

"Well, we just lost our only mode of transportation," said Mitchell, looking over at their destroyed jeep. Peering out from under the rocks, he tried to discern where their attacker was going to come from next.

"I'm open to ideas," said Jackson, looking up into the sky for the helicopter.

A smile emerged on Mitchell's face. "Nate, see if you can find an intact jerry can of gas on the back of the jeep and then dump three-quarters of it out."

Jackson shook his head. "You can't be serious. That only worked once before and that was because copious amounts of alcohol were involved."

"Do you have any other ideas?"

Jackson shook his head, darted over to the smoldering jeep and hauled off the only intact jerry can of gasoline. Unscrewing the cap, he quickly dumped the gas onto the ground, screwed the lid back on tight, and then sprinted back to Mitchell just as the helicopter flew overhead. Bullets tore up the sand, missing Jackson's feet by mere millimeters.

"Ok, we get one shot and one shot only at this," said Mitchell, looking along the horizon for the MI-8. "He's come at us from the west and east on his last two approaches. I suspect he's figured it out by now exactly where we are, so if I were him, I would come at us from north to south straight down this gully and try flushing us out."

"That makes sense, but your plan doesn't," said Jackson. "However, since I don't have anything better to offer, let's do it," Jackson said, holding the jerry can tightly in his hands.

The sound of rotor blades cutting through the air somewhere in the dark signaled the beginning of another run by the chopper.

Jackson took a deep breath, stepped out from under the cover of the rocks and into the open and started to rock the jerry can back and forth between his feet, gaining momentum with each swing.

Moving to where he could see straight down the gully, Mitchell pulled his rifle in tight against his shoulder and took aim about twenty meters into the air above Jackson.

The helicopter suddenly dove down out of the dark.

"Wait for it…wait for it…" said Mitchell calmly, trying to judge the right time.

Dropping lower, the helicopter raced towards the gully, intending to finish them off.

Mitchell counted to three and then yelled, "Now!" at the top of his lungs.

Without looking, Jackson, with his arms straining, swung back and threw the jerry can over his shoulder. Like a rock thrown at some Highland Games, the can shot up into the air.

Jackson instantly dove for cover.

Gritting his teeth, Mitchell pulled the trigger, sending a sustained burst of 7.62 mm rounds into the can. The phosphorous from a burning tracer round struck home, instantly igniting the fuel-and-air mixture built up inside the can. In the blink of an eye, a bright orange fireball lit up the night just as the MI-8 flew straight into the expanding explosion.

Kolikov felt the helicopter vibrate as the twin side-mounted machine guns fired towards their trapped prey. With a crooked grin on his face, he knew that there was no way anyone could survive such firepower. A small dark object suddenly appeared in front of the helicopter. Before his mind could even register what was happening, the cockpit was engulfed in a blazing fireball. A stream of burning gasoline shot in from a hole in the damaged windshield straight at the pilot's face. A terrified scream escaped the pilot's lips. Letting go of the joystick, the pilot panicked, trying to beat out the fire engulfing his face.

Kolikov felt his stomach drop as the helicopter instantly banked over to the left. They were flying so low there was nothing he could do to stop the inevitable. A moment later, the helicopter's rotor blades struck the edge of the dry riverbed's bank, shattering into hundreds of deadly projectiles that flew back along the side of the chopper, decapitating an unlucky door gunner. With a loud crunch of collapsing metal, the side of the MI-8 struck the rocky ground, causing it to roll over several times before coming to a sudden halt against a massive boulder, splitting the helicopter in two. Anyone not buckled in was pulverized when the chopper tumbled along the ground, sending their battered bodies flying around inside the interior of the cabin.

For a minute, the destroyed helicopter lay there silently covered in a cloud of dust. Inside, Kolikov slowly opened his eyes and to his dismay saw that he was hanging upside down, still fastened into the co-pilot's chair, his arms uselessly dangling down in front of him. Gritting his teeth, he tried raising his arms. Pain shot through his body. Kolikov swore. He had broken both arms when the chopper smashed into the ground. He knew he had to do something. If he stayed hanging upside down, he would surely black out and death would follow. He painfully wiggled back and forth in his chair, trying to escape the restraining device securing him to his chair. That's when he smelled it: volatile aviation fuel was leaking all over the place. A dark, foul-smelling puddle had already formed below his head. Panic crept into his mind as he tried frantically to escape his seat.

Behind Kolikov, a spark from the MI-8's smashed-up radio system caused the fuel-soaked interior to suddenly burst into flames. Screaming, he flailed desperately in his seat as he was roasted alive.

Mitchell lowered his rifle and watched the crashed MI-8 as it burst into flames.

"You owe me one hundred dollars for that," said Jackson as he watched the helicopter burn.

"We never bet," objected Mitchell.

"Well, I did, and I want my money when we get back home."

Mitchell shook his head at his friend. Standing there for a moment, he watched the fire consume the helicopter when it struck him: he knew exactly how he was going to rescue Jen and her mother.

"We need another jeep," said Mitchell, looking forlornly at the remains of their ride lying all over the dry riverbed.

"This area will shortly be crawling with bad guys," said Jackson. "All we need to do is go to ground, and when the time is right, we can borrow another one."

"All right then, find us a good spot to go to ground, but first you need to salvage what we can from the jeep while I give Yuri a call," said Mitchell.

Ten minutes later, Mitchell finished outlining his requirements to Yuri.

With an armload of ammunition, food and water, Jackson led the way to a small copse of brush about five hundred meters away from the burning Hip. In minutes, with their tracks covered, Mitchell and Jackson disappeared from sight and waited for someone to come along the trail that ran past their position.

Lying under the bushes, Jackson took a long swig of water and then handed Mitchell the bottle. Looking over, he saw a dogged determination in his friend's eyes. No matter what Mitchell was planning, he did not doubt that he could pull it off. No matter how foolhardy it may be, Mitchell was not the kind of man to fail.

26

Romanov oil refinery
Atar, Mauritania

Stale cigarette smoke wafted out of the sea container like a noxious fog escaping from a polluted swamp.

It was all starting to be too much. Alexandra Romanov bit her lip while she nervously paced back and forth. She hated being there. The odious smell from the never-ending stream of cigarettes was overpowering, but Alexandra wanted to supervise the bomb preparations personally. This was her part of her father's plan, and she did not intend to let him down. There could be no margin for error. Alexandra's hair was pulled back in a tight bun on the top of her head. She was dressed in long dark-green coveralls with a pair of very expensive, handmade Italian leather boots on her feet. The light from the container gave her complexion an almost deathly pale look to it.

Alexandra had spent most of the night on a secure line talking with her father's contacts who were guiding the nationalist's activities in Russia. The government had finally taken off the gloves and unleashed the army on the rebels. Government forces, recently supplied with Western intelligence, were hammering the rebels all across Russia. They were begging for more money and resources to continue the fight. She knew that it was better to keep them strung along with promises of support rather than actually giving them what they needed. The rebels were more useful to her family if they fought for a little while longer, rather than being allowed them to topple the government before her father was ready to assume power. She knew the people of Russia were clamoring for an end to the violence, and if President Ivankov could not provide it, they were willing to let another take his place. Alexandra grudgingly agreed to a new influx of money, but kept it to the bare minimum. The rebels would have to make do until her father was ready.

The tension of waiting galled Alexandra. Not able to take it anymore, she spun about on her heels, walked inside the container, and was almost stopped dead in her tracks from the wall of foul-smelling cigarette smoke. Through the haze, Alexandra could see a thin, anorexic-looking blond-haired man hunched over one of the bombs. A lit cigarette hung limply from his lips. Alexandra thought the man looked to be in his mid-forties; a pair of silver-rimmed glasses sat perched on his slender hawk-like nose. His face was narrow and covered in multiple scars from several almost-fatal mishaps over the years. The man was wearing a set of loose-fitting worker's coveralls and a dirty red baseball cap perched back on his head. Hearing Alexandra approaching, he stopped what he was doing, laid his tools down on the bench beside him, and looked up at her.

"Good morning, Miss Romanov," said the man in the coveralls. "Please let me introduce myself. My name is Ivan Markov," said the man as he offered Alexandra a dirt-covered hand.

Alexandra reluctantly took the hand and shook it. Markov instantly gripped her hand and locked his pale blue eyes with her. Alexandra bristled at the arrogance of the man. She had no time for the childish games inferior men seemed to enjoy playing with one another and pulled her hand free.

"Mister Markov, I am pleased to make your acquaintance," said Alexandra as she looked into the cold eyes of the man standing before her. "Your reputation precedes you."

She knew from her dossier on the man that Markov was a former captain in the Russian Army. He had been a combat engineer by trade; however, he had grown bored with peacetime soldiering in Russia. Deciding to strike out on his own, Markov found that his talents were in high demand in the shadowy world of international terrorism. He happily sold his services to the Iraqi insurgents, teaching them how to make larger and more powerful IEDs. His deadly skills were soon in demand throughout the world. He did not come cheap, but Markov had never failed to deliver. Recruited through Colonel Chang's underground contacts, Markov now had the ultimate challenge of preparing two nuclear bombs for detonation and several million dollars to add to his already substantial Swiss bank account.

"You are too kind, Miss Romanov," said Markov, stepping closer to Alexandra. "Please, let's not be so formal with one another. I would like it if you called me Ivan," said Markov, flashing a smile with his yellow tobacco-stained teeth.

Alexandra thought the disgusting man looked like some kind of unnatural ghoul. Her instincts told her that the man was as cold and deadly as a viper. He was someone whom she could never trust, and would have to be eliminated the second he was no longer of value to her father.

"Mister Markov, do not flatter yourself, nor waste any of my precious time," Alexandra said irritably. "Colonel Chang recommended you to us for a very specific job, and don't ever forget that. You are working for my family, not with us, and frankly, I could not care less what your first name is. Do your job well and you will be paid well."

"As you wish, Miss Romanov," replied Markov, his voice guarded and angry. His face was blank, but his eyes showed that he was unimpressed at being spoken down to by a woman.

"Now, Mister Markov, when will you be finished?"

"I will be finished by mid-afternoon. All I need to do is check a few more things and then ensure the arming devices are ready. You can move the bombs any time after that."

"Very well then, I won't keep you any longer," said Alexandra, peering down at her rose gold and platinum Rolex watch. "I will make the necessary arrangements to have the container moved at last light tomorrow to avoid any prying eyes."

Markov said nothing. Showing his growing contempt and displeasure, he turned his back on Alexandra and went back to work.

Stepping out of the container, Alexandra took a deep breath of fresh air. She detested men who thought themselves her equal. Hers was a life destined for grandeur. She knew that she would take great pleasure in ordering Markov's death.

Her cell phone rang. Looking down, she saw that it was her sister. Alexandra thought it odd that Nika should be calling so early in the morning. Answering the call, Alexandra froze in her tracks. She could not believe what she was hearing: an attack had occurred at the dig site and her father was ordering the entire plan accelerated by a day.

Changing the plan now would be difficult but not impossible. Alexandra knew that pushing back would be pointless as her father always got what he wanted. Jamming the cell phone away, Alexandra walked towards an office located by the entrance of the building. Inside, she found her secure sat-phone. Taking a deep breath to collect her thoughts, Alexandra dialed a number from memory. Thousands of kilometers away in Iceland, the call was answered. Quickly passing on her orders, Alexandra terminated the call and then stared out across the hangar floor at the container, wondering if they were moving too fast. Her timetable had been worked out to the hour; altering the plan was fraught with danger. Still, it was all achievable if the West could be convinced to push Ivankov out of power in the next couple of days. With a smile on her face, Alexandra Romanov looked over at the bombs and knew that they had the means to bring the West to its knees. With or without their help, she knew her father was destined to rule Russia.

27

Dig site
The Eye of the Sahara

D mitry Romanov sat behind his desk, his fists clenched so tightly that his knuckles had turned white. Someone had penetrated their camp and he wanted answers. Standing in front of him were Teplov and Chang. The mood in the tent was tense as Chang and Teplov glared accusingly at one another for last night's fiasco. Colonel Chang turned to face Romanov and reported his deputy's death along with a half-dozen men and the loss of a Mauritanian army MI-8 helicopter.

Anger boiled deep inside Romanov. He didn't care about the men or material he had just lost. He wasn't the kind of man to allow someone to mess with him or his family. People who had foolishly dared to stand up to him the past had quickly learned to bend to his will or had simply vanished without a trace.

Teplov waited for Chang to finish before speaking. He told Chang and Romanov about seeing Mitchell and another man leaving the site. He had no doubt in his mind that they had come for Miss March. Why they hadn't left with her was a mystery to him. To be safe, Teplov had doubled the guards around her tent and had told the Mauritanian security forces to arrest or kill Mitchell on sight. A search of the desert by a company of soldiers was underway. He was confident that it was only a matter of time before they found Mitchell.

Romanov shook his head. He didn't know whom to blame for this fiasco, he just knew that he wanted someone to pay. Mitchell had dared once again to interfere with his plans. The man was proving to be quite the irritant. Romanov could feel a tension headache building in the back of his head. Before too long the pain would be indescribable. He vowed to see the man and his accomplices flayed alive and then fed to the sharks once he caught them.

With the site compromised, Romanov ordered that all work other than the excavation of the jewels to halt immediately. He wanted the crown jewels found now; anything else dug up was of no value to him. Only the jewels mattered. Having them would solidify his hold on the fanatics and guarantee their unwavering loyalty before he took pleasure in double-crossing them. The rest of the sizable treasure still waiting to be found at the dig would go to Mauritania's president for his support and unquestioned use of his military.

Outside, the burning heat from the noonday sun turned the desert into a shimmering sea. Nika Romanov stood at the lip of the depression. Her uncaring eyes focused on an exposed portion of the *Goliath's* frame. Looking at a schematic of the airship, Nika saw that the tired, dusty and sweat-covered soldiers had at last uncovered the airship's freight storage compartment, just where Jen had said it would be. Nika knew that this was where the valuables of the passengers would have been stored for the long voyage. She refused to admit it, but her father's faith in the American woman had saved them days, if not weeks, of back-breaking labor to find the resting place of the crown jewels.

An enthusiastic cry went out, as several mangled wooden boxes and blackened pieces of luggage were uncovered.

Nika threw her schematic aside and leapt into the hole, sliding down on the loose sand until she came to a stop at the bottom. Pushing several men out of the way, Nika, her heart racing away, walked over to the find. The boxes and storage trunks were covered in burn marks from the fire that had doomed them all over eighty years ago.

"Roberts! Find anything belonging to Lord Roberts!" yelled Nika excitedly at the soldiers in fluent French.

Like men possessed, the soldiers dug and pulled out the battered remains of the freight compartment. Debris soon covered the sand. After five minutes of digging, two men uncovered a large black trunk, their muscles straining as they pulled it out and laid it on the sandy ground at Nika's feet.

Etched onto the lid of the trunk in large gold lettering was *Lord Frederick Roberts.*

Nika almost leapt for joy. Ordering the heavy trunk to be hauled up to her father's tent without delay, Nika spun about, climbed as fast as she could out of the hole, and then sprinted to tell her father the good news. She could have screamed when she saw Jen and her mother sitting at a table with her father, drinking lemonade and eating some sandwiches as if they were enjoying a pleasant picnic together. She had grown to loathe the two women and could not wait to deal with them herself.

Two sweat-covered soldiers placed the trunk beside the table and then left.

Romanov stood; his heart began to race in his chest. He almost could not believe that they had actually done it that he was actually going to lay his hands on the Romanov crown jewels.

Nika, seeing the look on her father's face, bent down and flipped open the trunk.

Anticipation filled the air. Even Jen and her mother stood and stared inside the blackened trunk.

Carefully, almost reverently, Nika emptied the contents of the trunk onto the table. She placed several items of clothing and smaller jewelry boxes, and then stood up holding a small crown encrusted with sparkling diamonds that looked as new as the day it had been made.

"The consort's crown," said Romanov as he took the crown from his daughter's hands and held it aloft, the sun glittering through the diamonds that covered its surface.

"My God, the stories are true," said Jen, shaking her head as she watched Romanov stare intently at the glistening crown on his hands. She was surprised to see a tear well up in his eye and then fall slowly down his face.

Nika reached down into the trunk and then placed a massive crown carefully upon the table, closely followed by an imperial scepter and orb.

Romanov delicately placed the consort's crown down, reached over, and picked up the sovereign's crown last worn by

Czar Nicholas II. His hands were shaking as he held it. He felt something race through his body; it was unlike anything he had ever experienced throughout his life. He thought about it for a moment and realized that it felt like absolute power.

Jen saw the new look in Romanov's eyes and felt her stomach turn. He had what he wanted and now their lives were his to take. Turning to look over at her mother, Jen felt sad that she was going to die because of her. She had not told her mother about talking to Mitchell last night in case some of Romanov's thugs had decided to interrogate them. The shooting had gone on for some time and Jen feared that Mitchell had been hurt, but after seeing how pissed Teplov had become, she knew that he had gotten away.

Romanov took a deep breath and then respectfully placed the crown back onto the table. Looking over at Nika, he gave orders for them all to leave within the hour. Instantly, the camp turned into a beehive of activity as equipment was stowed away and preparations were made to depart. The site was going to be abandoned to the Mauritanian army as it was of no further use to Dmitry Romanov. He had in his possession the instruments that he needed to bring his family to the throne and there was nothing and no one to stop him now.

28

Abandoned airstrip
North of Atar – Mauritania

A young barefoot boy with black curly hair walked beside a couple of gaunt-looking goats, gently steering them with a narrow stick while singing softly to himself as he headed home. He paid no heed to the world around him as the sun started to dip below the horizon, painting the sky with a pinkish hue. An odd sound in the distance made the boy stop in his tracks. Raising a hand to his eyes, he peered up into the sky. Looking around, the boy saw nothing, when suddenly the noise seemed to fill the very air around him. Yelling in fright, the boy threw himself to the sandy ground, covering his head with his hands, just as a helicopter seemed to appear out of the sun. It flew straight over him, missing him by mere meters. The startled goats bleated and darted for their lives back out into the desert, fleeing from the terrifying noise.

Yuri Uvarov checked his hand-held GPS one last time. He then banked the helicopter over and aimed it towards a long-abandoned military airstrip a few kilometers north of the Romanov oil refinery, where he expected Mitchell and the rest of the team to rendezvous with him. A minute later, Yuri saw a couple of parked vehicles with people milling about outside of a derelict hangar. Landing the helicopter on the open tarmac, Yuri switched off the engines and then jumped out. He was surprised to see Fahimah, Sam, and Cardinal standing there without Jackson and Mitchell.

179

A horn sounded from behind one of the battered old hangars. A few seconds later, Mitchell and Jackson turned the corner in a decrepit-looking sand-colored Toyota truck that looked like it had four mismatched tires on it while a cloud of steam poured from its over-heated engine. With a loud squeal from its worn brakes, the truck came to a shuddering halt beside the helicopter.

"Anybody order a pizza?" said Jackson as he got out of the driver's-side door.

With a grin on his face, Mitchell climbed out the window on his side, as the door had long since stopped working. Jumping down to the hot tarmac, Mitchell walked over and filled in his compatriots how he and Jackson had eluded several army patrols until they came across a grizzled old farmer trying to fix a flat on his truck. Bartering with the man, they traded away the borrowed AKs and some U.S. currency for the jeep, a deal the man seemed to think was in his favor. Driving mainly cross-country to avoid the police and the army, Mitchell was amazed that their ride had made it this far.

Seeing Yuri standing there with his greasy black hair tied in a ponytail and a cigar hanging from his mouth, Mitchell walked over and shook his hand. With a smile, Yuri opened the passenger door of the helicopter and pulled out several long wooden boxes and a dirty green duffle bag full of the equipment that Mitchell had earlier asked him to get his hands on.

"I hope whoever is paying for all of this has deep pockets. This stuff cost me a fortune. I had to cash in several favors to get everything," complained Yuri as he placed another duffle bag, this one full of clothing, onto the hot, dusty ground.

"Don't worry, Yuri. You'll get your precious money back," said Mitchell. "Besides, just think about it as money well spent."

The unhappy look on Yuri's unshaven face said he did not agree, but he knew he could trust his friends and would see his substantial investment returned with interest.

Yuri dug around inside the chopper until he found a map of Romanov's refinery. He handed it to Mitchell, who studied it for a few seconds before laying it out on the hood of Sam's jeep. Calling his friends over, Mitchell quickly outlined his plan and then, as he always did, he asked his team for feedback. Aside from Jackson saying he would send flowers to Mitchell's funeral, no one offered any changes. Everyone knew it was a plan made in haste, but sometimes simple was better when dealing with the unknown.

Yuri's sat-phone rang. Answering it, he chatted away in Russian for a few seconds before hanging up. "My contact says that Romanov is on his way back to the refinery. Just so you know, my dear Ryan, that call just cost me ten grand in hard U.S. currency," whined Yuri.

"Yuri, for God's sake, will you give it a rest," said Cardinal. "My great-grandfather's family emigrated from Scotland. I'm supposed to be the cheap one, not you."

"You are cheap," threw in Sam. "I've had many a dinner with you, and I can say without a doubt that you are tight with your money."

A chuckle spread through the group at Cardinal's expense.

"Ok, folks, it'll be dark soon. Stay alert out there and let's all RV back here safely in a couple of hours' time," said Mitchell with a determined look on his face, as he slapped a fresh magazine into his 9mm Berretta and then placed it into his shoulder holster.

Their preparations complete, Mitchell, Sam, and Yuri boarded the helicopter while Nate, Cardinal, and Fahimah drove off in Sam's jeep towards Romanov's oil refinery.

Right away, Mitchell could see that Yuri had managed to get his hands on a bargain-basement helicopter. The seats were held together with duct tape, and the battered-looking instrument panel had grease pencil instructions written all over it in Cyrillic for Yuri to read.

Mitchell had changed into a uniform similar to the one the mercenaries at the dig-site had been wearing. It was not an exact copy, but in the dark, it would have to do. His uniform, along with several days of growth on his face, should fool the workers at the refinery into thinking that he was one of Romanov's thugs. That was, unless someone took a good look at him.

"Yuri, I told you to not be cheap. Where did you get this death trap?" asked Mitchell into his headset as the helicopter seemed to fight taking off from the ground, as if it somehow knew better.

"I look for Eurocopter," replied Yuri into his headset, "but I only find this old French Army piece of crap."

Mitchell looked over his shoulder at Sam sitting behind him, her face a mix of horror and anticipation as red hydraulic fluid leaked from the roof of the cabin onto the seat beside her, coating the empty gold spray paint cans piled up on the chair.

If the helicopter made a return trip, it would be a miracle, thought Mitchell. Yuri banked the helicopter over and then made for the bright lights of the refinery, shining like beacons, illuminating the desert sky.

29

**Romanov oil field
Atar, Mauritania**

lexandra stood beside a couple of idling jeeps surrounded by a half dozen soldiers. With a proud smile on her face, she watched as her father's helicopter quickly descended from the night sky, covered by two circling Mauritanian Army gunships.

The instant the helicopter's wheels touched down, Romanov jumped out followed closely by two of his personal bodyguards carrying between them the crown jewels in a secure box. Walking over, he warmly embraced his daughter and together they climbed into the closest jeep while a second helicopter circled the refinery and came into land.

Nika, Jen and Mrs. March were helped out of the second helicopter by some of Chang's men just as Romanov's jeep pulled away, leaving them alone on the helipad. The poisonous look in Nika's eyes towards her sister departing with their father was not lost on Jen, who reached over and pulled her mother closer to her, keeping her safe by her side. Nika swore up a storm at her sister and then ordered Jen and her mother to get into the last vehicle. Jen looked up into the night sky and saw another helicopter come out of the dark, bank around and then start to descend towards the helipad. Seeing that it was in the golden color of the Romanov Corporation, Jen paid it no heed. Holding her mother's hand tightly, Jen said a silent prayer that this would be their last night as hostages of Dmitry Romanov.

"There! Down there!" Mitchell yelled into his headset,

pointing towards the ground. "Get us down as fast as you can. It's Jen and her mother, damn it, and they're leaving in that bloody jeep," said Mitchell as the jeep began to speed up and then drove away from the helipad. Flinging off his headset, he knew that they were mere seconds too late to help them. If he could have, Mitchell would have jumped from the helicopter. He had to follow the jeep quickly, before he lost sight of it somewhere inside the maze of roads and buildings of the city-sized refinery.

Yuri quickly brought the helicopter down beside the other one on the helipad and then switched off the engines. In a flash, Mitchell leapt from the chopper and hunched over as he ran out from under the rotor blades, his eyes scanning for Jen's jeep. Spotting an idling truck sitting unguarded alongside a nearby shed, he sprinted over and jumped in the driver's seat. Then, with a squeal from the tires, he sped off after Jen as she disappeared from view around a massive storage building. As per the plan, Yuri and Sam would stay with the chopper until needed.

A warm wind buffeted Cardinal as he climbed the outside of a hundred-meter-tall metal communications tower. Below, Nate and Fahimah stood alongside their jeep, keeping a wary eye out into the desert. After a couple of minutes, Cardinal crawled out onto a wide metal platform and slid the Russian-made Dragunov SVD sniper rifle off his back. Quickly making the necessary adjustments for distance and wind to his scope, he crawled forward until he had a commanding view of the massive refinery. Sweeping his telescopic sight back and forth, Cardinal soon acquired the helipad and saw a truck leaving in a hurry. Seeing Mitchell behind the wheel, he followed the vehicle. Cardinal knew his job for now was to watch, report, and if required to keep the opposition away from Mitchell.

Pulling up outside the hanger where they had been two days earlier, Jen was surprised to see people running about, busily preparing something. Several soldiers were busy clearing the way for a large yellow Caterpillar truck crawling along with a sea container cradled in its powerful metal arms. A thin man in coveralls walked slowly beside the container; a smoldering cigarette hung loosely from his lips. When the vehicle was one hundred meters from the hangar entrance the man turned and waved for the container to be carefully placed onto the ground.

Nika Romanov, still fuming, jumped from her jeep, and yelled at the closest mercenaries to come over and escort Jen and Mrs. March inside the building. She made it explicitly clear that they were to be placed inside a locked and guarded room until she came for them.

The women warily climbed out of the jeep. Under guard, they walked inside the brightly lit hangar. Quietly they followed their guards to a conference room at the far end of the hangar. The instant they were inside, the door was closed and locked from the outside.

Mrs. March grabbed Jen's hand tightly. She was shaking.

"What's wrong, Mom?" said Jen, wrapping her arms around her mother to calm her.

Mrs. March seemed to be unable to find the words. She just stood there staring at the locked door as if expecting the angel of death to walk in at any second.

"Don't worry. It's all going to turn out all right," said Jen soothingly as she led Mrs. March over to a couch, where they sat down together.

"Jen, I'm scared. I heard that awful woman talking with some of the guards earlier. They have what they want. We're now expendable to them," said Mrs. March as tears filled her tired eyes.

"Mom, it's not hopeless. Trust me," said Jen, taking hold of her mother's hand.

"How can you say that?" asked Mrs. March.

"Mom, I've kept something from you," said Jen. "We're not alone. Ryan is here."

At that, her mother sat straight up. Hope flooded into her eyes. "Are you sure?"

"Yes, he's coming for us. We just need to keep calm and stay alive, as long as we can," Jen said resolutely, wondering where Mitchell could be.

Speeding around the corner of the hangar, Mitchell slammed on the brakes. His truck came to a screeching halt. In front of him was at least a company of Mauritanian soldiers milling about watching an old-looking sea container. Instantly throwing the truck into reverse, Mitchell backed out of sight. *Whatever's inside the container is important enough to guard*, thought Mitchell. He was curious, but tonight only one goal mattered to him. All else would have to wait.

Markov pulled the cigarette from his mouth and threw it to the ground, crushing it with his heel. With a snap of his finger, several soldiers ran over, climbed up onto the container and were handed heavy-metal chains from below by their comrades. Quickly, securing the chains into reinforced metal eyelets in the four corners of the container, they hurriedly moved back to the center and secured the chains together onto a large metal hook and waited, looking up into the night sky.

The sound of a large helicopter approaching out of the dark made Mitchell stop and look up into the sky as a huge Russian-made MI-26 heavy lift chopper came into sight. It slowed down and then slowly descended towards the sea container. The sound from the helicopter's powerful engines was deafening. One of Chang's men stood directly in front of the container using a pair of bright yellow paddles to guide in the helicopter. Configured to take a sling load, the helicopter hovered for a moment as the thick metal chains from the sea container were placed into a massive steel hook hanging underneath the chopper. With its cargo ready to lift, the MI-26 increased its power. The powerful engines strained at first and then slowly pulled the container up into the dark night sky.

Parking his truck beside the hangar, Mitchell grabbed his AK, climbed out, and then made his way back along the side of the tall building. Cautiously, he peered around the corner of the hanger. The sea container was gone, and the soldiers had begun to drift off to other assignments. He was reassured when he saw Jen's jeep still parked out front; it could only mean that she was somewhere nearby. Seeing that the front entrance was crawling with soldiers, Mitchell looked back the way he had come and saw a door about fifty meters further down the side of the hangar. Deciding that this was his way in, Mitchell jogged over to the door, turned the handle, and breathed a sigh of relief when he found it open. Carefully stepping inside, Mitchell looked down a brightly-lit corridor with numerous offices on either side of the long hallway. Knowing that he had to start somewhere, he slung his AK over his shoulder and then nonchalantly, walked over to the first office, opened the door, and peered inside. It was dark and empty. Closing the door, he moved to the next office.

Nika sprinted up the stairs, taking two at a time as she made her way up to her father's makeshift office overlooking the spacious hangar floor. Throwing the door open, Nika stormed inside. To her disgust, she saw her father and sister standing there with champagne flutes in their hands.

"Ah, Nika, I am so happy that you are here. Now we can all celebrate together," said Romanov as he reached down and grabbed another glass.

"Why did you both leave the helipad without me?" snarled Nika, baring her teeth like a wild animal.

A puzzled look crossed Romanov's face. "Your sister wanted me to see the bombs before they were taken away, that is all," Romanov said, taken back by Nika's outburst of anger.

"My sister," Nika said mockingly, "how nice that she wanted to show off her work to you."

Alexandra's dark eyes narrowed. "Easy, my dear sister, Father wanted everything moved up a day. I just wanted him to see that his plan is still on track to succeed," said Alexandra, her voice dripping with venom.

Romanov moved between his daughters. They had always vied for his attention, but tonight seemed almost too much, even for him. A tension unlike any he had ever seen before from his daughters filled the room.

"Now, my dear daughters," said Romanov calmly as he raised his flute, "let us toast to our continued success."

Like a pair of alpha wolves warily eyeing one another, they grudgingly toasted and drank their champagne.

"Just so you are both aware, I have made arrangements for us all to leave within the hour," said Alexandra.

"That is excellent news," Romanov said. "The sooner we are on our way, the better."

"What about the American women?" asked Nika. "What do we do about them?"

"Miss March has brought me luck, perhaps that luck will continue. Her mother, however, is now redundant," said Romanov casually. "Kill her and then see to it personally that her body is incinerated. Erase her from the face of the earth."

An evil smile broke out on Nika's face. "With pleasure," said Nika.

Romanov patted the case containing the jewels. Looking over at Nika he said, "Once you have done away with the woman, I want you to ensure that the jewels and Miss March are loaded onto my helicopter."

Nika smiled at her father, ordered two of Chang's men to pick up the box, and then, singing happily to herself, she spun about and went to dispose of Jen's mother. She had hoped to kill both women today, but was resigned to the fact that she would have to wait to kill Jen later.

Jen sat straight up. She could hear footsteps coming down the hallway. Taking a deep breath to calm her racing heart, Jen watched uneasily as the door opened and two armed men entered the room. A moment later, Nika stepped inside with a look of sadistic pleasure in her eyes.

Jen felt her stomach knot. They had run out of time.

Mrs. March looked into Nika's eyes and felt a chill run down her spine. The woman seemed devoid of any feelings.

"Stand up," said Nika.

A man stepped forward and pointed his AK at the women.

Jen stood. She took her mother by the hand.

"Now, Miss March, you will accompany my men to my father. As for your mother, I promise that I'll make sure it will be quick and painless," said Nika coldly.

"No!" screamed Jen loudly as she threw her arms around her mother, holding on to her as tightly as she could.

Nika pulled a pistol from her belt and aimed it right at Mrs. March's head. "Let go of your mother, or I will shoot her right in front of you."

"It's all right, dear," said Mrs. March, trying to console her daughter. "Please do as the woman says."

Tears streamed down Jen's face. "No mother, I can't! I won't," said Jen.

Nika pulled back the hammer of the pistol with her thumb. "Now," she said coldly.

Mrs. March reached over, kissed her daughter on the forehead and then let go of her.

Looking deep into Jen's tear-filled eyes, Mrs. March said, "Stay alive."

Jen lost her voice; she meekly nodded as a guard moved over, grabbed her roughly by the arms, and forced her outside of the room.

Mrs. March stood there with a defiant look on her face. She could hear her daughter crying as she was led away. Turning her head, she looked over at Nika. She had never hated a person so much in her life. The vile woman standing before her deserved to die. Mustering up her courage, she raised her head and looked straight ahead. There was no way in hell she was going to give Nika the satisfaction of seeing fear in her eyes. Stepping out into the hallway, Mrs. March saw two more guards standing there, carrying a large case between them. Holding her head up, she fell into line behind Nika.

Before they had gone five feet, another mercenary came around a corner and walked straight towards them.

The guards carrying the case saw the man approaching, but paid no attention to him, until it was too late. In a flash, the man smashed his rifle's butt straight into Nika's face, shattering her nose with a loud crack. Blood instantly streamed down her face. Staggering back in pain, Nika instinctively raised her hands to protect her face. In a fluid move, her assailant savagely shot the butt of the rifle into her face, sending her tumbling onto the floor.

Corrine did not know what was happening and recoiled in horror.

"Down!" yelled the man as he brought his AK to his shoulder.

Throwing herself to the floor, Corrine covered her head with her hands.

Before the men carrying the case could drop it and pull their slung weapons off their shoulders, the man opened fire, cutting them down. Spinning on his heels, the man dropped his empty

AK and drew a pistol from his shoulder holster, looking for more targets.

Corrine's heart was racing inside her chest. The sound of the gunfire rang loudly in her ears. She tried to scream but found she had no voice.

The smell of cordite hung heavy in the air.

A hand reached down and touched her shoulder.

Shaking all over, Corrine looked up, straight into the blue-gray eyes of Ryan Mitchell. Instantly, a tidal wave of relief flooded over her.

"Come on we have to get moving," said Mitchell as he helped Jen's mother up onto her unsteady feet.

Corrine stood and looked down at the bodies lying on the floor. She saw Nika lying in a spreading puddle of blood on the floor. Corrine did not feel anything for the woman. In fact, she hoped that the revolting woman was dead.

"How did you find us?" asked Corrine as she looked at Mitchell's dirty mercenary uniform and disheveled appearance.

"Dumb luck, I was trying doors further down the hallway when I heard voices."

"The jewels," said Corrine as she looked down at the container lying on the carpeted floor. Dropping to one knee, she quickly threw the box open and grabbed the first thing she could. Holding the consort's crown in her hands, she stood and looked over at Mitchell. "We may need this," she said. "They took Jen."

"I came as quick as I could. I'm sorry that I'm late."

"We need to find her," said Corrine. "She's being taken to a man called Romanov."

"Trust me, Corrine, I want her back to, but we have to be careful. I have no doubt that people must have heard the gunfire," said Mitchell.

Corrine nodded and stepped behind Mitchell.

"They didn't take her this way," said Mitchell, pointing back from where he came. "So let's try this way," Mitchell said as he headed down the hallway, his reloaded AK at the ready.

Clutching the crown in her hands, Corrine said a silent prayer for Jen. They had something she wanted, and now she had something that they so desperately wanted.

Romanov looked down at his watch. He was growing more and more impatient by the second. Nika should have been back by now. His helicopter stood by waiting to take them all to his yacht anchored off the coast. To Romanov time was precious; every moment that went by was lost forever. Having moved the timetable up by a day, Romanov knew that one slip-up now could irrevocably derail Alexandra's carefully worked out plans.

He could wait no longer. Romanov ordered that Alexandra with some of Chang's mercenaries would leave immediately and depart via one of Romanov's commercial transport jets from the capital. They would head directly to Iceland in order to make sure the site was secure for the bombs' imminent arrival. Looking down on the hanger floor from his office, Romanov's temper almost flared when he saw one of Chang's men dragging Jen with him as he made his way to an armored Hummer parked outside of the building. Nika was still nowhere in sight. *What on earth could be keeping Nika? She should have dealt with the older American woman and been back by now.* Those who knew him knew that patience was not one of Romanov's better qualities. Turning to Teplov, he ordered him to go find Nika and tell her that if she was not at the helipad in ten minutes that he would leave without her. Teplov nodded. Calling for a couple of Romanov's close protection detail to accompany him, he swiftly left the room.

Mitchell turned the corner with his assault rifle tight against his shoulder. He was relieved that there was not a soul in sight. With Corrine close behind, Mitchell cautiously worked his way forward, always ready should someone suddenly step out of the many offices on either side of the hallway.

"Ryan, we're moving too slow," pleaded Corrine. "We're going to lose Jen if we don't hurry."

Mitchell felt the same way, but one inattentive moment could cost them their lives. "We'll get her back," said Mitchell, trying to reassure Corrine.

They moved down the corridor as fast as Mitchell dared. Coming to a door at the far end of the hallway, Mitchell was about to open it when it suddenly opened. An unsuspecting guard stood there holding the door; his eyes widened at seeing Mitchell standing there with an AK aimed squarely at his chest. The guard instantly froze in his tracks barely an arm's length away with his hand hovering over his holstered pistol. From behind him, another man almost ran into the guard's back.

"Move out of the way, you damned fool," said the man behind the stationary guard.

Adrenaline instantly shot through Mitchell's veins; he had heard that voice before.

The guard in front of Mitchell saw the momentary hesitation in Mitchell's eyes when he heard Teplov's voice. With lightning-fast reflexes, he reached for his pistol holster, hoping to get the drop on Mitchell. He was quick, but not fast enough.

Mitchell fired a short burst into the guard's chest. His body flew straight back onto a stunned Teplov, sending both men tumbling to the floor.

The sound of the AK firing inside the narrow corridor was deafening. Corrine screamed and brought her hands up to cover her ears as she moved tighter behind Mitchell for protection.

Barely a second later, another guard appeared at the open door with a drawn pistol in his hand.

Mitchell had anticipated the move and fired once, hitting the guard square in the forehead. His head snapped back, a crimson mist spraying the wall behind him.

Mitchell looked over the sights of his AK for any more targets. Seeing none, he turned and then grabbed Corrine by the hand. "We can't get out that way," said Mitchell as he started to run down the hallway the way they had come, dragging Corrine with him.

Teplov struggled to pull his weapon from his holster to get a shot off at Mitchell, but the dead man was just too heavy for him, pinning him to the floor. Cursing aloud, Teplov started yelling at the top of his lungs for help.

Corrine's heart was heavy in her chest. She knew that she had lost her daughter, but she did not intend to give up. She knew they would have another chance if they could get out of the building alive.

Turning a bend, Mitchell slid to a halt. Corrine, close behind, almost tripped over him. A couple of Mauritanian soldiers were standing at the end of the corridor, idly chatting away with their weapons hanging loose by their sides. Seeing Mitchell and Corrine, they foolishly fumbled for their AKs. Mitchell did not bother to aim. Flipping the selector switch to automatic with his thumb, he fired a burst into the soldiers, killing them both in a bloody swath.

Mitchell swore as more soldiers suddenly appeared at the far end of the corridor. Their escape route was blocked.

Mitchell pulled Corrine back around the corner for protection. Keying his throat-mic hidden under his shirt, Mitchell spoke. "Sam…Nate…this is Ryan, over."

Both instantly responded.

"I've lost Jen, but I've got her mother," reported Mitchell. "However, I've got a bigger problem than that now. This place is full of soldiers. I'm not going to be able to get back to the helipad. At least, not by the way I got in."

"We can come and get you," said Jackson, knowing his friend would never abandon him.

"No way, there are beaucoup bad guys between me and you. Stay where you are, I'll figure out a way to come to you," replied Mitchell.

Sam spoke. "We can't just sit here and do nothing. We have to help."

Mitchell knew his team would want to charge in like the cavalry riding over the hill to save the day, but there were just too few of them and far too many soldiers waiting outside to turn them into mincemeat if they got too close. "Listen up, everyone," said Mitchell. "I want you to stick to the original plan. I'll figure a way out of here. If I am not at the helipad in ten minutes, then leave without me, no arguments." Mitchell ended the discussion.

Mitchell looked over at Corrine, her deep brown eyes full of concern. "Don't worry, Mrs. March. We can do this," he said before leading her towards a set of stairs that led up to the second floor of the warehouse.

Sam silently stood there staring towards the hangar while she angrily stewed over the last order. Her friend and teammate was trapped inside and she'd been told to do nothing about it. White-hot anger built up inside her small frame. "Screw this," muttered Sam under her breath. She turned to face Yuri with a determined look in her eyes and said, "Yuri, I'm changing the plan. Get this thing ready to take off." Sam opened the passenger door and grabbed her AK74. Quickly, she slapped home a magazine and loaded the weapon. She locked eyes with Yuri; both knew what was going to happen next.

Sam keyed her mic. "Gordon, my love, clear a path for me," she said as she sprinted away from the helicopter towards a line of heavy construction vehicles parked a couple of hundred meters away.

Cardinal acknowledged Sam, pulled his sniper rifle tight into his shoulder and followed her through his scope as she ran towards the parked vehicles. When she was almost there, a soldier stepped out from behind a truck after taking a leak, still fumbling with his fly. Seeing Sam running towards him, he panicked and tried to pull his slung rifle off his shoulder. Taking up the slack on the trigger, Cardinal fired one round, striking the man in the side of his head, killing him instantly. His lifeless body crumpled onto the ground at Sam's feet as she leapt from the ground onto the ladder on the side of a monstrously large yellow two-story service truck.

"What's happening?" asked Jackson from the base of the tower.

"Looks like Sam's found herself a truck," said Cardinal. "But I'm fairly certain that she's never driven anything like it before in her life."

Jackson shook his head and said, "What was that?"

Cardinal watched through the rifle's scope as Sam climbed up into the cab of the enormous truck. "Nate, the truck Sam just stole is larger than my house."

"Good Lord. Can she drive it?"

"We'll soon find out," said Cardinal.

Mitchell stopped at the top of the stairs, quickly looking left and right down the hall, making sure they were alone. His earpiece buzzed.

Corrine could see a smirk on Mitchell's face. "What's that look for?" she asked, not seeing the humor in their predicament.

"My people aren't the best at following orders," said Mitchell, knowing that he would have done exactly the same thing had he been in their shoes. "Come on, we need to find an exit."

The sound of voices and running feet on the stairs below them caught Mitchell's attention. They weren't alone anymore. Opening a pouch on his dirt-encrusted vest, Mitchell retrieved a small old-fashioned Russian F-1 hand grenade. Swiftly pulling the safety pin, Mitchell tossed it over the side of the railing on the stairs. He heard it bounce once or twice on its way down. A second later, the grenade came to a halt at the bottom of the stairs. With a loud bang, it exploded, sending lethal shards of razor-sharp shrapnel tearing through the bodies of the half-dozen hapless soldiers closest to the blast.

The sound of the explosion echoed through the cavernous hanger.

Romanov turned his head towards the sound of the blast. Smoke was already beginning to pour from the open doors at the far end of the building. His face knotted in anger. He didn't have to be told that their security measures had been compromised once again.

"You have to leave now, sir," said an authoritative voice from behind him.

Romanov stood fixed in place, staring at the debacle unfolding before him.

"Sir, now," said the hard-edged voice.

Romanov turned to see Chang standing there with a futuristic-looking black plastic FN-2000 assault rifle cradled in his arms.

"I thought I told you to leave earlier," said Romanov, staring at into the eyes of the mercenary team leader. The tough, cold killer's eyes stared back.

Chang never replied. Stepping forward, he grabbed Romanov by the arm and then pulled him away from the vulnerable glass windows towards the stairs leading down to the waiting Hummer. At the bottom of the stairs, two of Romanov's men moved to protect their boss. Seconds later, Romanov was inside the armored vehicle and driven away.

Chang turned towards the open hangar. The sound of automatic gunfire echoed through the air. More Mauritanian soldiers ran past him to join the battle. With the bombs gone and Romanov safe, this was not his fight anymore. A smile emerged on his narrow face. Whoever it was, he was really messing things up for Romanov. For once, Chang did not mind that at all. Kolikov's death in the desert and Romanov's indifference to it had pissed him off. Deep down, Chang was starting to respect their opponent; he was tough and resourceful. It would be a shame to have to kill him.

Teplov took a deep breath to fill his aching lungs as a couple of soldiers hauled the body of the dead guard off him. Struggling to his feet, Teplov looked down the corridor at the smoke coming down it like a dense dark fog. Pulling his pistol out, Teplov fell in line with a squad of Mauritanian soldiers, his mind fixated on one goal and one goal only—killing Ryan Mitchell.

Sam climbed inside the cab of the enormous truck. Taking a quick look around, she happily saw that it was configured like any normal pick-up truck, only considerably larger. Quickly adjusting the seat so she could reach the gas pedal and the brakes, Sam searched the dash for the starter. She couldn't believe her luck: someone had left the keys in the ignition. Sam turned the keys over, instantly, the powerful diesel engines roared to life. Thick black clouds of smoke burst from the exhaust as Sam revved the monstrous engine. Dropping it into drive, she gently pushed down on the gas. Sam felt the huge vehicle slowly edge forward and then pick up speed by the second. Turning the steering wheel hard, Sam aimed the two-story vehicle towards the hangar, where she knew Mitchell was fighting for his life.

Bullets ripped into the roof at the top off the stairs. Pieces of debris rained down on Mitchell and Corrine. Their opponents at the bottom of the stairs had not given up yet. Firing wildly, the Mauritanian soldiers, badgered on by Teplov, were preparing themselves for another rush up the stairs. Mitchell had already used up his three grenades, but that did not seem to stop them at all. The soldiers' courage was never in doubt; like lions, they clawed their way ever upwards. The stairs were soon painted deep red with blood from the dead and dying soldiers littering the narrow staircase.

Mitchell crawled forward until he was near the lip of the stairs. Extending his arms fully, Mitchell pointed his AK down the flight of stairs and pulled the trigger. With a loud burst of automatic gunfire, Mitchell held the trigger down until the entire thirty-round magazine was empty. Rolling back towards Corrine, Mitchell pulled out a fresh magazine. It was his last one; they were running out of time.

"We appear to be trapped," said Corrine.

"It only looks that way," replied Mitchell, trying to sound confident as he looked back towards the stairs. He had probably killed a few more soldiers with his last burst, but that only bought them a few more seconds; the Mauritanians seemed to have an inexhaustible supply of men willing to risk their lives. Mitchell suddenly noticed that it was oddly quiet below. He knew that could only mean they were once again clearing the dead and wounded off the stairs. They had less than a minute's reprieve before the soldiers tried again. With only one full magazine remaining, Mitchell knew he could not hold them back for very much longer.

Suddenly, a voice came over Mitchell's earpiece. "Where are you guys?" asked Sam.

Mitchell grinned from ear to ear. "We're on the second floor of the hangar," he said as he helped Corrine to stand.

"Which end?" Sam asked.

"Southwest, I think," Mitchell said, not entirely sure of their exact location.

"Hang on, I'm on my way," said Sam. "I'll be there in thirty seconds or less."

Mitchell quietly pointed to the far end of the hallway. Corrine nodded and then dashed off, leaving Mitchell standing alone beside the battered staircase. Pointing his AK down, Mitchell fired off a quick burst to keep their attackers pinned for a little while longer, before sprinting after Corrine.

Sam spun the wheel in her hands and saw the hangar race towards her. Aiming for the corner of the building, Sam had no plan other than to use the massive truck as a battering ram; she was going to smash her way inside the hangar. Looking down, Sam saw a couple of cars parked outside of the hanger. She did not intend to try to drive around them. Relying on the sheer weight and brute power of the truck, Sam braced herself and jammed her foot down hard on the accelerator. The roar from the massive engine of Sam's stolen truck drowned the sound of crunching metal and breaking glass as she rode up and over the parked cars, reducing them to flattened debris in a matter of seconds. The corner of the hanger loomed large. Sam gritted her teeth and grabbed on tight to the wheel as the building filled her windshield.

Teplov had had enough. Pushing past the lead Mauritanian soldiers still pulling the bloodied bodies of their dead and dying comrades back down the stairs with them, Teplov grabbed a blood-smeared AK. He checked that it was loaded and then sprinted up the stairs, easily taking them two at a time. Suddenly, the entire building rocked back and forth, as if an earthquake had hit it. The hangar sounded like it was being torn apart. Teplov reached out and grabbed the railing to stop himself from being thrown back down the slick stairs by the unnatural swaying of the building.

Blinding dust and debris filled the air.
Mitchell staggered back and forth on his feet. Looking down, he saw that Corrine was lying on her back, knocked off her feet by the impact. Turning his head towards the far corner of the hanger, Mitchell could just make out the cab of some outrageously large truck through a jagged hole ripped into the side of the building. Inside the cab, Sam was waving at him to get moving. Mitchell bent down and helped a bruised Corrine up onto her feet. Together they carefully picked their way over the debris strewn across the floor. Stepping to the edge of the opening, Mitchell could see that Sam had wedged her truck into the side of the hanger. All they had to do was step out and over onto the narrow metal platform running along the outside of the driver's cab.

"Come on, Mrs. March. It's time to leave," said Mitchell as he stepped aside and helped Corrine climb her way through the debris and onto the side of the truck.

Seeing her coming, Sam opened the door to the cab and helped Mrs. March move in beside her.

Mitchell was about to jump over when the crack of a bullet striking the wall beside his head startled him. Instinctively spinning around, Mitchell dropped down onto one knee, his AK raised. Looking down the weapon's sights, he saw two soldiers charging towards him, screaming like demons and firing their weapons from the hip as they ran. Following closely behind them was Teplov. Mitchell took aim at the closest man and pivoted as he fired down the hallway, cutting the men down as if they were wheat under a scythe. The bolt to his AK locked back; he was out of ammunition. Tossing the empty weapon aside, Mitchell turned and then leapt over onto the cab of Sam's truck. His feet had barely touched metal when Sam threw the vehicle into reverse and jammed her foot down on the gas pedal. Mitchell felt the truck move and had to quickly grab onto the side railing to prevent himself from being tossed over the side of the truck as it pulled away from the mangled side of the hangar. The sound of tearing metal was deafening as wreckage pulled from the side of the hangar rained down to the ground. As soon as the truck was free, the wrecked corner of the hangar collapsed like an avalanche where the truck had once been. Opening the cab door, Mitchell shot Sam a smile of appreciation and then jumped over her, landing in a heap beside Mrs. March.

"Sam has them both and they're on the move," said Cardinal calmly into his throat-mic as the truck drove straight back from the building, smashing anything in its path to pulp.

"It's too dangerous now to use the chopper," said Jackson, his mind working out a new escape plan for the team. "Yuri, take off and head back to the old airbase. We'll RV with you there and make arrangements to get us out of the country ASAP," he said with a reassuring wink at Fahimah.

Yuri responded. His helicopter, already warmed up, leapt into the air and away from the mayhem.

Jackson spoke, "Cardinal, guide Sam back here to us."

"Can do," replied Cardinal as he calmly dropped a couple of soldiers aiming an RPG at Sam's truck.

Standing at the end of the demolished second-story hallway, staring unbelieving at the escaping truck, was a bloodied Teplov. One of Mitchell's bullets had gone straight through one of the soldiers and into his left shoulder. Gritting his teeth in pain, Teplov raised his pistol and pulled the trigger. He screamed like an enraged animal as his aimless bullets flew into the night. Hate filled his dark heart. If it took him the rest of his life, Teplov vowed he would have his revenge on Mitchell and his family. He would hunt them all down and see that they died painfully.

Sam acknowledged Cardinal's directions to their link-up point and with a loud squeal from the massive tires, she swung the truck around so she could see where she was heading. Being two stories up, Sam could not really see what was directly below the truck until she either smashed into it, or drove straight over it. Panicked refinery technicians and workers scrambled out of the way of the enormous vehicle that was ploughing its way through the refinery like a maddened bull elephant charging through the wilds.

Suddenly, a jeep with three soldiers in it raced out of a side street, chasing after the rampaging truck. Mitchell looked out the side mirror and saw that one of the men had an RPG in his hands, the grenade already loaded and primed. Mitchell's blood ran cold; he could see that the RPG gunner was trying to get a clear shot at the cab. Mitchell knew Sam could not see them from her side of the cab, and it was doubtful if Cardinal perched high up on his tower could either.

"Sam! Do you have a gun with you?" asked Mitchell as he watched the jeep race towards them. He figured they had ten seconds or less until they were fired upon. There was no way the cab could survive a hit from an RPG; he had to deal with them right away, or they would all be dead.

"Yeah, I've got an AK74 beside my seat," said Sam, her eyes glued to the road in front of her. "Why do you ask?"

Mitchell instantly reached over and grabbed it. "I need to get rid of some unwanted guests," replied Mitchell as he crawled over Corrine, opened the passenger-side door, and then jumped out onto the platform running the length of the cab. Looking down, Mitchell saw the jeep speeding up. In a matter of seconds, it was almost parallel with the cab, the gunner ready to fire his deadly missile. A soldier in the jeep looked up and saw Mitchell. He tried pointing him out to the soldier with the RPG, but was too late. Mitchell pulled back on the trigger. Bullets sprayed around inside the back of the open jeep, killing the two men before they knew what was happening. Quickly changing his aim, Mitchell fired off a burst into the driver. A moment later, the jeep slowed, and then swerved towards Sam's truck. Mitchell watched as the doomed vehicle disappeared underneath the gigantic truck. A second later, Mitchell felt and then heard the massive rear tires riding up and over the doomed jeep, flattening it and everyone inside of it. Realizing that they had dodged a close one, Mitchell opened the door and crawled in beside Corrine. In the distance, like a lighthouse showing them the way to safety, was Cardinal's sniper tower.

"Come on down, Cardinal," said Jackson into his throat-mic. "Ryan and Sam will be here shortly, and we can't afford to dog it here any longer than we have to."

Cardinal acknowledged the order and then made one last sweep of the area with his scope to make sure that the road was clear. Slinging his rifle on his back, he started to make the climb down the long metal ladder leading to the ground as fast as he could.

Fahimah cursed. She could see a dusty brown jeep coming their way. She called Jackson over and pointed towards the jeep driving cautiously in their direction.

"Stay behind me and don't do anything to draw unwanted attention to yourself," said Jackson calmly to Sam as he stepped in front of her.

The jeep stopped ten meters away. Both men got out, their hands on their holsters. They were dressed in cheap-looking khaki uniforms. The men suspiciously eyed Jackson and Fahimah standing beside their battered old jeep.

"Who are you, and what are you doing here?" asked the older of the two guards in Arabic.

"We're a little bit lost and stopped to ask for directions," replied Fahimah, knowing she was just playing for time.

"You're not allowed to be in here," said the guard

suspiciously. "There's been trouble at the refinery tonight. There are foreign saboteurs lose."

"We haven't seen any," replied Fahimah.

"You two, you don't belong here. You're going to have to come with us," said the older guard as he drew his pistol and pointed it at Jackson and Fahimah.

Jackson raised his hands and stepped forward, blocking their view of Fahimah.

Both guards warily approached with their weapons aimed at Jackson's midsection. Jackson could see that they were not professionals; most likely they were underpaid security guards employed by the refinery. It was a deadly pairing: poorly-trained amateurs with nervous hands on their guns. Holding his arms out in front of him as if he were surrendering, Jackson waited for his chance to strike. Seeing Jackson stop, the young guard stepped forward with his cuffs in his hands. With a burst of speed that neither man expected, Jackson lunged forward and smashed the two guards' heads together with a loud thud that reminded Fahimah of two coconut halves hitting together. A second later, both men dropped to the ground, unconscious.

"Help me cuff these men," said Jackson to Fahimah, as he reached down and threw the guards' pistols away into the dark.

Cardinal jumped down from the ladder with his rifle clutched in his hands.

Fahimah shook her head in disbelief at Cardinal as he walked past her. "Couldn't you see they had guns? They could have shot Nate. You could have easily killed those men. Why didn't you?"

Jackson reached up and gently touched Fahimah's arm. "Now's not the time, Fahimah. Just let it go. It's a sad fact, but killing becomes easier the more you do it. Cardinal is a true professional, he only kills when he has to. Besides, I had them."

Fahimah opened her mouth to say something, but decided that she still had a lot to learn as she bent down to help Jackson cuff the two sleeping guards.

A minute later, the ground seemed to shake as Sam's truck came into view. Jackson moved over beside the road and quickly flagged them down. Parking the massive truck to block the road leading out from the refinery, Mitchell, Sam, and Corrine climbed down and were met by a smiling Jackson. He never doubted his friends could pull it off, but smashing their way in and out of a building with a construction truck, that was a new one.

Fahimah walked over with a sat-phone in her hands. "Yuri just called in. He's in position and there's no one in sight."

"Time to go," said Mitchell.

With Sam and Cardinal leading in the guards' confiscated jeep, Nate, Mitchell, Corrine, and Fahimah followed close behind. Behind them, chaos and devastation gripped the refinery. It would take until first light before they could even attempt to assess their losses from the night before. It was time that Mitchell and his team desperately needed to escape the country.

30

Nouakchott International Airport
Nouakchott, Mauritania

T
he cold gray light of dawn slowly crept up on the horizon as the seemingly endless night gradually slipped away.

At the far end of a side runway used exclusively by Mauritania's military leaders sat a Lear jet painted the golden color of the Romanov Corporation. Parked beside it was an L-100, a civilian version of the venerable military transport workhorse, the C-130 Hercules. A company of Mauritanian soldiers with several armored cars guarded the airstrip.

Colonel Chang wrapped his khaki scarf around his face as the cool wind coming off the Atlantic whipped the reddish-colored sand across the airfield, stinging his exposed skin. It had been a long night. He stood there and quietly watched as the sea container holding the two nuclear bombs was carefully loaded aboard the L-100. With their security infiltrated twice in as many days, Chang had convinced Romanov that his plan needed to be re-adjusted. The bombs were now going to be flown to Iceland. It was obvious that the people had only been after their American hostages, but he could not risk the second and far more important part of their operation being discovered, even by accident.

His eyes narrowed as he observed a Mauritanian army helicopter descend from the gray sky and land less than 100 meters away. Out climbed the thug, Teplov, and Nika Romanov, both bandaged and moving gingerly across the windswept tarmac towards the waiting Lear jet. Chang smiled at their discomfort; to him, they were a pair of meddling irritants that had cost him dearly in loyal and trained men. He checked his watch, satisfied that they would make the new timetable and be on their way to Iceland within the hour.

Nika slowly climbed up the stairs of the jet. Her head was killing her. She began to wonder if she had a concussion from the butt stroke her to the head. Her nose had been set and purplish-yellow bruises had begun to form under her bitter-looking eyes. Looking inside the interior of the plane, Nika saw Jen fast asleep under a blanket, her hands tied securely to the chair. Sitting across from Jen was her father; staring out the window, he looked exhausted. His once-intense eyes were now bloodshot and glassy from fatigue. Nika could see that he had not shaved in days. The stress was beginning to show on them all, but now was not the time to slow down, not when they were so close to accomplishing their dreams. She carefully lowered herself into a chair across the aisle from her father, trying not to move her aching head too much, while Teplov found a seat at the front of the plane.

"Father," said Nika gently, trying to get his attention.

Silence was all she got in return.

Nika tried again. This time her father looked over towards her; his face instantly changed from despondency to concern at the sight of the bandages on Nika's head.

"My God, Nika! What on earth happened to you?" asked Romanov.

"Ryan Mitchell, that's what happened to me," said Nika, her voice bitter and angry. "He took the consort's crown, wrecked an entire building, killed who knows how many soldiers and somehow managed to shoot Teplov in the shoulder as well." Nika nodded her head towards the front of the plane.

"Colonel Chang told me about the escape, but he forgot to tell me that you had lost the consort's crown," said Romanov.

"Must have slipped his mind," said Nika. "Don't worry father, we can get it back," said Nika, looking over at Jen.

"What are you thinking?" asked Romanov.

"Mitchell seems driven to protect this woman. Perhaps we can use her as a bargaining chip. A simple one for one trade," explained Nika.

"Perhaps?" pondered Romanov.

"Where is Alexandra?" asked Nika, not seeing her sister in the plane.

"I sent her ahead with a small detail of men to prepare for our arrival. With things changing hourly, I wanted to ensure that we did not have any further needless delays or interference. Forty-eight hours from now, the world will watch as I become the next President of Russia, all thanks to a group of misguided nationalist thugs and a couple of well-placed nuclear bombs."

Nika felt fatigue taking hold of her tired frame. Closing her eyes, she reclined her seat all the way back. In seconds, she was fast asleep, oblivious to the world around her, while Chang and his men finished their preparations. On schedule, they took off, leaving the sand-strewn shores of Africa, flying towards their rendezvous with destiny.

31

Hilton Hotel - Algiers
Algeria

The ringing at first seemed so distant, but it would not go away; in fact, it seemed to grow closer and louder by the second. Struggling through the sleepy haze in his mind, Mitchell rolled over and searched for the phone on the bedside table. Fumbling, he picked it up. "Mitchell here," he said, his mouth cottony-dry.

"Wake up, sleepy head," said Jackson, far too cheerily on the other end of the line. "Haul your ass into the shower and meet me in the restaurant for breakfast."

Mitchell tried to focus his weary eyes on his Casio Pathfinder watch and saw that it was already past seven in the morning. Sitting up, he rubbed the sleep out of his eyes and stretched out his aching back. He had not planned to sleep that long, but his exhausted body must have needed it.

Quickly showering and changing, Mitchell made his way down to the lobby and joined his friends in the hotel restaurant for a breakfast buffet. The women grabbed a healthy mix of yogurts and fruit while the men, led by Jackson, heaped eggs, sausages, and fried potatoes on their plates. Taking a table in the corner of the restaurant, they sat down and ate their meal in relative peace.

They had arrived in Algiers late the night before. Their journey out of Mauritania was fast and uneventful. They had flown to an airstrip on the border with the Western Sahara, where a plane belonging to one of Yuri's contacts was waiting for them.

From there, they carried onto El Aaiun, the most populated city in the Western Sahara, where they caught a commercial flight to Algiers. Mitchell spent most of the flight filling in O'Reilly on what had happened in Mauritania and asked for help in tracking down where the Romanovs could be heading. Tammy Spencer arranged for them to stay the night in a hotel before deciding what to do next.

Mitchell sat at the breakfast table, checked his watch, and took into account the time change. General O'Reilly wanted them to check in as soon as they could. Only Jackson, who acted like he hadn't eaten in weeks, had to be coerced into leaving the buffet. Together, they all headed upstairs to Fahimah and Mrs. March's room. Mitchell ordered up some more coffee from room service, while Fahimah established a secure line over her laptop with the Polaris Complex.

The screen came to life. Sitting in the main briefing room in Albany were General O'Reilly and Fahimah's immediate supervisor, Mike Donaldson. O'Reilly looked relieved to see Mitchell's entire team sitting around looking relatively healthy and mostly unscathed after the recent events in Mauritania. Mitchell quickly made the introductions between Mrs. March and the people back in the States.

"Ok, Ryan, two things," said O'Reilly. "First, I'm happy to see all of you sitting there in one piece. The second thing is that the State Department has gone absolutely ballistic over your antics in the Romanov oil refinery."

Mitchell sat up, puzzled by the news. "Why the hell would the State Department object to us trying to rescue American citizens being held against their will?"

"It's not that. It's Dmitry Romanov that has them all up in arms," replied O'Reilly.

"Sorry, General, but I'm not following you on this one."

"Folks, while you've been away the situation has really deteriorated throughout Russia," explained Donaldson. "President Ivankov has let the army loose, but with many generals now openly siding with the nationalists, it could go either way. The country has almost reached a tipping point; one good solid nudge and it could conceivably fall to the rebels."

"Still not following," said Mitchell.

O'Reilly spoke. "Ryan, my sources tell me that the president is prepared to ask Ivankov to step down so a new president can take charge of the country. It would appear that the administration's ace in the hole, so to speak, is Romanov."

"General, they can't be serious. He's responsible for everything that happened to Miss March and her mother. Only one of whom we have been able to free so far, I might add," said Mitchell, trying to keep his cool.

"I know, Ryan; I was fully briefed by Mike and his people when I came in this morning. I called some of my friends in the administration with this information and to be blunt, they don't care. The stability of a nuclear-armed state is more important to them right now," said O'Reilly.

Mitchell sat there for a moment, not sure what to say. It all seemed to fly in the face of logic. Handing that SOB the keys to a country with nuclear weapons made absolutely no sense to Mitchell.

"Mike, did you read the report Fahimah and I put together yesterday for you?" asked Mitchell. "Unbelievably, Miss March helped Romanov find the Russian royal family's missing crown jewels. Aside from the name, is he a descendent of Czar Nicholas II? The way he was operating in the desert has me baffled. It was as if he didn't care if anyone found out what he was up to."

"I have looked into Romanov's family history, but I have to admit that I'm not a genealogist. The case he's put forward seems a little too clean, but Romanov claims that some newly-found family records will prove his claim to the throne," said Donaldson.

"Sounds dodgy, if you ask me," said Mitchell.

"For now, I think it might be better for all of us if you avoided any more contact with Romanov," said O'Reilly. "At least until the situation in Russia settles down. Once it's quiet over there, we can try prodding the State Department to ask for Miss March's safe return."

"Sir, please. These people have my Jen," said Mrs. March, her voice strained. "She's all I have. They're are monsters, once they no longer need Jen, they'll kill her."

O'Reilly took a deep breath. "I'm sorry, Mrs. March, but I'm getting a lot of pressure from Washington to bring you folks home right now. Unfortunately, there's not a lot we can do to help her, other than ask the State Department for assistance once this all dies down. Right now, we don't even know where she is."

Mrs. March fought the urge to lash out at the bureaucratic mentality of the government. "This isn't right, General," she said, trying to stay calm. "She may be one person when compared to what's going on in Russia, but she's my girl, and she needs your help."

Mitchell reached over and tenderly squeezed Corrine's hand.

"Sir, are you really going to let the State Department tell you what you can and can't do?" asked Mitchell.

O'Reilly took a deep breath and then smiled at the screen. "Ok, I'll see what I can do," said O'Reilly, knowing that he needed to find a way to get the administration to listen. "But I've got to be forthright here. Washington isn't really interested in my badgering them again but you have my word that I'll try. Until then, just relax where you are, and we'll get back to you as soon as we can."

Mrs. March bit her lip and nodded.

A cellphone went off, breaking the tension in the room. Yuri rose from his seat and dug through the collection of jackets and bags piled on the other bed. Finally finding the buzzing phone, Yuri saw that it belonged to Mitchell. "Ryan, you have call coming in," said Yuri, looking over at Mitchell.

"You take it," said Mitchell, too focused on the discussion with General O'Reilly to care who could possibly be calling him.

"Dah, Ryan Mitchell's phone, Yuri speaking," said Yuri, trying to sound professional but failing miserably.

A voice answered in Russian; the color instantly drained from Yuri's face.

"Ryan, it's for you," stammered Yuri, looking down at the phone in his hand.

"Take a message," replied Mitchell without looking over at Yuri.

"No, Ryan, I think you really need to answer the call," said Yuri, holding out the phone.

Mitchell turned and saw the pale look on Yuri's face. The room went silent. Standing, Mitchell walked over and took the phone from Yuri.

"Hello, who is this?" asked Mitchell.

"Good morning, Mister Mitchell. My name is Nika Romanov. You should remember me. The last time we met you gave me a large bump on the side of my head and broke my nose," said Nika. "I hope you and your friends slept well."

Mitchell's blood ran cold.

"I'd hoped the knock to your noggin had killed you," replied Mitchell.

"That's not very civil of you, Mister Mitchell," scolded Nika. "Now, just to put your mind at ease, your girlfriend is all right. In fact, I got your number from her."

"Thanks for the update," said Mitchell. "Now, why did you call me?"

"Ah, I knew you would be the direct type. Mister Mitchell, I want to make you a proposal."

The hair on the back of his neck shot straight up telling him to tread lightly. "What kind of proposal?"

"Don't play games with me, Mister Mitchell, we both know what you have, and my father is willing to trade Miss March for the crown that you stole from me."

"What if I don't have your precious crown anymore?" said Mitchell, trying to see what she did or didn't know.

Nika laughed aloud. "Please, Mister Mitchell, don't be foolish. We have Miss March, and you have the crown," said Nika.

"Ok, so we have the crown. What do expect me to do? I'm not just going to mail it to you and hope that by the grace of God you'll release Jen."

"No, of course not, Mister Mitchell. I expect you to board the next available flight from Algiers and make your way to Keflavik, Iceland, where some of my father's employees will meet you and escort you to a location where the exchange can take place. Once we have the crown, we will return you and Miss March to wherever you want to go unharmed."

"What if I were to call BS on that one?"

"I figured you would say that," said Nika, her voice growing cold. "So listen closely: this offer is good for twenty-four hours only. If you are not here by then, I will personally put a bullet in Miss March's head and drop her corpse into the Atlantic Ocean."

Mitchell fought to control his boiling anger and hatred for this woman and her evil family. "Now you listen closely. If you harm just one hair on her head, I will personally gut you and leave you to bleed out," said Mitchell, leaving no doubt in Nika's mind that he meant what he said.

"Then I look forward to seeing you again," said Nika, before hanging up.

Mitchell stood there staring at his phone, his eyes burning with anger.

"What is it, Ryan?" asked Jackson, seeing the look on Mitchell's face. "What's going on?"

Mitchell stood there silently lost in thought. Tossing his phone on the empty bed, Mitchell strode over and looked down at the image of General O'Reilly on the laptop.

"Ryan, I've seen that look before," said O'Reilly, seeing the rage in Mitchell's eyes. "What the hell just happened?"

"General, I am going to do something that the blessed suits in the State Department aren't going to like," said Mitchell. "If you like, we can terminate this discussion now, and you will have total deniability should things go badly."

"Ryan, I have never let my people do something I wasn't willing to take responsibility for, and I don't intend to do so now," said O'Reilly firmly. "What's going on?"

Mitchell quickly relayed the phone call conversation to O'Reilly and told him that he intended to go and get Jen back before they followed through on their threat and killed her.

"Ryan, these people are starting to piss me off too. You do what you have to," said O'Reilly resolutely.

"Thanks, sir," replied Mitchell.

"Now, is there anything you need us to do other than keep State off your back?"

Mitchell sat there for a moment, rubbing his bristly chin thoughtfully. "Mike, I need you to identify any and all of Romanov Corporation holdings in and around Iceland," said Mitchell to Donaldson.

"I'm already on it," said Donaldson as he looked away and instantly started surfing the extensive Polaris database for information.

O'Reilly leaned forward and spoke. "Ryan, I'd like a back

brief within the hour on what you're planning."

"Will do sir, and thanks for the support," said Mitchell, waving to O'Reilly through the laptop.

"Ryan, I've got the info you're looking for," said Donaldson. "The Romanov Corporation has very limited holdings in Iceland, but they recently negotiated the right to drill for oil offshore and currently have an oil exploration vessel located off the island of *Dragon er eldur*, Dragon's fire," explained Donaldson. "I've emailed Fahimah all the relevant info."

"Ok, at least that's something to go with for now," said Mitchell. "Take a close look at their activities around that island and feed that info to Fahimah as well. Thanks again, Mike."

"Ryan, I know you'll do what you think is right and that's good enough for me," said O'Reilly with a quick nod as the feed was terminated.

"Ok, Ryan, now that you and the boss seem to be making nice," said Jackson. "If you think you're just going to run out on us and leave us here, you're sadly mistaken."

Mitchell smiled at his friend. For the next half hour, Mitchell and his team discussed the call from Nika and their options to help Jen. No matter how limited they were, no one suggested abandoning her to the Romanovs. By the time they called General O'Reilly back, Mitchell had the genesis of a plan and briefed it to O'Reilly, who, seeing no realistic alternatives to the foolhardy plan, gave it his blessing.

Minutes later, Mitchell was on his way to the airport, knowing that this was probably nothing more than a ruse to get him to Iceland where the crown would be taken from him. After that, they could kill him at their leisure. Not for the first time in his life, Mitchell was counting on his friends to help when all else looked grim. It was a trust that Mitchell knew he could count on.

32

Keflavik International Airport
Iceland

Blowing snow whipped across the landing strip as the blue
and white Icelandair 757 came in to land. Passengers
heading out for the Christmas holidays excitedly departed
the plane. Mitchell took his time waiting until the plane was
empty before heading into the terminal to retrieve his luggage.
He'd barely had time between flights in Barcelona to purchase
some warm clothes to wear in Iceland. Mitchell stood there
wearing blue jeans with a dark-blue sweat top, with a pair of
worn hiking boots. He looked around; he had anticipated a
reception committee of some sort, but so far, he had not been
bothered inside the terminal. Grabbing his old army knapsack
along with a black hardened plastic carrying case, Mitchell stood
there looking around, wondering what to do next. He did not
have to wait long as three severe-looking individuals entered the
terminal and walked straight towards him. One man carried
under his arm a down-filled jacket, toque, and gloves. Mitchell
noted that there were two men and one woman in the group.
They all looked like ex-police or military to him, tough and gritty
professionals. Quickly handing the clothing to Mitchell, one of
the thugs smiled and then took possession of his meagre luggage.

"Get dressed, it's cold outside. Then come with us and don't
try anything," said a white-haired thug with a strong Russian
accent.

"Wouldn't think of it," replied Mitchell with a smile as he
pulled on the dark gray winter jacket.

Following the white-haired man out of the terminal, the freezing cold wind blasting in Mitchell's face was a nasty reminder that he was not in Africa anymore. Bundling up, he stood and waited in the frigid air, when out of nowhere, a dark-green minivan came to a screeching halt. Mitchell got inside the vehicle, closely followed by two of the thugs, while the white-haired leader jumped into a silvery-gray BMW X-5 Jeep that had pulled up behind the minivan.

"Where are we going?" Mitchell asked the ex-policewoman in the van with them.

She looked over, her eyes cold and dangerous. "To the other end of the airport where Mister Romanov has a helicopter waiting for you there. No more questions," said the woman brusquely.

Two minutes later, the vehicles pulled up in front of a small office building at the far end of the near-empty runway. Mitchell was quickly escorted inside at gunpoint.

The white-haired thug stepped inside, reached inside his blue ski jacket, pulled out a Glock 9 mm pistol, and aimed it at Mitchell's heart. "No funny business, ok?" warned the thug.

"I already said that I would behave," said Mitchell.

"We need to check you out before we leave," said the thug, waving towards the washroom with his pistol.

Ten minutes passed. Mitchell was dressed once more. His clothes and personal possessions had been thoroughly inspected for hidden weapons or transmitting devices. Finding none, the thugs only confiscated his cell phone and, grabbing a sat-phone, the head thug made a call. Almost immediately, the sound of a helicopter's rotor blades rhythmically beating away vibrated through the small wooden office. Outside, a gold-painted commercial Bell 430 helicopter swooped out of the gray sky and came in to land, its powerful rotors churning up the snow, creating a near whiteout just outside the office building.

"There's your ride," said the white-haired thug, pointing at the waiting chopper.

Mitchell knew there was no going back. With a smile, he walked out to the waiting helicopter and quickly buckled himself in. Mitchell watched as his luggage was fastened to the floor of the helicopter. With a loud thud, the side door slammed shut, sealing him in as surely as if he were trapped in a cold, dark crypt. A shiver ran down Mitchell's back at the thought. The three thugs had remained outside and crept back from the helicopter as it slowly edged its way skyward. With a powerful rev from its engine, the helicopter banked over, rapidly picking up speed as it flew away from the airport and headed south, over the dark-gray waters of the Atlantic Ocean.

Mitchell sat in silence as they flew into the unknown. He knew he was taking a huge gamble, but there was no alternative if he wanted to get Jen back. Leaning over, he looked out the window at the water racing past beneath him, knowing that if they had to ditch the chopper that they would all die from hypothermia in minutes in the near-freezing water.

After about thirty minutes, Romanov's luxury yacht, *Imperator,* came into view on the horizon. Mitchell looked out the side window at the opulent ship. He had never seen anything quite like it in his life. He had no doubt that this was their destination. The helicopter began to slow down as the pilot brought them in for a landing on the yacht's helipad. A well-dressed deckhand with bright orange paddles appeared on the helipad and helped guide the helicopter in for a smooth landing. No sooner had the wheels touched down, when two well-armed men ran up onto the helipad, their high-tech-looking FN-2000s levelled at the side door of the chopper.

The instant it landed, Mitchell reached over and slid the door open. Bitingly cold wind rushed inside the cabin of the helicopter. Seeing Mitchell sitting there, both armed men tensed. Their hands gripped their weapons tighter as if expecting a fight. Mitchell raised his hands to show that he meant no hostile intent and then slowly climbed out of the helicopter.

Mitchell turned to reach for his luggage.

"Leave it," snapped one of the guards. "You have no need for it right now. We'll bring it to you later."

Mitchell did not believe a word, but stepped back slowly, keeping his hands where the nervous thugs could see them.

"Follow us," said the guard, waving his assault rifle towards a set of metal stairs at the side of the helipad.

"Ok, just do what the polite gentlemen with the big guns want," said Mitchell to himself, as he followed his guards down off the icy platform and inside the warm interior of the yacht. They descended several decks until they came to a long hallway. At the end was a polished oak door inlaid with gilt in Cyrillic writing. The guards led him to the door and then abruptly halted.

Checking that the guards were looking toward the door and not at him, Mitchell nonchalantly reached over and pressed the indigo light on his watch three times quickly, activating a tiny, but strong, transponder built inside.

One of the guards stepped forward and opened the door. Mitchell stepped inside. In the center of the room, he could see sitting behind a long mahogany desk were Jen, Dmitry Romanov and his daughters. Alexandra was dressed in a black jumpsuit while Nika wore a matching teal blue.

Mitchell looked over at Jen. The worried expression in her eyes sent a warning through his body.

"Hey, asshole," said a threatening voice from behind Mitchell.

Mitchell tensed as he spun about on his heels. He was a fraction of a second too slow as the butt of an AK smashed against the side of his head, sending him tumbling on to the floor.

Jen screamed as Teplov stepped out from behind the door, an AK clasped in his hands and a twisted look of hate on his face. Mitchell's vision blurred. Agonizingly slow, he got up on his hands and knees, fighting through the pain and waves of nausea rippling through his body. He tried to rise, but was hit hard again, this time on the back of his neck from a viscous blow from a snarling Teplov. His world rapidly shrank into a narrow dark tunnel and then into merciful blackness.

"I owed you that, you son of a bitch," spat Teplov as he hovered over Mitchell's body. Hauling off with all his might, Teplov kicked Mitchell in the midsection, sending his body across the carpeted floor.

"Stop it," yelled Jen. She couldn't take it anymore. Her heart filled with rage at Teplov's cowardly attack on Mitchell. A guard lunged from behind, grabbing Jen by the shoulders, pinning her to her seat.

"Enough!" bellowed Romanov. "Leave him be."

Turning his head, Teplov glared at Romanov. Gripping his

AK tight in his hands, Teplov grudgingly stepped back from Mitchell.

Jen was not going to be scared into submission. Pushing the guard's hands from her shoulder, she stood and ran to Mitchell's side.

Romanov stood. With a snap of his fingers at the nearest guard, he said, "Take Mister Mitchell to the doctor and see that he gets treated for his injuries before being locked up in a room that is easily guarded."

The guard nodded, bent down, and then dragged Mitchell's unconscious body out of the room.

Romanov looked over at his henchman. Teplov was starting to become a liability. He knew that he would have to re-examine his relationship with him once the mission was over. "You can go as well, Teplov," said Romanov, brusquely dismissing the man from his sight.

Teplov opened his mouth to say something, but saw the look of displeasure growing on Romanov's face. Knowing he had no option but to obey, he turned and stormed out of the room.

The door slammed shut. An awkward silence filled the room.

"Miss March, I honestly mean you and Mister Mitchell no harm," said Romanov disingenuously.

"Like back at the oil refinery, when you sent your bitch of a daughter to take me away and kill my mother?" said Jen defiantly as she stared into the cold dark eyes of Nika Romanov.

"Miss March, please believe me when I tell you that it was all a big misunderstanding," pleaded Romanov.

Jen shot Romanov a look of disbelief. He was lying, and she knew it. She just wasn't sure who he was trying to convince of his innocence.

"Mister Romanov, you have what you wanted, and yet you allowed your goon to almost kill Ryan," said Jen angrily. "If you are an honorable man, you'll keep your end of the bargain, please let us go in peace. You've won none of this matters to us."

"That may be so, Miss March, but Mister Mitchell is in no state to travel, not after Teplov's unfortunate temper tantrum," said Romanov. "Besides I want you both around tomorrow, when the real impact of what I am planning to accomplish comes to fruition. Since your friend has delivered to me what I want, I can't see the harm in you both spending another day with me before I let you go free."

Jen knew that Romanov was lying. Why, she could not fathom; nor did she care anymore.

A moment later, the door opened and a female employee, dressed like the other guards in a deep-blue police style uniform, stepped inside. Romanov gave her orders to escort Jen to her room and to stay with her until called.

Once Jen was gone and the door closed, Romanov proudly looked over at his two daughters. They were so close to achieving their goal. Now, barely twenty-four hours separated them from destiny.

"Nika, be a dear and take possession of the consort's crown from the guards," said Romanov.

"Of course, Father," replied Nika.

Turning his head, he looked over at Alexandra. "Now would be the opportune time for you to contact our rebel friends and tell them I want them to mass their forces and re-double their efforts. The government needs to be on its knees begging for Western assistance by the end of the day tomorrow, or I will cut off their funding. Make sure they understand that I mean what I say."

Alexandra smiled.

"Now, I need to know if the preparations for the placement of the bombs are going according to schedule," said Romanov.

"I spoke with Chang less than an hour ago," replied Alexandra. "Everything is going to plan. We can fly the bombs ashore just before dawn tomorrow, and within a few hours they will be ready for detonation."

"Superb news, my dear," said Romanov, relishing the thought of crippling the West's supply of North Sea oil while leaving just enough clues to lead the West's intelligence agencies back to the nationalist rebels in Russia. In one move, he would assume power in Russia, while making a new and very profitable sale of Russian oil to Western Europe to make up for the loss of their rigs up and down the Norwegian coast.

33

Safe House - Reykjavik
Iceland

"**H**is transponder just went active!" exclaimed Fahimah as she brought up a map of Iceland on her laptop screen. Quickly scrolling over to Mitchell's signal, Fahimah pointed to a satellite image of Romanov's yacht anchored off a small island's western shore. Mitchell's signal was coming from the ship.

Leaving Algeria by another route, the remainder of Mitchell's team, along with Mrs. March, had flown to Iceland and set up a temporary office in an apartment suite near the airport. Yuri had left almost right away to see about renting a helicopter or plane from a local company.

Jackson leaned over Fahimah's shoulder and stared intently at the image on the screen. "I had hoped they would be somewhere ashore," said Jackson. "It's far easier to get to them there than off some damn boat, especially this time of the year."

"He hasn't sent a distress code yet, so perhaps things aren't going too badly," said Sam.

"Sam, please; do you honestly believe that family of psychopaths is going to allow Mitchell to simply waltz out the front door with Miss March?" said Jackson, trying not to sound too blunt.

"No, but I can always hope, can't I?" said Sam with a shrug of her shoulders.

"So, I take it we'll need to look at two options for extraction," said Cardinal, "one by land and one by sea."

"Yeah, looks that way," said Jackson, wishing things were not so difficult. On the flight to Iceland, they had discussed the various options open to them to get Mitchell and Jen back. Now, faced with the prospect of mounting a waterborne rescue in the cold waters of the North Atlantic, Jackson's skin began to crawl.

"Shall I open a secure link to General O'Reilly?" asked Fahimah.

"Yeah, I'd better pass on the good news," replied Jackson unenthusiastically.

General O'Reilly's image came up on the screen a minute later. He looked haggard and tired. It seemed no one was getting any rest these days. Jackson filled him in on what had occurred since they had all left Algiers and the two options facing them to get Mitchell and Jen back.

"Sounds tricky, to say the least," replied O'Reilly, his mind still digesting the details of what Jackson had passed on.

"The ship looks like it's anchored a few hundred meters from shore," said Cardinal, looking down at a satellite image on the computer screen.

"So you could possibly use the island as a staging area," suggested O'Reilly.

Jackson nodded. "Right now, we're looking at taking a flight over there later today after Yuri finishes getting the gear we need. If they remain at sea, Cardinal will cover us from the island while Sam and I will make our way to the ship and try and quietly find Ryan and Miss March once we get the signal to proceed."

"Not the soundest plan I've ever heard," said O'Reilly.

"Sorry, sir, but it's all we've got to go on right now," Jackson said.

Donaldson joined the conversation. "Ok folks, here's what I've been able to determine so far. A couple of years ago, the Romanov Corporation leased the island from the Government of Iceland for exploratory mining, which they are conducting at the base of an extinct volcano. This arrangement, along with the Romanovs' ongoing quest to develop Iceland's nascent oil industry on the surrounding sea floor, should generate billions over the next ten to twenty years for Iceland's hard-pressed economy. So I doubt that his activities have been properly scrutinized, if at all, by the local authorities."

"Thanks, Mike," said O'Reilly.

"General, I hate to say it, but you look exhausted," said Jackson, looking into the bloodshot eyes of his boss.

"Yeah, I guess I do," O'Reilly replied stoically. "I haven't slept a wink since we last spoke. I've been working the phones with my former associates in the administration trying to get a better handle on what the president is planning to do about Russia. My sources tell me that the vice-president is planning to talk with Romanov about assuming the Presidency of Russia, should he be called upon to do so," O'Reilly paused, took a sip of water, and then continued. "From what I'm being told, the VP will be contacting Dmitry Romanov sometime before midnight tonight, to offer him the administration's unconditional support should the situation continue to deteriorate in Russia. In addition, poor old Mike Donaldson has been cashing in favors left and right with his friends in the intelligence community. He's been trying to find out the real, no bull truth behind Dmitry Romanov, and what he's uncovered is quite disturbing if it turns out to be even half true."

The screen split and Donaldson rejoined the conversation. For the next five minutes, he laid out the history of the Romanov Corporation, which as expected was a multinational corporation with holdings in the tens of billions of dollars.

Fahimah looked at Donaldson, slightly perplexed. "Mike, without being disrespectful, this is all open-source information. I'm not sure where you're going with all of this."

"I knew you would say that," Donaldson replied. "I did a little snooping around his corporation's financial department and found several irregularities relating to his stated profit margin. It would appear that for the past year, he's been moving large sums of cash ear-marked for his oil exploration operations in Iceland to an account in Switzerland." Donaldson took a sip of coffee, and then continued. "Using less than *legal* software provided to me by an old friend within the Treasury Department, I took a close look at these transactions and found that almost five billion dollars have been forwarded to dummy accounts and shell-corporations throughout the world."

"So, he's a tax cheat," said Jackson. "Name one honest

multibillionaire out there?"

Donaldson smiled and then said, "It's not that at all, Nate, some of these dummy accounts and shell-corporations are on the NSA and CIA's watch lists for suspicion of financing international terror. In short, I suspect that Romanov is in bed with the rebels fighting to overthrow the Russian Government."

"Good God," said Fahimah. "He's playing both ends against the middle. Does the State Department know this?"

"That's just it, I only have a really good hunch to go on right now," said Donaldson. "I don't have the proverbial smoking gun in my hands to tie him directly to the rebels, but trust me, I'm working on it."

O'Reilly chimed in, "I've told Mike to chase this down, no matter what. I'll personally take the flack should we run afoul of some archaic Swiss banking rules and regulations. This information needs to be brought to light if it is as bad as we think it is."

"Sir, the administration must be told," said Sam over Nate's shoulder.

"I have a meeting later tonight with the president's National Security Advisor. I'll lay out our case at that time. I have no doubt that I will not be in anyone's good books for a while after this," said O'Reilly. "Far too many people see Romanov as some kind of knight in shining armor, when he's actually a two-faced SOB playing everyone for all he can.

"Folks, I'm still not sure what Romanov is up to, but it sure smells to high heaven," continued O'Reilly. "Ryan is in far greater danger than I first suspected. I don't know what Romanov is doing off the coast of Iceland, but my gut tells me it's bad."

Jackson nodded his head. "General, Fahimah will be checking in with you once we're all established on the island," said Jackson confidently. "Don't you worry, we'll have them all back on a flight to New York within the next twenty-four hours."

O'Reilly thanked them all and then ended the transmission. His shoulders ached from the stress and fatigue of the past few days. He stood and stretched out his back as he walked back to his office, knowing that things were speeding along like an out-of-control train and were only going to get worse before too long. O'Reilly took a deep breath and then steeled himself for the coming struggle. It was a fight he knew they could not afford to lose.

34

**Imperator
Iceland**

T iny pinpricks of white light agonizingly shot into
Mitchell's mind like hot slivers of pain, reminding him
that he was still alive. Slowly opening his eyes, Mitchell
rolled over and felt the cold hard metal floor on his skin. A
rolling wave of nausea suddenly and painfully gripped his
innards. Unable to hold it back, Mitchell emptied the scant
contents of his stomach on the floor of his cell. Writhing in
agony, Mitchell realized that he must have received a more
severe beating from Romanov's goon than he had first thought.
Sitting back on the cool floor, Mitchell took in several deep
breaths to calm his turbulent stomach. One thing was for certain,
he was looking forward to giving a bit of payback the next time
his path crossed with Teplov.

Wiping the spittle from his face, Mitchell sat up and looked
around the tiny room that was his cell. Aside from a light switch
on the wall, the dull steel gray room was devoid of any furniture
or fixtures. Looking down at his wrist, Mitchell realized that his
watch along with his wallet was gone. Mitchell swore under his
breath; he was cut off, he now had no way of sending any
messages to his team.

Painfully struggling to rise, Mitchell staggered over to the
door, tried the handle, and was not surprised to find that it was
locked. Balling up his fist, Mitchell pounded on the door and
started yelling, hoping that there was someone outside he could
talk with. He had to know where Jen was, and if she was all

right.

A voice laced with a strong Russian accent spoke. "You in there, stop that."

"Make me," replied Mitchell defiantly.

Mitchell could hear voices yelling back and forth in Russian and then an odd silence.

He waited a minute and then, with nothing to lose, decided to carry on smashing the door. Suddenly he heard a key in the door lock. Stepping back slightly, Mitchell prepared himself in case the opportunity to try an escape presented itself.

The door swung open.

Mitchell stepped forward warily. "Hey out there, what the hell is going on?"

"Place your hands on your head and then slowly step out," ordered an unseen voice.

"What if I don't?" said Mitchell.

"Then I will be forced to throw a tear gas grenade inside your room and make you do as I say."

Mitchell knew there was nothing he could do. Stepping out into the hallway, Mitchell was not surprised to see half a dozen of Romanov's men with their weapons trained on him. Falling into line with the guards, Mitchell walked upstairs until they came to the main deck of the *Imperator*. It was dark outside. A cold wind swept up over the deck of the ship, making Sheppard shiver. Cautiously, the men led Mitchell to the helipad and then stepped back, forming a ring around him. A moment later, a down-filled jacket was passed to him. Slowly dressing, Mitchell ran a hand through his hair, and then stood there wondering what was going on. Seeing a thin sliver of light creep up in the east made Mitchell realize that he had been out cold for at least twelve hours. Looking over at the nervous-looking guards, he doubted that he was going to be shot at dawn; there was something else on the go, but what? He did not have to wait long for his answer as Dmitry Romanov soon bounded up the stairs, full of energy, and walked over to where Mitchell stood.

"Good morning, Mister Mitchell," said Romanov. "I am so happy to see that you don't look the worse for wear."

"I wish I could share your enthusiasm, but I have a splitting headache and I'm sorry to say that I left my last meal all over the floor of my cell," Mitchell said. "Aside from that I suppose I can't really complain."

Romanov smiled at Mitchell's bravado. "That is good news. I wouldn't want you to miss out on today's activities."

"Miss out on what?"

"Come now, Mister Mitchell, you wouldn't want me to tell you, would you? It would positively spoil the surprise for you," teased Romanov. "Let's just say that because of your persistent meddling, you have become an integral part of my plan and by the end of today, you will become part of history."

"Seriously, I haven't a clue what you're going on about. Why not just tell me and I'll promise to look surprised later."

Romanov waved a finger at Mitchell. "No more questions, Mister Mitchell. I can assure you that you will be truly impressed later, of that I have no doubt." With that, Romanov walked away, leaving Mitchell to ponder what was going on. Whatever it was, Mitchell knew that it could not be good; he had to find Jen and then together find a way off the ship as fast as they could.

A voice called out, "Ryan, thank God, you're alive!"

Turning, Mitchell saw Jen push her way past a couple of guards and then run straight towards him. She threw her arms around him and embraced him, never wanting to let go. Her lips reached out and met his.

"What are you doing here?" asked Mitchell, looking down into Jen's deep- brown eyes.

Jen looked over at the helicopter on the helipad. "Romanov told me that we were all leaving right away. We're flying over to his mining camp over on the island," said Jen, looking over towards the unwelcoming dark silhouette of the volcano towering over the island.

A feeling of foreboding fell over Mitchell. "I don't think that's a good idea," he said, looking into Jen's eyes. "Something bad is going to happen over there today, and you need to be as far away as possible from it."

The distinctive sound of an assault rifle being loaded made Mitchell freeze in place. Turning his head, he saw a thug aiming his rifle at Jen.

"In the chopper now," ordered a blonde-haired thug, pointing at the helicopter.

"I think it's out of our hands now," said Jen, trying to smile at their predicament.

Taking a deep breath, Mitchell calmly escorted Jen to the open doors on the side of the helicopter, its engine whining loudly as it warmed up. Two minutes later, the helicopter leapt up into the air and then swung over the deck of the ship, heading towards the island outlined against the gray light of the dawn sky.

35

Romanov mining camp
Dragon's Fire

D ragon's Fire is a midsized, barren, ice and rock covered island, which from above resembles a giant horseshoe with a long-dormant volcano jutting out to sea in the middle of the landmass. Reaching up almost a kilometer and a half, the volcano's last recorded eruption was in the fifteenth century, the result being the formation of a large fracture on the eastern edge of the volcano. Because of the cover afforded in its sheltered bay, a thriving fishing and whaling community used the island for several hundred years. The Danes had constructed a tall, circular, stone Martello tower overlooking the bay in order to protect their ships and keep the island safe from the Royal Navy during the Napoleonic Wars. Aside from a few birds that called the island home, not a soul had stepped foot on the island for decades until it was leased to the Romanov Corporation who had built a small mining camp at the base of the volcano, near an old long-abandoned whaling camp.

A recent snowfall covered the island in a thick white blanket. In the dark, three shapes moved cautiously forward along the windswept side of the volcano. In the lead, Jackson dropped to one knee while he took a good look around them. So far, they had not seen a soul, but that didn't mean that the people in the mining camp did not patrol the island during the night. Behind him was Sam. In her hands was her M4 carbine and on her back was a stripped down med-kit. She hoped to keep it shut the whole time, but experience had told her to be ready at all times. Pulling up the rear was Cardinal, also carrying an M4; however, strapped across his back was a Barret .50 cal sniper rifle capable of hitting a man at two kilometers in the hands of a good sniper, and Cardinal was among the best.

Yuri, flying barely a meter above the waves, had flown a long and circuitous route to the island, dropping them off just after two in the morning on the far side of the island. Hoping to avoid detection by the *Imperator's* radar, Yuri headed back out over the Atlantic. First flying east and then north to a small fishing community on the southern shore of Iceland, he and Fahimah now anxiously waited for a signal from Jackson to return to the island to pick everyone up. Mrs. March had remained in the safe house in Reykjavik, awaiting word of the mission's fate. Sitting alone, she knew it would be the longest day of her life.

Crawling forward on his stomach, Jackson crept along until he reached a rocky outcropping looking down into Romanov's mining camp. His winter white uniform easily blended in with the frozen terrain. Carefully, bringing up his thermal imaging binoculars, Jackson swept the darkened camp. He could see an electrified fence running the entire perimeter of the camp. Looking like bright glowing spirits against a cold dark background, Jackson watched two men with guard dogs as they walked along the fence, chatting away as they strolled along, not paying any attention to the world outside of the camp.

Jackson smiled; he loved amateurs.

Looking back towards the center of the camp, Jackson saw several prefabricated office buildings, with a few snow-covered all-terrain vehicles parked in the open. A dirt road from the camp meandered up to a darkened tunnel dug into the side of the rocky volcano. A couple of dump trucks and a bulldozer rounded out all that Jackson could see from his vantage point. Calling Sam and Cardinal forward, Jackson quickly oriented them to the ground.

Without any change in signal from Mitchell, Jackson was still planning to try to rescue him and Jen from the *Imperator* later that day. Seeing that the Martello tower had a commanding of the mining camp as well as an unobstructed view of

Romanov's ship, Jackson led his small team back off the ridgeline and down into the low ground. Moving along as quickly as they could before the sun began to creep up on the horizon, they made their way over to the old tower. Stopping at the base of the fortification, Jackson could see that it in its time it would have been an imposing defensive position. It stood over a dozen meters high and was ten meters in circumference, with walls that looked about three meters thick. Popping his head inside an opening where a wooden door had once stood, Jackson took a quick look around. The ground floor was empty. He could imagine at one time that the tower's supplies were stored there. A set of stone stairs led up. With a nod, he led Sam and Cardinal to the second floor, which surprisingly still had several wooden tables sitting there, as if expecting the soldiers to return and have their breakfast meal. Sam smiled when she saw an old brass cannon still sitting there, aimed out over the bay. Looking around, they saw another set of stairs leading up to the roof. Cardinal carefully made his way up and out onto the open roof, where a wooden roof had once covered the top of the tower. As expected, Cardinal could see for kilometers in any direction. With a smile on his face, he knew this would do just nicely.

Deciding that they would rest there for the day, Jackson checked in with Fahimah and told her what they were planning. With a wish of good luck, Fahimah told Jackson that she would contact O'Reilly and pass on what was going on. Now all they could do was get as comfortable as possible and wait for dark.

Cardinal took the first watch, scanning the camp through the scope of his sniper rifle, taking the time to identify possible future targets. His watch soon passed without incident. He was about to head below and wake up Sam, when he heard the unmistakable sound of rotor blades closing in fast. Grabbing up his binoculars, Cardinal scanned the gray sky for any sign of the intruder. Seconds later, a large shape appeared. Cardinal was not surprised, after what they had been through, to see that the helicopter was flying without its running lights on. As it grew closer, Cardinal could see that slung underneath of the helicopter was something large and rectangular. A cold shiver raced down Cardinal's back. He did not know how, but he was certain that this was the same sea container that he had seen airlifted out of

Romanov's oil refinery in Mauritania. *There's no way this could be a coincidence*, thought Cardinal as he quickly made his way down below to wake Sam and Jackson, only to find them already up and looking out the cannon's firing port, searching the sky for the helicopter.

"Company coming?" asked Jackson.

"Yeah, there's a heavy-lift chopper coming towards the mining camp," said Cardinal. "It looks like it's got a sea container slung underneath."

At the camp, infrared strobe lights, naked to the visible eye, came to life, marking the landing zone for the helicopter. With a practiced move, the helicopter slowly came in and smoothly deposited its precious cargo on the ground. Seconds later, men ran from the office buildings and swarmed all over the container, releasing it from its chains. With a slight rev of its engines, the chopper banked off to the left and then quickly disappeared out to sea and away from prying eyes.

The instant the helicopter disappeared from sight, a group of heavily armed men emerged from the tunnel entrance. A lean, tough-looking man with thick dark hair and an eye patch surveyed the area and then spoke into a Motorola. Instantly, all of his men readied their weapons and quickly fanned out throughout the camp.

Sam said, "I wonder what the hell is going on down there. What could be so important to them that they had to fly it in here at the crack of dawn?"

"Not sure," said Jackson. "Not sure I really want to know, either."

36

Mitchell was happy to be back on solid ground. He was comfortable flying in all sorts of helicopters, but their ten-minute flight had been choppy and his body still felt raw after the beating he had taken from Teplov. Jen walked silently beside him as several of Romanov's goons led them away from their helicopter towards one of the mining camp's buildings. Once they were inside the small empty shack, the door was locked behind them. Mitchell quickly slid over to the window and looked outside. He saw four men standing there, weapons cradled in their arms. Moving over to the other side of the office, Mitchell repeated the drill and saw even more men outside.

"Looks like we're going nowhere for a while," Mitchell said, taking a seat on the floor beside Jen.

"Well at least for once we're together," said Jen, giving Mitchell a quick hug and a kiss upon his cheek.

"Yeah, I guess that's something."

They sat in silence for a few minutes, while outside the sound of heavy machinery starting up and moving about filled the air.

Sam watched through her binoculars as the golden helicopter came into land. Figuring it was another group of workers coming to maintain the equipment, she was about to look at something else, when she saw Mitchell and Jen climb out under guard. Keying her throat-mic, she passed on the news to Jackson and Cardinal, who both quickly made their way to the top of the tower. Crawling over, they laid down alongside her, observing what was going on as Mitchell and Jen were led over to a small pre-fab building.

"Well, that changes everything," said Jackson as he turned his binoculars towards the mercenaries guarding the container. "How many bad guys do you think there are?" he asked Cardinal.

"I count over thirty. A mix of mercenaries and hired thugs from Romanov's ship," replied Cardinal. "Don't forget those are the ones I've been able to see; I have no clue how many people are still inside the tunnel."

"Swell, at least ten to one," commented Sam.

"Well, at least we know where they are now, and we don't have to try pulling them off a ship anymore," said Jackson.

"Great silver lining thinking," said Sam with a smile. "Well, I need to get some intel sent back to Fahimah without delay." Sam dug out a small camera from her pack and then set it up on a tripod that barely peered above the top of the tower. Carefully adjusting the picture with her palm-sized tablet, Sam soon had a steady feed sent straight back to Fahimah and on to Polaris Headquarters.

"Ok then, I'd better come up with a new plan," said Jackson as he crept away from the wall and made his way downstairs. Sitting on the cold stone floor, he peered out of the open gun port and pondered his options. He knew Mitchell would never hesitate to come to his aid, and he did not intend to let his friend down either; it was all just a question of how and when.

Sitting still and waiting for things to unfold chafed at Mitchell. Curiosity was starting to get the better of him. Standing, he made his way to the front window, pulled up the blinds and watched as two eight-wheeled off-road vehicles, both pulling trailers, drove up and stopped in front of a sea container guarded by at least a dozen tough-looking mercenaries. A feeling of dread seeped inside Mitchell's consciousness. Something was wrong, very wrong.

"Jen, do you know what was inside the sea container that was flown away in the middle of the night from the refinery in Africa?" asked Mitchell.

"No, why?" said Jen.

"Because it looks like they've brought it here with them."

Jen stood and joined Mitchell looking out the window at the container. "I never saw what was inside, and they never spoke about it around me, not that I would have been able to follow what they were saying in Russian," said Jen.

"Well, I don't mind telling you that I don't like the look of all that security guarding whatever it is they have in there."

Voices from right outside the door caught Mitchell's attention. A second later, the door was unlocked and flung open. A woman stepped inside wearing a tan-colored winter jacket, with matching toque and blue jeans, her jet-black hair braided in a ponytail down her back.

Mitchell looked over and said, "I know you, but where's the bandage on your nose?"

"Wrong sister, Mister Mitchell," said Alexandra Romanov bluntly, as she lithely stepped aside, allowing a couple of guards inside the room, their weapons pointing at Jen.

"Don't tell me. There are two of you?" Mitchell said. "I must have missed that detail before being sucker punched in the back of the head while we were still on the ship of fools."

"I have no time for adolescent games, Mister Mitchell. My father is waiting for you. Come with me," ordered Alexandra. "Miss March will remain here."

Jen reached out and grabbed Mitchell's arm, her eyes betraying her fear.

"It's ok," said Mitchell with a smile. "I'm sure he just wants to talk sports or something. I'll be back before you know it and then we can go on a nice long holiday somewhere together."

"You'd better be, mister," said Jen as she watched Mitchell walk out of the room; the door was quickly closed and locked behind him. Jen's heart suddenly felt empty as if part of her soul had just left her. She realized that for the first time in her life, she was falling hard for someone. Tears filled her eyes.

Mitchell walked over to the sea container escorted by Alexandra and a couple of men, who, not trusting Mitchell, kept well back with their weapons trained on him at all times. A minute later, the sound of a helicopter's rotor blades split the air. Looking up, Mitchell saw that it was another one of Romanov's choppers coming in to land. The powerful downdraft from the rotors sent a bitterly cold wind whipping across the open ground, stirring up the fresh snow into a mini-blizzard. Mitchell turned away as the chopper landed. As soon as it was on the ground, the engine switched off. Looking back, Mitchell observed Dmitry Romanov climb out, accompanied by Nika and their goon, Teplov. A serious-looking Asian mercenary with a black eye-patch walked over and started to talk with Romanov. They were too far away for him to hear a word. Romanov thanked the man and then walked towards the sea container where Alexandra Romanov stood waiting for her father.

On order from Chang, the doors to the container opened. A loud protesting screech from the rusty hinges rang out.

"Come with me, Mister Mitchell. I want to show you something that will change the world as we know it," said Romanov as he walked towards the entrance of the open container.

Stepping forward, for the first time Mitchell saw inside. Instantly, a chill ran through his body. Securely fastened into metal cradles were two long cylindrical bombs. Mitchell instantly knew they were nuclear. Spinning on his heels, Mitchell locked eyes with Romanov. "What the hell are you doing with two nuclear bombs?"

Romanov grinned. "I knew there would be no fooling you, Mister Mitchell. You are quite correct; I have in my possession two nuclear bombs."

"Where did you get them? And for God's sake, please don't tell me you were able to buy them on the black market."

"Unfortunately no. The Russian Mafia and the Pakistani military both rebuffed my offers, oddly enough. So I had Colonel Chang appropriate a couple for me," said Romanov, walking over beside the bombs. "They are South African, a little old, and somewhat crude, but still quite functional. They are more than sufficient for what I have planned."

"And just what is that?" asked Mitchell, trying to get something, anything, useful out of Romanov.

Romanov pursed his lips and shook his head at Mitchell. "All of your questions will be answered in good time, Mister Mitchell. You must remember when I said you were an essential part of this operation. Trust me, I meant every word. Now, no more idle talk. Chang and his men have a lot of work to do over the next few hours."

Mitchell thought about making a lunge for him, but knew that he would not make more than a meter before being cut down by one of Romanov's goons. Frustration grew inside him. He had to do something before this mad man actually tried to use the bombs that he had in his possession.

Teplov turned to one of Chang's men and said, "Cuff Mitchell to the lead eight-wheeler and make sure that two men remain with him at all times. If he escapes, I'll hold you responsible."

Chang stepped forward until he could look into Teplov's cold eyes. "My services are contracted to Mister Romanov, not you. I'll give the orders to my men from now on," said Chang, thinking back to the wasted death of his deputy in the desert.

Seeing the look of anger in Chang's eyes, Teplov could tell that Chang hated him and if given the chance, would enjoy killing him. Taking a step back, Teplov said, "Fine, have it your way. But I still want Mitchell secured and guarded." With that, he walked away.

With a nod from Chang, two men roughly grabbed Mitchell by the arms, forcibly dragged him over to the ATV, and cuffed him to the ATV's roll bar.

Mitchell stared defiantly at the two guards and pulled hard on the cuffs. As he expected, they didn't budge at all. Mitchell had to admit to himself that he was going nowhere fast. Letting go of his building frustration and anger, Mitchell stared back into the container at the bombs and tried to figure out what Romanov was planning. He would not have brought them here if he intended to use them on a major city in Russia or another target in the West. He could have easily shipped them into a busy port and detonated them there before anyone knew what was happening. There had to be another reason. Looking around at the camp, Mitchell saw the tunnel dug into the base of the tall ice-covered volcano. Some of Romanov's men were busy clearing the snow from some of the equipment around the entrance of the tunnel. Looking back at the bombs, Mitchell broke out in a cold sweat. He suddenly knew what Romanov was going to do. If he wasn't stopped, millions of people would be dead in the next few hours.

37

S am sat there, intently staring down at the image on her tablet. Moving her finger delicately along the pad, she adjusted the zoom of the camera and brought up a picture of Mitchell sitting under guard at the side of an ATV. She could see that he looked less than enthused about his situation. Cardinal took over keeping watch on the roof, methodically identifying and recording his targets, while Sam moved below with Nate. She had heard from Fahimah in the past minute and was relieved to hear that Yuri had managed to refuel the helicopter, and that they were both anxiously waiting on a quiet airstrip. She reported that Yuri was already strapped into his seat, ready at a moment's notice to fly his rented Bell 204 Huey helicopter to their location the instant that the word was given.

Jackson lowered his binoculars and said, "Looks like Jen is still under guard at the closest pre-fab office building, and Ryan is having tons of fun being cuffed to that ATV in front of the sea container."

"Getting them out will be a lot harder now that they're split up," observed Sam.

"I'm open to suggestions," said Jackson as he surveyed the metal fence running the perimeter of the camp, looking for the best place to try to cut their way through.

Up above, Cardinal raised his rifle and looked through the scope, looking around the camp for potential targets. As his sight moved past the sea container, Cardinal's heart skipped a beat. His hand fumbled for his throat-mic. "Folks," stammered Cardinal, "take a look at the sea container. They're moving a couple of devices outside and they sure as hell don't look friendly."

Jackson moved over beside Sam and looked down at the image on the small tablet while Sam focused the camera on the container. Both instantly swore.

"Are those what I think they are?" asked Cardinal incredulously.

"My God, they've gotten their hands on a couple of nukes," said Jackson, not believing what he was seeing on the screen. "By the looks of them, I would say that it's something in the order of ten kilotons destructive power per bomb."

"Jesus, what the frigg are they doing with them here?" Sam said as she watched while a bomb was placed onto a trailer behind Mitchell's ATV.

"Sam, get in touch with Fahimah ASAP," said Jackson, wondering if the day could get any worse.

On an airstrip, just over one hundred kilometers away, Fahimah almost fell out of her seat as the images from Sam's camera appeared on her laptop. Her heart raced like a jackhammer in her chest. There was no doubt in Fahimah's analytically-trained mind that she was looking at two nuclear devices in the hands of Dmitry Romanov. Her hand still shaking, Fahimah instantly opened a line to the Polaris Complex and passed on the data for immediate analysis and feedback. Looking down at her watch, Fahimah realized that the graveyard shift was still on duty. Only a couple of junior analysts would be working at the complex this early in the morning. Grabbing her cell phone, Fahimah dialed Donaldson's home phone.

It started to ring.

"Come on…come on," said Fahimah, nervously chewing on her lip.

Donaldson groggily answered.

"Mike, it's Fahimah here. I need you to open your secure Internet line this instant."

Less than two minutes later, Donaldson was still dressing as he jumped into his car and raced towards the Polaris Complex. Across the city, General O'Reilly was also on the move. Mitchell's team had stumbled onto every government's worst nightmare.

Jackson sat there looking over into Sam and Cardinal's faces. He had just finished outlining his plan to rescue Jen and Mitchell and was waiting for their thoughts, but neither one said a word. They were ready, and it showed in their eyes. He knew it was a risky plan made on the fly, but doing nothing until someone showed up to help was undoubtedly a worse option. When they nodded their heads, Jackson knew they were ready. Leaving Sam and Cardinal alone for a minute, Jackson moved over and checked the equipment in his knapsack, making sure that he had enough explosives for the mission.

With Cardinal covering them from the top of the tower, Jackson and Sam made their way downstairs and out into the cold. Moving stealthily, they silently made their way down through the snow-covered rocks, towards the nearest edge of the mining camp. High above them, Cardinal made his .50 cal sniper ready and started to zero in on his targets. He knew that he had to make every shot count if Jackson's plan stood the remotest chance of working.

38

Mitchell sat there growing colder by the minute; his breath hung in the air while internally he stewed about his inability to do anything as the first nuclear bomb was securely placed onto the trailer at the back of his ATV and then quickly covered with an old canvas tarp. Two men in grungy-looking blue coveralls, led by a thin man wearing an old red baseball cap, jumped in beside Mitchell. Turning the engine over, the ATV drove slowly to the tunnel entrance. Staring into the uninviting darkness, Mitchell could see that the cold, damp tunnel seemed to go on for hundreds of meters before unnervingly disappearing down into pitch-blackness. Parking just inside the tunnel, the man with the red baseball cap got out of the ATV and moved back beside the bomb. Mitchell could see that he was checking and re-checking a box on the top of the bomb, which Mitchell surmised was an electronic arming device.

A few seconds later, Mitchell heard a jeep pulling up. Turning his head, he saw Romanov and his daughter Alexandra get out. Accompanied by several bodyguards, Romanov strode over and stopped beside the bomb with a smug look of satisfaction etched on his face.

"Still confused as to what is going on, Mister Mitchell?" asked Romanov.

"No, not at all," said Mitchell, turning his head so he could get a better look at Romanov's arrogant face. "If you are planning on doing what I think you are, then you intend to detonate these nuclear bombs inside the volcano in order to trigger a massive landslide that will send a mega-tsunami of almost unbelievable destructive power hurtling towards the shores of Europe; to be precise, towards the United Kingdom and

Norway."

Romanov clapped his hands and said, "I should have hired you instead of some of my other people. Not only are you an unbelievable irritant, but you are also quite intelligent, Mister Mitchell. Not what I would have expected at all from a man who works for a glorified security guard company."

"I'm flattered by the offer," said Mitchell insincerely. "But the fact of the matter is that I don't work for psychos. Also, I watched a special on the *Discovery* channel about mega-tsunamis last month, so I'm not actually all that bright."

A look of disgust flared in Romanov's eyes at Mitchell's insolent remarks. He took a deep breath and then continued. "Just think about it for a moment, Mister Mitchell. When the bombs go off they will superheat the ice trapped in the rocks throughout the eastern face of this volcano, causing it to tear itself apart in a spectacular explosion that will be heard around the world. I have been assured by my experts that something in the order of twenty cubic kilometers of rock, the equivalent of—"

"500 billion metric tons," said Mitchell, interrupting Romanov's thought.

"Yes, of course. 500 billion metric tons will, within seconds, drop straight down into the Atlantic Ocean, causing a massive tidal wave to begin. In less than four hours, a wave up to one hundred meters high, travelling at close to eight hundred kilometers an hour, will hit western Norway and Scotland. The destructive power of all that water should travel for tens of kilometers inland before the wave finally dies out. I expect that at least five million people will die from the tsunami, but that is not the best part. The wave will race down the North Sea between Norway and Great Britain, destroying every oilrig from here to the coast of the Netherlands. The entire oil-producing capacity of western Europe will be eliminated in a single day. With winter gripping Europe, they will naturally turn to Russia to give them what they need or face freezing in the dark. A Russia, I might add, that will be led by me in the next twenty-four hours."

Mitchell had thoroughly misjudged the man's megalomania. "Ok, I'm impressed. So how much will it cost the West for you to not explode your bombs?"

Romanov laughed aloud as if Mitchell had just a good joke. "No, Mister Mitchell, it is all far too late for that. As we speak, your vice-president is on his way to meet me at my yacht in order to discuss my orderly transition into power as the next President of Russia. Naturally, I will agree to his more than generous offer of support. Unfortunately, just before I can assume power, rogue rebel forces will detonate these bombs, thereby crippling the West for decades. However, my first act in power will be to set things right, by handing back to the people the crown jewels of Russia and accepting their invitation to become its ruler. After that, through an undisclosed, but thoroughly reliable source, I will leak to the Americans where the hidden rebel bases are. Within hours, planes from the mighty U.S. Navy, with token Russian military support, will crush the remaining rebels, thereby allowing my family to assume control over a major portion of the world's oil supply, which I will then sell to the West for a phenomenal profit."

"You do realize that this blast will be thoroughly investigated, and the radiation signature on this island will be detected. Each one is unique; you do understand that, don't you?" said Mitchell. "They will eventually trace it back to you."

"Mister Mitchell, your State Department has by now been informed of the theft of two South African nuclear bombs by an unknown terror organization. I made sure that sufficient information was leaked to tie the theft to one of the more radical nationalist groups tearing Russia apart right now. In the post-9/11 world, a state of paranoia has probably already set it in. I must admit that you and your government are so predictable."

Mitchell shook his head in disgust. "Why the hell are you doing this?"

Romanov stepped close so he could look deep into Mitchell's eyes. "Because I can, that is why."

Mitchell had heard enough. Like a coiled cobra, he shot his head forward and smashed his forehead down onto Romanov's nose, shattering it and sending blood gushing down his surprised victim's face.

Instantly, a rifle butt flew into Mitchell's head, snapping it back. Stars filled his eyes; his vision blurred for a moment, but thankfully, this time he did not black out.

Romanov staggered away from Mitchell, his jacket covered in a slick patch of his own blood.

"Bastard!" screamed Alexandra as she pulled out her pistol, pulled back on the slide and then aimed it at Mitchell's head.

Mitchell sat there staring into the cold dark eyes of Alexandra Romanov, waiting for the gun to go off.

"No, not that way," said an enraged Romanov, as he wiped the blood off his face with a white silk handkerchief. "I want him to agonize over the fact that there is nothing he can do to prevent the inevitable. Cuff him to the bomb," ordered Romanov.

Hands reached out and manhandled Mitchell away from the ATV and onto the trailer. Seconds later, he was cuffed to a railing running down the side of the bomb.

"If he even so much as blinks, kill him," said Romanov as he walked back to his jeep, got in and then drove towards his waiting helicopter.

39

Marine One
En route for Camp David

President Donald Kempt sat back reading over a file that had been hurriedly handed to him by his chief of staff before boarding the marine helicopter bound for a weekend at Camp David. The president and his wife were planning to spend a quiet weekend away from the troubles of his office with their daughter, her husband, and their newborn child. Putting the file on the latest budget figures aside, President Kempt removed his reading glasses and rubbed his tired eyes. He knew the press would make his time away from Washington into something it was not. Undoubtedly, his chief rival would be on TV tonight, complaining that not enough was being done to help Russia. He would expound that an administration run by him would naturally do things better. Shaking his head at the non-stop spin that was the news these days, President Kempt felt tired. He needed forty-eight hours away to recharge his batteries. His staff had assured him that nothing else could be done right now to help President Ivankov and with Vice-President Grant getting ready to meet Romanov in Iceland, all he could do was sit back, try to relax, and wait.

Kempt was about to close his eyes and get a few minutes sleep, when his cell phone buzzed. It was Dan Leonard, the president's National Security Advisor, calling him. Barely thirty seconds into the call Kempt sat there, his jaw clenched tight. He had been played, they had all been played for fools. Quickly ending the call, the president turned to the head of his security detail and told him that they were returning to Washington immediately. His wife, Deborah, would just have to entertain without him.

Quickly calling his chief of staff, Kempt ordered the National Security Council to convene immediately; any ships they had in the North Atlantic needed to be steaming for Iceland immediately.

Sitting back in his leather-bound chair, President Kempt looked out the window at the lights of the homes passing by underneath his chopper as it raced back to the capital, wondering how many millions of lives they could save and if he was already too late to do anything about it.

40

Romanov Mining Camp
Dragon's Fire

S am lifted her head ever so slightly and watched the two-man guard team amble by completely oblivious to her hiding spot behind a snow-covered boulder only a few meters back from the electrified fence. Waiting until they were out of sight, Sam leapt up with her silenced M-4 snug in her shoulder. Panning around, Sam made sure it was safe. "All clear," said Sam, barely above a whisper.

Jackson's large frame appeared as if from nowhere. Stepping forward, he knelt and studied the fence before rummaging through the pouches on his chest-rig until he pulled out a small aerial spray can. Starting at the base of the fence, Jackson sprayed the concentrated liquid nitrogen onto the fence in an arc until he reached the other side. The metal instantly froze and cracked. Without being touched, the fence buckled and then fell quietly onto the snow. With lightning-fast relaxes, Sam dove through the opening and took up a fire position on the far side while Jackson barely managed to fit his larger frame through the hole.

"Don't say a thing," huffed Jackson. "I know what you're thinking. My wife's gonna put me on a diet as soon as we get back to the States."

Sam shook her head; she knew better. Jackson had been promising to lose weight for years. Keying her throat-mic, Sam spoke. "Ok, Cardinal, we're both in."

Cardinal acknowledged and took deliberate aim at the thugs

nearest Sam and Jackson, just in case he needed to deal with them right away.

Jackson looked over at Sam with a broad reassuring grin on his face as he extended his hand. "Good luck, Sam. Stay safe, and I'll see you back at the tower shortly," said Jackson.

Sam shook Jackson's hand. "You too, and remember to keep that big ass of yours down," replied Sam. With that, she winked at Jackson and, like an Olympic sprinter, dashed off towards the cover of the nearest building.

"I don't have a big butt," mumbled Jackson to himself as he peered towards the entrance of the tunnel where Mitchell was being held. "Now, what I need is a new set of duds," said Jackson to himself as he quietly crept after the men who had just walked past.

Teplov rode up to the tunnel with the second bomb. An overconfident smirk emerged on his lips when he saw Mitchell cuffed powerlessly to the first nuclear device. Leaping from his still-moving ATV, Teplov walked over beside the bomb specialist, Markov, who was standing to one side busy checking and double-checking the weapons' remote arming devices as usual. A smoldering cigarette hung limply from his mouth.

"Markov, are we ready to go?" asked Teplov impatiently.

Markov did not bother to look up from what he was doing. "This isn't a simple roadside IED that we are playing with here. Give me five more minutes to ensure the triggers are fully functioning, and then you can place the bombs," said Markov.

Teplov shook his head at the aggravating technician. He was going to kill Markov the instant the bombs were detonated. After Markov's last impertinent remarks, he was looking forward to it.

Alexandra Romanov got out of her jeep at the entrance to the tunnel and joined Teplov inside the darkened passageway. Removing her designer sunglasses, Alexandra gazed down the length of the angled shaft as it led deep into the heart of the volcano. It looked as cold, dark, and uninviting as a tomb. She did not consider herself claustrophobic, but standing there looking into the bowels of the earth made her skin crawl. It was a feeling of dread and impending doom. Shaking off such unwelcome thoughts, she looked over at Teplov and said, "How far into the volcano does this tunnel go?"

"The tunnel goes for about a kilometer and then it branches off into two different directions for about another kilometer on either side, which is where we will plant the two bombs," explained Teplov.

"Have you driven the tunnels before?" inquired Alexandra.

"No, but Chang has and he says with the ATVs pulling the additional weight of the bombs, it shouldn't take more than ten minutes to get the devices into position," replied Teplov. "However, Markov the damned perfectionist, has asked for an extra half-hour once the bombs are in position to ensure that the devices are good to go, and then we will return to the surface. Your father's helicopter will be back by then, so we will be safely onboard the yacht hours before your father remotely detonates the bombs."

"What if they are discovered before we can activate them?"

An evil gleam shone in Teplov's eyes. "That possibility is quite remote, considering no one can come here without your company's permission. However, should someone decide that today would be a good day to come sniffing around, Colonel Chang isn't in the loop as to the exact timeline for detonating the bombs," Teplov said coldly. "Let's just say that he and his men will still be here guarding the nukes when they go off, eliminating the threat of anyone ever speaking to the authorities and saving your company tens of millions in payments at the same time."

Alexandra smiled. It seemed like everything was ready. All they needed to do now was place the bombs and leave.

Sam edged to the corner of an abandoned wooden shack and cautiously peered towards the building where Jen was being held. Outside the front entrance, Sam could see two tough-looking men standing guard, their weapons cradled in their arms. The ground from where she was to the building was open and sparse. There was no way she could make her way over to the other building without being seen. Swearing to herself, Sam pulled back behind cover and quietly keyed her throat-mic, "Gordon, I've got two ugly mothers outside of Jen's building. Can you see them?"

"I'm already laid on them," replied Cardinal into Sam's earpiece.

Sam did not expect anything less. "Ok, my love, once Nate starts the fireworks, I need you to clear them out of the way so I can make it over there in one piece."

"Consider it done," said Cardinal, his voice trailing off.

Sam knew something was up and waited.

"Fahimah's just heard back from General O'Reilly. The cavalry is on the way. ETA to our position is just over two hours," reported Cardinal.

"Who did they find out here? Iceland doesn't have an army," said Sam.

"Seems a marine amphibious ship was on exercise with NATO naval forces off the coast of Scotland and is now steaming our way. When they're close enough, they're going to launch a company of marines to assist."

"Sweet, they're gonna show up when we don't need them."

"Enough chatter. Focus on the task at hand," said Jackson, ending it for everyone.

Pumping her legs expectantly like a professional sprinter waiting for the race of her life to begin, Sam took a deep breath and readied herself for the inevitable clash coming their way in the next few minutes. Nervous tension filled her body. Waiting for the first round to be fired was always the hardest part for her. Once it started, Sam knew that she was ready to do her part.

41

Mitchell watched as the second ATV pushed past and pulled ahead of the one he was cuffed to. A few seconds later, Alexandra strolled past him with her head haughtily held high as she climbed aboard the lead ATV. Riding in Alexandra's ATV were Markov and two of Chang's men. Another bomb specialist and three more mercenaries jumped onto Mitchell's ATV. The man who had cuffed Mitchell to the bomb sat propped up on the back of the ATV, his FN-2000 resting on his lap, its short barrel aimed at Mitchell.

Seeing that all was in order, Teplov walked outside the tunnel and took out his cellphone to make a quick call to Dmitry Romanov.

No matter how hard Mitchell tried, he could not make out what was being said. Mitchell was certain that Teplov, the ever-loyal goon, was reporting in and getting the final go ahead from Romanov to place the nukes. Looking back over his shoulder towards his guard, Mitchell gave the stone-faced man a smile and tried to wiggle his hand out from the tight cuff restraining him to the bomb. No matter how hard Mitchell tried, he was getting nowhere. All he was doing was rubbing his skin raw. Grinding his teeth in frustration, he knew he had to get his hands on the keys to his cuffs if he was going to escape.

A faint noise seemed to seep inside the tunnel, growing louder by the second; Mitchell knew that it was the sound of a helicopter flying over the island, but whose?

Several of Chang's men jumped off their ATVs, made their way to the entrance of the tunnel, and watched disbelievingly as two dark-blue police helicopters swooped down to land in the open area in front of the camp.

Mitchell knew that the police did not stand a chance against the small army of trained killers guarding the bombs. If shooting erupted, which Mitchell knew was only seconds away, the fight would be horribly one-sided.

Teplov finished talking and snapped his cellphone shut and, with a look of disbelief on his face, watched the two helicopters land. Grabbing the nearest Motorola, he hurriedly spoke into it. From out of the mining camps' buildings emerged a couple of local thugs hired by the Romanov Corporation to keep an eye on the camp. Walking over, they were soon engaged in an animated discussion with the police as they climbed out of their helicopters. The police ignored the guards and pushed right past them, intent on approaching the tunnel. It was obvious to Teplov that their cover had been blown. Spinning around, he glared at Mitchell. Although he couldn't prove it, he suspected that the pain in the ass former soldier had somehow contacted the local authorities. Biting his lip in anger, Teplov tasted the coppery taste of his own blood. Grabbing the Motorola, he yelled at Chang to deal with the police.   A second later, a volley of anti-tank rockets slammed into the police helicopters, blowing them to pieces and instantly killing anyone still inside. Hundreds of bullets tore into the stunned police officers from Chang's well-concealed men. In less than five seconds, the area outside the tunnel became a bloody funeral pyre. A tall thick black cloud shot up into the brilliant blue morning sky, warning others that death waited for any who came.

Mitchell watched in horror as the police were mowed down. They'd never stood a chance. His blood boiled at his inability to stop the massacre. Tugging as hard as he could at the restraint no matter how much it hurt, Mitchell knew he was going to free himself, even if it meant tearing his hand off to do so.

At the far end of the camp, a backhoe exploded, sending shrapnel and debris flying into a couple of luckless guards, tearing both men apart. The sudden explosion made Chang's men duck and look around for their unseen assailant. Jackson watched as fear and confusion gripped two inexperienced guards who quickly panicked, dropped their weapons, and fled for the safety of an old cement mixer. Waiting a couple of seconds to allow the growing panic to spread out of control like a disease, Jackson pressed down on the remote detonator in his hand; the cement mixer detonated, turning those who had sought cover behind it into red mist. His only regret was that he was a minute too late to help the police officers lying dead in the snow. Walking out from his hiding spot, a smile crept across Jackson's face as he dropped the remote to the ground, slung an appropriated FN-2000 over his shoulder and nonchalantly made his way towards the entrance of the tunnel, his "borrowed" guard's gray uniform bursting at the seams.

"Now, Gordon," said Sam into her throat-mic, as she darted from behind the cover of her building, her legs pumping for all they were worth. She figured it would take her less than ten seconds to cover the distance, but that was an eternity to her as she sprinted across the open ground. A guard turned and saw Sam in her white camouflage uniform emerge out of nowhere, sprinting towards him. Instinctively, he raised his weapon to take a shot; however, he never had a chance. A half-second later, his head exploded in a bloody crimson spray of bone and blood. The other guard died with a hole torn straight through his chest by Cardinal's well-aimed .50 cal sniper rounds.

Jen sat on the floor with her arms wrapped around her legs. The sound of firing and explosions outside rocked the flimsy building as if it were made of paper. Closing her eyes, Jen prayed for salvation. With a loud crack of snapping wood, the front door burst open. A second later, a white-clad figure holding a weapon slid inside and came to a stop just in front of Jen. Closing her eyes, Jen was certain she was going to die.

"Miss March, it's all right, I'm a friend of Ryan's," said a female voice.

Opening her eyes, still fearing the worst, Jen looked into the grinning face of Sam Chen.

A wave of relief washed over Jen. Fighting back tears, she looked past Sam at the two bodies lying bloody on the ground outside the office. For a brief instant, she hated herself for being relieved that they were dead; the feeling quickly passed when she realized that she was now safe.

"Come on," Sam said, looking back over her shoulder at the mayhem tearing through the camp. "We have to get out of here, while all hell's still breaking loose outside."

Jen nodded and stood, ready to follow Sam wherever she went.

Making their way to the open door, Sam quickly scanned around for any hostiles. Seeing none looking their way, she told Cardinal that she had Jen and was on their way back to his location. Waving for Jen to follow, Sam jogged back the way she came with Jen following close behind her.

Cardinal followed the women through his scope. He knew it would take them a good half-minute to make it back to the hole in the fence, but once there they would be under the cover of the rocks. Out of the corner of his eye, he saw a bloodied guard stumble out from behind a building. Seeing Sam, the guard went to raise his rifle to fire. Cardinal aimed dead center on the man's chest and pulled back on the trigger. The guard never knew what hit him as his body was cut in two.

At the hole in the fence, Sam guarded Jen as she made her way through the opening. Sam then dove through the gap, rolled over her shoulder, and came up on one knee. Feeling satisfied that things had so far gone to plan, Sam took the lead and quickly led Jen into the safety of the low ground.

42

*T*heir plan was rapidly falling apart, thought Alexandra Romanov as she watched the black smoke from the destroyed police helicopters float, like an escaping genie, ever higher into the sky. What had begun as a day that would see her father propelled into power now looked to be in danger of failing. The sound of firing swept the camp as Chang's men fought back against their unseen attackers. *Still, if we can detonate the bombs, then something could be salvaged from the debacle*, thought Alexandra.

Grabbing Teplov by the arm, Alexandra pulled him towards her. "Leave Colonel Chang and his men to deal with the infiltrators. We need to place the bombs without delay."

Teplov nodded, snatched up his Motorola, and quickly told Chang to find and destroy their attackers, no matter the cost. Without another thought, he turned his back on the men he had left to die while they rushed to place the bombs. With a wave of Teplov's hand, everyone climbed back on their ATVs. Taking a quick look over his shoulder to make sure that they were ready, Teplov turned to his driver and told him to drive.

With a dull roar from the lead ATV's engine, the vehicle began to slowly crawl forward. Within seconds, the two vehicles and their deadly cargoes disappeared from sight into the long gloomy tunnel.

Mitchell felt the vehicle pick up speed as it descended deeper into the volcano as if heading down towards the pits of hell itself. The tunnel became cooler and darker the more they travelled from the light at the entrance of the tunnel. Tugging at his restraint, Mitchell's wrist had become a slick, bloody mess from the painful twisting and turning he had subjected his hand to. If he had another ten minutes perhaps, he could do it, but Mitchell knew that he probably did not have the time. Turning his head back towards his guard, Mitchell tried lifting his bloodied arm. "Hey you, you got a bandage or something?" he said, trying to get his guard's attention.

The bored-looking man turned his head, smiled at Mitchell's dilemma and dismissively spat on the passing ground.

So much for that, thought Mitchell. Looking at the bomb, he saw that it was secured to the trailer by several wide canvas straps. Reaching over with his good hand, Mitchell started to pull at the nearest strap to him.

"Hey, you! Stop that!" bellowed the guard with a strong Scandinavian accent.

"Screw you," replied Mitchell, still pulling and twisting the strap, trying to get it to loosen.

Jackson ignored the gun battle going on behind him as Cardinal, from his position atop the tower, dropped anyone foolish enough to stick their head out in the open. Taking a deep breath, he walked calmly towards the entrance of the tunnel. Most of Chang's men had learned their lesson and had moved under cover, forming up into fire teams. It would not be long before they figured out where Cardinal was and made a move against him. As much as he wanted to help, Sam and Cardinal would have to deal with the mercenaries by themselves. Right now, he had to save Ryan and stop the nukes from being detonated. Stepping inside the darkened tunnel, Jackson saw a thug sitting on a four-wheeled ATV, a cigarette hanging from his lips; his weapon lay across his legs, while he dug around in his jacket looking for his lighter. Walking over to the guard, Jackson waved at the man to get his attention. The guard simply nodded in greeting. He was too busy looking for his lighter to realize that Jackson was not one of them. With one powerful punch, Jackson sent the luckless guard tumbling off the ATV and up against the far rocky wall, coming to rest in a heap on the tunnel floor. Grabbing the man's rifle, Jackson threw it into the back of the ATV and jumped onto the four-wheeled vehicle. Turning it on, he quickly changed gears, turned it around, and charged off down the tunnel.

The ATVs separated. Teplov and his vehicle turned down the left-hand tunnel while Mitchell's went right. Helplessly, Mitchell watched what was happening. Gritting his teeth against the pain, he frantically tugged at his restraint. Time was running out.

"Quit it," ordered the guard.

"Come over here and make me," taunted Mitchell, trying his best to piss the man off.

With a loud huff, the thug pulled himself up and warily stepped over onto the bomb trailer. "I said stop that," said the guard threateningly. "I was told to keep you alive until we reach the bomb site, but no one told me that you couldn't be hurt." The guard he raised his rifle, aiming at Mitchell's bloody arm.

Mitchell took one quick look past the guard; he could see that everyone else was still looking forward and not paying the slightest bit of attention to what was going on behind them.

The guard carefully edged forward until he towered over Mitchell. "Hold still, and I'll try to only put one hole in you," said the thug with an evil grin on his face.

Mitchell knew he only had one chance. In a flash, he shot out his legs, sweeping the legs of the guard out from underneath him. With his arms flailing about, trying to grab onto something, the large guard tumbled down onto the trailer. Instantly bringing his right leg up, Mitchell rammed it as hard as he could into the stunned man's face. Blood flew as the man's nose shattered. Mitchell's heart was racing. Quickly peering past the man, he was relieved to see that no one had heard a thing over the sound of the ATV's powerful engine vibrating off the tunnel walls. Scurrying on his rear a little bit closer to the wounded guard, Mitchell wrapped his legs around the man's throat and, like a boa constrictor, started to squeeze the life out of the guard. The shocked guard struggled to break Mitchell's hold, but he didn't stand a chance. It was only a matter of seconds before he would black out and die.

Suddenly, a voice rang out. "Günter!" shouted one of the guards on the ATV. Scrambling to his feet, the guard tried to raise his weapon when his head snapped back, a bloody hole in the center of it.

A loud crack echoed down the tunnel.

Turning to look back over his shoulder, Mitchell saw a bright headlight racing towards him. A moment later, Mitchell could not believe his eyes as Jackson sped past him, one hand on the ATV's handlebar, the other holding out an assault rifle as he fired a short burst into the body of another guard, sending him tumbling over the side of the ATV.

"Nate, for God's sake, don't shoot the bomb tech!" yelled Mitchell, trying to get his friend's attention.

Leaning over, Jackson grabbed onto the larger ATV's roll bar and hauled himself over onto the speeding ATV. The last of Chang's mercenaries, a broad-shouldered red-haired man sitting beside the driver, lunged at Jackson, trying to grab him by the waist. Jackson had anticipated the move and brought his hands down onto the man's back. With a loud grunt, the guard's legs buckled and he dropped back in his seat. Trying to finish him off, Jackson swung at the man's head. However, the red-haired man pulled his head back at the last second and scrambled over his seat, trying to get his hands on Jackson. The driver, seeing the melee going on beside him, tried to grab his holstered pistol. His momentary lapse of attention caused the ATV to crash into the side of the tunnel, sending both Jackson and his attacker tumbling over the side of the ATV and onto the hard, rock-strewn floor of the tunnel.

Mitchell watched in dismay as Jackson and the thug rolled past him, locked in a struggle to the death. With one hard tug of his legs, Mitchell heard the last gasp of air escape from his adversary's shattered nose. Reaching down with his free hand, Mitchell grabbed the dead man's shirt collar and dragged him closer. Immediately Mitchell started to rummage through the pockets on the man's shirt, desperately looking for the key to the restraint.

The tunnel grew dark as Mitchell's ATV sped away. The only light now was from the overturned four-wheeler that Jackson had abandoned further down the mine, casting eerily long shadows as Jackson and his assailant desperately grappled with one another. Fists and elbows flew as both men tried to cripple the other; it was like a gladiatorial fight to the death. Struggling to free a hand, the guard flung his hand towards

Jackson's face, his fingers clawing for his eyes. Pulling his head back as far as he could, Jackson waited until the man's hand was as close as it would get. Reaching over with his mouth, Jackson bit down hard on the thug's hand and tasted blood. With a howl of pain, the goon pulled his hand free. Letting go of Jackson, he recoiled and hurriedly scrambled to his feet. Jackson, displaying unexpected agility for a large man, jumped up on his feet. Stepping back out of Jackson's reach, the red-haired goon pulled a six-inch blade from his belt that, in the light of the tunnel, gleamed menacingly. With a loud snarl on his lips, the man stepped forward and thrust the blade towards Jackson's exposed midsection. The man may have had a weapon, but Jackson had years of experience and training on his side. Turning on his heels, Jackson shot out his right hand and grabbed the thug's extended hand in a vicelike grip, squeezing it as hard as he could. The man yelped in agonizing pain as Jackson turned the man's arm over, snapping his wrist. A second later, the knife dropped to the dirt. With a swift thrust of his free hand, Jackson brought his large fist straight down on the man's jaw, knocking him to the ground, unconscious.

Mitchell's hand felt something cold and metallic...*yes*. Wrapping his fingers around it, Mitchell pulled out the keys to his restraint from the dead mercenary's shirt pocket. As quickly as he could, Mitchell opened the cuff. His bloody wrist ached in pain, but that was not going to slow him down, not now. Reaching over, Mitchell grabbed the dead man's assault rifle, pushed the dead body off the trailer, and jumped over onto the fast-moving ATV. The only passengers remaining on board were the driver and the bomb technician, both of whom were in no position to stop Mitchell. Slamming the butt of his rifle down hard into the side of the technician's head, Mitchell watched him slump over before he jammed the cold muzzle of his weapon into the back of the driver's neck.

"Stop this vehicle, now!" said Mitchell firmly.

The vehicle quickly slowed and came to a halt.

Mitchell ordered the driver to place his hands on his head and slowly climb out of the vehicle. The driver, his eyes wide and scared, did as he was told. Mitchell smiled at the guard just before butt-stroking the man in the head with his rifle. The guard flew straight back onto the rocky floor like a dropped sack of potatoes.

Mitchell had just finished hog-tying the guard when Jackson drove up on his four-wheeler with a broad grin on his face.

"Where's your guy?" asked Mitchell.

Jackson pointed over his shoulder. "He's back there looking as pretty as yours," replied Jackson, looking at the tied-up guard lying face down on the ground.

Mitchell walked over and grabbed his comrade by the arm. "Nate, I need you to stay here and get that specialist over there to disarm the nuke," said Mitchell, nodding towards the woozy technician.

"What if he doesn't want to help?"

"Then kill him and try to disarm it yourself," Mitchell said loud enough that the unsteady technician could hear.

"I help, I help, just don't shoot me," the terrified technician said meekly, with a strong Russian accent.

"Ok then, come here and no screwing around," said Mitchell, pointing his weapon at the battered man.

"Jesus, Ryan, what the hell is going on?" asked Jackson. "Why the hell do these people have a couple of nukes?"

Mitchell turned and looked back down the darkened tunnel. The other bomb would soon be in place. "Sorry, Nate, there's just no time to explain right now. You have to disarm this bomb, or millions of people will die." Mitchell climbed onto Jackson's borrowed four-wheeled ATV. "I have to stop the other bomb from being armed."

Jackson nodded, reached behind his back, and handed Mitchell a Glock 9mm pistol. "You might need this," he said.

Mitchell thanked Jackson, took the pistol, revved up the ATV's engine, and sped off down the long dark tunnel.

Jackson watched his friend disappear from view. Turning his attention to the terrified Russian engineer, Jackson walked over to the man, easily towering over him. "How long to disarm this mother?" asked Jackson, looking over at the bomb.

"Uh, three minutes perhaps," stammered the technician.

"Well, I'll give you two, before I put a bullet in your head."

The man practically tripped over his feet to get to the bomb.

43

The noise from Cardinal's .50 cal tore through the air. One of the thugs' vehicles was on fire, after a well-aimed round had torn through its driver, sending the jeep smashing into another parked vehicle. Using what cover they could, Chang's men began to advance towards the tower overlooking the camp. Neither side was backing down from the fight; everyone there knew that it was a fight to the finish.

Chang lowered his binoculars and swore. At the rate his men were taking casualties, it would not be long before he would not have enough men to storm the tower. If more attackers were to arrive, then Chang knew it would all be over. As far as he could tell, it was only a few well-armed men firing at his men from the old Martello tower. Even the anti-tank rockets were proving useless against the thick walls of the tower, exploding harmlessly on the hard exterior. Although the snow-covered ground was littered with the bodies of more than a dozen of his men, Chang was still confident that his well-trained team could take the tower if they could only get close enough. The area from the camp to the ridge where the tower stood was just too open. His men would not make it half the distance to the rocks before being picked off one by one. Looking about, he searched for a way to even the odds. A moment later Chang saw the answer to his prayers. With a loud whistle, he pointed towards a large yellow tractor. A quick wave by one of his men let Chang know that he knew what to do. Grinning as he looked up at the tower, Chang wondered just who it was who had managed to screw up the Romanovs' plan. If circumstances had been different, he might have even offered them a job; they were that good.

Cardinal scanned the mining camp through his sniper scope and guessed that there were about fifteen mercenaries still in the fight. Most of Romanov's men were all either dead, or cowering from the fight. Not expecting a protracted fight, Cardinal had carried what he thought was enough ammunition, but with the firefight gaining in its intensity, he was beginning to run low. At least he still had his M4.

"Hey there, how's it going?" asked Sam, startling Cardinal.

Peering over his shoulder, Cardinal saw Sam's head sticking up from below. "We're doing ok, I guess, but I'm starting to run low on 50. cal ammo," replied Cardinal. "Do you have Miss March with you?"

"Yeah, she's safe and sound down below. Have you seen any sign of Jackson or Mitchell?" asked Sam.

"None, Nate disappeared into the tunnel a good ten minutes ago."

The sound of an anti-tank rocket slamming against the side of the tower made both Sam and Cardinal duck.

"Ok then, I guess we're gonna hold up here until the cavalry arrives," Sam said, trying to sound optimistic. "I'm gonna send an update to Fahimah and find a good firing port to help you from."

"All right, but keep your head down," replied Cardinal as he looked over at Sam. Neither said a word. For a moment, they locked eyes, both knowing they would die for the other. With a quick wink, Sam dropped down the stairs and out of sight. Turning his head back so he could see through his weapon's telescopic sight, Cardinal saw three men making a dash towards the tunnel entrance. Seeing weapons in their hands, he swung his sniper rifle over, took aim, and cut down one of the men before the others dove for cover behind some old rust-covered 45-gallon drums.

44

Mitchell hunched over the steering bar of the ATV. Rocks scattered everywhere under the vehicles' tires as it tore around the narrow corner of the tunnel. He looked down the long dark tunnel, but saw no sign of the other vehicle and its deadly cargo. Gunning the accelerator all the way, the ATV leapt forward like a prized stallion racing down the track. Mitchell slung his rifle on his back and drew Jackson's pistol, knowing that he could not be that far behind Teplov. The thought of Romanov's thug made Mitchell's blood boil. The sooner he dealt with him, the better.

The long eight-wheeled ATV came to a gradual halt at the end of the tunnel. Teplov jumped off and looked back down the tunnel; only cold unforgiving darkness seemed to stretch into the distance. The cool, damp air made him suddenly shiver. Shaking his head, he turned back towards the bomb. Teplov ordered the guards with him to unhitch the trailer and get the ATV turned about so they could leave as soon as Markov had finished his final inspection of the bomb.

Alexandra slipped her cold hands into her jacket pockets and walked over beside Teplov, a sour look on her narrow face. "It looks like we will have to remotely detonate the bombs well ahead of schedule," she said bitterly. "Father won't be happy, but it can't be helped."

Teplov looked down at Alexandra. "Don't worry," he said with the hint of a smile. "Once the bombs go off, the West's ability to mine oil in the North Sea will be obliterated, Russia will soon once more belong to your family, and you will be rich beyond your wildest dreams. It will be as your father planned, just a few hours early, that's all."

A light flickered down the passage.

Teplov had not expected anyone else to be coming down the tunnel. Gently, he moved Alexandra behind him, using his body to cover hers. Reaching down, he grabbed his Motorola and called the other bomb team.

Silence answered him.

The sound of an approaching ATV's engine echoed down the long, narrow tunnel.

"Perhaps it's the other team? Or one of Chang's men coming to report?" asked Alexandra.

"Maybe," replied Teplov, unsure. "You two come here," he said to the guards.

Stopping what they were doing, the two men walked over beside Teplov.

"I'll help Markov. You two see what the other crew wants," said Teplov, edging back behind the mercenaries. His gut told him that something wasn't right. Taking Alexandra by the arm, Teplov walked behind the bomb, trying to put as much distance as he could between them and the approaching ATV.

Mitchell saw the light from the larger ATV illuminating the far end of the passageway. He could see several men standing there, silhouetted in the light. Leaning over the handlebar for support, Mitchell brought up his pistol and took aim.

Teplov was about to chalk it all up to his nerves, when a shot rang out. Instantly, one of the two guards' head snapped back, his lifeless body falling backwards onto the ground. Before the other man could react, two bullets pierced his chest. Grabbing at the bloody holes, the man dropped onto his knees and tumbled over onto the cold, rocky ground.

Teplov pushed Alexandra back and drew his pistol, making it ready.

The blonde-haired Markov turned in horror as a vehicle sped towards him, out of the dark as if it were coming out of the grave to seek vengeance upon him for his many sins.

Slamming on the brakes, Mitchell turned the vehicle's handlebar all the way to the right. The ATV came to a sliding halt right beside the dead bodies of Chang's men. Jumping off the ATV, Mitchell strode straight towards a petrified Markov, his pistol aimed straight out in front of him.

Markov, seeing the look of anger in Mitchell's eyes, instantly dropped onto his knees, threw up his hands in the air, and pleaded not to be shot.

"Disarm this, now," growled Mitchell, jamming his pistol hard into Markov's face.

Trembling, Markov got to his feet, meekly nodded and turned towards the bomb.

Seeing only two dead guards, Mitchell instantly began to wonder where Teplov and Alexandra had disappeared to. A gnawing in Mitchell's stomach told him to be wary. They had to be close. A sudden movement in the corner of his eye made him turn on his heels. Standing there was Teplov, with his pistol aimed at Mitchell; behind him was Alexandra.

"Drop it," said Teplov to Mitchell.

"It'll be a cold day in hell when I drop this pistol," replied Mitchell.

"Markov, is the bomb prepared?" asked Teplov, looking past Mitchell at the bomb specialist.

Markov stopped what he was doing and nervously fumbled for a cigarette. Lighting it, he spoke. "Yes everything is in working order. I was about to—"

The sound of Teplov's pistol firing inside the narrow tunnel was deafening.

Blood and gore sprayed all over the bomb casing as Markov slid to the ground, a hole blasted straight through his temple.

Mitchell fired.

Teplov felt the bullet pass by his head as he ducked back behind the bomb, leaving Alexandra standing there, a perplexed look on her face. Ruthless to a fault, she had never expected to be abandoned and left to the mercy of others.

Mitchell ducked. Ignoring Alexandra, he fired off a couple of quick shots under the bomb trailer, hoping to kill or at least wound Teplov, who he knew was hiding somewhere in the dark.

Within seconds, it grew deathly quiet inside the tunnel. The only sounds Mitchell heard were his own breathing and the rocks crunching under his feet as he slowly edged his way towards the end of the trailer. His heart started beating fast in his chest as he turned the corner of the trailer. Raising his pistol to fire, he froze and swore loudly. There no one was there.

Mitchell was about to move down the other side of the trailer, when the hair on the back of his neck shot up. Stepping back, Mitchell barely had time to register the dull flash of metal as a shovel blade reached out from the dark, hitting his already-bloodied hand. Blinding pain shot up his arm as his pistol was knocked from his hand and tumbled away under the bomb trailer. Mitchell cursed. He was certain that his right wrist was broken. Reaching over with his left hand, he grabbed the shovel's wooden handle and pulled as hard as he could. Teplov stumbled forward off balance with his hands still firmly gripped around the shovel. Letting go of the shovel, Mitchell balled up his left hand and sent it straight into Teplov's face. Lesser men would have dropped from such a blow, but Teplov, fueled by hate, simply dropped the shovel to the ground, stepped back, shook his head, and arrogantly spat out the shards of several shattered teeth from his bloody mouth.

With a loud cry, Teplov dropped his head and charged straight at Mitchell, hitting him in the stomach. Both men flew backwards onto the rock-strewn ground. Struggling, both men fought to break the other's hold. Twisting his body, Mitchell brought up his right leg and tried kicking Teplov off him.

Sensing the move, Teplov turned his body slightly, so Mitchell's leg missed him completely. Snarling like a rabid animal, Teplov bared his jagged teeth and lunged with his head for Mitchell's face.

Mitchell recoiled, repulsed by Teplov's primal attack. Pulling with all his strength, Mitchell broke his left hand free and sent it flying into the side of Teplov's head. A loud satisfying thud filled Mitchell's ears as Teplov's head flew to one side. Thrusting his leg once more upwards, this time into Teplov's stomach, Mitchell flipped his assailant up and off him. Scrambling to his feet, Mitchell sent his right foot flying into Teplov's head, knocking him back down onto the ground. Quickly looking about, Mitchell saw under the bomb trailer that his pistol was lying just out of reach, barely ten meters away. Turning to run, Mitchell nearly tripped as Teplov, bloodied and injured but not yet out of the fight, shot his hand out and grabbed Mitchell's nearest leg. Hauling off with his free leg, Mitchell kicked as hard as he could into Teplov's ribs. The sound of escaping air being painfully forced out of Teplov's lungs and a rib or two breaking were barely drowned out by Mitchell's heart pounding away in his ears.

With a moan, Teplov let go of Mitchell's leg. Struggling to catch his breath, Teplov painfully got up on his knees and looked over at Mitchell. He had expected to have been struck again while he was down, as he would have hit Mitchell without hesitation.

Something was wrong; something had made Mitchell hesitate.

Turning his pounding head over, Teplov looked over at Alexandra. A weak smile crept across his bloodied face when he saw that Alexandra was standing there. In her hand was Mitchell's pistol. Slowly he stood; his feet were unsteady underneath him. Teplov, his heart still consumed with anger, staggered over to Mitchell and with a cry on his lips he smashed his fist into Mitchell's face, sending him staggering back against the rocky wall of the tunnel.

Mitchell's jaw felt as if it had been hit with a baseball bat. Struggling to remain standing, Mitchell shook his head, took a deep breath, and looked over at Alexandra and Teplov. He had to play for time. "I've already stopped the other bomb from going off, so you might as well give in," said Mitchell.

Teplov let out a chuckle. Blood and spittle trickled down his chin. "Give it a rest, Mister Mitchell. I helped Alexandra plan this entire operation from beginning to end. Do you honestly think I would not have thought of that possibility? All we really need is one bomb. The second is a mere insurance policy. Besides, once this one goes off, the other will explode by sympathetic detonation."

Mitchell bit his lip. Teplov was right; his plan was almost foolproof. "Bravo for you two psychos," said Mitchell, inching ever closer. "But I doubt that your band of thugs outside will be able to hold off the army who are on their way to this island as we speak."

"I think you are bluffing, but it is not important. Chang and his men need only last as long as it takes for Alexandra and me to leave," replied Teplov.

"Take another step, Mister Mitchell, and I'll shoot," said Alexandra, stepping back and away from Mitchell.

"Enough of this crap," said Teplov gruffly. "Kill him now and let's get the hell out of here."

Alexandra smiled and raised the pistol, aiming it at Mitchell's head.

The sound of something tumbling through the air made Mitchell turn his head. A split-second later, Alexandra's body violently lurched forward with a bloody pickaxe blade protruding through her chest. Her eyes glazed over, a look of shock and disbelief on her face as her legs buckled. Alexandra turned to look at Mitchell. She tried to say something, but only a bloody gurgle escaped her lips as she fell forward onto the tunnel floor. The pistol bounced out of her hand, landing at Mitchell's feet.

Seeing the pistol lying there, both men dove for it. Mitchell was faster. Snatching it up off the ground, Mitchell did not even bother to aim. Pulling the trigger repeatedly, he emptied the magazine into Teplov, his body twitching every time a bullet struck home. He was dead long before his body hit the ground. The smell of acrid smoke hung thick in the air. Mitchell looked down at the corpses and turfed the pistol away into the dark. Anger and disgust filled his heart. So many people had died, and for what?

Jackson stepped out of the shadows, looking down at the lifeless body of Alexandra Romanov.

Mitchell looked over at his friend. "Thanks, Nate," said Mitchell. "You had a gun, why didn't you just simply shoot them both?"

"You were in my line of fire. Besides, I wanted to make sure that she got the point," said Jackson, grinning at Mitchell.

Mitchell shook his head at Jackson's dead-pan humor. "What about the other bomb?"

"It's disarmed," replied Jackson. "I left Igor, or whatever his name is, tied spread eagle on top of it, so he wouldn't get any ideas of heroics."

"Great, but this nuke's still live and can be remotely detonated at any time by Romanov."

Jackson stepped over to the bomb. The arming device looked far more complicated than anything he had ever seen in his life. The thought of tinkering with it instantly left his mind when he saw that it had what looked to be an encrypted code built into the arming pad.

"I'm going back to the other bomb and I'll bring Ivan back here to disarm this one too," said Jackson as he jumped back on the ATV and took off down the tunnel.

A cellphone vibrating in the dark caught both men's attention. Looking around, Mitchell realized that the sound seemed to be coming from Alexandra's body. Bending down, Mitchell pulled out an iPhone from Alexandra's jacket. Holding it up, Mitchell saw a message in Cyrillic on the screen. Mitchell cursed himself for letting what Russian he knew become horribly rusty, but the one thing he could read was that it was from Dmitry Romanov. The man was obviously expecting his daughter to send him an update. Mitchell could imagine him sitting on his yacht, going out of his mind as he wondered what was going on. Placing his broken wrist inside his jacket to give it some stability, Mitchell turned and looked down the tunnel. The sound of gunfire from outside made him realize that it was not over yet.

A couple of minutes later, the ATV came to a halt, with only Jackson on it.

"Where's the bomb expert?" asked Mitchell.

"He told me that he doesn't know the code," replied Jackson. "He had the code for his bomb only, and the other specialist knew the codes for both. It would appear that trust was not this crew's greatest asset."

"Great, the dead one is the one we need," said Mitchell, looking over at Markov's corpse.

"So now what do you recommend we do?"

Mitchell held up Alexandra's phone. "Daddy dearest sent a text message while you were gone."

"What's it say?" asked Jackson.

"Damned if I know," said Mitchell, putting the iPhone away in his shirt pocket. "But one thing is for sure, I'm fairly certain that this one was Daddy's favorite and I doubt that he intended to bring billions of tons of rocks down on his own flesh and blood.

Come on, we need to get out of here and stop this bomb from being detonated."

"How are we going to do that, pray tell?" asked Jackson as he followed Mitchell towards his still-idling ATV.

Mitchell jumped on behind Jackson. "With this," said Mitchell, holding up Alexandra's iPhone, "along with Fahimah, Yuri, and the support of the navy. First, though, I think Sam and Cardinal may need some help."

Jackson nodded, turned the ATV around, and jammed his foot down on the accelerator. In an instant, they sped off down the tunnel, leaving Alexandra and Teplov on the cold, lonely ground.

45

Dark gray smoke filled the air, blocking out the sun. The sound of automatic weapons firing combined with the smell of cordite filled Chang's senses while he edged forward, calmly ignoring the sound of bullets whipping past him. They had one chance and one chance only to take the tower. If the fight kept going the way it was for much longer, he would be out of men. The sound of heavy machinery starting up made him look back over his shoulder at the large yellow earthmover as it made its way down towards the camp. Chang smiled. His men had seen the terrible precision from the sniper perched atop the tower and had placed a row of 45-gallon drums inside the earthmover's large shovel, hoping to absorb some of the impact from the deadly .50 cal rounds.

Calling his surviving men over, he quickly outlined his plan of attack. They would wait until the large earthmover passed them, then they would fall in behind and use its mass for cover as it made its way towards the tower. With a quick nod from his men, Chang ejected the magazine from his rifle and slapped home a new one. He knew that when they got to the tower, the fight would be short but deadly, and his men would come out on top, of that he had no doubt.

Rolling on his side, Cardinal dug through his breast pockets until he found what he was looking for, his last full magazine of ammunition. Quickly placing it on his rifle, Cardinal pulled his weapon tight into his shoulder as he scanned the ground below him for targets. Smoke from burning vehicles and buildings obscured his view. All he could see were those mercenaries he had already killed. It may have been a cold winter's day, but

Cardinal's throat was parched. He thought it felt worse than some of the hottest days he had spent lying in wait in Afghanistan. Reaching back, he was fumbling for his canteen when he heard the sound of a heavy machine's engine rumbling somewhere in the burning camp. Forgetting his thirst, Cardinal peered through his sight and sought out the source of the noise. Barely a second later, the massive earthmover emerged from the smoke with its shovel held high, protecting the driver.

"Clever bastards," muttered Cardinal to himself when he saw the row of drums inside the long shovel.

Sam's head popped up from below. "Do you see what they've got?"

"Yeah," replied Cardinal, as he took aim where he figured the driver would be and pulled the trigger.

A loud metallic clang split the air as the .50 cal round sailed through the 45-gallon drum but came to an abrupt stop against the extra plates of steel the driver had placed behind the drums. With a satisfied grin on his face, the driver slowed down slightly, allowing Chang and his men to dash over behind the tracked vehicle as it clawed its way towards the tower.

"It didn't stop," observed Sam dryly.

Taking a deep breath, Cardinal took aim and then pulled back on the trigger. A loud bang filled the air as the rifle fired. Looking through his sights, Cardinal cursed. He didn't have any armor piercing rounds with him, and that was what it would take to stop the vehicle.

Rolling over on his side, he looked over at Sam. "You and Miss March better make a run for it while you can. I'll try to hold them as long as I can," said Cardinal, knowing that they had at best a couple of minutes before the tractor made its way to the base of the tower.

"Like hell," was all Sam said before disappearing from sight.

Shaking his head in frustration, Cardinal looked back at the tractor as it ground its way towards them like some kind of unstoppable mechanical beast coming to finish them all off.

Dropping down onto the stone second floor, Sam dashed

over to the open gun port and peered outside. She could see that the tractor was still a few hundred meters away, but soon it would turn onto the road leading up to the tower. Spinning about, she looked around the room, desperate to find something to stop the tractor. Seeing Jackson's bag lying on the floor, she picked it up and began to rummage through it.

"What's going on?" asked Jen, seeing the look of desperation in Sam's eyes.

"Unwanted company's coming," replied Sam without looking up.

Turning her head, Jen looked out the window and saw as the large yellow earthmover came into view. Stepping over beside the old cannon, Jen shook her head. They had come so far; there had to be a way to stop them.

"Do you think we could use this cannon?" Jen asked Sam.

Sam pulled out a block of C4 and several detonators from Jackson's bag. "Sure, I don't see why not. I can use this as the propellant, but I don't see any cannon balls lying around."

"Not cannon balls...rocks," said Jen as she tore past Sam, taking three steps at a time as she ran to the bottom floor and straight out the open door of the tower. Looking about, Jen could feel her heart racing as she tried to find a rock that would fit down the barrel of the old cannon. Dropping to her knees, Jen dug through the snow, growing desperate to find a projectile when she heard the sound of automatic gunfire erupt from above. She didn't know it, but Cardinal was out of sniper ammunition and was now using his M4 to try to slow down their enemy. Jen's hands were becoming raw and stinging from the bitter cold as she clawed at the snow and ice, when suddenly her hands felt something hard. Digging as fast as she could, Jen found a couple of rocks frozen to the ground. Pulling at them with all of her strength, Jen let out a cry as they came free. Cradling them in her arms, she sprinted back inside the tower.

Sam heard Cardinal open up with his M4. She knew that was not a good sign. Turning to look out towards the tractor, Sam realized that the mercenaries were no longer firing at the tower, which could only mean that they were all jammed behind the massive vehicle. Seeing her chance, she threw herself on top of the cannon and crawled forward until she was half in and half out of the tower. Grabbing her expedient charge, she rammed it as far as she could inside the barrel of the cannon. Her arms were too short to jam it all the way home. Swearing, Sam crawled back inside, sprinted over to the nearest old wooden table, and in one swift kick, knocked one of its legs off. Dashing back, she took the wooden leg and then stuck it inside the barrel, ramming home the charge. She was about to crawl back inside when she heard Jen bounding up the stairs. Turning her head, Sam called out for whatever Jen had in her hands.

Jen, her hands numb from the bitter cold, looked down at the three rocks in her hands. Quickly deciding that the middle one was the best, she handed the rock to Sam, who jammed it into the barrel and rammed it home.

"Move," cried out Sam as she crawled back inside the tower. Looking down at the cannon's mount, Sam saw that there was no way to elevate or depress the cannon. She would have to wait until the tractor was almost upon them to fire it.

Jen stood there rubbing her hands together, trying to get some warmth back in them when Sam turned and, with a serious look on her face, dug out her pistol, pulled back on the slide and then handed it to her.

"In case this fails," said Sam.

Taking the pistol, Jen felt its weight in her hands. She had never used a weapon in her life. Jen knew that if their plan failed that there would be no other way to stop the mercenaries and she did not intend to die without a fight.

Jackson, his hands gripped tightly on ATV's handlebar, had expected a welcoming committee the instant they sped out of the tunnel. The bright sun rising up in the sky momentarily blinded him; however, the path in front of them was empty. Hearing the sound of firing off to his left, Jackson jammed his foot down on the gas pedal. His friends were in danger and he was not going to slow down for anything or anyone.

"Over there," called out Mitchell as he pointed towards the gaggle of men using a large tractor for cover as it closed in on the tower.

"Hang on," said Jackson as he turned the handlebar hard over, the wheels of the ATV clawing at the icy ground as it slid sideways for a few meters before suddenly gripping the rocky path that led down from the volcano towards the destroyed mining camp.

Speeding past the still smoldering remains of the two police helicopters, Mitchell changed the magazine on his pistol and then looked up at the tower. He knew his friends were fighting desperately to protect Jen. Kicking at the floor of the ATV, Mitchell cursed at the vehicle to move faster. He wanted to be in the fight before it was too late.

Cardinal was trying his best to ricochet rounds under the spade of the tractor, hoping to hit the driver. He doubted he was doing anything but wasting ammunition, but he had to try something. Ejecting his empty magazine, Cardinal could see that the tractor was less than one hundred meters away and closing. Quickly jamming a new magazine home, he decided that he would make his stand with Sam on the floor below. Crawling back on his stomach, Cardinal quickly made his way to the stone staircase and then dashed down below, only to have a pistol unexpectedly thrust into his face.

"Jesus, you should have said you were coming down! I could have shot you," said Jen as she slowly lowered her pistol. Her hands were shaking so much that she thought she was going to drop the gun.

"Sorry," replied Cardinal, his heart jack hammering away in his chest.

"I suggest everyone lie down on the floor as I'm not sure if this is going to work," said Sam as she held up a remote detonating device in her hand.

Cardinal and Jen dove to the floor.

Taking one last look out of the window, Sam saw the tractor looming large.

"What are you planning to do?" asked Cardinal.

"This," replied Sam as she depressed the button on the remote. In the blink of an eye, the C4 inside the cannon detonated, sending the rock flying out of the barrel and straight at the uplifted shovel. First striking the top of one of the 45-gallon drums, the rock easily sliced through the metal and then tore a hole into the top of the shovel, sending razor-sharp shards of metal flying into the face and neck of the driver, killing him. His foot slipped off the gas pedal. A few seconds later, the tractor came to a shuddering halt about fifty meters short of the tower.

Chang saw the blood trickling down the side of the tractor and knew that his driver was dead. Shaking his head in anger, he was about to climb up and over into the cab, when a man behind him called out in pain and dropped to the ground. Turning his head, he could not believe his eyes as an ATV came charging towards them, the driver and the man beside him firing away like mad men. His blood boiled when he recognized Mitchell. At that moment, he knew the plan to detonate the bombs had failed. With bullets cutting men down where they stood, discipline among his men evaporated in an instant. They had had enough. Men dropped their weapons and ran for their lives, some foolishly towards the tower, only to die in a deadly barrage from Sam and Cardinal, while others tried running back towards the camp. They never made it either as they were shot in their tracks by the men in the ATV. Throwing himself under the tractor, Chang crawled out of sight. It was over. He did not see the point in dying when he did not have to.

"Don't stop," yelled Mitchell over his shoulder at Jackson, as he emptied his pistol magazine into the panicked crowd of mercenaries.

Jackson had no intention of stopping. Firing his weapon on automatic, he sprayed the area in front of them with bullets.

In seconds, it was over. Not a single mercenary was left alive.

Tearing past the stopped tractor, Jackson brought the ATV to a sliding halt in front of the tower. Both men instantly leapt from the vehicle and ran towards the open door of the building, met by Jen, Sam, and Cardinal as they made their way outside.

Seeing Mitchell still alive, Jen, with tears welling up in her eyes, threw her arms around him and pulled him in close.

"Ow," mumbled Mitchell as Jen crushed his broken wrist in her vicelike grip on him.

"Is that all you've got to say?" said Jen as she let go of Mitchell and then wiped the tears away from her face.

Mitchell smiled. Jen's face may have been covered in tears and dirt, but to him she was still the most beautiful woman he had ever met. "We can talk later," he said as he looked over at Sam. "Get Yuri and Fahimah here ASAP."

Nodding, Sam dug out her phone to make the call.

The sound of rotor blades made Mitchell look skyward. With a smile on his face, he watched five V-22 tilt-rotor Ospreys came in to land.

"God bless the United States Marine Corps," said Jackson.

"Come on, let's go and greet our party crashers," said Mitchell.

46

"Mister Mitchell, I presume?" said a short, broad-shouldered Hispanic-American Marine Colonel wearing full battle gear.

"Yes sir," said Mitchell, offering the man his left hand in greeting.

"Looks like we arrived a little late," said the colonel as he looked around at the smoldering remains of the camp, and the several dozen bodies strewn about. "Some fight. My headquarters told me to pass on that General O'Reilly sends his regards. My name is Colonel Robert Santiago. Are the bombs secured?" asked Santiago anxiously.

Mitchell was relieved that General O'Reilly had been able to get someone to listen to him about the bombs. "Sir, unfortunately we only managed to defuse one," replied Mitchell.

"It's down the tunnel and to the left," said Jackson. "You'll find a cranky little Russian tied to it," he added.

"The other bomb?" asked Santiago.

"It was armed before we could stop it," Mitchell said.

"I have a top-notch bomb disposal team with me; they have experience from Afghanistan. They can disarm it," said Santiago.

Mitchell shook his head. "Sir, I'm sorry, but it won't be that easy. It's not a complex IED. It's a nuclear bomb with an encrypted arming device on it that's set to be remotely detonated," explained Mitchell, pausing to choose his next words carefully. "Colonel, no disrespect to your men, but they will most likely trigger it before disarming it."

Santiago looked up towards the immense volcano. "All of this is sheer madness. I still don't understand what the hell is going on."

"Sir, I'll gladly tell you what I know," said Mitchell, "but in order to save millions of lives, I'm going to need your help."

A puzzled look grew on Santiago's face. "Son, this is a military operation now," said Santiago. "Fill me in and my people will deal with it."

"Sir, please, this isn't the time for us to get into a pissing contest. The longer we delay, the more likely it is that Romanov will detonate the bomb. I've been on board Romanov's ship; have any of your men?" asked Mitchell.

Taking a deep breath, Santiago looked over at Mitchell; the look in his eyes told him that he could trust the other man. "I haven't a friggen' clue who this Romanov character is, but you've got my attention. Ok, mister, I'm listening," said the colonel.

Mitchell quickly outlined his plan. Santiago stood there with a look of incredulity on his face after Mitchell finished. Knowing their options were limited, Santiago nodded and instantly called for his radio operator.

47

A great skua banked over and looked down at the snow-covered island she called home. Below she could see a small group of people standing together behind the burned-out remains of a wooden building. Suddenly, the air seemed to come alive with noisy vibrations. Looking towards the sea, the large seabird saw a golden object approaching, appearing as if from thin air, racing towards her home. Deciding for the moment that it was getting far too crowded, with a loud screech the bird turned and headed back out to sea where it was a lot safer and quieter.

Flying over the white caps of the dark gray waves, the helicopter pilot quickly checked his dash-mounted GPS to ensure that he was in the right spot. Seeing the flat icy ground below him, the pilot smoothly brought his helicopter into land. Sitting beside him was a dangerous-looking man, dressed in the distinctive blue uniform of Romanov's personal security detail.

"We're in the right spot, so where the hell are they?" asked the pilot nervously, looking through the glass windshield at the devastation and bodies strewn throughout the camp. Keeping his hand on the joystick, the man was about to radio back to the *Imperator* when, as if on call, two people emerged from behind the nearest building and began running towards the helicopter. The pilot could see two men carrying a woman in a blanket as they ran towards the helicopter. Looking closer, the pilot recognized Alexandra Romanov's coveralls, but now they seemed bathed in blood.

"Get out and help them in," ordered the pilot to the security man. Panic filled his voice. Their employer would go berserk if they failed to help his daughter. The consequences would be too horrible to imagine.

Unbuckling himself, the security guard hurriedly opened his door and then stepped out. Hunched over to avoid the rapidly spinning rotor blades, the guard turned and opened the side door of the helicopter, sliding it open to receive Alexandra. The people were only meters away, when the guard felt something amiss. He did not recognize either of the men carrying Alexandra Romanov. Assuming they must be all that was left of Chang's mercenaries, the guard stepped forward to help with Alexandra when the lead man let go of Alexandra's feet, brought a pistol up, and pulled the trigger. A single bullet tore through the guard's chest, sending his body flying back into the open helicopter door.

Mitchell did not even wait for the guard to fall, before sprinting around the front of the helicopter, his pistol aimed directly at the helicopter pilot. With a look of stunned disbelief on his face, the pilot slowly raised his hands in surrender. From behind him, a voice spoke in Russian. "I'll take the controls now, please." The pilot looked over his shoulder into the rough-looking face of Yuri, as a pistol slammed into his face.

Ten minutes later, with everyone loaded, Mitchell stepped away from the helicopter. Standing there were Jen, Cardinal, Fahimah, Colonel Santiago and several soldiers guarding the miserable-looking chopper pilot. Walking over, Mitchell stopped in front of Jen, her face masking her feelings.

"I'll be back in an hour, two tops," said Mitchell reassuringly, looking into Jen's deep brown eyes.

"Ryan, why do you have to go?" asked Jen, fighting back her emotions.

"Jen, if I don't, millions of people could die," said Mitchell, taking her hand and tenderly squeezing it. "We have to stop Romanov from detonating the bombs. As long as he thinks his daughter is still alive, he won't set them off, and that gives us a chance to stop him."

Jen leaned forward and kissed Mitchell on the lips, her heart racing in her chest. She knew that she would never be able to convince him not to go. "For luck," she said, letting go of Mitchell.

Mitchell wanted to say something more, but knew it would have to wait. His right wrist was splinted and taped up so it could not move. After a shot of Demerol for the pain in his wrist, Mitchell was as ready as he could be. Turning, he looked over at Cardinal. "Look after Jen for me, and keep General O'Reilly in the loop as to what we're up to," Mitchell said, shaking his friend's hand.

"Not a problem," said Cardinal. "You just make sure that Sam comes home. We have a vacation planned after this," Cardinal looked past Mitchell at Sam as she buckled herself in beside a couple of tough-looking marines.

"It's a deal," replied Mitchell.

Colonel Santiago walked over. "Ok, Mitchell, seeing no other viable alternative, the Chief of Naval Operations is willing to give you what you requested," he said.

Mitchell grinned. "Thanks, Colonel. I hope to be flying home for some well-deserved beers in an hour's time."

Santiago's face turned serious. "Captain Mitchell, if you are not off that ship in thirty minutes, they will sink her, if need be, and you with it."

"Colonel, hitting it with an airstrike is no guarantee that Romanov won't survive long enough to detonate the bombs."

"I know.

"Sir, you do what must be done to stop the detonation of those nukes, our safety is secondary," replied Mitchell, his voice strong and determined. Both men firmly shook hands. With a quick wave, Mitchell sprinted for the helicopter's passenger door; he jumped in and then closed the door behind him.

Jen stoically stood there, her hands resting by her sides, tears in her eyes, as the helicopter took off, quickly raced over the top of the volcano, and disappeared from sight.

"Time to leave," said Santiago to his radio operator. Ten minutes later, Santiago, Jen, Fahimah, and Cardinal were airborne and heading at full speed for Iceland. Looking out her window, Jen said a silent prayer for Mitchell and everyone else. After what had happened today, she knew that they needed all the help they could get.

48

Dmitry Romanov sat despondently at his desk, his head resting in his hands. The silence from Alexandra gnawed at his soul. He knew something had gone wrong. Deep down, he knew that his carefully laid-out plans were not going as he had wanted. Unexpectedly, the US Vice-president had cancelled their meeting and on the news, it was being reported that the President of the United States himself was flying to Russia to meet with President Ivankov for an emergency summit in Moscow. Until half an hour ago, he had no idea if his daughter was alive or not, when a text message had arrived asking for a pickup. Instantly dispatching his best pilot, Dmitry Romanov agonizingly waited for word from his daughter. So far, there had been no message whatsoever from the helicopter crew, adding to Romanov's growing anxiety.

The door to his private office opened and Nika stepped inside. "Father, the helicopter is approaching and there is still has been no word from the pilot, but I just received a text from Alexandra," said Nika nervously.

"What did she say?" asked Romanov, slightly raising his head.

"That the bombs are in place and that there was fighting between Chang's men and some police," said Nika

"Anything else?" asked Romanov, seeing the hesitation in Nika's eyes.

Nika paused and then said, "Alexandra wrote that she was shot in the leg, but she says she's okay."

Romanov stood, all thoughts of defeat suddenly erased. "Tell the captain to have the ship's doctor waiting for the helicopter. Once we have Alexandra safely on board, we will detonate the bombs and then set course for Algeria," said Romanov, his eyes burning with vengeance.

"Very well, Father," said Nika, walking over and picking up the ship's telephone to pass on her father's orders.

Romanov took a deep breath and then sat back down. With the North Sea oil industry gone, the US and Europe would have to come back around and offer him the control of his homeland. They just needed a little inducement.

Ten minutes later, Nika stood impatiently on the back deck of the yacht, looking expectantly towards the gray horizon. Anchored in a quiet bay with tall cliffs to protect it from the coming blast, the ship's radar had told them that the helicopter was only minutes away, but Nika still could not see it. She was about to head below deck to warm up when a low-moving object approaching the stern suddenly caught her eye. Looking, Nika saw that it was her father's helicopter flying towards them. A wave of relief washed over her. Spinning on her heels, Nika ordered the doctor to see to her sister the instant the helicopter landed. Not wanting to waste another moment, Nika dashed inside to tell her father the good news.

The helicopter slowed down and, like a giant golden eagle, it seemed to hover for only an instant above the helipad and gently landed. Its engine instantly switched off. The long sharp rotor blades began to slow and then stop. The ship's doctor, a thin Indian gentleman, accompanied by two security personnel manhandling a stretcher, made his way along the slick deck towards the helicopter's side door. The door suddenly slid open and an assault rifle was thrust out.

Jackson pulled the trigger, cutting down the two guards before they could draw their weapons. Jumping out, he yelled "Swim!" at the terrified doctor, who nearly tripped over his own feet as he dashed for the side of the boat. Freezing water or not, the man never stopped, quickly disappearing over the side of the ship.

Mitchell joined his friend. "That's really subtle, Nate," reproached Mitchell.

A klaxon horn sounded.

"So much for the element of surprise," said Mitchell, turning to face his team. "Ok. Sam and the marines, get to the operations room. Nate, plant the charges below deck, and no heroics—that means you Nate," said Mitchell, eyeing his friend. "We all meet back here in ten."

No one said a word as they all sprinted off in separate directions. Only Yuri remained on deck with a pistol in his hand should he need it.

Mitchell took two stairs at a time as he sprinted down into the bowels of the ship straight towards Romanov's office. A guard racing from the opposite direction did not even see Mitchell before almost smashing into him. With a swift stroke from his rifle into the guard's chin, Mitchell sent the guard flying off his feet straight back onto the floor. Bending down to grab the man's pistol, Mitchell edged towards the corner of the hallway and peered in the direction of Romanov's office. Outside stood two guards, their hands firmly wrapped around their FN-2000s, nervously looking at the roof as if they could see what was happening above them. Stepping back, Mitchell looked down at the unconscious guard and said, "How about doing a solid for the good guys?"

With the two marines in the lead, Sam advanced, her M4 tucked tight into her shoulder. Moving down off the helipad, the marines edged forward down the deck. Suddenly, a door in front of them opened. A man stepped out, saw the marines, and went for his holster. Two shots rang out. The man dropped to the wooden deck, blood pooling underneath him.

"That's got to be the ops room," said Sam to the marines, pointing at the door that the dead man had just exited.

"Ok, stay close," said the lead marine, a young red-haired sergeant, as he cautiously crept towards the closed door. Reaching down, he placed his hand on the doorknob. Looking back at his African-American partner, the sergeant lifted his hand, showing three fingers. Sam and the black marine nodded their heads. After silently counting down from three, the door was flung open and the sergeant stepped inside. "Move an inch and I'll kill you all," yelled the sergeant in fluent Russian.

Every head in the room turned at once and then froze.

With a loud thump, the body of the unconscious guard hit the golden-carpeted floor. Both men outside Romanov's office flinched and looked down at the body. Neither man was prepared when Mitchell turned the corner and then calmly shot both men with one shot to the chest each. Dashing forward, Mitchell turfed the guards' weapons back down the hallway without bothering to see if he had killed either man. He knew he did not have time for such things. He had only one thought: to stop Romanov. Hauling off, Mitchell kicked the door to the office in. Diving forward, Mitchell rolled over and came up on one knee, his M4 tight in his shoulder. Looking over the weapon's sights, Mitchell was surprised to see Dmitry Romanov sitting there with an almost serene look on his face. The Russian crown jewels lay in front of him on the mahogany table.

"You can't stop me now, Mister Mitchell," said Romanov, lifting his hand to show a small remote detonator. "All I need to do is press one button, and it is all over."

"You don't have to do that," said Mitchell, wondering if he could kill Romanov before he pressed the button. He doubted it.

"Yes, I do. The rules of the game have changed, and I want to turn them back in my favor. Now, Mister Mitchell, since you are standing here, I suspect that Alexandra is no longer with us," said Romanov with a hint of sadness in his voice.

"That's correct," replied Mitchell.

"How did you manage to contact the ship?"

Mitchell tossed Alexandra's cell phone on the table; it slid across the polished surface until coming to rest by Romanov's hands. "I simply had one of my people send you fake messages, making you think she was alive, so you wouldn't set the bombs off."

"Clever of you," said Romanov, as if the words let a bad taste in his mouth. "How did my Alexandra die?"

Mitchell locked eyes with the megalomaniac and coldly said, "Your precious daughter died with a pickaxe stuck in her chest."

Sadness instantly turned to blind rage in Romanov's eyes.

A disconcertingly familiar voice from behind Mitchell spoke. "Father, I've heard enough. Drop your gun, Mister Mitchell."

Turning his head, Mitchell saw Nika standing there with a pistol in her hand, aimed squarely at his head.

"Now!" shrieked Nika.

Mitchell dropped his rifle. "I should really learn to look both ways when entering a room," said Mitchell, realizing that he had screwed up.

"Take a seat," said Romanov, indicating to the chair opposite him.

With a feigned smile on his face, Mitchell sat.

Romanov looked at his daughter. "Nika, I doubt that we will now be able to leave in peace," said Romanov wearily. "Head below and prep the submarine, and I'll join you shortly."

"You have a sub? Who the frigg are you, Doctor Evil?" said Mitchell, alluding to the Austin Powers films.

"Money buys many things," said Romanov. "Now, Mister Mitchell, I doubt that you are here alone."

"That's correct," replied Mitchell, playing for time. "Currently my people are accessing your financial records, while another is going to ensure that you, your daughter, and this ridiculously over-priced dinghy end up on the bottom of the Atlantic Ocean."

"No need to be so crass at the end, Mister Mitchell. I intend to let you live long enough to see the bombs detonate, thereby letting you and your oversized ego know that you have failed. After that, I will put a bullet in your head to erase you from my mind," said Romanov, pulling a pistol from his desk drawer.

"Kill me if you want," said Mitchell. "But you're finished. There will be no place in the world where you will be safe. You will be hunted down, and like Bin Laden you will end up a dead man."

Romanov smiled and shook his head. "You just don't get it, do you? The world needs oil, and I am the man who can deliver it. Your government will never come after me; I am their only hope for long lasting peace and stability in Russia."

Mitchell gritted his teeth; unbelievably the man still thought he could buy his way out of the stinking hole he had dug.

"From the look in your eyes, Mister Mitchell," said Romanov, "it is only now that you see I am right. All of your foolish heroics have been for nothing."

Jackson stepped down off the metal stairs and guardedly looked around the dimly-lit engineering room. It seemed deserted, but his experience and the gnawing in his gut told him otherwise. Moving slowly, Jackson turned 360 degrees to make sure there wasn't anyone lurking in the shadows, before pulling a couple of charges of C-4 explosive from his backpack and lying them down on a steel worktable. Setting the timers for five minutes, Jackson made his way to the nearest wall and securely placed the charges onto the hull of the ship. Once they exploded, the hole torn into the side of the yacht would be fatal. The ship would sink in minutes.

A faint noise echoed in the shadows.

Jackson spun about, just in time to see a man edging towards him, his hand raised with a wrench clenched in it. Firing from the hip, Jackson fired one round into the man, hitting him squarely in the arm. With a loud clang, the wrench hit the metal floor; the man stood there wide-eyed holding his bloodied arm.

"Now, why did you have to try that?" said Jackson, looking at the injured man. "I hope you can still swim."

Looking down the business end of Jackson's weapon, the man stepped back and eagerly nodded before edging his way to the stairs. Realizing that he wasn't going to be shot in the back, the man turned and hurriedly fled up the stairs.

Movement further down the room caught Jackson's attention. Realizing that his rifle was more of a liability than an asset in the cramped space, Jackson drew his pistol and then warily moved towards the other end of the engine room.

The red-haired sergeant, a Russian immigrant to the States, sat behind a computer console, his eyes speedily going through Romanov's business correspondence. A terrified computer operator had been "coaxed" by Sam into opening up the Romanov Corporation's private files for the marine. Emailing anything and everything of value directly back to the computers at the Polaris Complex, the sergeant was laying bare Romanov's duplicity, his double-dealing with the Russian insurgents and his plans to cripple the West economically. It was all there.

"Two minutes, then we've got to go," said Sam to the marine as she checked her watch.

The young man nodded without looking up from the computer screen. He intended to use every second he had to finish the traitorous Romanov.

Flying twenty meters above the white-capped ocean waves, two ghost-gray U.S. Navy F-18s closed in on the *Imperator*. The lead plane flew towards the yacht, as if it were going to fly straight into it, while the other plane banked away and started to climb into the dark gray sky. At one kilometer out, the lead pilot reached down and flipped a switch on his console and with a deafening roar he flew right over the *Imperator*, its wake rattling the ship as if it were a toy in a child's bathtub.

The sound of the rapidly approaching plane penetrated deep inside the *Imperator*. Dmitry Romanov nervously ran his thumb over the remote detonator, his mind suddenly filled with doubt. Had Mitchell been a decoy to give someone time to sink his yacht? Looking over at Mitchell, Romanov was disconcerted to see him sitting there with a confident grin on his face. *I've had been set up*, thought Romanov. Rising from his chair, Romanov looked at Mitchell with hate in his eyes. Slowly he brought up the detonator and then pressed the button.

For a second, Romanov held his breath, expecting an explosion as bright as the sun to flash on the horizon, but nothing happened. Repeatedly smashing his thumb on the detonator, Romanov stared down at the impotent device in his hand, a growing bewildered look on his face.

"It's useless," said Mitchell standing. "The plane that just flew over your yacht was configured to do an electronic warfare burn. Every device from your detonator to your ship's navigational computers were all fried in an instant. You lose, Dmitry Romanov."

Blinded by his anger, Romanov swore and hurled the detonator towards Mitchell.

Ignoring the flying remote, Mitchell dove straight at Romanov, smashing him in his chest, sending him flying over the wide wooden desk. His pistol flew out of his hand and fell onto the floor. Mitchell quickly glanced about for the pistol but could not see it anywhere. Pushing a chair out of the way,

Mitchell reached down and grabbed Romanov by the collar. Hauling him to his feet, he sent a fist into Romanov's stomach, painfully forcing his opponent to double over.

The sergeant swore as the screen flashed and then went blank the second after the plane, piercingly loud, shot over the yacht. "Thirty more seconds, I just wanted thirty more seconds," he said.

Sam laid a hand on his shoulder. "Time's up, marine, we have to go."

Standing up, the sergeant turned towards the cowering computer operators, and in Russian said, "Time to swim. If you can't, take a life preserver with you, but you are all going over the side, right now!"

The men nodded. With their hands still in the air, they scurried out of the room, rats off a sinking ship.

Pulling a charge from her satchel, Sam placed it on the computer mainframe and set it for three minutes. With the marines once more in the lead, Sam started to make her way back up to the helipad and safety.

The heat inside the engine room was almost unbearable. Jackson was dressed for the freezing temperatures outside. Rivers of sweat poured down his clean-shaven head straight into his eyes. Thick clouds of steam made visibility near impossible. The smooth metal floor soon became slick and dangerous. *Someone must have opened the valves*, thought Jackson. Trying his best to blow away the annoying sweat, Jackson made his way deeper into the bowels of the ship, looking for the intruder. The sound of chains rattling caught his attention. Edging forward, his pistol aimed into the thick gray cloud, Jackson mentally counted down in his head. He had barely two minutes before his charges exploded, flooding the engine room and him with it. Edging around a turbo, Jackson stopped in his tracks, not believing what he was seeing. An athletic-looking woman in a snug-fitting dry suit was preparing to launch a submersible from a hatch built into the bottom of the boat. For a brief moment, Jackson almost thought he saw a ghost, but he remembered that Jen March had said there were two Romanov daughters.

"Going somewhere?" asked Jackson, stepping out so he could be seen.

Nika stopped what she was doing, looked over at Jackson, and then smiled unnervingly.

Jackson stepped forward with his pistol trained on Nika's chest. "What's so damned amusing?"

"You must be one of Mister Mitchell's friends."

Jackson nodded slightly.

"You are such a big man; while you chased shadows in the steam, I snuck around you and changed the timers on your charges."

Jackson hesitated. Could she have been that fast? Looking at her undeniable physique, he knew she was not lying.

Less than a second later, the charges detonated, knocking Jackson off his feet and sending him crashing against the hull. Thousands of liters of ice-cold water instantly rushed in from the mortal wound torn into the hull, quickly flooding the engine room.

Staggering unsteadily to his feet, Jackson looked over towards Nika, but she was already gone. The sound of air escaping the submersible indicated that it was diving. Firing off one shot in rage, Jackson turned and found himself already struggling through freezing cold knee-deep water. By the time he made it to the stairs, it was up to his waist.

The explosions rocked the yacht from side to side. Mitchell had to let go of Romanov to prevent himself from smashing against the side of the ship.

Although battered and bruised, Dmitry Romanov was still a powerful man. Seeing a chance, he dove towards the table. Scooping up the long golden scepter in his hands he spun around and brought it up, intending to swing it down like a deadly mace towards Mitchell's head.

The flash of the scepter arcing through the air made Mitchell turn his body. The rod flew past his head by mere millimeters, striking Mitchell in his collarbone and sending an agonizing jolt of pain down his right side. Mitchell jumped back to avoid the scepter as Romanov skillfully brought it back up in one smooth movement. Reaching behind him, Mitchell felt a chair. Wrapping his hands around it, Mitchell hauled it around and threw it at Romanov. Seeing the chair coming, Romanov weaved to the side as it flew harmlessly against the hull of the ship, shattering to pieces.

"You may have ruined everything, but I will at least see you go to hell," snarled Romanov as he brought up the scepter, aiming to send it crashing into Mitchell's head.

Pivoting on his heels, Mitchell turned sideways as the heavy gold rod barely missed him. With lightning-like reflexes, Mitchell grabbed Romanov's over-extended arm and twisted it as hard as he could.

Surprise shot into Romanov's eyes as his arm painfully twisted over. He had no choice, but went with his arm and fell to his knees, writhing in agony. The scepter fell to the green-carpeted floor, away from his limp hand.

Already the ship had begun to list. Mitchell struggled to keep his balance as the ship slipped deeper into the cold gray water.

Mitchell had had enough. Smashing his knee into Romanov's head, he sent his opponent tumbling to the floor. Bending down, Mitchell grabbed the scepter and before Romanov could get up off his knees Mitchell, with a loud yell of rage on his lips, smashed the scepter straight into the side of his opponent's head. He heard the sound of bone cracking as blood flew from a deep gash in Romanov's head.

The color from Romanov's face instantly drained. His disbelieving eyes went blank. He tried to say something, but no sound escaped his dying lips.

"You wanted it so bad," said Mitchell as he tossed the scepter onto Romanov's body as he struggled to catch his breath, "you keep it."

"I would have said he who lives by the sword, dies by the sword," said Jackson, from behind Mitchell.

"It's not a sword, it's a scepter," said Mitchell, shaking his head at his friend's joke. Turning to look at over at Jackson, Mitchell saw him standing there, his soaked clothes dripping water all over the deck.

"What happened to you?" asked Mitchell.

"I went for a swim," said Jackson. "Come on, boss, we need

to get off this wreck before we go with it."

Another explosion tore through the yacht as Sam's charge destroyed the operations room. The ship was beginning to list heavily to port. Both men knew that it had minutes to live before it began the crushing descent to the bottom of the ocean. Running as fast as they could, they made their way up towards the helipad.

Having switched off all the power on the helicopter, Yuri had spared the craft's electronics when the F-18s flew over the ship. Now sweat drenched Yuri's forehead as he fought to keep the chopper level. The ship already began to sink from underneath the helicopter's wheels. Keeping the helicopter hovering just above the deck, Yuri inched it over to avoid the rotor blades from striking the deck of the yacht as it sank to one side.

"Do you see them yet?" nervously asked one of the marines over the chopper's intercom.

"Not yet," replied Sam, sitting in the passenger seat beside Yuri.

"If Ryan and Jackson are not up here soon, they will have to swim. I can't keep the helicopter like this much longer," Yuri said with his eyes focused on the steadily titling deck.

"There! There they are!" Sam almost screamed for joy as Mitchell and Jackson emerged from below deck.

The black marine edged over, slid open the side door, and looked out. The ship was sinking faster by the second, threatening to turn over and capsize, and take Mitchell and Jackson with it.

Mitchell and Jackson fought against the doomed ship; each step was a struggle as they made their way over the debris-strewn deck towards the hovering helicopter. The sound of the ship slipping below the waves was overwhelming as air blasted out from below deck.

Yuri, seeing them move closer, increased the pitch, and prepared to take off the instant Mitchell and Jackson were inside the helicopter.

"You first," said Mitchell to Jackson. "I'm a better swimmer than you."

Jackson fought the urge to say something, but turned and jumped up into the open door of the helicopter. Squirming on his belly with the marines pulling him along, Jackson made it inside. Rolling over, he instantly thrust his arms down towards Mitchell just as the ship began to roll over.

Mitchell leapt up and grasped Jackson's powerful arms just as the deck slid out from under his feet.

Applying full power, Yuri struggled to raise the helicopter away from the stricken ship. For a moment, Yuri thought he had waited too long, and then ever so slowly, the nose of the helicopter began to rise. Praying and swearing up a storm in Russian to anyone who would listen, Yuri pulled back on the joystick as the helicopter clawed its way into the sky.

With a loud grunt, Jackson pulled with all his strength. A second later, Mitchell's head popped up. Dashing over, Sam reached down, grabbed Mitchell by the collar of his winter jacket, and together they all pulled him up and into the open door.

"Thanks," said Mitchell, lying on his back, looking up at everyone in the chopper. "I really wasn't looking forward to a swim in the North Atlantic this time of year."

Looking down, Mitchell dispassionately watched as the *Imperator* disappeared from view. A bubbling, foaming froth soon marked the final resting place of Romanov and his twisted dreams of power.

Yuri banked the helicopter around and headed for shore.

49

Polaris Operations Complex
Albany, New York

The flight home was blissfully quiet. A U.S. Air Force Lear jet, courtesy of the government, picked up Mitchell and his team the instant they landed in Iceland. Arriving home in the middle of the night, all Mitchell wanted to do was sleep, but several police cruisers and two sleek black government armored SUVs were waiting for them at the airport. Whisking them through traffic, the column of cars made their way upstate to the Polaris Complex, where General O'Reilly and several very interested parties from the State Department impatiently waited to debrief them all.

Mitchell and his team accepted the debriefing as an unwelcome, but necessary, part of the assignment. Mitchell was thankful that Jen and her mother had—under escort—gone home shortly after arriving.

Leaving no stone unturned, the debriefing seemed to go on forever. If it were not for Tammy Spencer and her homemade coffee and delicious sticky buns, Mitchell doubted that he would have remained awake much longer.

"The use of an electronic warfare burn over the ship was sheer genius," said General O'Reilly, looking proudly at his fatigued people.

"Not really, sir," replied Mitchell. "We used it a fair bit to fry the electronics inside IEDs in Iraq and Afghanistan. I hoped that it would work and thanks to the navy, it did."

"Sir, what about the information on the rebels that was sent back here?" asked Fahimah, stifling a yawn.

"It was relayed to the State Department," said Mike Donaldson. "They in turn fed it to the Russians who struck back at the insurgent forces all across the country. Romanov's plot is all over the news over there. President Ivankov is looking pretty good right now."

"The rebels are finished, thanks to you people," said a stern-looking woman in a dark-blue suit from the State Department. "The Russians have them on the run and the information provided on Dmitry Romanov's financing of the insurgency was the nail in the coffin for them."

"What about the other daughter?" said Jackson, trying to remember her name. "You know, the one that got away."

"Nika," said Mitchell.

"Yeah, any news on her?" queried Jackson as he reached over for another donut.

O'Reilly looked over at the people from the State. None returned his gaze.

"I guess she's still at large," said O'Reilly.

The government people stood. The stern-looking woman smiled at O'Reilly, shook his hand, and then locked eyes on Mitchell's people. "I need not remind you that this whole affair is to be considered a matter of national security. Any word of what has happened will be considered an act of treason with the penalty of life in prison should you be found guilty, which you would be," said the woman harshly.

"Charming," muttered Cardinal, who earned a sharp look from Sam.

"Have a nice day, Ms. Early," said O'Reilly as he ushered the government people out.

Ten minutes later, Mitchell and General O'Reilly sat alone in O'Reilly's office drinking more of Tammy's coffee. The remainder of the team had already scattered to the winds: Sam and Cardinal had gone to Sam's parents' place in Hawaii, Jackson to his wife and kids on the outskirts of New York, Fahimah to her parents' home, and Yuri, as was his style, had simply vanished.

"I don't mind telling you that you look like hell," said

O'Reilly, looking over at Mitchell's bandaged wrist and bloodshot eyes.

"I feel a hell of a lot worse than I look," Mitchell said honestly.

"Well, you're all home now."

Mitchell put his cup down and leaned forward. "Sir, what was with the all the muscle and the threat from the State Department?"

"No one's happy about being played like a gang of fools, especially this administration," said O'Reilly with a shrug of his shoulders. "Nuclear bombs don't go missing every day and the thought that they could have fallen into the hands of terrorists could have started a panic. That's why this never happened."

"The Government of Iceland knows. They lost people on the island," said Mitchell.

"Only a select few do," O'Reilly said. "The story circulated in the press will be about terrorists using the island for training; the police and government will come out of this looking like heroes, in the long run."

Mitchell shook his head; he was tired and had no time for the games played by politicians and bureaucrats.

"I see that look in your eyes, Ryan. Don't let it get to you. If you do, you won't last long in this business. The bureaucrats make the rules, and that is all there is to it. Be proud of yourself. You and your people worked miracles out there. You all deserve a long break," O'Reilly said, consoling his protégé.

"If you say so, sir," wearily replied Mitchell.

"Any ideas of what you might do now? You know you're still on leave," said O'Reilly.

Mitchell ran his hand through his unkempt hair. "I guess I owe some ladies a holiday. So, if they're willing, I'm hoping to take Jen and her mom to Jamaica. It's the least I can do for them."

O'Reilly smiled at Mitchell. For the first time since he had met him, O'Reilly began to wonder if Mitchell was ready to settle down, but decided for now to keep such thoughts to himself.

"Sounds like a plan," said O'Reilly. "Come on, Ryan, I'll give you a lift into the city myself."

Five minutes later, O'Reilly was on the road, and Mitchell was slumped over in his seat snoring loudly enough to wake the dead.

50

**Romanov Warehouse
Tunis, Algeria**

The doors to the darkened warehouse closed behind the Hummer SUV, blocking out the sandstorm racing through the city, covering it in a thick brown haze. Two of Romanov's remaining loyal bodyguards warily got out of the SUV and scanned around for any sign of a threat. Seeing they were alone, the closest guard reached back and opened the rear passenger door. Nika Romanov stepped out, dressed in a tight-fitting dark gray leather outfit, her hair pulled back on her head.

"We leave for the airport in ten minutes," said Nika curtly to the guards before striding over to a staircase leading up to the second floor. The clicking sound of her high heels on the concrete floor echoed through the cavernous hangar. Reaching the top of the stairs, Nika turned and walked towards a locked office at the end of the hallway. Looking back over her shoulder, Nika opened her purse, dug out a key and then quickly opened the door. Stepping inside, Nika reached over, flicked on the light switch, and froze in her tracks. Her father's picture was not in the middle of the wall where it always had been. Instead, it lay on the floor. The door to the hidden wall safe was open and the contents of the safe were missing.

The sound of a pistol's safety being unlatched made Nika turn her head. Instantly, her blood turned to ice. Sitting in a darkened corner of the room was Colonel Chang. In his hand was a silenced pistol aimed right at Nika.

"The last time I checked, there were just over twenty million dollars in that safe," said Nika.

"Nineteen million, eight-hundred thousand, to be precise," replied Chang.

"A small price to pay," said Nika. "I can get more, plenty more if you need it."

"I don't need any more," said Chang coldly. "I came for the remainder of the money you people owed me, which I now have. I have outstanding expenses and one too many widows to pay off, thanks to you and your family."

Nika tried to swallow, but fear had turned her mouth dry. "Don't play me for a fool, Colonel Chang. You knew what you were getting into when you agreed to serve my father. Losses are an inevitable part of your business."

"You are quite right, Miss Romanov; losses are to be expected," Chang replied. "However, betrayal is not. You cannot deny it. You did not intend to pull me or my men off that volcano before it exploded, wiping us all out. I was just too slow to realize it and it cost me and my organization dearly in men and material."

Nika's stomach gripped itself in knots. "Think about it, Colonel, you can't escape. My men downstairs will surely kill you if you shoot me," said Nika insolently.

"Wrong," said Chang, firing one bullet square into Nika's forehead, blasting out the back of her skull. Blood and brains splattered the wall behind her as her body fell to the floor. "Your men are dead already," said Chang as he removed the silencer from his pistol. Standing, Chang placed his pistol away into his shoulder holster. Stepping over Nika's lifeless body, he switched off the light and quietly closed the door behind him, ending his contract with the Romanov Corporation.

51

Corrine March's home
Charlotte, North Carolina

Mitchell sat at the kitchen table, knowing that it was better to keep out of the way when a woman was busy running around packing things. Corrine March sat at the table with him. Both sat there enjoying a beer, while Jen hurried around the house.

"Are you sure you won't come with us?" Mitchell asked Mrs. March.

"No, after all I've been through, I think some time with Jen's brother Derek and his family in Chicago is in order. He has three little ones I can spoil rotten for a couple of weeks before coming back home," replied Mrs. March. "Besides as they always say: two's company, three's a crowd."

Jen stepped into the kitchen holding up a couple of shirts in her hands for her mother to help her decide what to pack.

Mitchell, seeing her standing there, instantly stood and wrapped his arms around Jen's slender waist, pulling her towards him. He took in a long intoxicating breath of Jen's perfume.

"Easy does it, Mister Mitchell," said Jen playfully. "Mom is in the room."

Mitchell shook his head. "You do know we're going for a week, not a month, don't you?"

"A girl's got to look her best," replied Jen.

Letting go of Jen, Mitchell raised his hands in surrender and sat down. From out of nowhere, a chill ran up Mitchell's spine. The room grew quiet. Shrugging it off, Mitchell reached for his beer, but stopped in mid-reach. Standing there quietly was Jen; her head was turned away as if she was intently listening for something far away.

Mitchell reached over and gently touched her hand. "Hey sweetheart, what's wrong?" he asked. "You look like you've just seen a ghost."

Slowly, Jen turned towards Mitchell, a calm look on her face. "No, I didn't see a ghost, but for some reason, I feel I don't have to be afraid anymore."

Mitchell sat there holding her hand, wondering what Jen had meant. Knowing it would serve no purpose to ask Mitchell simply squeezed Jen's hand and sat there in the room, knowing that he would always be bound to the woman who had just entered his life.

- END -

Printed in Great Britain
by Amazon.co.uk, Ltd.,
Marston Gate.